BAD

INTENTIONS

BAD

INTENTIONS

JACK
GRUBBS

ZONE PRESS
Denton, Texas

BAD INTENTIONS
Jack Grubbs

Published in the United States of America
By Zone Press

www.ZonePress.com

an imprint of
Rogers Publishing and Consulting, Inc.
201 North Austin
Denton, Texas 76201

Any resemblence to actual people and events is purely coincidental.
This is a work of fiction.

Editing and Design: Randy Cummings
Cover Art: Jayme Grubbs

ISBN: 978-0-9796698-2-8
ISBN: 0-9796698-2-0

Dedication

To Mom and George. You are missed terribly.

To Judy and all my girls.

Prologue

Sand danced beneath turning wheels. Above the dance, Martha Stetly's attention meandered between the intermittent stripes dividing Texas Highway 35 and mental tapes playing out her station in life. She, husband Joe, 12-year old twins Andrew and Ben, and little Amanda, three days short of turning five, were returning from a weekend of fishing off the jetty at Port Aransas. Gone were the days when world-class tarpon massed at the pier, but the reds and specks remained plentiful enough for a large haul by the boys. The late-afternoon Texas sky, stained pink, orange and purple, stretched majestically over her left shoulder. Joe slept peacefully against the passenger door of their Wolfpack recreation vehicle, having turned the driving duties over to Martha. He and the boys had been on the jetty since four in the morning. The twins nestled in the overhead compartment, breathing in unison the untroubled rhythm of deep sleep. Amanda curled up on the dinette seat cushion. Martha smiled unconsciously at a yellow Piper Cub passing overhead, sharing her peace with the unknown pilot. Her gaze moved to her husband. A spirit sprang from her breast, born from thoughts of spending her life with this very gentle man she had loved since the seventh grade. A girlfriend's scribbled note, 'Joe Stetly was asking my brother about you. What's up?' rested in a memory box at their home in Galena Park. Physical excitement coursed through her body as it had 22 years earlier. She moved her hand and placed it, unfelt, on his hip, then spoke gently in her mind. *Hello friend – I love you.* Driving due north, Martha made out the faint yellow glow on the traffic light facing the westbound traffic. Her timing, based upon many journeys to Port A, seemed perfect; she pressed on the gas pedal and the RV surged into the intersection with Stryker Avenue just as her light turned green.

She barely noticed the tractor-trailer. No screeching brakes, no turning away.

Only a thud, much like a dropping pumpkin, accented the collision. In an instant, four of the five were dead.

The sand danced.

●

"Two eggs over easy with wheat toast."

"And you, sir?" The pleasant Cracker Barrel waitress finished pouring coffee.

"I'll have an Uncle Herschel's Favorite. Thanks." He turned back and continued the discussion. "It happened late yesterday afternoon. If there was ever the perfect situation, this is it."

"Yeah, I know." Almost a whisper.

"Look, you can back out now. Just say so and it's over." He glanced at the other diners, then back. "But let me tell you right now, tort reform's coming to Texas. It's just a matter of time."

He paused briefly, sipped the hot coffee, and continued. "I have people in place. Right now they have no idea of any other involvement. They'll do as they're told. If we go for it, they will never know you exist. You need to take this over. It's the perfect link. You make a national statement about the trucking industry. I'll bring my suit to the front while yours is white hot. You go in October and I'll follow in November. They'll fit together like two spoons in a drawer." He tapped his fingers on the cup and waited.

"I understand the timing. That's the easy part. I'm not so sure of the outcome."

"Listen to me. I've been in this business a long time. I know what brings wealth and I know what brings power. These events will bring both."

"Maybe."

His eyes tightened. "Let's cut the bullshit. I intend to do this once. You need to tell me now." Another deliberate pause. "Yes or no?"

A lingering silence.

"Yes."

1

"Hello, this is Tom Seiler. Susie and I must be out and about so just leave a number and we'll get back to you just as quick as we can . . . beeeeep."

Tom screened his calls before answering, if he answered at all. He had a love-hate relationship with the telephone; hated the frequent interruptions yet realized the phone linked him to his profession.

When asked, Tom's explanation of an accident reconstructionist was simple. "Medical examiners autopsy dead people. I autopsy accidents."

Happenstance brought him to the profession; an ability to dissect accidents of almost any nature carried him to success. By proper title he was an expert witness; other titles included ambulance chaser, gunslinger or corporate whore.

"Tom, this is Travis. We got the Stetly case. Time to crank it up." Excitedly, the lawyer spoke of a high-visibility case in which, win or lose, his firm would make money.

Tom Seiler looked at the clock resting on the desktop. The red digital display read 22:10. No special reason why he used military time - just easier to use all 24 hours of the day. He had to pick up his daughter at Houston Hobby Airport at 10:30 and was thankful that Travis had called - but he didn't have the time to hear the gruesome details.

He picked up the phone. "Hey compadre, what's up?" Tom leaned back in his chair, staring at a perfect scale model of an old steam engine locomotive. The 3985 painted on the cab identified the Challenger series – and stirred a quick vision in Tom's mind of days gone by.

Travis repeated himself. "We got the Stetly case and you're the expert witness."

"Stetly. The family killed on Texas 35?"

"That's them."

Tom mentally replayed the graphic photos from the Chronicle. Not pretty.

Travis continued eagerly. "We need to get together right away. This is big time."

Tom focused again on the carnage to a family of five . . . only a surviving daughter. Then he remembered, *Pick up Paige at Hobby.* He interrupted, "I'll take a look at it. Can't talk now. Gotta pick Paige up at Hobby in 20 minutes."

Travis barely broke stride, "Hard to tell who's to blame on this one since everyone seemed to be running red lights. The parents and two boys were killed instantly. Both boys died from broken necks. A little girl survived."

Travis White, a Houston lawyer for 25 years, met Tom at a Little League coaches meeting in 1984. A year later Travis, aware that Tom was a mechanical design engineer at NASA, asked Tom to help him with an analysis of a fatal accident in which a dozer rolled off a flatbed, crushing the operator. They won the case. Then came a successful analysis of an airplane crash. The jobs started to roll in. Tom's engineering skill and basic honesty complemented Travis' grasp of law and human behavior. They were a formidable team. Tom had more than three decades at NASA when the cutbacks in the space program, lucrative early retirement packages and his gradual movement into the world of accident analysis led him to a decision to retire.

"The D.A.'s office announced today that criminal proceedings will be filed against both the driver and Belton." With an air of disgust, Travis continued. "What's more, Colter, Fisher and King were out there damn near before they picked the bodies up and have convinced grandma and grandpa to sue both Wolfpack and Belton Trucking for negligence. They're citing substandard hiring and training policies by Belton and poor construction of the RV. Like they even have a clue. Anyway, we need you to . . ."

A sense of urgency tugged at Tom. He broke in, "Travis, I'll check it out tomorrow, I need to make tracks. Fax me everything you've got and I'll call you once I've read it. Adios." He hung up the phone, stepped into his loafers while slipping on a World Cup '94 athletic shirt and headed down the stairs from the loft that served as the executive suite for Seiler Engineering - Accident Analysis.

"Susie, I'm off to pick up Paige. Be back in time for Letterman's Top Ten." On most occasions he would give Susie a quick kiss, but he was in a hurry to pick up his only daughter, a beautiful young woman from his first marriage. Susie was Tom's second wife. During the height of Mardi Gras 1962 he met a girl from Baton Rouge and married her two months later. They had three children, two boys and a girl - Paige. At birth, Paige's most distinguishing feature was an amazing tangle of jet-black hair. Her dark features prompted them to nickname her "Rod" for the

Mexican name "Rodriguez." She was sandwiched between Tom, Jr., and Steve. In spite of a marriage that folded after 22 years, Tom, Sr., had a special relationship with his children. The home in Clear Lake, near the Johnson Space Center, was the gathering place for the Seiler kids and their friends. Everyone liked Mr. Seiler. It was Tom who took kids up for airplane rides and it was Tom who would volunteer to chaperone high school parties. It was also Tom who would tell one of his children's friend when he or she was acting stupid. Tom made it clear, through word and action, that real families get involved with each other. Tom Seiler was not perfect, but he got that part right.

On the Gulf Freeway Tom placed his '90 Buick Le Sabre on cruise at, as always, 55 miles per hour, moved into the right lane and relaxed. Even in a hurry, he was a slow driver. The bright lights of a tailgating car caught his attention. The car swerved around him and accelerated. He looked to his left to see three teenage boys laughing at something uproarious. *Youth. You better enjoy it.* The youngsters triggered a memory from Tom. A smirk appeared on his face as he pulled the story from his past. The image was as clear as the night it happened:

●

Three teenaged boys, indistinguishable from the moving shadows of trees blowing in the warm Texas wind, crept behind a row of planted hedges. Reaching the base of the huge concrete façade, they climbed a small ladder in silence. The threat of being seen from the nearby highway was enough that each boy felt his pounding heart would burst.

They crawled silently over the concrete ledge onto a landing eight feet deep and 70 feet long, regrouped next to a small door hidden in the blackness of night. Jack, the older of Tom's two younger brothers, briefed Tom and classmate Haygood Wikan on the two-minute mission. They hid in the temporary safety of darkness; yet, once started, the plot had to be carried out in total illumination. Jack disappeared inside the door while Tom and Haygood moved to their assigned stations. After 30 long seconds Jack appeared carrying aluminum cargo. Gently, he placed each piece of metal in the exact position it needed to be along the top of the ledge. Each boy felt the exhilaration born of the risk of being caught and the thrill of escape. Jack thrust his thumb into the air and the operation began. Tom looked up and saw the bright letters above him - ALAMO DRIVE IN. He leaned over the ledge and looked down at the letters on the marquee. Vertigo, caused by the upside-down perspective, swept over him. He read the feature movies for the weekend:

JAMES STEWART IN "THE STRATEGIC AIR COMMAND"

DANNY KAYE AS "THE COURT JESTER"

While Haygood clumsily removed IR and JEST at one end of the marquee, Tom took STE and AYE from the other end. Jack, the former ticket attendant during his first two years in high school, placed the needed letters and rearranged the spacing in less than 40 seconds. Jack finished the final touches of the masterpiece as Tom and Haygood crawled back over the ledge and down the ladder. Unable to see the letters, yet knowing what would be in store for them, the two at the bottom looked at each other first with grins, then with quick staccato belches of muffled snorting, and soon, uncontrolled, bellyaching laughter. His mission finished, Jack quietly descended the ladder and, with Tom and Haygood alongside, ran to the exit road. They sprinted up the incline and across the Austin Highway, disappearing into a grassy knoll 100 yards from the drive-in. As they crossed the highway, each turned to see the fruits of their work. There it was for the entire world . . .

JAMES WART IN "THE STRATEGIC ASS COMMAND"

DANNY COCK AS "THE COURT FUCKER"

●

The vision of long lines of cars thronging to the next night's movie and the exasperation of the owners filled his mind. He mentally rejoined the three teenagers howling until their stomachs hurt. The boys relished their slightly tarnished reputations as fun loving hell raisers – no risk, no fun. Tom laughed out loud with the boys in his mind, but the laughter faded as another image came to his mind - a young paratrooper of the 173d Airborne Brigade dying in a rice paddy near the Vietnamese hamlet of Vo Dat. December 1965. A black Christmas.

If he hadn't flunked out of Texas . . .

Tom turned off at Airport Boulevard and, since he was now 15 minutes late, drove directly to the doors at baggage claim. The ritual had been the same since Paige entered Tulane University in New Orleans 10 years earlier - Tom arrives on time and meets her at the Southwest Airlines arrival gate; Tom arrives late and meets her outside of baggage claim. They mostly met at baggage claim. Paige was waiting.

"Hey lady, need a ride?" Tom reached over and opened the passenger door. Paige tossed the red vinyl travel bag into the back, eased into her seat, squeezed

Tom's hand and exhaled: "One hundred and forty passengers and I get the one with bad breath. The guy wouldn't stop talking. Gross."

Paige graduated from Tulane as a structural engineer. Tom hadn't been red hot about her being an engineer, but Paige remained adamant. A strong work ethic led to solid grades. Her personal stock was bankrolled in a generally upbeat attitude about life, a large chunk of common sense and healthy good looks. Her four years in New Orleans – always enticed by the ambiance of the most unique city in America – taught her how to balance entrees on the great menu of life. All six companies with whom she interviewed offered her a position. She chose to go with Tenneco because she wanted to return to Houston. Her rising reputation as a design engineer was based on competence. Paige was very much a chip off the old block.

"So, how's Seiler Engineering these days? I'm ready to read some more depositions."

"Good. Almost too good." Tom smiled. "Cases out the gazoo. Seems the lawyers love an old NASA engineer."

"Maybe they just like a competent, honest engineer who tells it like it is."

Tom shrugged off the compliment. "Just before I came down here I may have landed a very big one. Travis wants me to take a look at an accident at Stryker and Texas 35. It sounds pretty much like the one that killed Erin Foster."

Paige turned away from her father, staring at the passing lights. *Two girls – best friends – laughing and talking over cokes and fries.*

"Damn. I didn't mean to be so matter-of-fact." Tom gently patted her arm.

"It's O.K. Dad. I can't believe it's been 12 years." A lump in her throat momentarily cut the words off. "Why did she have to die?"

A black thought passed through Tom's mind. His oldest son. His brother. Tom fought against the anger.

"Let me change all this around. Tell me about Ross."

"Dad, he's wonderful. Not the extrovert you are, but he's got a sense of humor that catches you off guard all the time. And I'll tell you what else. He's not only a looker, he's just plain nice. I'm not in any hurry to get married, but he's up there fighting for that special category."

Tom smiled, tempered slightly by a tinge of sadness. The inevitable passage of time.

Their conversation focused on Ross for a few more minutes then flowed comfortably back to the accident. They pulled into the driveway shortly before 11.

Before opening her door, Paige offered, "If you need some finite-element analysis on the vehicle, I'd be glad to work on it."

Without reply, Tom exited the car. He took two cans of Miller Lite from the garage refrigerator, popped the top on one, walked to the kitchen door and held it open for his daughter.

Susie was asleep in front of the TV. Tom's remark about returning in time for Letterman proved prophetic. Dave was commenting about ten indications that your job is not going well.

"Number three. When the word 'sucks' appears eight times on your performance appraisal."

2

Saturday morning. The hot, humid Houston sunrise was half an hour into history. Rays of light reflected off the white walls of the bedroom, leaving a series of horizontal bars outlining the partially opened blinds of two large bedroom windows overlooking a small but pretty backyard. In summer, a huge dome of high pressure over the Gulf of Mexico serves as the source of a general clockwise flow of warm, moist air gently flowing into the Texas Coast from the south and east. Houston is a major target of the hot, muggy air. By early June the Canadian cold fronts have lost the energy to bring relief of dry, cool days to the Deep South. The weather pattern is a monotonous daily routine of solar heating, parcels of hot air rising and cooling, and eventual condensation into clouds that, because of the release of further heat as water vapor condenses, boil upward into towering thunderheads. It is a hit or miss situation in which torrential downpours, spectacular but sometimes deadly lightning and gale force winds play Russian Roulette with towns and cities of South Texas. Today would be typical. Praise God for air conditioning.

Tom, awake but still in bed, sorted through the events from the previous day and actions to be accomplished this day. He wanted to take the Stinson for a quick flight over Houston Bay, but first had to get to the 13 pages he received from Travis the night before. He visualized the truck-RV accident and reflected on the fact that Travis' firm of Duffy, Guyer, and White was representing Belton Trucking and not Wolfpack. At the request of Belton Trucking, the law firm would also represent the driver of the tractor-trailer in the criminal proceedings. His thoughts, shifting towards an afternoon flight, were interrupted by the delicious aroma of freshly brewed coffee. With a playful grab of Susie's fanny and a gentle "Love ya kid," Tom hopped out of bed and into his running shorts. He made a quick stop in the

15

bathroom, and then headed for the kitchen.

"Coffee's on and I'm buying." Paige was at the kitchen counter, already pouring.

"You're up mighty early." Tom took the hot cup and leaned over to give Paige a quick kiss on the cheek.

"Woke up thinking about Erin." Paige spoke without looking directly at Tom.

Tom sat down in front of the large TV screen, searching beneath a cushion for the remote as Paige joined him. She continued. "Actually, I woke up a couple of hours ago and since you were still sleeping I passed some time looking over those faxes from Mr. White."

Tom broke in. "Call him Travis."

Paige continued. "I couldn't get Erin's death out of my mind and I wanted to see if the same thing happened this time."

Tom squeezed the remote tightly.

"Dad, I just can't shake it. Guess I never will. You know, she really was a nice person. Nice to everyone. I can't get the 'why?' out of my mind."

Tom placed the remote down on the glass coffee table, blew on the coffee and searched for a reply . . . "Yeah, I know."

Nothing was left to say, only the quietly held grief that would never go away.

Tom diverted their thoughts. "So what did you think about the accident? Can we defend the trucking firm or are they in deep trouble?"

Tom and Paige talked forensic engineering over two more cups of coffee. The faxes consisted of the police report of the accident, several fax-fuzzy photos and some preliminary information on the specifications of the recreational vehicle. The photos were clear enough to show complete destruction of the driver's compartment. Also highlighted was damage to the overhead compartment caused by the two boys being thrown through the upper window. Though detail was lacking, failure of the sheet metal could be seen at all of the four rounded corners of the window. Tom placed his finger on top of one of the window corners.

"What's this tell you about the two boys."

Structural integrity was Paige's forte. While in school, Paige read many of Tom's depositions and court testimony. Paige studied the photo carefully, zeroing in on the fractured corners. "My take is that if the compartment had held them in, both would have survived. I'm speculating, but my gut feels pretty strong about it. You ?"

Tom leaned back, coffee cup in hand. "I agree. For one thing, the little girl was about the same distance from the bathroom bulkhead as the boys were from the overhead window. She came out of it in good shape. Not exactly the same circumstances, but pretty close."

Paige nodded, waiting for Tom to continue.

He sipped from the cup, then sat up. Turning to his right, Tom looked directly into his daughter's eyes. "You mentioned doing some finite-element analysis of the RV last night. I'd like to hire you to do it. I've seen your work. No nepotism, I'm after professional work. I'll clear it with Travis. Standard rates based on billable hours. No major discounts – you get paid the same as others. Forty-eight bucks an hour."

Paige's disappointment from Tom's non-response the night before switched to controlled euphoria. Already intrigued with the accident, she jumped at the offer. "I'll take it. I need to do it part-time, but I'll do it right. What's the time frame?"

Tom answered her question with another one. "The basic question to be answered is 'How much force was required to fracture the window corners?' My suspicions are that it didn't take much."

Tom methodically outlined his approach to accident analysis. He concluded with Paige's contribution to the effort. "Let me get the detailed information on the RV specs and I'll reconstruct the accident. Once I round it up, I'll turn you loose on the analysis. If we can show what strength was needed to keep the boys in the overhead compartment and then show that the folks at Wolfpack didn't even come close, then I think we can certainly make a case that, as a minimum, they're, say, 50 percent at fault. Anyway you slice it, the extended family is going to end up with a great deal of money to ease their grief."

The clock read 9:00, well past Tom's scheduled start time for a weekend jog. During his tenure at NASA he usually ran at noon in defiance of humidity and temperature readings often exceeding 90 degrees. Since his retirement Tom ran as early as possible. The cooler temperatures and lack of traffic suited him now. He needed to run. "Gotta go. It's going to be another bear. I'll get started on my part and hopefully get everything to you by the end of the week. Oh, one thing I need you to do is to make the results of your analysis jump out at the jury. I doubt any of them has a clue about what finite-elements really are. I need you to give me results and a simple methodology that I can explain in clear, basic terms." Tom rose and walked to the kitchen, took a new cup from the cupboard, added half-n-half from the refrigerator and filled it with coffee. He raised his voice slightly. "Oh yeah, the time frame is about four weeks. And you've got free liberty to think out-of-the-taco-shell all you want."

Paige was elated. She knew that his offer was real. He would not make it had he not considered her competent. *Four weeks? I'll have something to you in four days.*

Tom disappeared into the bedroom with the fresh cup of coffee, placing it on the nightstand next to Susie. He sat quietly on the bed and put on his socks and running shoes, then made another trip to the bathroom. This time he stopped long enough to brush his teeth and look at the aging man in the mirror. At just under six feet, with thinning black hair, the old man sneered at Tom. *Hair half gone, wrinkles all over, hanging skin everywhere. Shit.* The only saving grace was that he was a pretty fair runner. Sixteen straight Tenneco Marathons and a memorable run in Boston allowed him to rationalize. On his way out, he gently patted Susie's fanny and whispered, "I still love ya kid." She smiled.

●

Tom was in his late 30s and a heavy smoker when he was introduced to jogging. If they started right on time and ate sandwiches concurrently with playing, his small group of NASA engineers could get in several hands of bridge during the 45-minute lunch break. During a particularly exciting hand in July 1978 one of the young engineers walked through the smoke-filled room in running shorts. Tom chastised him.

"What the hell are you doing? It's 100 degrees out there. Come on in and play a man's game."

Bill Ellers faked a choking motion and responded. "Thanks for nothing. I prefer to live past 40."

"What's the big deal about running around in tights? You look like a sissy." Tom inhaled deeply, filling his lungs with delicious smoke. On exhaling, he declared, "Three no-trump."

Bill challenged him. "Twenty bucks says you can't jog half a mile."

Tom loved a challenge. "You're on sucker. Just bring your wallet tomorrow."

It wasn't even close. Tom lost the bet before making it 500 yards. The day after, he excused himself from the bridge game and ran almost half a mile. Nine months into his new life, Tom Seiler ran through Austin in the Capitol Ten Thousand. He never played bridge and he never smoked again.

●

Tom stretched his legs and groin beneath the basketball goal, settled into his car and drove to the NASA back gate. He stretched again, placed his car keys on top of the driver's side front tire and began what usually was a six-mile jog. It would eventually turn out to be almost 13 miles. The heat index was already well into the 90s, but the sky was beautiful and the traffic very light. It provided him the perfect opportunity to do what he wanted to - jog and think. He took a right on Park Shadows and another right on Bay Area Boulevard. Once he settled into a smooth stride and was able to cast off the daily struggle with his aging body, the questions appeared. *How fast were they going? What's the overhead compartment made of? Did the trucker run the red light or did the Stetly lady? Was there any drinking involved? Sort it out with the police report. Who's the expert witness for Colter?* Tom allowed himself to be a little distracted by the scenery at Armand Bayou Park. The half-mile loop passed a mixture of shade trees, little league ballparks, soccer fields and picnic tables. He stopped briefly at the public drinking fountain for a full drink and returned to the run. By the time he completed the loop for a second time his mind had returned to the business at hand. *Does the D.A.'s office have any additional information? What other factors exist to take blame from the driver and the trucking firm? How soon do we have to be ready?* He tried on different plans of action. *Need to talk to witnesses. Must call the D.A.'s office - and the Houston Police Department. Paige can help with a good analysis - must be understandable. Get with Travis.* Left - right - left. Each stride fell effortlessly onto the pavement. Northeast to Red Bluff, then southeast to Kirby. The analysis lasted over six miles before Tom's mind demanded that he move on to other things. The sky beckoned him. The weather would be good with only scattered thunderstorms. *It's a great day to fly. A flight to Matagorda Island would be great.*

Tom slowed to a brisk walk 200 yards from the back gate, having finished a half-marathon. Al, the guard, wasn't there to provide his normal greeting. It was Saturday.

He drove home slowly, the cool air soothing his tired, already aching, body. Entering the back door, Tom announced plans for the day, "Hey Susie Q, Paige, I'm back. Let's fly down to Matagorda Island this afternoon. Maybe we can spot some pirates."

3

Saturday afternoon.

A tractor-trailer, its flatbed loaded with steel tubing, rested on the apron of the abandoned airstrip.

Towering thunderclouds roamed the late afternoon coastline, but none had brought any relief to this parcel of pure hell. Searing heat from the cruel Texas sun blistered the concrete and backs of two men standing between the forklift and the Peterbilt rig. Undulating vertical lines of heat rose from the distant pavement. The concrete pad once served as part storage facility and part runway. At 2800 feet in length and varying in width from 80 feet at the west-end to 300 feet at the east, the airstrip proved to be an ideal training facility. It was abandoned in 1980 following the fourth major hurricane making landfall on that exact section of the Texas Gulf Coast. The only other sign of human existence was a small plane flying peacefully towards Cavello Bay. Seagulls waltzed high above the men.

One mile to the northeast lay the remains of Indianola; 10 miles to the northwest was Port Lavaca; Cavello Pass and the northern tip of Matagorda Island were another 10 miles to the southeast. With something less than 100 hearty souls, Indianola was nothing more than a memory of what could have been. Three centuries had passed since Rene Robert Cavelier, Sieur de la Salle, first set foot on what appeared to be an idyllic landscape. Indianola later became the finest seaport on the Gulf of Mexico. In 1866 a storm struck at the heart of Indianola causing great damage and some loss of life. The resilient folk rebuilt and life settled down for a bustling, growing city. But no one was prepared for September 17, 1875. The most powerful hurricane known at that time used Indianola as its bull's-eye. Monstrous waves, raging storm surge and shrieking winds reduced the area to rubble. Nearly 1,000 perished. Maybe it was insanity, but Indianola made another comeback as stronger, deeper port facilities were constructed and homes slowly began to dot the shoreline. The final death knell came in 1886. The fury of the third hurricane, more severe than the first two, made it clear that Nature did not intend for human beings to occupy this land in large numbers. None of the structures remained standing; most of the townspeople had perished; the few that survived left forever. The only significant construction that had taken place in more than three-quarters of a century was the airstrip and two sheet metal hangars built in the late '60s. Some hope for a new Indianola still lingered. Ironically, even though the eye of Hurricane Allen passed well to the south of Corpus Christi, another 85 miles down the Texas coast, a small tornado spawned from the storm destroyed one of the hangars and each of a dozen aircraft that may have precipitated a rebirth of the town. Save a few small cottages and shrimp boats, Indianola was dead.

Jud Weems exclaimed, "goddamn thing better work this time." The taller of the men, and, for what it was worth, the leader of the gang of two, was hot, tired and irritated. Beads of perspiration rolled from his head to his temples, cheeks and nose, forming small rivulets cascading in meandering patterns along his neck and upper back. Dark, half-elliptic patterns of sweat formed under the armpits and neck of his light blue T-shirt. Habitually, he dragged his upper teeth up and over the stubble of whiskers that had been growing under his lower lip for the past day and a half.

"Fuck you. This is dangerous shit and I ain't killin' m'self 'cause you got a hard-on 'bout gettin' hot. I'll move it up one notch at a time."

A short, burly man of 46, Buck Tallant enlisted in the Marine Corps on the day of his seventeenth birthday. Nine months later he was given a dishonorable discharge for selling stolen property - property he had stolen from his fellow Marines. The court-martial was a piece of cake compared to the beating he endured when other Marines caught him rifling a wall locker. Following a series of odd jobs throughout the Houston area, Buck caught on with Flagg Brothers, International, a trucking firm specializing in citrus produce from the Valley areas near Harlingen to markets in Dallas, Houston, Atlanta and St. Louis. The company expanded in the 1980's with the acquisition of 50 flatbed trailers and added heavy equipment, concrete and structural steel tubing to its inventory of goods hauled.

Jud glared at Buck. "Look Buck, this thing has been moved up. We either do it now or sit on our asses forever."

Jud drove a tractor-trailer for Bettis Trucking. Until recently, his marriage to a woman from Alvin had been meaningless. The marriage provided Jud with a place to sleep; it provided his wife, Sybil, a substantial medical benefits package. Jud purchased two $500,000 life insurance policies through the company with each spouse being the beneficiary of the other. Once the plan was underway Jud told Sybil that he didn't need as much as she did. They agreed to reduce her policy to $200,000 in January. Sybil worked as a waitress in Galveston, 25 miles south of Alvin. Her older sister and two younger brothers did the same. Sybil would walk in her house five minutes on either side of 2:45 on six out of seven mornings every week. Monotonous.

Jud locked eyes with Buck. "Make the fucking run."

Buck returned to the rig, climbed in, started it up and pulled out in an arc that came within two feet of the forklift onto which Jud had climbed. Buck shot him the finger as the rig accelerated west to the end of the concrete apron. The rig, with a crimson red cab on which was painted a waving Texas flag with the word *'FLAGG'* trailing in dark blue lettering shot down the pavement in the form of a huge, ominous, guided missile. It reached 60 miles per hour before Buck realized that he was almost at the end of the runway. He slammed on the brakes, causing the rig to nearly jackknife, and ran some 40 yards into the sand and dirt before making a semi-circle and aligning it in a due easterly direction. He stopped on the concrete momentarily, then with a guttural "try this you bastard," accelerated the Flagg Brothers rig in a straight line along the northern edge of the apron. Peering through the slits of his eyes, Buck aimed the 32-ton missile at its target. He passed the forklift at 62 miles an hour, continued to accelerate to a speed of 68 miles an hour at the instant he reached a line of black paint that arched in a long, smooth curve changing in heading from east to southeast. He executed a smooth turn to the right. Two seconds into the turn the rig passed over a red stripe, ten feet in length, painted perpendicular to the black arc. Exhilarated and raging, Buck gave the steering wheel a hard turn to the right as the red paint passed beneath the cab. He sensed the entire rig wanting to continue forward while the wheels churned relentlessly into a turn ill-suited for the load of steel tubing stacked on the flatbed. The rig began to rotate counter-clockwise, initiating an impending rollover. Buck knew he was going to die and mentally pictured his head dangling out of the window as the cab caught him between the top of the roof and the concrete. He imagined his head being crushed and breaking into large mottled fragments of red bone and brain matter.

Physically sensing the counter-clockwise listing of the rig, Jud leaned to his right in an unconscious effort to right the monstrous machine. Then something caught his eye. The front tiedown strap gave way first, two feet above the left side forward lifting shackle. In a split second, the strap shot out, up and away from the steel tubes in a slingshot manner. It was followed immediately by straps two, three and four. The immense inertia of the tubes wanting to continue forward controlled the unfolding sequence of events. As the straps split one by one, the steel tubing shot off of the left side of the flatbed. Each piece of four-inch diameter steel tubing was a 132-pound missile. Each joined the others as a giant beehive artillery round being fired at a soon-to-be disemboweled enemy. The tubes rocketed forward, bouncing, rolling, almost leaping through the air as they lethally covered the concrete.

Death consuming his imagination, Buck lost control of the steering wheel. With the instantaneous release of the steel tubing, the cab immediately righted; the loss of the load gave stability to the flatbed. In sensing the return of stability, Buck instinctively turned the steering wheel slightly left, pulled his feet away from the accelerator and brake and let the rig, minus its steel load, coast to an eventual stop nearly half a mile from where he started the turn. He placed his head on the steering wheel between his hands, closing his eyes. Save his labored breathing, Buck sat motionless.

Jud jumped up and down like a school kid and laughed in total delight.

"Incredible, simply fuckin' incredible. I don't believe it. That was so fuckin' beautiful. Incredible, incredible . . ."

He half ran, half skipped, to the rig. He jumped up on the running board and simultaneously reached in and slapped Buck on the back. "Buck, it was beautiful, simply fuckin' beautiful . . . ain't no one gonna live through that."

4

The office suite of Seiler Engineering - Accident Analysis was the second floor loft in their three-bedroom condominium on Bay Harbour Road. Mauve carpeting complemented light gray walls. The mahogany railing overlooked a spacious living room below and, visible through two large vertical windows facing east, a peaceful view of the small tributary emptying into Clear Lake. Two desks, one for Susie and one for Tom, sat side by side facing and almost touching the railing. Each had a workstation. Tom never served in the military, the critical designation of his work at NASA precluding it. Yet, he loved flying. The walls were accentuated with framed pictures of aircraft - mostly World War II fighters. The P-51 Mustang, P-47 Thunderbolt and P-40 Tomahawk each had a three-dimensional look offering Tom that sense of freedom known only to the pilot.

"Here you go Babe."

Susie cleared the top step to the loft. In her left hand she held two hot cups of coffee, one black and one with half-n-half and sugar. In her right were letters, bills and advertisements just removed from the kitchen counter.

Susie looked much younger than her years. Light reddish hair accentuated sparkling blue eyes. Her trim body had not yet lost to the half-century march of time. Tom and Susie met at the Johnson Space Center in 1988. She worked as a secretary in the JSC Clinic in Building 8 while Tom worked in Building 7 as a senior design engineer. The strength of their relationship had been forged in a casual friendship long before they started dating. Both had been divorced. Tom lost a brother in Vietnam and his firstborn son in a boating accident. Susie parented two children. Her daughter, Carrie, excelled in high school and had gone on to the University of Texas, eventually graduating from the Medical School as an ob-gyn. The jury was still out on her son. Bubba lived up to his redneck name. He often skipped school, seldom studied and was in a continual state of being in trouble with someone - the school, the law or the irate parents of some girl of whom he had taken advantage. Yet, he too had managed a remarkably good freshman year at Stephen F. Austin State University in Nacogdoches. Hope springs eternal.

It was Monday morning.

"Thanks honey." Tom took the coffee, his second cup of the morning, moved his chair to a position where he could cross his legs over the middle mahogany railing, opened a manila folder and prepared to brief Susie.

Susie sat down on her chair, kicked off a pair of pink slippers, also crossing her legs as she stretched them out on the carpet. She folded her hands on her stomach and prepared to listen. The ritual was always the same. Tom got up early, made his coffee and worked on the current case. Generally between nine and ten o'clock he would be ready to present his ideas to his partner.

Tom began. "I've looked at Travis' stuff closely, including the photos of the RV and the accident scene." Tom paused to put structure to everything in his mind. "My first thought is that the driver of the truck screwed up big time. He just plain ran the light. The photos don't show any skid marks from the rig. That makes it tough for us since we'll be defending the trucking firm as well as the driver."

Susie had questions but didn't respond. It was the ritual again – and it worked. She did log the questions, one by one, into her mental register.

"Hell, Susie, it's as though they were playing chicken. Why would they just plow into each other?" Tom hesitated long enough to move his first page of notes to the back of the stack. "I need to look at the accident from two different perspectives. First, can I reconstruct exactly what took place with the truck driver? Why didn't he stop? Was he drunk? Tired? How fast was he going? Where was the sun? Was the radio on?" The logical questions that Tom formulated on his run two days earlier were now on paper.

"Secondly, can I reconstruct exactly what the lady was doing? This will be tough since I can't talk to her. She just ran that RV broadside into the truck. But beyond reconstructing the chain of events for the RV, I'm going to look very closely at the construction of the overhead compartment. I know the two boys would have made it if there were any structural integrity at all in that upper window." He sipped his coffee. "What've you got?"

It was now Susie's turn. She ran the business end of SEILER, Inc., yet Tom always asked her to provide one more perspective to the investigation. She had strong intuition. Susie asked well thought out questions; Tom either answered a question outright or both chewed on it for a while. Today she asked few, being content with a medley of interesting thoughts.

Her first thought held the most weight. "You seem more puzzled about this accident than most. That, and nothing else, tells me that the key to this thing is something out of the ordinary. You need another view of the accident, something external to the physical evidence."

"You're right. I'll gather any and all info I can whether it fits any mold right now or not." He jotted a note reflecting Susie's wisdom and moved to the next page.

"My schedule's going to be normal. Travis today, then I can pick you up on the way out to the accident scene around sundown. Need to take our own photos of the vehicles. Travis is sending the police report over today. I'll have him set up a meeting with HPD. I need to call Bill Acker right away to get all the detailed specs on the RV."

Bill Acker owned a small company specializing in providing specifications on any vehicle using the American highways. As always, the bill for his services would be sent to Duffy, Guyer, and White.

"Once I go over Bill's report I'll send some of it to Paige so she can analyze it on Super-SAP," Tom said, referring to a computer program that used finite-element analysis. 'SAP' stood for 'Structural Analysis Package.'

They kicked a couple of other questions around. The last sip of coffee was cool.

●

The offices of Duffy, Guyer and White, Attorneys-at-Law, were at Two Houston Center on Fannin in the heart of Houston. Tom exited left from the elevator on the 33d floor, walked to the end of a long corridor and entered through glass-plated double doors. Fifteen feet beyond the doors sat the executive receptionist, Lynn Hargrove, an exquisitely beautiful girl whose light Texas accent and friendly smile would make any client want to return.

"Hi, Tom, Travis is waiting in room five." Lynn moved her head slightly over her right shoulder as to point to a suite of rooms along the left side of a wide corridor ending at a magnificent polarized gray window overlooking the Houston skyline.

Room five had a conference table for 12, with captains chairs covered in cowhide. Plush hunter green carpeting was standard and a chandelier hung from a 12-foot ceiling. Tom studied the ceiling, his mind deducing that the 34th floor was used for storage since this room encroached at least two feet into it. A movie screen was set up behind a set of drawn curtains. A small room behind the screen contained multi-media equipment capable of showing VCR, DVD, transparencies and CD-ROM audio/video; it had a stereo system with a four-barrel speaker system. At six-foot-five, Travis' frame dwarfed the chair at the end of the table nearest the screen.

Travis welcomed his friend into the room. "Hey compadre, what's up?"

"Not much amigo, but once again I'm here to pull your ass out of a fire."

Travis laughed, gesturing Tom to join him at the table. As Tom walked forward, Travis got right down to business.

"If we can get Belton and their driver off the hook on this one, we'll land them for everything they need in the future. Beyond the criminal trial, we guess the civil suit will be in the neighborhood of $40 million. If we lose, Belton loses a ton of money and we might lose Belton."

Tom sat down across from Travis and took out a tablet and mechanical pencil. On the top line, he wrote in caps:

BELTON VS. RV: WHITE VS. HOUSTON D.A./COLTER

Tom rubbed his right hand across his forehead, massaging from the temples to the bridge of his nose. "What've you got so far?"

"I had one of our junior legals go out and take some more pictures of the scene and of the RV. These are the originals that I faxed you Friday night." He handed Tom two sets of envelopes containing some 20-plus color photos. "Also got three photos from the Chronicle."

Tom thumbed through the photos more as a gesture than anything else. He responded, "Anything else that I don't have?"

"Couple of things. First, the media has really dug into the background of the Stetly's. From every source they were the nicest people on the planet. Active in the Baptist Church, kids soccer and basketball coaches, volunteers for Special Olympics and just about every other good thing a family could do. Even the kids are good kids. They sound like the Cleavers to me."

Tom was in a hurry. "Gotcha on the Stetly's. What about the accident?"

"Sorry, didn't mean to ramble. As for the accident, the police got a full statement from the truck driver. Also, they took some photos and VCR of the scene. Probably not much but you might want to see it anyway. Some were taken shortly after the accident and more at exactly the same time a couple of days ago. Since the weather was the same, it might give you something to work with."

Tom added new entries to a growing list, speaking as he wrote. "What's the driver got to say?"

"The D.A.'s office hasn't released the initial report yet. Only thing they told me was that the driver admits he ran the light. We've asked for everything, including a copy of the VCR tape. Told 'em you'd be by to pick everything up. I did ask that you be allowed to talk to the investigators and the guy who took the VCR. You're on for 4:00 Wednesday."

Tom continued to fill the pad of paper.

Travis added, eyebrows askew, "They called back to let us know the D.A. wants you to stop at her office first."

Tom looked back at Travis, a question mark on his face. "What's that all about?"

"Don't really know. Probably going to be high visibility."

There was a pause. Tom returned to the photos, analyzing out loud. "There were no skid marks, and look at this." He pointed to a news photograph showing most of the intersection, a few feet of the approach to the intersection and, in the distance, the rig on the side of the road. "What's it say to you?"

Travis got up and moved to a position at the end of the table and looked at the photo, eyeballs tracing the slight movement of Tom's index finger.

"It doesn't say shit. What's it saying to you?"

"It's a long rig. I think he hit the dilemma zone at the worst possible time. That could be key if we go to trial."

"Friend, there's no 'if' about it. No settlement. They're going all the way with it. Criminal and civil"

Tom continued, "No real skid marks from either vehicle means that the trucker made the decision to beat the light. If the woman had been stopped I'm sure she would have noticed the truck. Hell, in her mind she had a green light and no concern at all for the truck. She didn't see it."

Deep wrinkles appeared on Travis' brow in a manner directly proportional to their chances in the lawsuit. "Do you think she just went brain-dead?"

"Could be, but it's hard to tell. Puts us in a hell of a bind but, still, she should have seen him coming. My top choice is that she was distracted by something."

●

Joe Stetly was asking my brother about you. What's up?

●

Tom jotted his thoughts on the notepad:

- *Dilemma zone - bad decision*
- *No skid*
- *Woman - no concern for truck*

- *Why?*
- *Fault breakout - RV overhead, trucker ???*
- *Distraction – to what degree?*

His mind would put structure to the notes soon enough. For now, he had more information to gather.

"I'll head out to the scene later this afternoon. I'll probably take some vehicle photos, depending upon the quality of these. Matter of fact, I will regardless. Paige is doing some analysis on the overhead compartment. You need to give her billable hours for this."

"It's a deal."

Tom rose, inserted the photos in the envelopes and placed them with his notepad into a black leather briefcase. He walked to the door with Travis, past Lynn with a quick "See ya, beautiful," and down the hallway to the elevator.

Travis, hands in his pockets, walked to the elevator with Tom. As the door started to open, he asked, "Is it winnable?"

Tom stepped into the elevator and turned to Travis. His body blocked the beam of light from reaching the receptor that would allow the door to close. He replied, "Don't think so." A small twinkle emerged in his eyes. "But we'll cut some losses in both the criminal and civil trials." He backed to the rear of the elevator, disappearing behind closing doors.

That's what Travis wanted to hear.

●

The pay phone on Calhoun Street rang at exactly 2:30, ending Jud Weems' 15-minute wait. He lifted the receiver.

"Yep." He spoke with a twangy Texas drawl.

The voice at the other end was polished and succinct. "Make a full timing run tonight, without the load. I'll call at 3:30 tomorrow. Questions?"

"Nope."

The caller hung up. Jud placed the phone in the receiver, took a deep breath, and walked out into the hot midday air. It was refreshing compared to the inside of the phone booth. The time had come to get all this over with.

5

Tempering business with pleasure is the way to go. After surveying the accident scene, Tom and Susie were to meet Ross and Paige for dinner at the New Bay Brewery in Seabrook. Ross was forewarned that it would be a working dinner, but he knew that the work part would give way to the relaxing effects of several Miller Lites. Bill Acker sent the specifications on the van to Tom via fax. Tom would give copies to Paige at dinner.

Tom and Susie arrived at the intersection of Stryker Avenue and Texas 35 shortly before 8:00. Given the phenomenon of sidereal movement, Tom timed their arrival 22 minutes earlier than the actual time of the accident. The timing allowed them to survey the scene with the sun at an identical angle from the horizon as on the day of the accident. Weather conditions were similar, mostly clear, the setting sun backdropping occasional puffs of cumulus clouds. Another gorgeous Texas sunset entered the books.

They passed through the intersection from east to west, drove another 100 yards down Stryker Avenue and parked in an open area. Tom exited the car, moved around to Susie's side and opened her door. Chivalry wasn't dead quite yet. There were times when she opened the door herself, but on most occasions Tom continued to display the simple courtesies demanded of him as a boy. Susie hopped on the right fender next to Tom. Earlier he had separated photos of the scene from the later photos taken at the salvage yard.

Tom backed against the car, Susie peering over his shoulder.

"A rough guess, based on the damage patterns, says they were both going over 40, he probably 50 or so. Let's check it out." Tom gave the photos to Susie, took a small notebook and pen from his shirt pocket and stepped away from the car. Susie slid off the fender and walked with him to the innocent-looking intersection where

31

four lives had been lost.

At the northwest corner of the intersection they watched the traffic. Everything was normal. Tom made his way across Texas 35. He walked east to a position along Stryker Avenue where he estimated that the truck driver might have started checking for north-south traffic. Looking south along Texas 35 Tom visualized the Stetly family traveling north. He asked himself the big question, *Why did she keep going?*

He walked back to Susie. She was fixated on the roadway. They were quiet. It was obvious that they would not be able to verify a set of skid marks that belonged to the accident. Besides, the initial police report indicated that neither party had applied their brakes prior to impact. Tom found it strange since the black marks on the roadway clearly showed that many drivers had seen the need to apply brakes rather than collide with another vehicle in the intersection. Intrigued, Tom took out a pen and placed more entries into the notebook:

> BELTON vs RV: White vs Houston D.A./Colter
> - Open - visible area
> - Skid marks - many. None for RV?
> - Intersection accident history

"Anything new?" Susie inquired as Tom closed the notebook.

"Yeah, seems to be tire marks everywhere, but neither of our drivers hit the brakes. Still looks like they were playing chicken. How 'bout you, anything?"

"I just wonder if something was blocking their view." Susie, sensing she had missed the final chapter of a great novel, sighed, "We'll probably never know."

They repeated the process, looking at the accident scene from all four quadrants of the intersection. Tom added a few notes concerning possible speed, potential distractions, fatigue, and the degree of illumination. The visit was over by 8:30. They returned to their car. As Tom closed Susie's door, a shot of adrenaline jolted him - the sound of screeching brakes and an immediate blasting of a car's horn pierced his brain. He could not understand the cacophony of Tex-Mex profanity being hurled between a pickup truck and an RV similar to Martha Stetly's. Tom did understand the symbolic gesture of middle fingers being thrust into the Texas sky by occupants of both vehicles.

"This is one shitty intersection. Hope Paige has already ordered me a beer."

●

The New Bay Brewery was indeed new. Occupying a place of prominence overlooking Galveston Bay, the two-floor wooden structure was an exact replica of an earlier version, the Bay Brewery. Like its predecessor, the New Bay Brewery sat perched atop reinforced concrete pilings designed to let storm surge pass harmlessly underneath the restaurant. The open area would serve as a parking facility until the arrival of a hurricane. Patrons negotiated wooden steps up to the lower of two restaurant sections. An open-air porch surrounded the main restaurant area, providing a spectacular view of sailboats playing in the bay beneath formations of white pelicans. Three round tables with wooden rocking chairs occupied the southeast corner of the porch. The New Bay Brewery lay one-quarter mile north of the original location across the Clear Creek Channel from Kemah, Texas and its well-known restaurant complex. Graced with Texas charm, its own microbrewery and delicious food, the New Bay Brewery would not have to survive on the overflow from Kemah. On many nights the oppressive heat of August would drive even the heartiest Texans inside. But this night was warm, clear and blessed with a gentle, yet constant, breeze complementing ice-cold beer and anything Cajun. The timing was perfect as the standing-line had dissipated and luck offered Paige and Ross the round table in the corner of the deck. Paige ordered Miller Lites for everyone.

"Dad, Susie, over here." Paige signaled her parents' arrival.

Tom and Susie both waved and walked to the table.

Ross stood, reflecting good South Texas manners.

"Evening Mr. Seiler, Mrs. Seiler."

Tom thought, *good, ought to be a little gun-shy,* then quickly shook Ross' hand, pulled back a chair for Susie and immediately grabbed the Miller Lite. It was half-gone before he sat down.

The conversation was light, concerning new jobs and the new relationship between Ross and Paige. The four rocked leisurely, comfortably together.

Tom asked Ross, "Are they going to let you stay in Houston?" Tom would be ready if Paige married Ross and moved away, but it was a possibility he did not relish.

"I think so. They're headquartered here in Houston and that's where most of the CPAs work." Ross was more hopeful than convincing.

Paige broke in, allowing Ross to drink his beer. "What he didn't tell you is that he's already moving up the corporate ladder. He's been asked to work on a brokering project of some sort. He's in charge of a financial analysis team." Paige smiled as Ross shifted uncomfortably in his seat. She continued. "He also got a call from AEP wanting to know if he was open to another job opportunity."

Tom thought out loud. "Sounds like the hounds are on the trail." He looked at Paige. "How's that play out with you?" Tom's inference of separation caught

Paige unprepared. She recovered nicely.

"I'd like to see him stick around here." She looked Ross in the eyes and put her hand on top of his.

Ross glanced at Paige quickly, then returned his focus to his beer bottle.

Tom saved Ross. "I'll drink to that." He held up his bottle in a toast.

Tom and Susie noticed Ross grabbing his bottle with his non-drinking hand. Some beer sloshed out of the bottle and he choked on the rest. They loved it.

The situation was quite clear to Tom and Susie: Paige was probably falling in love with Ross; Ross was totally, reverently, in love with Paige. They would get married someday. They ordered one fried catfish and three Cajun crawfish dinners. With the arrival of Tom's third beer he directed the conversation to the accident.

"Let's talk accidents. Here Paige, look at these." Tom gave Paige a 19-page packet containing information as to the specifications of the RV, photos, an analysis of the structure of the overhead compartment and general conclusions. Tom waited a few seconds while Paige scanned the pages. Then he continued.

"My basic conclusion is that they did a pissant job of providing sufficient structural integrity in the front window portion of the overhead compartment. The photos show fractures at all four of the window corners." As he talked Tom searched through the pages to the appropriate photos. "I'll be taking some more photos tomorrow. Inside and out."

Paige asked, "Does this report give details about the materials and the construction methodology?"

Tom showed excitement. "Yeah, check this out." He quickly turned to one photo showing a close-up view of one of the corners.

"The corner is made out of thin-gauge aluminum and Styrofoam." He stuck his finger at the corner of the photo. "Here, you can see where some vinyl-covered plywood is bonded to the Styrofoam from the inside. This is really bad news." Everyone saw the eagerness in his eyes, a result of an intangible sensing on his part. He found an indicator that someone other than his client was to be partially at fault. For a chess player, it was that look at the board that said *'Checkmate'*. "Can you model this accurately?"

Paige smiled. "My senior research involved finite-element modeling of a surface of contact problem. I can do it." She had an incredibly pretty smile. "I'll start tomorrow night. I've already thought about how to attack the problem and it looks like I've got all I need to do it. I'll give you a call by Thursday to go over the details. Sound good?"

"Damn, I raise smart kids. Ross, you're in the company of genius in action."

Ross did not answer immediately. He could only focus on an insatiable sensation in the pit of his stomach. He started awkwardly, "Yessir . . . ," then recovered beautifully, ". . . must be in the genes." Tom and Susie looked at Paige and smiled.

Tom tilted the beer and finished it off as the waitress arrived with four plates of Southern delicacies. "Remember," he smiled to the waitress, "the tip is dependent on always keeping a full beer to my front."

The waitress remembered Tom from before. "Sweetie, I'm in for my usual big tip tonight." With the announcement she set a single, full, Miller Lite in front of Tom. "How 'bout everyone else?" They ordered another round of drinks.

It was almost midnight when they parted company.

6

Twenty-two miles, as the crow flies, to the southeast of Seabrook, Sybil Weems was serving a final order of beer and Cajun shrimp to a table of four at Landfall 1900, named after the 1900 hurricane that took 6,000 lives.

"Here you go. Best shrimp on the island." Sybil smiled at her customers.

Her feet ached. On this typical slow Monday night she was bored and ready to return to her home in Alvin. On Monday nights Sybil and her sister Marla each waitressed six tables. Slow nights were not good for either of them. On Wednesdays, Fridays and Saturdays both women enjoyed their work. The customers were pretty good people; other than an occasional nasty drunk, Sybil and Marla found the company generally pleasant. Unlike some restaurants, they did not pool their tips with other waitresses. They paid the two busboys $10 each out of their tips and kept the rest. A good night brought in more than $100. On top of the tips came an hourly wage of $2.50. They were also paid an additional $15 each night to close. A year's wages came to better than $30,000, not bad for two women who did not finish high school.

The two couples at her table continued eating their shrimp and downing beer over small talk and bad jokes.

"Nate, you need to pray for my Grandmother," one of the men exclaimed.

"Well, what the hell happened to her?" Nate wrinkled his eyes in a quizzical frown.

"Those damn thunderstorms we had last week were terrible. The water came up and washed her right off her porch and into the cypress swamp."

Nate, with a poker face, egged his partner on. "Did they find her?"

"Yeah, but she was dead, pinned underneath a cypress stump."

"Vern, that's sure as hell a big bummer."

37

Vern, with a serious look accentuated with exaggerated wrinkles in his brow, exclaimed, "Well, it's not all bad. When they found her she had 20 blue crabs on her - we're gonna run her again tomorrow!"

The two men hooted and hollered, stomped their feet and gave each other a high-five. For their part, the two young women rolled their eyes toward Heaven in mock disbelief. "That's disgusting, Vern."

They told a few more jokes. Would it ever end? Finally, the two comedians and haggard dates got up, left a tip far larger than was expected and sauntered off for the streets of Galveston.

Marla watched them leave and commented, "Now there go two guys who won't get laid tonight. Damn, I'm tired."

The two waitresses began their final charge of the night. They cleaned off the tables, refilled the condiment containers, placed chairs on top of tables and vacuumed the indoor-outdoor carpeting. After vacuuming they returned the chairs to the floor and set each of the tables for the next day. By the time they finished it was 1:00, early morning - it seemed later.

The ritual played out night after night. Sybil drove the '86 Ford Taurus to Frasier's, next door to Landry's Oyster Bar on 15th Street. Like their sisters, the D'Arcy brothers had worked the restaurant since the late 1980's. Their early arrival afforded both women the opportunity to relax at a small table. The stale, dank smell of the empty bar was thick. The auxiliary lights were on, the room too bright for drinking beer. Hank D'Arcy, the oldest brother, walked over and placed a Coors Light in front of each sister. He gently scratched the top of Sybil's head before moving off to finish closing up the bar. The youngest of the four was named Zebulon, nicknamed 'Zip' by family friends. They were the only four remaining at Frasier's.

Hank cold-rinsed the last few beer mugs. "Syb, you still thinkin' 'bout leavin' him?"

"Yeah, it's all over. He knows it, I know it. Hell, we don't talk no more'n two words a day when he's home. I need something more out of life."

Zip added, "Once a jerk, always a jerk. I knew Jud was a scum-bag when I first met his sorry ass."

"Well, least he never hit me. All I do is clean 'is clothes. But the bad thing is bein' lonelier when he's around than when he's gone. Let's change the subject. Better yet, let's go." She took one last sip from the half-full bottle, grabbed Marla's empty bottle, and placed them on the bar.

Hank emptied one into the sink, then dropped the bottles in a recycling bin and joined his sisters.

Marla, Sybil and Hank walked out onto Seawall Boulevard. Zip zeroed out the register and placed money and receipts in a safe built into a desk in the manager's office. He felt good that the owners trusted him to handle the money. Similarities among the four were remarkable. The age difference from Marla to Zip was five years. The two girls were the protectors up until Hank entered junior high school. Sibling squabbles had been rare. Their father died of lung cancer when Marla was a high school senior. She dropped out of school to earn money for the family, demanding the others finish school; Sybil didn't, the brothers did. All four worked hard – paper routes, waiting on tables, service station attendants, whatever it took – and all were disciplined. Though higher education and wealth had eluded them, the D'Arcys were good, honest, people.

Zip closed and double-locked the restaurant door and caught up with the other three by the time they reached the car. The women climbed into the back, Sybil on the left and Marla on the right. Hank drove and Zip rode 'shotgun.' The rule was that both riders in the front stayed awake. The duties of driver, shotgun and sleepers ran on a weeklong schedule, rotating on Wednesdays of each week.

The car had seen a thousand trips between Galveston and Alvin. They turned north on 15th and then west on Broadway. The women were tired. Sybil's head and body leaned left; Marla's leaned right. They were in a deep sleep by the time the blue Taurus entered I-45, also known as the Gulf Freeway.

"Got a smoke?" Hank pushed in the lighter simultaneously with asking the question.

Zip reached into his shirt pocket and pulled out the remains of a pack of Camel cigarettes. He tapped on the end of the bottom of the pack, forcing two of the three cigarettes to rise out of the opening. He gripped one gently with his teeth and offered the other protruding cigarette to his brother. Zip used the final cigarette as a roller around which he wound the remainder of the paper pack, a habit from his junior-high days.

It was after two in the morning when they passed over the Galveston Causeway separating East Bay and West Bay. Five minutes later the car left the Gulf Freeway at exit 7 and picked up Route 6 at Bayou Vista. Alvin lay in an almost straight line, 22 miles to the northwest. Save a few cars passing off into the distance along the Freeway, traffic was nonexistent.

"How 'bout some fishin' Sunday? Alex is takin' his Cobia out and me an' him's going' for Reds." Hank spent the bulk of his free time either fishing off the pier at Galveston or in the Gulf when the opportunity presented itself. "Alex'll cover the fuel and me and you can split the beer and sandwiches."

"Don't have nothin' else t' do. Count me in." Zip was not a fishing zealot, but he did enjoy being out in the Gulf. The open water gave him a sense of freedom and he knew Hank would bring equipment for both of them.

Hank continued discussing fishing, partly because he truly loved it and partly because he was more tired than usual. They entered Algoa at exactly 2:30. Neither Hank nor Zip was aware of a car parked along the side of what had once been a service station. They traveled another quarter of a mile before the car and its single occupant eased onto Texas 6, accelerated gently, soon reaching a speed equal to that of the Taurus. The open country between Bayou Vista and Alvin is flat as a table, spotted with occasional buildings of different sorts and a few stands of trees. Hitchcock and Santa Fe were barely large enough to command a few streetlights. Visibility, day or night, is unlimited. Zip found it necessary to fight sleep by tightly tracing and closing the thumb and middle finger of his open right hand from the temples, across his eyebrows and finally closing onto the bridge of his nose. He squeezed for three seconds and simultaneously shook his head while slowly blinking his eyes in exaggeration. He could only respond to Hank's questions with one-syllable words. Hank had been there many times himself and appreciated the loyalty of his younger brother trying so hard to stay awake.

●

Texas 35 and Route 6 intersect on the eastern side of Alvin. The Ford turned south on Texas 35. As soon as it passed beneath the trestle of the Atchison, Topeka and Santa Fe Railway, the driver of the trailing car spoke into the handset of a CB, "Mark one." Jud Weems followed his wife and her siblings from less than 800 yards, unnoticed.

A reply came over another CB, "Mark one."

The car traveled along Texas 35 for exactly two miles. The highway gently curves clockwise so as to circle the eastern half of town. Once it reaches the southern extremity of Alvin, Texas 35 curves back to the left and moves to the south-southwest in a straight line. At the high point of the curve, Farm Road 1462 intersects it. Hank slowed and turned right onto 1462.

"Mark two."

"Mark two."

Jud slowed and turned right on Mustang Road. He would travel aimlessly around Alvin for 30 minutes and then drive to the small, faded-white, house on South Park that he sometimes shared with Sybil. Sybil would be asleep before he arrived.

Farm Road 1462 approaches Alvin from the west-southwest. It runs for seven miles without so much as a trace of a curve. As though designed in a manner to deflect boredom, the road enters the town with a sweeping curve to the right, then back to the left and finally back to the right where it ends at the Route 35 intersection. At the beginning of the first curve Farm Road 1462 intersects at an angle with State Road 172, also known as Parker School Road. Some called it Parker Road for short.

The diesel engine of the Peterbilt increased in pitch as the driver pulled onto Farm Road 1462 from the right shoulder. The sequence of acceleration and shifting of gears had been rehearsed in detail many times. The start point was exactly one and a quarter miles west-southwest of the Parker Road intersection.

From Texas 35 it took the Taurus two minutes and 12 seconds before slowing at the Parker Road - Farm Road 1462 intersection. A small forested area on the south side of Farm Road 1462 obscured Hank's view beyond the curve. As he slowed and prepared to turn right on Parker Road, unusual patterns of light pierced the trees. There was something different in the movement of the lights that seemed to catch Hank off-guard. In an instant the huge tractor-trailer entered the curve traveling at a speed that seemed to Hank to be in excess of 100 miles an hour. He was both mesmerized and paralyzed as adrenaline shot through him as never before.

The empty rig drifted over the centerline of the roadway and aimed at the defenseless car. Less than one hundred feet from impact, the driver cut deliberately hard to the right. The vibration and wind vortex buffeted the car with tornadic fury. Hank could do nothing more than look up into the cab above him. A face, intense with both purpose and odd curiosity, glanced down at the victims. It passed by no more than three feet away, spewing rocks, sand and diesel fumes onto the car. The rig swayed as it accelerated, then corrected itself and negotiated the two remaining curves leading to Texas 35. It disappeared into the night as sand and gravel danced their dance. Hank was in shock. He could not recognize the make, color or license of the rig. He was only aware that some crazy bastard had nearly killed him.

●

At 3:30 Tuesday afternoon the pay phone on Calhoun rang. Jud Weems was ready.

"Yep" - again with a Texas drawl.

"Successful?"

"Yep."

"Your wife driving this week?"

"Yep. Starts tomorrow."

"Friday night. I'll handle the cargo. Questions?"

"Nope."

The caller hung up. So did Jud.

7

Tom loved solving problems; he disliked trips to places such as the Harris County District Attorney's office. He looked up at the massive structure and pondered those working in its bowels. There are sterling souls who labor in law enforcement for all the right reasons. Thank God for them; otherwise the country would disintegrate from greed, corruption and chaos. Yet, every time he made the journey Tom ended up asking himself *Why are so many of these people such assholes?* His mind could not shake the images of his youngest brother lying in a hospital bed, under arrest, with a gaping gunshot wound to the leg. The circumstances behind the shooting by a Houston cop were not important. That he met exactly one cop who treated him with respect during the episode was important. Tom felt a tug of remorse that he never thanked the officer. He hoped the young man had remained on the force.

Tom looked at his watch. *Fifteen minutes early.* Early arrival would not speed his seeing the District Attorney. Arriving late meant not seeing anyone at all. Because of the potential for criminal charges against Belton Trucking, Wolfpack and the driver, District Attorney Elizabeth Harker would be directly involved. To most people, a private meeting with the Houston District Attorney was a big deal. To Tom, it was a meeting, no more, no less. He was mildly surprised that the D.A. would be personally involved. *Why would she meet with me? Why not one of her underlings?* He dismissed the questions and began to focus on Elizabeth Harker. He gave her high marks for her relentless pursuit of wrongdoers. He gave her low marks for bedside manner.

Tom presented himself to a nondescript receptionist and took a seat on an old wooden Deacon's bench. He opened his briefcase and took out the manila folder with 'Stetly vs. Belton' printed neatly in ink at the top. He perused the individual

43

pieces of information he had gathered and the structured outline notes formulating an explanation as to what actually happened on that unfortunate Sunday.

"You can go in." The receptionist was neither warm nor cold.

Rising, Tom glanced again at his watch. It was 4:20, a short wait. He walked in the door without knocking and proceeded to the large oak desk behind which sat the District Attorney. She remained seated.

"Good to see you again, Ms. Harker." Tom lied. "I appreciate the opportunity to talk to you about the Stetly case."

Head down, eyes trained on a sheet of legal paper, she intentionally did not acknowledge his presence. *This is billable time.* The thought floated through his mind. He was in no particular hurry.

After probably half a minute, Elizabeth Terese Harker looked up, put down a pencil and rose from behind the desk. She turned her back towards Tom and walked to the large windows overlooking traffic just below the second floor office. The late afternoon sun cast her as a dark, thin statue, both hands at the back of her neck, grasping the rope of brown hair cascading down her back. Tom mused at the amount of energy she used when her guard was up. He had never seen her when she wasn't 'on stage.'

"Your driver murdered four people." Elizabeth Harker spoke with seething clarity. "Your trucking company is just as guilty since they couldn't care less about the drivers they hire. Beyond the criminal charges, the family deserves more than your clients could ever pay." She returned to her chair and leaned forward, resting on her elbows with hands interlocked, supporting her chin.

The D.A. did not offer Tom a chair. He sat down. He acted out his role and she acted hers. She played the ball to his court.

"How can you sleep at night knowing what your clients have done? Of course, I guess the pay is good."

"I'm here to clarify the whole incident as to what physically happened. I trust the court's judgment to sort it all out." His return of serve was deliberately soft. "I was told that I would be able to talk to the investigating officer and view a VCR of the accident scene. Is that possi . . ."

"Who told you anything about a VCR?" She seemed caught slightly off-guard but recovered quickly. "I didn't know we had some film until this morning. I haven't even seen it." She was lying.

"I don't really remember anyone specifically talking to me about it. It must be in some of the notes I received from D, G and W. Possibly the investigation report." He was lying.

Her interest in the videotape automatically made it a significant piece of evidence, although he did not know why.

Tom deliberately changed the subject. "How long did it take the police to arrive on the scene?"

"Don't ask me, ask the cop, he's on the fourth floor. Officer Newton." Liz Harker was irritated. She continued. "I have work to do."

Tom rose, thinking to himself, *A two minute meeting? I don't get it.* "Thanks for the help. I appreciate it."

As he closed the door behind him, Tom could hear the plastic-on-plastic sound of the District Attorney fumbling with the phone. He ignored the receptionist and found his way to the stairs leading to the fourth floor.

Room 414 was a maze of cubicles. Plexiglas panes rose from three-foot high metal partitions. Two pathways provided for a row of small offices on each side of the room and a double row, touching back-to-back, down the middle. Senior investigators owned the outside cubicles with windows. Tom asked for directions to Officer Newton and was pointed to the second cubicle on the far right. He arrived just as the policeman was putting down the phone receiver.

"I'm Tom Seiler, hope you got the word that I would be stopping by on the Stetly case."

The officer rose quickly, precipitating a quick grimace followed by a genuine smile, and extended his hand. "I'm Bill Newton; if you can handle the mess, let's talk. Coffee?"

"Thanks. Black is great."

Bill Newton went for coffee; Tom thought to himself, *nice guy*. Tom noticed a limp and conjured up a shootout in a drug sting gone badly. He retrieved his notes and a list of questions concerning the death of the Stetlys.

Their discussion focused on why the two drivers were so unaware of each other. Bill Newton gave Tom a copy of his final report. A few minor additions to the initial report, nothing earth-shaking.

"Yeah, I'd say that it was no later than 8:20 when I arrived. There was still some light in the sky."

"Did you see anyone alive?"

"No, but the paramedics were working on Mrs. Stetly. She and her husband were both inside the cab. His head was crushed, probably killed instantly. She had been bleeding from the mouth and ears and I saw a lot of blood on her shirt and Levi's when I looked in. They took her out first and were attempting stabilization even before they put her in the ambulance. I was told at the scene that a good Samaritan took a little girl directly to the hospital. I never saw her. The husband and two boys were gone. The boys were twins, both with broken necks. It was a strange sight, especially the angle their heads were resting relative to their upper bodies. The exact same. I remember thinking 'identical in life, identical in death'.

One of them landed on top of the flatbed and into the equipment that was being hauled. It was a large diesel generator with some peripheral support items stored in packing crates. The other boy hit the side of the flatbed, probably with his head, and was lying partially under the rec vehicle. I can only conclude that somehow he spent a short time attached to the flatbed and then fell off as the two vehicles came to a stop."

"No skid marks?"

"None that seemed to fit braking." Bill continued, thinking out loud. "There were tire marks from the front of the rec vehicle from where it wedged into the side of the rig. Truck driver dragged the Stetly's van with him after impact. As for other skid marks, there were lots of them all over, but not from either of these vehicles. Really strange." Newton's forehead furrowed with concentration.

Tom broke in, "What about the VCR tape? What'd it show?"

"Not much really. My partner, Fred Murray, and I took the video. Two parts. The first part I took at the scene that night. Shows the vehicles, three of the bodies and a panorama of the intersection. Took it 360 degrees to capture anything that might be useful. I probably screwed up somewhat by not filming the driver of the truck more than I did. He was stone sober - nervous as hell, but stone sober. I did catch some of his mannerisms. You'll be able to see them – shaking his head, confused look and the like. Fred took the second part two days later. I drove. It consists of several drive-through scenarios from both directions traveled by the vehicles. He tried to replicate what either driver had seen. Nothing conclusive."

In addition to the investigation report, Tom asked for copies of any notes Bill may have jotted down. He also asked to see the VCR tape.

"No problem, got it right here. Hang on." He picked up the phone and placed an interoffice call.

"Ma'am, it's Officer Newton, we're going to take a look at the Stetly tape." After a short pause, he responded into the phone, "Yes, ma'am, in the video room. Yes ma'am."

Bill turned to Tom. The ravages of nearly three decades on the force showed in multiple wrinkles at the eyes and forehead. His drooping posture took considerable height away from a former six-foot-five frame. "Let's go check it out. The D.A. wants to view it with us."

"I thought she'd seen enough of it."

"Well, I'll give her credit for being thorough."

I thought so, mused Tom. They rose and walked through doors at the end of room 414. Inside were four rows of chairs, a rectangular table in the front, a small podium, a screen in front of a blackboard and a large screen TV, with internal VCR, placed at an angle to the front right corner of the room. Bill offered Tom a seat in the second row nearest the TV. The front row was for the District Attorney.

Another 20 minutes passed before she arrived. The two men passed the time in light conversation covering minor additional details of the accident, the sometimes unpleasant nature of the District Attorney and general anecdotes about their personal lives. The focus fell mostly on Bill's life. Bill Newton had grown up in Houston. Following graduation from Jesse Jones High School in 1969 he enlisted in the Marine Corps. In April 1970 he deployed to Vietnam as a rifleman with Echo Company, 2d Battalion, 7th Marine Regiment, 1st Marine Division. A single round from an AK-47 was the fork in the road for his life. Most of the time Police Sergeant Bill Newton did not think about his limp. Occasionally, a sharp hot sting returned him to the Que Son Valley. August 19, 1970 . . .

"I'm hit. Oh God, I'm hit."

Marine Corporal William Newton, his head ringing, looked up. Through the dissipating haze of smoke and dust, he began to see the clear blue sky of an early Vietnamese morning. Popping sounds and human voices invaded his senses. So did searing pain in his right leg and right elbow.

"Oh, help me, I'm hit." The three marines had huddled too close together when the grenade landed next to Lance Corporal Casey Carns' leg. The explosion killed Carns instantly and blew the other two marines in opposite directions. Private Johnny Sims lay in an open area that, except for the grace of God, should have been the place of his death. The blistering fire from multiple AK-47's tore through the brush, the ground and into the marines. Beyond the shards of fractured steel that found their way into his buttocks and left leg, Sims had taken one round in his shoulder and another through his left side. Disciplined marines, they responded to the withering fire within seconds. Chaos reigned. An unknown unit of the 2d NVA Division had caught the second platoon of Echo Company in an 'L' shaped ambush.

Shit. I've got to get him. Oh, God.

Immobilized by the fragment lodged in his right elbow, the young corporal acted out of Marine Corps instinct. Using his left arm and leg, Bill Newton inched his way to his fallen comrade. He dragged himself next to the upper torso of the dead Casey Carns, actually using the fallen marine's body for protection. Newton, for a split-second, recalled watching Casey and other young marines laughing at a bar in Koza, Okinawa, playing the game 'Bears Around the Icehole.' Gasping for air, directly in harm's way, Bill Newton reached Sims after almost two minutes in the open. His only option, given his wounds, was to push with his head in Sims' upper side.

"Move yourself. Help me out. Move your leg! You've got to move your leg!"

The desperate marines struggled sideways for 20 feet towards the relative safety of a small depression. Had safety been two feet closer, Bill Newton might have gone to Marine Officer Candidate School, commanded a marine amphibious force battalion in Desert Storm and finished an illustrious career as a Major General commanding the Corps training base at Camp LeJeune. But he wasn't two feet closer. As he moved his huge frame into the depression, a single round tore through both legs, taking away almost two inches of his left femur before lodging in his right hamstring. With both legs and his right arm useless, the young marine corporal garnered his last reservoir of strength to pull himself into the depression. The blue sky faded to white haze . . . and then to emptiness.

●

Two days later Bill Newton woke to excruciating pain. His recuperation in the VA hospital at Valley Forge lasted 16 months. Private Sims retired from the Corps 23 years later as a lieutenant colonel.

Bill Newton married an army nurse in 1972, the day following her separation from the service. Two children and a few small jobs as a salesman provided the backdrop to their first three years. He fought hard for a physical disability waiver and was accepted into the Houston Police Academy in 1975.

●

Elizabeth Harker walked in the room and took a seat in the fourth row, furthest from the TV. "Let's see the tape."

The tape lasted 18 minutes. The portion taken shortly after the accident was exactly as explained by Bill Newton. The filming commenced immediately after the ambulance departed for Ben Taub with Martha Stetly. The film clip began with a view of the two vehicles taken at eye level from a distance of 10 feet. The passenger side of the driver's compartment was wedged at an angle to the rig. It appeared almost fused to the bed of the trailer, some five feet behind the fifth wheel. The camera zoomed in on Joe Stetly. His position was upright, but only because the right side of the RV had the appearance of having been sucked into the side of the rig. A violent blow, probably caused by a 6x6 inch wooden extension to the tiedown system, had crushed his skull. From the side, Joe Stetly's head resembled a half-deflated football. The camera lingered uncomfortably on the remains of Joe Stetly, suggesting Bill Newton had become mesmerized at the scene, forgetting that he was filming an accident.

Liz Harker was not pleased with the amateurish filming. "Let the photographers take the pictures."

The camera caught the two dead boys. They resembled mannequins in a grotesque department store window display. The bodies, Andrew's on the trailer and Ben's on the pavement, lay with heads angled almost 90 degrees to their bodies. The orientation of their bodies paralleled the 18-wheeler. Arms down along each torso and legs extended. Save a few tendons maintaining a meaningless attachment to his body, Ben Stetly's right leg was completely severed just above the knee. Again, the camera spent more time recording the carnage than was necessary. This time, however, the camera was shut off before surveying a new scene. The quality of camera work improved with time. The angle of the RV with respect to the tractor-trailer and its damage pattern corroborated the initial finding that the RV impacted the rig perpendicular and, in the process of being wedged, was spun in a counter-clockwise motion causing the additional depth of crushing damage to the passenger's side. The impending darkness made the parallel tire marks difficult to detect. The next shots taken of the RV were made from the flatbed. The camera angle looked down on the final orientation of the front of the RV and the broken overhead compartment window section, each corner torn as a strip of paper. The camera then panned down to two men, one a policeman, Bill's partner; the other John Schrauder, driver of the Belton tractor-trailer. John Schrauder was clearly confused and distraught. His head hung down over a stooped frame, arms behind his back with his hands each in a back pocket of his jeans; he seemed almost as pathetic as the lifeless bodies prostrate on the ground. Always looking down, John Schrauder continually shook his head from side to side as though saying "No" to each question. He seemed unable to comprehend the totality of what had just happened. The first segment ended with the filming of the intersection, taken both from the flatbed, 130 feet west of the point of impact, and finally at the exact collision point in the middle of the intersection. The traffic light was functioning normally, ignored by drivers being directed by another policeman. There were no visual obstructions for either driver.

A new scene, taken two days later from inside a patrol car, appeared on the screen. Bill Newton stopped the tape. "That's the first part ma'am. Would you like me to replay any of it?"

"No. Keep playing."

The movie rolled on. The first segment, three minutes in length, depicted what Martha Stetly might have seen. A second segment consisted of three runs, consuming another three minutes, in the direction driven by the tractor-trailer. The first run was a simple drive-through of a green light. As the patrol car passed through the intersection the camera panned left to an almost empty road showing only a single car coming to a stop at the light. The second run was taken with the camera pointed due west. The light turned red and the car stopped. While stopped, Bill's companion traced 180 degrees from south to north. Again, nothing that would divert or impair one's view of all oncoming traffic. *It just doesn't track.* Tom couldn't put it all together, but he did sense Elizabeth Harker's watching his reaction more than the film. The final segment was taken as the patrol car again drove west. The camera focused first to the south, swung slowly right, and then re-centered on the traffic light and an oncoming eastbound truck. As they neared the intersection the camera revealed the light changing to yellow. A quick rise and fall in the camera picture, caused by the driver accelerating the car, caught the light as it changed to red. The final second focused on a truck heading south at a speed probably in excess of the posted limit. The TV monitor went to static. Bill stopped the VCR and waited this time for the D.A. to speak.

"Any questions Mr. Seiler?"

Tom suppressed a desire to smile. "Not much to help solve the puzzle, but I do thank you for giving me access to the investigation." He, of course, knew that she was required by law to give him access to all evidence.

"Fine, I have work to do." She left the room.

Bill put the VCR on rewind, shook his head and laughed lightly. "Touché, Tom. She's smart as a whip, but politeness is not her strong suit." He tried to defend a case of bad manners. "Sometimes she's pleasant. Probably a little too taken with her position."

"Doesn't bother me. I guess PMS is an all-month affair for some." Both men smiled. "OK to take a copy of the tape?" Tom had prepared himself not to react to anything important on the tape. Now he needed to watch it again, without the D.A. watching him.

"Sure, I've got two additional copies. Did anything jump out at you?" Bill hadn't noticed anything that would solve the riddle of the four fatalities.

"I'm not sure, but there's plenty of information on the tape that may help." Tom smiled, holding out his right hand, palm down, and added, "Actually, I was more concerned with Mother Superior smacking me with a ruler."

The men returned to the small cubicle representing the stature that three decades on the Houston Police Force had given to Bill. Several citations for bravery, two bullet holes, one in the abdomen and one in the shoulder, intense loyalty and absolute honesty had not been enough for him to rise to lieutenant. Yet, in his mind and in fact, he had made a difference. Tom knew little of Bill Newton, but he liked what he had seen of the huge cop.

Bill gave Tom a copy of the videotape and offered another cup of coffee. Tom declined the coffee, put the tape in his briefcase and left.

Tom walked briskly to Lowe's Parking, dissecting the VCR viewing with each step. He was eager to play it at home. He would let the District Attorney ponder his interest in the film. *She doesn't know shit about what I saw.* He gave his ticket to the parking attendant, then made a call on his cell phone.

A quiet voice interrupted the fourth ring. "John Schrauder."

●

Two men sat in a corner booth at Sodbuster's Country Steakhouse. Their quiet conversation blended into the late-afternoon din of waiters, diners, kitchen noise and country-western music.

"I did what you told me." Buck's eyes sparkled with pride and anticipation. "Booked for Wednesday after Labor Day out of Corpus. A week at the Renaissance Aruba Beach Resort, where ever'n the hell that's at." The travel agent had conjured up very vivid, very accurate, images of pristine sandy beaches, friendly people, a private island, gambling at the resort casino, marvelous eating and spectacular entertainment. Arubans had named themselves the inhabitants of One Happy Island. Anyone who had ever celebrated New Year's Eve in Aruba knew the title to be true. "Hell, I've never been nowhere but Mexico, and then just t'get laid. Wish I was goin' for real. But after it's done, I'm going everyfuckinwhere." Buck took a large swig from his bottle of Lone Star, belched slightly and smiled in anticipation of many vacations – beaches, gambling, liquor, women, the high life – he would soon be able to afford.

"O.K., have a ball. But do your job first. You'll load Friday afternoon. Only thing to postpone it will be a call from me." Jud looked around the room, then added, "But don't expect a call. This is all tied to the case going on in Houston. The family killed out on 35." He looked around again. "The closer we are to that trial, the more money we're looking at. Don't ask me why, but I've been told. So, do everything exactly the way we planned. Don't fuck it up. We hit on this thing and in less than a year we both retire to any place on Earth." Jud worried about Buck's ability to convince the police that he was an unlucky participant in a tragic accident. He was more worried about Buck's mouth.

The plan was straightforward. Steel tubing ejected from a tractor-trailer traveling too fast tragically destroys a car with a family of four. The driver has a real reason to be speeding. He began a haul from Houston to Corpus loaded with steel tubing. Outside of Rockport he realizes he's left his airline tickets and vacation vouchers in his rented apartment in League City. He decides to return for his vacation packet and makes a valiant, though naive, effort to make up some lost time. An animal in the road precipitates a defensive swerve by the driver. Unfortunately, the four siblings become targets of the steel missiles propelled from the out-of-control 18-wheeler. The driver stops to render assistance and even calls the highway patrol over his CB radio. The trial will be quick and decisive, as will be the civil suit against Flagg Brothers. Civil suit juries in Brazoria County tend to vote Democratic and give large awards to a sole-surviving member of a family destroyed by poor hiring and driver training policies and greedy corporate executives. As for the driver – no drinking involved, attempts to help at all levels – maybe six months at the most. Maybe nothing. A small price to pay.

In anticipation of his soon-to-be wealth, Jud gave the waitress a $10 bill for the two beers. "Keep it sweetheart."

Now that's a nice guy. Hope he comes back soon, the waitress thought to herself. She looked through the front window at the two men walking into the Texas sun towards separate cars.

●

"Hello, this is Tom Seiler, Susie and I must be out and about, so just leave a number and I'll get back to you just as quick as I can . . . beeeeep."

"Daddy, it's Paige, just wanted to . . ."

"Hi kid, what's goin' on?" Tom was first her father and then her best friend. Whether he would peacefully relinquish the latter role to Ross had not yet been answered.

"I just wanted to let you know that Ross and I will make it down to Port A on Friday afternoon. The analysis is dead on target. You ought to see the stress pattern I generated. Right out of the textbook. It'll be easy to show not enough structural integrity existed at the corners. We're going down to Galveston Beach with Brad and Sarah Davis for a Labor Day party so we'll have to leave on Sunday afternoon."

"Wish you could stay longer. Steve and Kelly will be with us. We're going to break from the pack and take them to dinner at Jay's Sunday night. Just a chance to welcome her into the family. Can't believe they eloped. Saved me some money and saved her dad a fortune." Tom smiled in his judgment that Steve had picked a winner. "By the way, bring some of your work with you. We can find a few minutes and see where things stand."

"O.K., the computer's still on and I've got more work to do. Ross says hello."

"He'd better. Catch you on the flip. Love ya kid." Tom hung up.

Ross put his arms around Paige, kissing the back of her neck. Paige turned around, giving him a long, passionate kiss. She reached her arms around his neck and lovingly told him, "Sorry lover boy, you don't constitute billable hours."

"Damn."

8

"He's here Sarah." John Schrauder called to his wife from the porch.

Tom pulled up to a small, wooden frame house on Huisache Street in Bellaire. A covered porch, simply decorated with two rocking chairs and a small, metallic-gray, round table, faced the street. John rose from the chair and walked to the wooden railing. Three flower boxes, with an assortment of buttercups, violets and angel's breath, adorned the railing. A wooden kitchen chair had been added for Tom's visit.

As Tom got out of his car, John walked down the steps. He met Tom on the sidewalk, extending his hand. They shook hands firmly as John spoke. "You must be Tom Seiler. Thanks for coming by."

"Glad to meet you John. Wish the circumstances were better. Nice place." Neither was adept at small talk. It was not the time for small talk.

The porch's northern exposure provided shade throughout the day, making it an ideal sanctuary for John and Sarah. In better times, they rocked the evenings away in pleasant conversations. Not much for television, the Schrauders had a two-hour per night rule for their two daughters. Once the homework was done the girls were always welcome to join their parents on the porch.

As the two men reached the top step, Sarah Schrauder appeared at the door. She placed a tray holding three glasses of iced tea on the table, wiped moisture from her hands and reached towards a new friend. "Hi Tom, I've heard some good things about you." Her handshake was strong, unexpected to Tom given her petite stature and the circumstances. At first glance one could see a woman who worked very hard over the years; a second look revealed a woman still graced with beauty. A gentle smile, a perfect nose and symmetrical blue eyes overpowered wrinkles at her eyes and premature streaks of gray.

"Probably heard that from Travis, so you might not want to hold too much stock in it." He tried a little levity.

Sarah smiled. "I did and I believe his version. Please have a seat. Care for some iced tea?"

How about an ice cold Miller Lite? "Thanks, I'd love some." In response to Sarah's hand signals, Tom sat down in a large New England rocking chair. The curved wood molded to his back. Very comfortable.

The tea was refreshing. A little too sweet maybe, but very soothing.

The conversation began with biographical sketching from both sides. John's description of life as a driver for Belton was the entrance to the real discussion.

"And then all this happened." John looked past Tom, aimlessly searching the street for answers.

Tom took over. "John, I need you to go over every second of what happened going into that intersection. Once we've looked at the accident from your perspective, I'll fill you in on my view."

"Tom, I just screwed up. I just screwed up."

Tom answered. "Probably did, to an extent. But what I'm really hunting for is the degree to which you are to blame for the accident. You might be glad to know that I don't see it as an open and shut case. I believe that Mrs. Stetly played a major role in what happened." Tom took a quick swallow and continued. "Without any prompting on my part, go over every detail, every little thing, that you can remember from about a mile away from the intersection." He put the glass down on the porch floor and took the small notepad from his shirt pocket.

John, sitting on the other rocking chair, crossed his legs. With both elbows resting on the arms of his chair, he held his glass gently in his left hand while rotating it with the thumb and front two fingers of his right hand. He thought. The scene – *the road, the setting sun, and the peaceful hum of the engine* – had almost been idyllic. Then it all rolled forward into his mind. The tightness in his face signaled his recall of the last few seconds.

"I remember being relaxed. As I do most of the time, I was enjoying the ride. Always looked forward to getting back. Funny, but I was thinking about sitting right here on the porch having a sandwich and talking to Sarah." He glanced quickly over to his wife, then back to Tom. He almost choked on the lump in his throat. "I don't think I was going very fast at all. Yeah, relaxed, I was relaxed. The sunset was beautiful and I remember looking directly at it. Wish I could say it affected my vision, but it didn't. I did notice the light was green. Then, when I got close to the light, it turned yellow." John stopped for a moment, trying to reconstruct what had happened in the next few seconds of that terrible late afternoon.

Tom jotted a series of single and double words on the pad. He did not speak.

"I was too close to stop, so I stepped on the accelerator in order to get through the light. I did have a quick tinge, but I think every time I have ever encountered a yellow light, whether I stopped or not, I got the same feeling. It didn't seem like a big deal." His face tightened again. "Then, out of nowhere, the RV came. I barely saw it out of the corner of my eye. Just as I became aware of another vehicle, she slammed into me. I couldn't believe it. I just couldn't believe it. It must have been instinct, but I looked in the rear-view mirror and saw it all wedged under my flatbed. I eased down on the brakes. I even remember not wanting to slam on the brakes so I wouldn't hurt anyone. As I was stopping, I steered gently to the right. Oh God. It was so terrible."

John talked into the glass, his voice muffled. "And that's about it. I keep thinking that maybe it didn't really happen."

Tom jotted a few notes while waiting for John to continue. He picked up the glass and emptied his drink. The extended silence prompted Tom. "John, in some ways my analysis ends with you coming to a rest on the shoulder. But I do think it's important to know what you did at that point. Can you remember what you did?"

John was confused, partly because he did not think it important and partly because he did not want to remember. Without speaking, Sarah took both men's glasses and walked into the house.

"I remember getting out and running to the driver's side of the RV. The woman, Mrs. Stetly, looked badly injured. I didn't see her breathing. I asked her if she was OK but she didn't respond." John's voice became more urgent as he recounted the events. "Then I looked over at the husband. He was sitting up but was still. I ran around the RV to him." John paused. "When I got there, I could see the whole side of his head was crushed. I knew he was dead. The windshield and side window were broken. Then I heard the crying of a little girl. 'Mommy, Mommy.' I will *never* forget it." His voice cracked.

Sarah, the men's glasses in her trembling hands, waited at the door. She couldn't walk through the door and face her husband's suffering.

"Her voice cut right through me. Then I realized that someone was alive. For some reason I turned around to my right – I just wanted to get to the girl. That's when I saw the two boys, one lying on the flatbed and the other one on the ground." John, lost in thought, asked instinctively. "Who are they? Where did they come from? Oh, God, no." He looked down at his feet, his head resting in his hands. He sucked in a deep breath, then mumbled something unintelligible. Tom remained silent.

"Oh, God. Why is this happening? I've asked myself a thousand times. Why?" John looked back up at Tom. "Sorry Tom. I just can't get it together." He focused again on the scene. "I could tell they were dead. I had to get to the girl so I ran to the door. Don't know if it was locked or not. I just got in somehow. The little girl was sitting on the floor crying. 'Mommy, Mommy,' that's all she kept crying." John's lips quivered. "*Mommy, Mommy.* Oh, God, I'll never forget it."

John hesitated again, gathering composure. "She didn't look hurt, more stunned than anything else. I told her something like 'It's OK, it's all OK.' And then picked her up in my arms. She didn't resist me. As I stepped out of the RV I made sure she couldn't see her brothers. I took her to the back and just tried to rock her. I do remember her putting her head into my chest. She quieted down, but never stopped asking for her mother. Then, all of a sudden, it seemed like a lot of people were milling around. I don't know how many. A woman who said she was a nurse took the little girl. I haven't seen her since."

John made a side comment. "Called her grandparents a couple of days later but the grandfather hung up on me." Eyes watering, he returned to the nightmare. "I went back to Mrs. Stetly. A couple of people were trying to bring her around. I didn't know what to do so I just stood back from them. Then an ambulance arrived, I think they were first, and then the police. That's about it."

John stood up and walked to the railing. Sarah opened the door and approached Tom.

Still sitting, Tom took his second glass of tea. "Thanks Sarah."

Sarah put the other glass next to John's rocker, then walked to her husband. She put her hand on top of his, not saying anything.

Voices erupted in front of the house.

"Granger has it! He's free! Fifty, 45, 40 . . . he's going all the way!"

Two young neighborhood boys, one with a football tucked under an arm, ran in front of the house. They laughed as they ran.

9

The temperature around Houston reached 93 as wet, sultry, haze blanketed the entire Gulf Coast. The Labor Day weekend is the best holiday of them all in Houston. Psychologically, it signals the end of another stifling summer. Tom, Susie, Steve and Steve's new wife Kelly flew to the reunion in Port Aransas.

Susie turned around from the copilot's seat and passed her headset to Kelly. Tom signaled for her to put it on. Uneasily, she placed it over her ears. Tom pointed to a small push-button device as he spoke.

"To talk to me all you have to do is push the button. Are you ready?"

She spoke out loud to Tom, ignoring the button. He reminded her. "Use the button. You'll get used to it."

Kelly pressed the button. "O.K., I'm ready."

"All right young lady, just listen in for a minute." He turned back to the front and requested permission to take off. "LaPorte tower, this is Stinson Echo 4597, requesting permission for take off."

"Roger Echo 4597. Runway 1-3-0 is cleared for take off. Have a great trip."

"Roger." Tom pulled back on the throttle, giving full power to the engine.

The plane accelerated, slowly at first, then with a surge as it descended down the runway. It lifted slowly but cleanly off the ground. Houses passed underneath and children at a small playground shielded their eyes as they watched the classic plane sail above them.

Tom owned two small planes, the 1947 Stinson and a 1940 Piper Cub J-3. His

59

restoration of the old Stinson drew envious praise from fellow pilots. Fiberglass cloth covered the steel tube fuselage. Its light beige coloring, accentuated with a dark brown stripe extending through the entire length, gave it antique elegance. The tailwheel landing gear made for an occasional interesting takeoff or landing. With two passengers a Stinson flies beautifully; with three or four, it handles as much like a boat as an airplane.

Near Port Lavaca Tom intercepted a freighter on its way to Corpus Christi. Speaking through the headset, he told Kelly, "Hang on, we're going in on a strafing run." He circled his right hand in the air several times. Susie and Steve knew the signal.

With Tom's pull on the steering wheel, the Stinson rose, nose up, into the sky. Then, abruptly, he pushed the wheel hard forward. With a sensation of a cresting roller coaster, the passengers each felt the tickle in the stomach that took their breath away. The Stinson barreled down towards the freighter until, under Tom's control, it turned hard starboard, flying alongside the 'Okeanos' at a height no more than the ship's bridge.

"Tom. Stop it!" Susie was not amused. Every time he did it, her stomach heaved.

Kelly said nothing; it's hard to speak when terrified.

Steve roared in delight. For the hundreds of times they had buzzed freighters, he still loved it.

Tom headed due west at Rockport, circled gently to the south and then east to approach the runway at Port Aransas heading into the daily onshore breeze. They taxied to the parking area and found the last spot having tiedown rings reaching out of the sandy soil. The late afternoon sun was alive and well in Port Aransas, Texas. The building cabin heat forced everyone immediately out of the plane. Steve off-loaded the two small overnight bags while Tom tied the Stinson down for the weekend.

"Sorry if I scared you. It's just one of those urges. My dad was a fighter pilot in World War Two and it must have rubbed off on me."

Kelly tried to be cool. "Oh, I really loved the flight," she said, then added, "but I could make it the whole way back without acrobatics."

Susie interjected, "Sometimes I love his youthful exuberance. Sometimes I . . . well, you know what I mean." She shook her head and shrugged her shoulders. "Boys will be boys I guess."

Tom looked at Kelly. "You're a great trooper. Just right for being a Seiler." He then said to the group, "O.K. guys, let's grab our gear and make tracks."

Tom and Steve loaded the travel bags onto a small portable dolly. The group walked directly across Highway 361 to the Executive Keys. The efficiency unit willed to Donald by their mother was the rallying point. The '83 Pontiac waited in the parking lot, slot 44.

●

The others came from everywhere. Nancy drove down from San Antonio with daughter Sally and two granddaughters. Donald and Sue flew in the week before from Ventura, California, with 18-year-old Jayme in tow. Their son Mike, with his wife Shannon and two children drove straight through from Durant, Oklahoma. Donald and his Texas Aggie classmates, Jerry Freeman and Mick Wheaton, along with high school buddy, John Grant, met in the Executive Keys parking lot each morning at 5:15 for the fishing ritual. Nothing soothed Donald more than watching the beginning of another day spread across the Gulf of Mexico. He enjoyed catching a 30-inch trout or six-pound drum, but Donald didn't care if nothing came his way. His 20-year bout against multiple sclerosis kept him from the end of the jetty, but Aggie Rock next to the UT research station suited him fine. John, Mick and Jerry were content just to spend time with Donald. A notorious hell-raiser in younger days, he was their focal point, always counted on when push came to shove. There had been plenty of push and plenty of shove.

The Executive Keys is a modest complex of two-story wooden buildings arranged in a herringbone pattern. The eight buildings, light blue with dark blue trim, surrounded a swimming pool usually full of squealing children. Most of the units had two bedrooms and two baths, a living room-dining room combination and a balcony overlooking the Gulf or the pool. Odd numbers at ground level, even numbers above.

Tom's entourage checked in at the lobby, dropped their small assortment of baggage in apartment 510 and sauntered off to apartment 116. Steve and Kelly were gone in a minute, destined for food supplies and beer.

Tom knocked on the door and walked in. Bubba, eyes half-closed, looked up from the couch. He tried to clear his head. "Hey Tom, hi Mom. How's it goin'?" The TV droned in the background.

"Hey there Bubba." Tom quieted. "Where's Donald?"

Bubba slurred a response. "He took 509 so they'd have room for Jayme."

"Thanks. See ya' later. Get some sleep, we party tonight." Tom and Susie backed out of the door. Bubba dropped his head, closed his eyes and returned to his siesta.

Tom and Susie ran into Don at the pool. The party officially began at 5:40.

●

"Sign both sheets." The gate guard, mindful that he was working late on a Friday afternoon, was agitated.

"Yeah. Got it." Buck Tallant signed a bill of lading and the required dispatch sheet at the exit of the yard. The crimson cab of the Flagg Brothers Trucking rig was dirtier than usual. Buck, unshaven and dirtier than the cab, was more agitated than the guard.

He pulled out of the loading yard at North Bay Steel Corporation in Baytown with a load of steel. Two stacks of steel tubing, the first consisting of 200 pieces of four-inch outside diameter pipe, each one 12 feet in length, and the second stack of 100 pieces had been loaded in tandem. A wall thickness of .262 inches dictated the 132-pound weight of each tube. The total weight of the payload came to 39,600 pounds. The front stack, weighing 26,400 pounds, was tied down with four Kinedyne nylon straps. Two straps secured the back stack. Each of the straps had a tensile strength of 18,000 pounds. Under control of a professional driver, the straps provided more than enough strength to hold the load securely; given an unsafe driver, and under conditions of being frayed or cut, the straps could be rendered woefully inadequate. As Buck pulled out onto Route 146, he looked to his left and noticed the company sign:

* Bar Stock - Hot and Cold Finish
* Structurals * Sheets * Plates
* Tool Steel * Stainless Steel
* Reinforcing Bars & Mesh
* Pipe

The time was 6:45, the 30th of August.

●

Small groups of family and friends gathered into one large party, broke apart as some participants strolled the beach, made bathroom calls or drove into town in pursuit of beer and shrimp, then would reform again. As always, the center of activity focused on the three Seiler siblings. The adults gathered outside of 509 while the children played impromptu games only children can make up. An almost full moon rose into the darkening sky. The sounds of the surf wafted on the quieting shoulders of the evening onshore breeze. Time for the stories.

"To Jane Seiler and her 45 caliber howitzer." Donald raised his hand in salute to an unforgettable woman.

"What's with the howitzer? That's one I don't remember." Jerry Freeman, hand raised in salute, had not heard the story.

"Happened right out there on the beach." Donald pointed his beer can in the direction of the Gulf. "I think it was '80 or '81. Late September. She goes out to a desolated beach, not bothering anyone. Some tattooed jerks," Don looked over at the tattoos on both of John Grant's forearms, then added a side comment, "No offense John, I love you man." Smiling, he continued, "jerks who happened to have tattoos, show up and decide to harass a little old lady. With ten miles of open beach they . . . there were five of them . . . pull right up next to her. I mean five feet between her car and their truck. They get out, straggly as hell, all swearing profanities that I never heard and turn on a boom box to the max. Mother tries to get along with people, but when she gets pissed, she gets pissed. Anyway, she asked them over the din of the boom box to please turn it down. Unfortunately, one of the jerks got in her face, eyeball to eyeball, and . ." Donald paused a little. ". . . excuse the language ladies, says 'fuck-off granny.' Now that's not what you say to my mother. Tough, smart lady, that Janie Seiler. She pretends she's in a huff, goes back to her spot – you know, five feet away – and picks up her towel. Then she goes and opens her trunk and pulls out Pop's World War Two 45 pistol and hides it under her towel." Donald added significance, "And, hey, that's a big pistol. The U.S. Army Colt 1911 .45 automatic. A powerhouse. Anyway, instead of getting into her car . . ."

Donald started to laugh, spilling beer on his stomach. He gathered some composure and continued. ". . . she walks directly to the front of their truck next to the boom-box sitting on the hood. Picture these scumbags lying around with smirks on their faces. In a voice loud enough to be heard over the acid music, she says, 'I'm sorry, but I asked politely.' She pulls the towel off the gun, points the gun at the boom box and blows the sucker away. I mean she blew it the hell away, including the windshield of their raggedy-ass truck."

Everyone, even those who had heard the story countless times before, howled uncontrollably.

Licking his lips, Donald continued. "A couple of the guys curled up in a ball; another one started crying and cowered under the front bumper. Then Mother asked one of them to move out of the way so she could shoot out the left front tire. He did and she did. Her final comment to the original wiseass was 'Thank you very much. Oh, by the way, I have five more bullets. Sometimes I just feel like killing bad people. You're bad people. I think you should apologize to me and then be on your way.' He quivered and slobbered like a baby as he apologized. Fantastic. Her only mistake was pointing the pistol right between his eyes. That didn't play too well in court."

The listeners leaned forward and circled around Donald. Those who knew the story hoped for a new and better ending. All were mesmerized. Donald continued for a few more minutes.

Janie Seiler was arrested, convicted and sentenced to two days in the county jail.

One more lick of the lips and Donald finished the story. "When the judge gave her jail time, the whole courtroom erupted in boos. Then, as they led her away, she received a standing ovation. That woman, my friends, was one great lady. To Janie Seiler." Again, Donald raised his beer to the sky.

Twenty-five beer cans rose towards Heaven.

The timing was perfect. Nancy called to the gathering, "OK everyone, supper's ready." She, Susie and Kelly handled the first night's menu. "Ross, you get the honors with the barbecue."

Boiled shrimp, jambalaya and barbecued ribs were spread among the rolls and salad on the kitchen counter. The boisterous crowd moved inside, Ross leading the way. Tom and Paige sat side by side on the lawn, complacent with being the last to eat.

Paige cut right to the quick. "I brought my analysis with me. Want to take a look at it while the feeding frenzy is on?"

Tom sensed her urgency. *Great,* he thought. Still, it was not the right time; he was having too good a time and the beer had dimmed his senses.

"Don't want to play down your work, but I've had too much to drink." Tom didn't want Paige to become discouraged at their first meeting. He made a counter-offer. Looking at his watch, he said, "I've got exactly an hour an a half until I consume my last beer. I'm taking Erin and Cristen Jane for a morning flight about 10. Let's meet at my place at 8:30. A deal?"

Paige understood. She also succumbed to the delicious aroma coming through the open apartment door. "Understood. The food smells great. I'm buying."

They walked in the door, moving aside as Mike, a former high-school All-American football player, exited with a plate piled high with great Texas cooking.

A medley of stories continued until midnight, the centerfold of this reunion being Janie Seiler. She was once named 'Profanity Jane' because of an inadvertent slip of the tongue while in a chorus line in Seattle. On countless trips from San Antonio, she fished and slept on the beach with Donald at Port A when he was a little kid. Little did they know she would return to live in Port Aransas for 16 years. During the '50s she packed the kids into their car and chased hurricanes along the Gulf Coast. The stories barely touched the tip of the iceberg.

The kids were strewn throughout the living and dining rooms, some on the couches, one asleep sitting up in a lounge chair, and others on the floor. Only Jayme and Cristen Jane were left standing, contentedly watching MTV.

One by one, people began to drift away, snatching a child or two and disappearing into the night. Eventually only Tom and Susie remained, surrounded by empty chairs. Tom stopped drinking at 10, exactly 12 hours before he was to take Nancy's two granddaughters for a plane ride. They sat, legs stretched towards the sea, looking into the sky.

Susie thought out loud. "I think tonight is the most peaceful night I've ever experienced out here. Look at that moon." She inhaled deeply and smiled at the brilliant globe shining above the sand dunes. "I just wish everyone could experience the peace I feel right now."

Some people enjoy the simple pleasures of life. Others don't.

10

"O.K. – let's get it done." Jud yelled up to Buck, sitting in the cab.

Buck gave a thumbs-up and pulled onto the highway.

Jud trailed the rig in a circuitous route from Baytown, along U.S. 59 to Ganado, south on Route 172, then east on Farm Road 616 to the outskirts of Blessing. The town's police officer - Bubba was his name - was a jovial man in his late 70s, a Korean War veteran. Officer Bubba generated revenue for the tiny town by ticketing those who rolled through the only stop sign within 50 miles. Buck and Jud knew of Bubba and both came to full stops at the stop sign before heading east on Texas 35. From a small knoll along the road, a police car waited in hiding. Bubba watched the vehicles drive by, unfortunately obeying the law. *Oh well. There'll be others.* At 10:15 they stopped at a roadside picnic area outside of West Columbia. They would remain there for two hours.

The men exited their vehicles and met at the left front tiedown strap on the rig. Buck carried a small flashlight.

Bright as it was, the moon was insufficient for Jud to see. "Shine it here first." Jud held the strap at shoulder height and rotated it.

Buck aimed the beam of light at the strap, highlighting the reverse side of the webbing. Still tight, the strap was restrained from moving vertically.

"Hold it here and keep the light on it." Jud directed Buck as though beginning surgery. An easy operation.

Jud pulled a small piece of thick manila paper, six inches long and the exact width of the tiedown strap, from his shirt pocket and held it down so that the light allowed him to see black horizontal markings. The manila paper served as a template for cuttings that needed to be exact. Jud placed the top of the template at shoulder height vertically along the strap. "O.K., keep it here." The light focused on his left hand and the paper.

Taking a cardboard box cutter from his jeans, Jud gently cut horizontal segments matching the black markings on the manila template. His face grimaced with each stroke. A single bead of sweat hung precariously from the tip of his nose. He finished the first cut, whispering to himself, "There, now the next."

Jud completed two outside cuts, then folded the strap lengthwise, creating a vertical crease. He made a small horizontal incision of almost one-half inch at the fold. Just as Buck had practiced the driving component of their plan, Jud performed the same cutting operation some 25 times using sections of identical tiedown straps. After cutting the strap exactly as planned, Jud took an oily rag and rubbed it lightly along the strap to a height as high as he could reach. He buffed the cuts. He cut the second strap using a similar procedure, the only difference being the pattern of the cuts. He changed the procedure for the third strap. He rotated the long-wide-handle and disengaged the ratchet. The flat-hook connector fell away from the rig allowing the strap to hang freely. Turning the strap around, Jud folded the loose strap to create a horizontal fold.

"Hold it still." Jud commanded the flashlight beam onto the back of the tiedown strap. One by one, beads of sweat fell to the ground. He used the box cutter with great precision and applied light pressure to each of the four strokes across the backside weave of nylon. "Got it."

The remaining straps were operated on the same as the first.

"That's it. We're a go." They were the only humans within two miles, but Jud continued to whisper. "Any questions?"

Buck, obviously nervous, returned the whisper. "No, let's just get this the fuck over with."

Jud was able to distance himself mentally from all that would happen in a couple of hours. He was more interested in his long-term future than on the specific events going on around him. "Good. Relax 'til I leave. The rest of this is easy. Don't get nervous on me."

"Easy for you to say. I didn't see you volunteer to drive the rig." Buck walked away, only to hear Jud behind him.

"How about turnin' off the light?" Jud turned towards his car.

"How 'bout fucking yourself." Buck was nervous, irritable and nauseous. He turned off the flashlight and climbed back in the rig. He tried unsuccessfully to take a nap.

Jud rolled down his window and smoked seven cigarettes. Buck spent most of his time visualizing the unfolding events and pushing the nightlight mode on his watch. He rehearsed his part of the plan numerous times in Indianola and timed his dummy run past the intended target a few nights earlier. Buck learned in the

Marine Corps that one of the great axioms of war is to rehearse, rehearse, and rehearse. He had rehearsed.

●

Shortly after one in the morning, Jud pulled around and alongside the rig, giving Buck the sign to begin the final phase of the operation. They traveled along Texas 35 to Angleton, then north to Rosharon where they picked up Farm Road 1462. The huge Flagg Brothers tractor-trailer, its cargo secured in place, pulled to the right side shoulder of the road, 50 yards past Briscoe Canal. To most people, the weather would have been ideal for an evening walk. It was stifling to Buck. Jud continued on to the abandoned service station in Algoa. Halfway there, Jud made one final call on the CB to test communications. No problems. At the service station he pulled up to what had once been the pumping island. He stopped, then backed the car behind the station next to two rooms which served as restrooms in days past. Both doors were missing; all the plumbing fixtures had been stripped within days of the station's closing. He turned off the ignition, lit a cigarette, inhaled deeply, and lowered his body in the front seat so that his neck was supported while still offering him a view of Route 6. Jud rested his left elbow on the bottom window opening while gripping the roof. In the dim night, he could barely make out the faded logo on the side of the service station - *It's Humble in Texas*. He waited.

●

Labor Day weekend officially starts on Friday nights in Texas. The party atmosphere builds through Saturday night, then quiets on Sunday in a sea of hotdogs, hamburgers, softball and beer. For the D'Arcys, the night had been financially rewarding and physically draining. Marla and Sybil accepted their lot as the 'front-seaters' for the drive home. Hank and Zip were asleep by the time the car reached Broadway.

Women's discussions are much different than men's. Nine out of 10 times there is more substance to what they talk about. Men speak of sex, sports and, sometimes, money. Women tend to talk of relationships and future possibilities.

Looking out over East Bay, Marla prodded her sister. "Syb, if you had it all to do over again, what would you change?"

Sensing loneliness, frustration and even a little indignation, Sybil tightened her grip on the steering wheel. "I'd either never been born or would have gone to college. I don't care about lots of money and fine things, but maybe I would've met somebody who was nice . . . real nice. I just hate my life."

"Yeah, guess I'd do the same." She paused, "Do you feel something?"

Sybil concentrated on her sister's question; yes, she felt a small but distinct vibration through the steering wheel. Not severe, but there was a definite bumping sensation.

"Damn, it's probably the wheel. Bet it's from when Zip hit that curb. Should we stop or try to make it home?"

Marla sensed her own tiredness and just wanted to be home. "I vote to slow down a little and we can make it home. Let the guys change it in the morning."

The Taurus slowed to 45 miles an hour. It didn't really matter to them that they would be a few minutes late getting home. Their discussion continued to address all the 'what ifs' in their lives. Linking the past to the future with 'what ifs' is to invite depression. Sybil voiced frustration that she and Mark Findlay hadn't gotten married. After three years in the Army, he had gone to Texas A&M, become very successful in construction and was happily married to a woman from Waxahachie. He would have married her, but Sybil wanted to wait until he got out of the Army. *How stupid.* He was such a nice person. *How utterly stupid.*

Marla thought of her own life. Different chapters, same story.

The bubble on the side of the right rear tire grew. By the time they arrived in Algoa, the constant bumping had awakened Hank. "What's wrong with the wheels?"

No sooner had he spoken than the tire blew. To their immediate right front was an abandoned service station.

Jud sucked a large volume of smoke into his lungs. He was about to inform Buck on the CB that the target car was late when he noticed the trace of light beginning to stretch before him. Suddenly the light beam turned towards the service station. The protective shadow from the front of the station extended no more than six inches beyond his right front fender.

"What the fu . . ." exhaled with cigarette smoke from his lips before Jud gained control of his senses. He cut the word off just as his upper front teeth lifted from his lower lip. A shudder rocked his entire body. *This can't be happening* was the only thought he could muster. Instinctively, he dropped the cigarette, still lit, on the floor mat and crushed it with the toe portion of his left work boot. He had no choice but to exhale the remainder of the smoke from his lungs. He decided against rolling up his window. It would make noise and, more importantly, he needed to hear what the car's occupants were saying. Jud turned off the CB radio, then lowered himself while shifting to the left, leaving him hidden, yet in position to hear some of what was going on.

"C'mon Zip, we got work to do." Hank clambered out of the back of the car and walked up to Sybil to get the keys to the trunk. "Syb, need the keys and get the flashlight outta the glove compartment."

Sybil responded with the keys.

Marla stretched and yawned simultaneously, then reached over the front seat and began looking for the flashlight. "No flashlight up here. Look in the trunk." Marla closed the glove compartment.

Zip, not yet fully awake, sluggishly got out of the right backside of the car, stretched his entire body and slumped against the car, head resting face down onto his crossed arms on the roof. "Shee-it."

Hank opened the trunk and searched for the tire tools in the faint glow afforded him from a streetlight a block up Route 6. He could barely see. "Zip, go check the station for a light switch."

Zip, still groggy, responded slowly and lumbered towards the cinder block derelict. He reached the station manager's office door; it was boarded up. Almost instinctively, he headed towards the side of the building shielding Jud's car.

Buck Tallant became uncomfortably aware that the entire timetable was falling behind. First quietly, then irritably, and finally with fear and anger, Buck called into the CB handset.

"Breaker, do you have a Mark?"

The response for no activity was to be a simple "Marker Zero." There was no response. Louder, Buck called, "Are you there? I need a mark now." Again, no response. "Give me a fuckin' answer now!" Only the silence of the warm Texas air answered his call. Buck was sweating profusely. Jud's CB was turned off.

"Zip, I found it . . ." reached Zip's ears as he stepped around to the side of the station. Glancing at the car hidden in the shadows, Zip almost made out the top of a man's head, then dismissed it from his mind with the welcome news that they had found a flashlight. He turned around and went back to help his brother.

Changing the tire took Hank 12 minutes. Oblivious to the car 40 feet away, the other three smoked while engaged in aimless chatter. Hank lowered the jack, placed it in the trunk with the remnants of the tire and closed the lid with both hands

"That's it. Let's saddle up." Hank turned towards Sybil. "Want me to drive?"

Her body screamed *Thank God, yes.* Sybil responded unconvincingly. "No. Thanks. My turn on the roster. But you can join me in the front. You care Marla?"

Marla knew she was only minutes from home, yet was glad to be offered a respite from staying awake. "Be my guest, but you owe me for this." All three smiled.

They climbed back into the car, Marla and Hank changing places. Changing the tire energized Hank to the point that he was fully awake. Sybil eased the car back onto Route 6. They had traveled a quarter of a mile when Jud pulled out of the service station.

The Texas sky was coal black, punctuated with a million stars. Hank rolled the window down and looked at the incredible display above his head. "Damn, it's beautiful out here. On a night like this seems you could almost reach up and pluck a star out of Heaven." He felt good. "Right now I'd be happy to drive forever."

"Yeah, it sure is." Sybil did agree, but she just couldn't muster the same sense of euphoria that her brother was experiencing.

They talked a little of what other places would be like. California, Florida, New York City. They even pondered how much the Eskimos enjoyed the North Pole where their only friends were polar bears and penguins. It didn't matter where penguins really live. Hank glanced at the image of car lights in the rear view mirror. It only slightly detracted from the mood. They turned south on Texas 35 and passed underneath the railroad trestle.

"Mark one." The call was louder than practiced.

Buck jumped at the message. Under the best of circumstances he would have been tense. Things were not going well.

"Where the hell've you been?"

There was no response. He realized there wouldn't be.

"Mark one." Buck knew that he had to regain control of his senses. He had less than four minutes until he would begin execution of his part of the project. The steady rhythm of the idling diesel helped soothe the tension. Buck talked to himself. *Do it just like you practiced. No different this time. Pretend to help. Call the Highway Patrol. You've done it all before.*

"Yeah, I'm gonna do some serious travelin' someday." Hank daydreamed out loud. "Gonna get me an RV and go from one end of the country to the other. I really need to do it soon. I don't want to be someone who talks and talks and talks about something but never does it. Matter of fact, I saw in a book a place out in Colorado called Black Canyon National Forest, or Monument. Something like that. It's beautiful. It's kind of like a gully except it's like no place I've ever seen. Syb, I'm gonna do it."

Sybil smiled. In her mind she knew he would and yearned to ask if he wanted company. She decided not to ask. She slowed the Taurus at Farm Road 1462. She turned to the right.

"Mark two."

Buck was trembling violently but, to his credit, responded into the handset, "Mark two."

Jud heard, then felt, terror and excitement of a voice mixing with sweat. *This is it. Time to get home.* Jud turned and, keeping within the speed limit, drove towards the house that he would share with Sybil Weems for less than two more minutes.

Buck inhaled deeply, sucking life from his cigarette. Handset in his right hand, Buck grabbed the cigarette left-handed. It was not a clean grab. The cigarette fell, hot embers breaking away from the main body and into the recesses of his crotch. Startled, Buck squirmed in the seat, brushing frantically.

"Jeez-us." The rig lurched forward. He slammed the break pedal, still brushing. It took precious time. He was behind schedule – critical seconds.

Buck, unaware of the effects of adrenaline, accelerated faster than during his practice runs. He looked at the speedometer as always, but it did not register in his mind that he was going 74 miles an hour, not 68. From his perch inside the cab, Buck saw the headlights reflecting through the trees that dotted the bending road.

Hank must have read Sybil's mind. He asked his sister, "Want to ride shotgun across the country? I really mean it. We can see that Black Canyon first-hand."

Sybil looked at her brother and smiled. "You bet I'd . . .."

Her response to Hank was interrupted by light on the highway - a bright light forging through the trees. Hank broke out of his daydream just as the tractor-trailer came into view. Déjà vu. He had seen the image before. *The tractor-trailer!* He immediately reached for the steering wheel. Sybil hit the brakes, waking Marla and Zip.

The huge tractor-trailer, aimed directly at the car, crossed halfway into the opposite lane. The car and its occupants slowed dramatically but made no apparent attempt to move out of the path of the oncoming rig. In reaching for the steering wheel, Hank inadvertently grabbed the lower portion and pulled it towards him. His actions countered Sybil's futile effort to turn away from the impending collision. It proved fatal.

The speed of the rig initiated physical consequences. The impact location changed. The car became more than a target; it was a danger. The combination of the car's position relative to the rig and the six-mile an hour differential in the programmed speed created a different scenario for Buck. He reacted badly. As the rig crossed over Parker Road, Buck, more in self-defense than deliberation, urgently yanked the steering wheel to the right. The enormous inertial forces created by the turn affected the load of steel tubing exactly as they had during all the practice runs at Indianola. The tiedown straps on both stacks of tubing split once again in a series of violent whiplash movements. The tubing, first almost as a single unit and then in a random, devastating, pattern, shot at the defenseless car. Under the influence of speed and a diminished turning radius, the tractor-trailer became critically unstable. The center of gravity moved outside of the wheels. Buck slammed his boot into the brake pedal. He compounded his first mistake with a second one. Buck took his foot off of the brake pedal, then slammed it back to the floor. Modern anti-lock brakes require steady pressure; once released the brakes are unusable for a second. An infinitely-long second.

The first piece of steel tubing hit the car at the hood. It drove into the thin layer of metal and entered the passenger compartment, exploding through the radio. As it impaled Zip in the back seat, other steel missiles initiated near total destruction of the car. Sybil was decapitated. In the infinitesimal moment it took the steel tube to pass through the windshield and into her face, Sybil was able to focus on the dark hole being punctured in the shatterproof glass. She died instantly. Marla was hit first by the same tubing that killed Sybil. It carried brain and skull matter into Marla's right side, taking part of her rib cage with it. She felt a searing bolt of pain through her body. It was taken away in a maelstrom of steel.

Simultaneously with the deaths occurring in the car, the cab, now well past the Taurus, began to roll over. Buck's mind returned to the first successful run on the airstrip. The same loss of control. The same fear of death. The tractor-trailer obeyed the physical laws of nature. Buck tried to lean away from the roll. The cab rotated faster than the trailer. The resulting stresses caused a rupture along the locking mechanism of the fifth wheel. Following the popping sound of the fracture came the violent slamming of the left side of the cab into the pavement. Buck could not stop his body from assaulting Farm Road 1462. His head made contact first, splitting his skull. In rolling over two-and-a-quarter times, the cab caught Buck's lifeless body part in and part out of the cab. It finally ended its rollover lying on the driver's side with Buck's body still partially in the cab. His head had been crushed and broken into mottled fragments of red bone and brain matter.

Destruction engulfed three-quarters of the car. One piece of tubing rotated slightly as it caught the driver's door, crushing Hank's left arm. He sustained multiple other severe injuries from debris that sprayed through the car like woodchips from a chainsaw. His chest cavity was partially crushed and both legs suffered compound fractures below the knees.

The battered car came to a rest on the shoulder of Parker Road. It lay nestled among individual sections of steel. One piece of steel extended through the entire length of the car, another imbedded into what remained of the front grill. Dust and small debris clouded the night sky as the small particles gently floated to the ground. All became still. The light Texas breeze continued its gentle stroking of tall grass and mesquite trees. It was quiet.

●

The ceiling fan quietly traced a gentle circular path through the hot humid air. Both bedroom windows were open. Jud lay naked on his back staring up at the barely visible image of the blades. His senses, still sharp from the reservoir of adrenaline that had driven his actions during the night, searched for telltale signs. They came. At first he thought it was his imagination. It could have been an animal baying in the fields. But, as if in ever increasing waves, the inescapable sounds of wailing sirens came into focus. The eerie cry of ambulances and patrol cars filled his imagination with visions of what surely had taken place. Unaware of the sweat soaking the sheets, Jud listened as the sounds grew closer and then faded off to the south. He thought triumphantly, *I did it.* Jud glanced at the nightstand. The red digital display of the clock read 3:05. Soon Jud felt tired, exhaustion finally dominating his body. He rolled over and fell asleep.

11

Paige knocked gently on the door, then tried the doorknob. It was unlocked. She walked in just as Tom reached the door.

"Coffee's on and the buns are in the oven." Not a trace of the previous evening's drinking remained with Tom. "Let's crank up before the hordes arrive. Susie's still down for the count."

Paige walked to the dining room table and placed her laptop and briefcase at the end nearest the one socket along a 20-foot wall. She made a beeline for the coffee and delicious cinnamon rolls. Tom poured a fresh cup for Paige and topped off his own cup. Her first roll was accompanied by Tom's second.

Munching on the roll, Paige attached the extension cord to the laptop and inserted the far end into the wall socket. She pushed the on/off switch and the quiet whir of the system signaled a clean boot. While the computer operating system did its thing, Paige took a stack of papers, some colored, some not, from the briefcase and placed them into three neat stacks along the near side of the length of the table. She sat in the left of two chairs; Tom sat in the right.

Tom surveyed the stacks of paper, then held up the brightly colored sheet on top of the right stack. "Nice looking work. What's it saying?" He took a huge bite into his roll.

Paige mentally rehearsed her presentation in bed before falling asleep the night before. "What I did was to draw the overhead panel that had the window in it. I used quadrilaterals for elements except at the corner edges." She pointed to the wire-framed sketch Tom held in his hand. "There I used smaller triangles just as we discussed last week."

Paige gave a step-by-step chronology of her solution to a problem asking what stresses should have been expected on the sheet metal at the rounded corners of the window panel. With the information, she and Tom could ask other questions about what professional engineers should have designed for in terms of structural integrity of the Wolfpack RV. Her understanding of both the power of computer architecture and the dynamics of vehicular collisions was surprising to Tom. She was a disciple of the use of finite-elements to solve complex engineering problems. The computer's ability to solve thousands upon thousands of simultaneous equations with incredible speed made it ideal as a solution tool to questions of structural dynamics. Finite-element theory had grown out of the needs of the aerospace industry in the 50s. In reality, computers themselves are quite boring. They do exactly what they are told - nothing more, nothing less. Computers don't even mind the fact that they are asked to perform the same task billions of times in repetition. As for the aerospace industry, mistakes about the stresses to be expected during flight had been causative in many fatal airplane disasters. Researchers used the computer to model aircraft by breaking the structural framework into a pattern of triangles or quadrilaterals. In effect, a mesh of individual, or finite, elements could be made. Wire frame models of automobiles shown elegantly in television advertisements are analogous to a three-dimensional finite-element model. Each corner of an individual element was identified as a node and, since one element could be connected to one or more other elements, several elements could share the same node. In its simplest form, finite-element theory allowed forces to be modeled at specific nodes. Data as to the specific location of each node relative to other nodes in the entire mesh could be stored in a database. Some nodes could be constrained so as not to move even as forces are applied. For a steel building, nodes along the ground could be modeled 'fully constrained' whereas nodes associated with a top floor would be 'unconstrained,' being allowed to 'float in the wind'. Properties relative to the material of each element were used to determine how much stress and strain each element would experience under a load. A piece of metal in the actual physical world would stretch according to the degree of stress. If the load is taken off, as long as the stretch did not exceed the elastic limit of the metal, the element returns to its original configuration. The computer allows each element to behave in a similar manner. Although the mathematics can be very complex, and certainly the subject of many doctoral dissertations, the basic theory is simple. Results were originally given in reams of tabular data. With improvements in computer graphics, models, both two- and three-dimensional, became highly sophisticated. The entire process occurs in three stages. The first stage is the modeling stage, also known as preprocessing, in which the computer generates a model of the object. The second stage is that of analysis. Given the dimensions, properties, and applied forces modeled in preprocessing, the computer 'does its thing' in solving equation after equation. The output comes in the form of data structures describing stresses and associated deflections, all stored in huge arrays. The final stage is that of post analysis, also known as post-processing. The result of post-processing is an ability to output the analysis data in many formats. It could be tabular or graphical in its format. Graphic displays could include two- or three-dimensional renditions, color coding to show intensity of stress, animation to depict displacement as a function of loading, or simultaneous display of 'before and after' models to capture the severity of displacement. In the hands of good engineers, finite-element analysis represents the future of sound engineering. In the hands of poor engineers, it is dangerous.

Paige and Tom knew they had a problem of delivery. For a finite-element analysis to be credible evidence, it must be explained to a jury in terms understood by non-engineers. The two engineers worked their way through an accident on a computer screen. The display on the screen allowed them to see what forces the sheet metal on the overhead portion of the Wolfpack RV had experienced. At times, it was mundane; other times, riveting. Her methodology in determining where the stresses would be greatest and, therefore, where additional reinforcement should be designed into a good product, was logical, straightforward and, from Tom's perspective, correct. The biggest question mark concerned the jury.

"Another cup of coffee?" Tom rose from his chair, stretching his arms as high as he could reach.

"No thanks." Paige continued looking at the results of her efforts on the monitor.

Tom poured a final cup of coffee. Sitting down he said, "We need to talk about the jury."

"Dad, we can do it. I've thought about the jury as much as the RV. We'll convince them that, first, they are all smart and can understand our version of the accident, and, second, that people who design for money over safety, the jury's safety, are totally negligent, which they are." She pulled two stapled pages from the center stack and placed them in front of Tom. The pages outlined the methodology to do exactly what he implied – to first teach, then convince the jury.

Paige continued, "I think you ought to start by telling them that, because they are smart, you are going to present the results of some high-tech engineering analysis. I'd emphasize that they will later see that what comes out of the computer replicates almost exactly what happened to the RV and that any responsible engineering design group would have known the dangers involved. Then . . ."

Tom interrupted, "Hang on. Have I showed any graphics by this point? I don't want them to get bored early." He swallowed another slug of coffee and reached for some stale peanuts from the night before.

"Oh, you'll do it real quick. I was thinking that as you talked, we could turn on a television monitor and . . ." Paige began a discourse concerning both product and process.

Tom marveled at his daughter, thinking to himself, *This is good stuff.* Not only was she a competent engineer, she already had her plan of attack on paper. In her words Tom saw Paige crawling inside the heads of the jurors. Her methodology focused as much on an expectation of jury personalities as on basic concepts of engineering. The engineering would be there, but in some cases it would be secondary to enlisting the jury to their side of the trial.

The two engineers, the two friends, the father and daughter, polished and restructured the basic plan until they were not only satisfied, but were proud of the product. The hour and a half passed quickly.

The sound of children knocking on the door ended the strategy session.

"Uncle Tom, will you take us for a plane ride? You promised." Nancy's two little granddaughters rushed in the door, giggling at the thought of their own private journey. The only possible delay might be the time it took them to split a hot, sweet, cinnamon roll.

He loved the kids – his own and anyone else's. If you know how to deal with them, kids can be great. Tom gave them a double thumbs up as he rose from his chair.

"Absolutely. We might even fly to the Moon today."

Erin stopped in her tracks. The Moon was a long way to go. "Let's just go for a short ride. OK, Uncle Tom?"

Tom and Paige looked at each other with cat's-got-the-mouse grins, then turned away to hide the laughing.

Tom regained his composure, then assured his great-niece. "OK, Erin. No Moon today, just a fun ride over the beach."

Erin smiled and proceeded towards a hot cinnamon roll.

As Tom and the two excited girls pulled out of the Executive Keys parking lot, the phone rang. Paige picked it up.

"Hello."

●

On the fourth floor of Ben Taub the trauma team finished its seventh hour struggling against Death over the body of Hank D'Arcy. Dr. Joseph George, in his 15th year as head trauma surgeon, was satisfied that the team performed well enough to give Hank a fighting chance of survival. He gave instructions to have Hank moved to the surgical intensive care unit. He then joined his colleague,

Dr. Will Smith, in the washroom. He was both surprised and pleased that Hank survived the surgery.

"I can't believe how much the human body can handle. He should have died on the spot. He's tough as nails."

"Sure is." Will added, "It's funny though. Did you hear about the bee sting yesterday? It just doesn't track." He referred to the other end of the spectrum - that of a 45-year-old construction worker who died within two hours of being stung by a yellowjacket.

Joe responded, "A hell of a way to go. But, you know, I think the bee sting guy may be the luckier of the two."

●

Tom dropped Cristen Jane and Erin off at their place with a promise to take them up each year they came to the reunion. He walked in the door and grabbed a beer from the cooler. "Hon, I'm back."

Susie walked in from the bedroom and gave Tom a quick peck on the cheek. "Did they enjoy it?"

"Sure did. Wanted me to buzz everything on Mustang Island. Maybe next year I'll show them how to cut up toilet paper with the propeller." He smiled to himself as he lifted the beer to his lips.

Susie remembered the phone call. "Oh, Travis called while you were flying. He wants you to call him back as soon as possible. He's at his office." She handed Tom a small piece of paper with Travis' phone number.

It struck Tom as odd that Travis would call during the Labor Day weekend. He surmised that the Stetly case had been moved. Thank God that Paige had done her work. He relaxed and picked up the phone.

Two rings and Travis was on the line. Tom was prepared to go to court whenever Travis needed.

"Travis White."

"Hey amigo, what the hell are you calling for today?" Tom grinned into the phone, expecting to be able to announce his thorough preparation on the Stetly case.

"Hey Tom, thanks for the call back." He spoke without his normal jocularity. "There was a bad accident last night in Alvin. Four killed, one about to die. Two brothers and two sisters in a car slammed by a rig. One of the brothers is at Ben Taub. Involved an 18-wheeler from Flagg Brothers that dropped a load of steel on the car. The rig rolled over and killed the driver. A real mess. I need you to take it on."

Business was almost too good. Still, Tom enjoyed his association with his old friend and the company of Duffy, Guyer and White. A slight uneasiness in his thoughts. *But, why now? Why on a Saturday morning?*

"I can look into it. But what's the rush? Why call me now?"

Travis, in jeans and sneakers, looked unconsciously towards the small town of Alvin, Texas. A vague picture of carnage settled in his mind. "Hell, Tom. The Flagg Brothers CEO called me at five this morning. He's real concerned about this one. Mentioned you by name. Remembered you from the Flagg-Wiggins case."

The Flagg-Wiggins case. Victory had been snatched from the jaws of defeat. A head-on collision between rigs from the two largest in-state trucking firms. So much at stake. Reputation, not liability, was the key issue. Flagg won because of the testimony of their expert witness. Tom Seiler.

"Besides . . ." Travis lightened up a bit, ". . . if they can hassle me over Labor Day weekend, I've got every right to hassle you."

Turning serious, Travis continued. "Actually, I would have waited until Tuesday but it was picked up by Fox. Lots of outside interest. You might want to check things out on Fox and the Corpus stations."

"Hang on Travis." Tom turned to Susie. "Susie, turn on the TV to Fox News."

Susie picked up the remote and soon had the Fox Saturday morning news."

"Got it. We can talk on Tuesday. I'll call you."

Tom changed subjects before ending the call. "One more quickie. Paige is earning her money from you guys. She spent this morning going over her analysis of the Stetly case. Really good stuff. She backed it all up with graphics and a plan for my presentation. I'll tell you, if we lose it won't be because you hired my daughter."

Travis replied. "Great. I figured she was a chip off the very old block. Give me that call on Tuesday when you get back."

"Gotcha. Adios."

"Adios."

●

Six lawyers, waiting since 7:30, engaged themselves in idle conversation outside of the Surgical Intensive Care Unit, SICU for short. Another bad night for the Astros. All were smokers. The lawyers, resplendently dressed in 'sincere suits' of dark gray or blue pin striping, were reluctant to leave lest the others get first offer at a legal case worth millions. One by one, the lawyers hastily exited the ward and searched out the smoking area. The slowest lawyer returned in 12 minutes.

A hospital administrator, not either of the principal doctors, informed the small gaggle in the hallway that Hank D'Arcy's condition was too critical for him to be interviewed. The lawyers reacted both urgently and irritably to the statement that no one, not even family, would be allowed in the room until authorized by the attending physician. In an amusing game of chicken, the lawyers collectively announced their departure, then, within minutes, each returned to the fourth floor smoking patio. When the sixth one appeared through the doorway, the laughter over their insincerity exploded. They smoked and talked lawyer-speak until finally accepting the fact that Hank D'Arcy would not be having visitors that day. Each left a card with the name of his particular law firm at the SICU nurses' station. They almost believed the cards would be delivered.

12

"I'll bet you Travis calls before I get back. He's relentless." Tom walked out the front door, a variation from his normal back-door ritual.

The run was a grueling masochistic exercise. Feeling more Miller Lites than he cared to count, Tom was tempted with every footfall to just call it a loss for the day. Putting one foot in front of the other at a pace identifiable as jogging was excruciating. Still, Tom slowly transitioned from the drudgery of shuffling waist deep in mud to the fluid strides that were his trademark some twenty years earlier. With each step his mind gave energy to images related to what had come his way - the almost certain lawsuit against Flagg Brothers. Two blocks from home he slowed to a fast walk, took a wet piece of Scot towel from his sweat-soaked running shorts and wiped each reachable part of his body. The refrigerator in the garage beckoned his return.

No sooner had Tom closed the kitchen door than Susie called down. Too early for her to have a beer, so he only held one in his hand.

"Hi honey, don't sweat on the carpet . . . and you get the gold star for that accident in Alvin. Travis called twenty minutes ago. He needs you to call him about that and the Stetly case. You've got time to take a shower first – please."

"Thanks hon." Beer in hand, Tom took the right turn through the living room and down the hall to the comfort of the shower. A slight headache gnawed away at his temple. The shower would be the true answer to healing his wounds from the impromptu Labor Day celebration. The warm water pellets massaged his head. The headache slowly faded, replaced by the Newton video. Ten minutes in a hot shower with a cold beer brought him partway back to life. He dried off and walked naked to the bedroom to dress. Screw looking at the aging man in the mirror.

Tom joined Susie at the top of the stairs, gave her a kiss on the top of her head while kneading her shoulders. They had been married five years, all of them good. Holmes and Watson. Don Quixote and Sancho. Red Ryder and Little Beaver. Bud Abbott and Lou Costello. Susie and Tom made a great team, often trading places between leader and sidekick. He was the technical strategist, she the intuitive thinker. In the short time that she had been Tom's partner, Susie had done well. Through on-the-job-training she had become a fairly competent engineer in her own right.

"O.K. Susie, it's showtime." Tom moved from behind Susie to the phone and dialed the number for Travis.

"Duffy, Guyer and White, how may I direct your call?" The voice was genuinely friendly and native Texan.

"Hi Lynn, it's Tom Seiler. I'd rather talk to you but Travis asked me to call him back."

"Hi, Tom. Hang on and I'll get Travis. Tell Susie hi for me."

Travis began, "Hey, compadre, how was Port A?" He didn't wait for a reply. "Great party last night; we missed you. Michelle didn't even get up this morning. If I had your luxury, I sure as hell wouldn't be here right now." Travis had his own headache. "Sounds like you and Susie had a great Labor Day." Travis finished his pleasantries. "Did you see anything on the accident in Alvin?"

"Yeah, I saw Flagg Brothers all over the screen. Looks like you've got a shitpot full of problems. Just ran and started brainstorming. Haven't had a chance to put it down on paper, but Susie and I'll start right away." Tom was eager. The thrill of the chase seized his imagination once again. To accurately reconstruct an accident based on bits and pieces of physical evidence went beyond engineering; it was art to Tom.

"Can you get out there right away? Randall Flagg called. He's worried about a civil suit since three members of a family - two sisters and a brother - were killed. Another brother is in the hospital and is an odds-on-favorite to die as well. Two brothers and two sisters killed in Brazoria County is bad news for Flagg." Travis' voice lacked the usual jocular tone.

"You already told me that. Where's the exact location and where did they take the wrecks?"

"At the intersection of Parker School Road and Farm Road 1462 on the south side of Alvin. I was told that the car was taken to Savage's in Alvin and the rig would be there too. They hadn't actually moved it when Flagg called."

"What about the tubing, tiedown straps, dunnage and other stuff?"

"Don't know. We'll find out and give you a call."

Tom paused for a second, then spoke. "Travis, you guys are jumping on this one fast. Any other items I should know about?"

"We've only got a few bits and pieces. Neither driver appeared to have been drinking. Rig driver goes around the curve too fast and dumps a load of steel pipe on the car. Flagg Brothers hasn't had an accident like this before. They had the Houston manager on the scene at four this morning. He's knowledgeable about accidents and is totally dumbfounded on this one. The driver was approaching Houston when he was supposed to be headed to Corpus. Add that to three or four family members killed in Brazoria County and they're scared shitless."

"O.K., I'll head out there in a few minutes. What's the salvage yard again?"

"Savage's. They're on Route 6, out by Mustang Bayou."

"I'll call you tomorrow with my first cut at it. Catch you later, amigo." He started to hang up.

"Tom, hold on." Travis almost yelled into the receiver.

"Yeah, what else you got?"

"We're going to court on the Stetly case. I don't know why it's moving so fast. We tried to hold it off but the judge put it on the docket for October 16th. Need to see you next week on it. How's that one going?"

Tom smiled at Susie. He visualized watching the VCR tape with the D.A. and Bill Newton. He reflected on his exuberant *hot damn* silently spoken during the video. "Travis, my good friend, I'll bring you lots of goodies. I'd like Paige to join us but I don't know if she can get off work. Can you make it late in the day? You call the date."

Travis had blocked his calendar. "Next Wednesday O.K. with you? If Paige is key, then we can go at six for her. How about our starting around four on the Flagg Brothers case? We can change to Stetly when Paige arrives. An hour and a half on Stetly and then we all go out with our better halves. What's Paige's boyfriend's name?"

"Ross. Great guy. Quiet like me."

"Yeah, right. We'll need a few laughs by then." Travis' voice relaxed considerably with Tom's revelation that someone other than Belton Trucking would shoulder significant fault in the death of the Stetlys.

Travis hung up feeling downright good.

●

The call came from the same public telephone.

"Colter, Fisher and King. May I help you?" Friendly, yet businesslike, the receptionist greeted Jud's call.

"I need Mr. Colter."

"Whom may I say is calling?"

"Lemme speak to Colter now!"

The receptionist recoiled at Jud's rudeness. She dealt with many abrasive people, but this caller was clearly over the line. She gathered composure, replying with a dose of syrup, "Just one moment please."

Barry Colter answered the intercom.

"Sir, an individual - he refused to identify himself - is on the line. He demands to talk to you now. Sounds nasty."

Experienced lawyers anticipate calls like this one. Barry Colter calmly replied, "Beth, I know exactly who it is and . . .," he pulled an authentic sounding chuckle out of the air, " . . . exactly why he's calling. I simply have no desire to talk to him, although I should for a few laughs. Beth, you may have to plug your ears, but tell him I won't be back until tomorrow. He'll be crude, but he's harmless. Thanks."

The levity at which one of the most influential lawyers in Houston, Mr. Barry Douglas Colter, Esquire, addressed the call disarmed the young receptionist. It didn't come naturally, but when he wanted to, Barry could tame an acre of mad snakes. Beth, sensing her invitation into a practical joke, returned to the caller. "I'm sorry, Mr. Colter will be out of town until tomorrow. May I take a . . ."

"The fuck he is!" Jud slammed the phone down and stepped out of the booth. Not knowing exactly what to do, he paused a few seconds and then turned towards his car. The pay phone rang. Jud knew who was at the other end.

"Yep."

"Do not ever call here unless I say so. Never. Get out there and be a good husband and brother. Get to the brother before he dies. Show that you care. I'll call tomorrow. Nine a.m., questions?"

"I gotta make a run tomorrow and won't be back 'til Thursday morning."

"Wait right there. I'll call you at exactly 2:45."

Both men hung up. Barry Colter waited 15 minutes before telling Beth he would be going out for lunch. Jud walked slowly to the Calico Cat, a small hole-in-the-wall two blocks down Calhoun, for a cup of coffee. He pondered the events of the last 20 hours and Barry Colter's admonition. *Dumb asshole* he thought to himself. *Be a brother and husband.* Jud was irritated. Jud remembered Barry saying, "Don't even think of going against the agreement." A clear threat. With his mushrooming distrust came a concurrent dislike. Using the same logic as that of the esteemed lawyer, Jud intended to use Colter for his personal gain. He also knew that Colter was cunning. Jud needed to protect himself. As he walked along Calhoun Street, he decided that he would make plans for the future, his future. Those plans would not include a lawyer, any lawyer. All in due time. *Let me do this one step at a time.* Mentally returning to the phone call, Jud realized that

Barry Colter wanted him to play the role of loving husband and loyal brother-in-law. Having already identified what remained of his wife took a lot out of him. Crocodile tears were not something Jud Weems had really mastered. *Now go play sad to Hank. I am sad . . . sad that he's still alive.*

The Calico Cat was not impressive, but it was clean. Six red cloth-covered tables, each with four wooden, tacky, upholstered chairs, were arrayed in a straight line along the right wall. A long counter with the cash register closest to the entrance took up the entire left side. Prints of cats in differing situations adorned the walls and the back of the establishment. The cleanliness of the bathrooms indicated that, although very simple in its furnishings, the Calico Cat probably served very good food and coffee. It did.

The coffee aroma had a delicious hint of mocha, but Jud was unaware of the quality of the coffee. Sitting on the last stool at the long, dark green, Formica counter, he rotated the handleless coffee mug in a counterclockwise manner, staring down at the ever-repeating rings of coffee generated by his middle finger tapping at the side of the mug. *Gotta keep it under control. Buck's dead. Good. Need to protect myself.*

He remembered his first encounter with Barry Colter. The call from a lawyer informing him of his rights when he had been involved in an accident. Though the truck was damaged enough to make the case that the truck was totaled, Jud Weems was not hurt - except for the whiplash injury manifested only minutes after Colter's first phone call. Winning the trial was no problem at all. The foam neck brace, the struggle to turn and face the jury and the obsequious 'yes sirs, yes ma'ams' painted a picture of Jud far removed from reality. Jud was unaware of the tightening of his jaw and facial muscles as he remembered the settlement. He received a small pickup truck and $2,000 out of a $40,000 victory. The lawyer's explanation of the fees made him aware that had it not been for Barry Colter, he would have received nothing. As it was, he did get the money and the truck. The muscles relaxed slightly as he focused on his meeting at Colter's beach house in Seadrift. Barry explained a plan in which, if all went well, Jud Weems could pocket a personal fortune of more than $80 million. Jud's mind diverted slightly to questions surrounding Barry Colter's ability to know so much about Jud's family. He didn't realize that he was the result of Barry Colter's two-year search.

"Is something wrong with the coffee?" A short, fifty-ish waitress with curly gray hair interrupted Jud's train of thought. It triggered a look at his watch. Five minutes until the call.

"No." Jud got up, grabbed $1.87 from his pocket and placed it on the counter. He made it back with one minute to spare before the phone rang.

He picked up the phone at the end of the first ring. "Yep."

"Now listen carefully. Go see D'Arcy. Remember everything you can about the room he's in, where his bed is located, how he looks. Find out from the nurses, or better, the doctors, if he has a chance to survive. Don't be too conspicuous, but find out everything you can about any treatment he's getting and the medicine he's on. Be smart. Just repeat what you did in the courtroom. In one hour I want you to call my office and request a lawyer to represent you, your wife and her brothers and sisters. At 6:30 call me again at . . .," he hesitated, ". . . take this down. Get a pencil."

"Wait a minute." Jud grabbed a pencil from his shirt pocket and tore a small piece of paper from the phone directory. "Go ahead."

"Call 466- . . ." He gave Jud the number. ". . . and give me every piece of information you can get. Any questions?"

"I'm no dumbass." Jud didn't appreciate Barry's holier-than-thou attitude. "You better remember that." It was Jud's first warning to Barry Colter that double-crossing the country bumpkin was not an option.

Barry ignored the warning. "One last thing. Be careful, there's going to be a video camera in the room. Find out exactly where it is, but don't be obvious."

"Six-thirty." Jud hung up.

Jud didn't feel the heat, was oblivious to the sounds of the city and ignored the passersby who nodded friendly smiles. He was keeping score of the unfolding deadly game. The three deaths in the car were good for the home team. Hank being alive constituted points for the opponent. He asked himself *What do I do about him?* Buck Tallant had died, offsetting Hank's survival. Basically the plan had worked pretty well. Buck wasn't worth sharing a lot of money with anyway. In a nutshell, it was a tie - but the game needed a winner. One thing was very pleasing to Jud. *Ain't no one got a clue on this. We can be home free. Just play it smart. Yeah, play it real smart.* His step picked up as a wry smile, not meant for the lady responding with a smile of her own, accentuated his face. He sauntered towards the parking lot, thinking back to his fortunate encounter with Barry Colter.

●

"Hey there, Mr. Colter. How're you doing?"

Barry Colter peered quizzically around the gasoline pump to the man on the other side of the island. "Hello. Please excuse me. I recognize you but your name escapes me."

Jud topped off his gas tank and replaced the refueling hose. "Name's Jud

Weems. You helped me out back in '93. An accident. I sort of hurt my neck."

Barry smiled heartily, replaced his hose and stepped between two of the pumps. He shook hands with Jud. "Can't remember all the cases." A hint of recollection appeared on his face. "Wait a minute. Weren't you going to use some of the judgment money to get married?"

"Yep, that's me. Used about half of it on a honeymoon in Cancun. The rest went to enjoying my recovery. Also got this here truck. Been a dream." Jud patted the small pickup truck gently.

Barry replied. "Great, glad I could help." He added, "How's your wife doing? Any kids around the house?"

Jud's facial expression negated any need to answer. A wry frown and eyes to the sky said it all. "Well, let's just say it was a great honeymoon. Never had no kids and that's been for the best."

Jud's reply rang sweetly in Barry's ear. "Well, you can't win them all." Barry turned to leave, speaking over his shoulder. "It's been good to see you. Hope all goes well." He started to move towards his car, then stopped as though something triggered his memory. "Hey, Jud."

Jud, in the act of returning to his truck, turned around quickly. He waited for Barry to speak.

"Listen Jud, I've been getting together with former clients to sort out how I can improve my batting average. Would you be interested in meeting for lunch someday soon? My treat." Barry spoke innocently enough.

Jud hid the surge of excitement. "Be glad to. You batted a thousand in my case. Tell me when and where."

"Hang on." Barry opened the passenger door and grabbed his jacket. He pulled out a stack of business cards, giving one to Jud. "Give me a call this afternoon and we can set it up."

"Sure. Be glad to."

They shook hands firmly and returned to their vehicles. Jud pulled away first. His senses heightened in anticipation. There's more to this than a free lunch.

Barry Colter stood at the island for a few extra seconds contemplating what might follow. He reached in his back pocket and pulled out his wallet. He placed his credit card into its designated slot, then took a small folded piece of paper from one of the hidden recesses. He unfolded it and glanced at it. He wet his lips and smiled. It read:

PROJECT
D. Salk
W. Tallant
J. Weems

●

Barry and Jud sparred for almost four months following their initial encounter at the service station. By the end of the first meeting Jud knew that Barry wanted to use his services and Barry knew Jud was willing, for the right price, to cross any line. Jud understood the basics before Barry made the final, blunt, offer. Jud and his wife Sybil barely spoke to each other. No fire. No emotion. Four siblings, all riding night after night in the same car. The late night scheduling meant timing would be no problem. If Sybil had a life insurance policy, make sure it was for a small amount. No need to arouse suspicion. Handled properly, the project would net Jud Weems millions in cold, hard, cash. Jud weighed the lives of four family members, including his wife, against untold wealth. The family came in a very poor second.

"You will receive a huge sum of money, not all of which will belong to you. Once taxes have been handled on the up-and-up you will be free to move money as you desire. That's when you will move 70 percent of it offshore. I'll give you instructions on transferring funds. Once I take over the funds, I'll take care of the driver. He's not as important as you are, so he won't get the same amount. I'd suggest you keep that information to yourself."

"No problem." Jud sensed Barry had little use for the driver once everything was finished. He wondered what Barry had in store for him.

Barry's eyes tightened. *"While we're making this official, you need to know that transferring of the money will be based upon an agreement. Don't even think of going against the agreement."*

Jud thought, *Don't threaten me, asshole,* then responded, *"No problem."*

Barry passed a thick envelope across the table. He whispered its contents. *"Five thousand. Not a drop in the bucket to what it will be."*

Jud took the envelope and, without inspection, placed it in his shirt pocket. He inhaled deeply, drawing his teeth over his lower lip. *"Tell me about the driver."*

●

Buck Tallant's recruitment was similar, though more disconcerting to Barry. After almost two years of searching for an appropriate prospect, only Buck remained. The other possibility, David Salk, was eliminated after the customary lunch. Barry's concern about Buck resulted from Buck's extreme eagerness and tendency to talk too much. Still, Buck was a driver for Flagg Brothers and Flagg Brothers was the biggest fish in the pond. Buck's only hesitation came when he realized that his participation included the physical risk of driving a tractor-trailer in a planned near-collision. He reasoned, however, that he was one hell of a driver. Recounting several near misses with vehicles and animals of all sorts, Buck prided himself in the way that he was able to avert disaster. He joined the conspiracy with a sense of challenge, as if he were undertaking a crusade of great courage. He had vivid, very distorted, images of an act of bravery that was never offered to him in the Marine Corps.

Barry could have sealed the deal with $1,000, but he gave the same $5,000; no need for dissention in the ranks.

●

Susie waited at the curb until Tom arrived. Twenty-five minutes later they entered the intersection of Parker Road and Farm Road 1462. Tom took a right on Parker Road and stopped 100 feet north of the intersection. They exited the car and scanned the area. A traffic light emphasized the intersection and sweeping curve. Tom jotted down a note verifying that the light was operational. A housing development backed up onto a small field on the north side of Parker Road. Across the intersection stood the Red Oak service station. The far off sound of children playing emanated from the red brick Alvin Elementary School on Robarton Road. Typical Americana. Trees extended from the far end of the service station along the south side of Farm Road 1462. Tom's first reaction focused on the field of vision. *It's clear. Only a few trees. He should have seen the car. He must have fallen asleep.* He walked past the intersection along Farm Road 1462. The virtual absence of traffic allowed Tom to walk into the roadway. No more than 50 feet from the apparent impact point black tire marks stood out clearly from the asphalt/ stone road. The driver's side tire marking started at least six feet into the oncoming lane. Both ended just beyond the intersection, indicating the cab narrowly missed the D'Arcy car. Tom looked down the road, visualizing the driver waking just before impact. The frantic swerve to the right came too late . . . but only by a fraction of a second. *He almost made it. Gave it all he had.*

"How do you see it?" Susie joined Tom in the middle of the road.

"He comes down 1462, probably dozing off. Sees the car after coming out of the trees, but it's too late. He was probably a good driver. I don't know how, but he managed to keep the cab and the rig from hitting the car. Unfortunately, the straps on the rig couldn't handle the force. They ruptured, throwing the tubes all over." A car appeared on the horizon, requiring the couple to move to the opposite side of the road. They walked to the service station. Tom continued. "Funny, but had he not tried so hard to save their lives he might not have rolled over. He'll never get credit for it, but the guy's a hero. What a helluva way to go."

Crossing the highway, Susie visualized the scene.

Manny stood at the checkout counter and answered their questions. "Yeah, it was built in '97. Do more business in candy and drinks than I do in gas. The school kids love the sweets."

Tom took the lead. "What about the night of the accident? Was anyone on duty?"

"Nope. We close at midnight. Just not enough people runnin' about at that time. We tried when we first opened but it just cost us money."

Tom and Susie waited while Manny helped an elderly woman retrieve a container of milk. She paid, smiled at all three and walked gingerly out of the store. Tom returned to his questions.

"How dangerous is the intersection?"

"Not dangerous at all. You can see very well and the light warns everyone of the curve. I've been here five years and this is the first accident." Manny seemed proud, as though he was responsible for the five-year safety record.

"So, the light was working?"

"Sure was. Other than a lightning strike last summer, light's never been out. It's on a timer so that at that time of night it would have been blinking yellow."

Susie asked, "How often do big rigs come through here?"

"Oh, now and then. Don't see many, but some come through."

Tom and Susie's questioning added very little to what they had already surmised. It was worth noting that there had never been an accident before. Tom's preliminary view of the accident matched their discussion with Manny. In payment for his services, Tom and Susie each bought a Payday candy bar.

Tom scribbled a few notes on the way back to the car. He opened Susie's door and she got in. "Next stop is the Chief of Police. Then the salvage yard on the way home."

Tom did a 'U' turn on 1462. Susie took a last look down the slow curving highway.

"Tom, that curve is very negotiable." Her intuition was at work.

The door leading from the entrance foyer to the offices of the Alvin Police Department clicked open and Chief of Police Mike Mercer stepped briskly towards Tom and Susie. Standing six foot two, impeccably dressed with civilian dress slacks, light blue shirt with dark blue pin stripes, a red and blue striped tie, and sporting well cropped hair and a neatly trimmed salt and pepper moustache, Mike smiled enthusiastically at his old friend.

"Tom, good to see you. It's been too long. He reached out and firmly shook Tom's hand, then turned to Susie. "Welcome, I'm Mike Mercer."

Susie reached forward and shook his hand. "Hi Mike. Tom's given you rave reviews. I'm glad to meet you in person."

The three conversed in the foyer, Mike taking time to explain the general construction of the building. Its open space design, abundant windows and high ceilings were top of the line for a small town and were purposely designed to provide a sense of openness between the police and the community. He guided them down the side of the building to a suite of offices. His office was comfortable and serviceable, not ostentatious. If larger than the remaining offices, it was not by much. He offered them seats and then sat down. They continued talking without breaking stride.

"I saw you a couple of times on T.V. lately and both times you were hauling in community service awards. I didn't see a bad guy in either story. And these are great." Tom pointed first at the wall to his right and then to a small bookshelf to his left. Among the diplomas and citations were pictures of Bill Clinton, George W. Bush, and, appropriately, Linda Carter of Wonder Woman fame. "I can tell you two things. First, it looks to me like Alvin has attracted national attention for good community relations and, secondly, you've got to be the most politically ecumenical cop in Texas."

Mike laughed and then spoke of joint efforts between the police and the residents of the town. For a community not much over 20,000, Alvin, Texas, had its collective act together. As an outgrowth of programs supporting victims rights, senior education and mentoring, anti-tobacco and anti-drinking education for teenagers, and with help from a volunteer group called the Alvin Citizens Patrol Unit, crime had declined dramatically, smoking among kids dropped like a rock and, until now, traffic fatalities were one fifth of a decade before. No less than nine chaplains, men and women of all denominations, were directly associated with the police department. Mike Mercer and his police department could be empathetic when appropriate and tough as a bear trap when necessary. But on this day, he was staring at a quadruple and possibly, if Hank D'Arcy were to die, a quintuple increase in fatalities over the previous year. To Mike, however, the statistics were insignificant to the loss of fine human beings.

Mike moved the subject to the incident at Parker Road. "As a matter of fact Tom, I think the last time we talked was after the Hoyt accident two years ago." Mike leaned forward and added, "It's probably time we got into this accident. I'm glad to see you're working the case. Any forensic insight you can shed would help us avoid something like this in the future. I've been here since 1977 and this is the worst accident we've ever had."

They talked for 45 minutes covering the police report given to Tom, speed and relative location calculations and backgrounds of the people involved.

"I knew the D'Arcys very well. They're, or they were, really fine people. Grew up here and bonded together when their father died during their teenage years. Their mother died two years later leaving Marla in charge. I never heard a negative comment about them. To the best of my knowledge, the only one married is Sybil."

Tom said, "That's the worst thing about my business. Through pictures, and on rare occasions in person, I get too close to human suffering."

Susie asked, "Was the driver from around here?"

Mike shook his head, "No, I think he's from the other side of Houston. I'm not certain. It's probably in some of our reports." He closed his thumb and index finger lightly over his moustache, gathering final thoughts of the D'Arcys. "You just hate to see this. The D'Arcys pretty much represent the fabric of this town. There's a lot more to Alvin than being the home of Nolan Ryan . . ." Mike hesitated a bit, then continued, ". . . matter of fact, in terms of character and grit, Alvin's got a bucket load of Nolan Ryans."

Tom's eyes brightened slightly. He sat back and told a quick story. "We know that. Last time we were here was on a Tuesday. We and another couple went to Joe's Barbeque Company. No sooner did Susie order a brisket of beef barbecue sandwich than one of the local women standing behind her told her to try the Tuesday night special instead. Susie did and I did and I'm here to tell you it was the best fried-shrimp plate I've had in years. We ended up staying until 10:00 with three Alvin couples. Even those neat ladies down at your Chamber of Commerce, Hope and Judy, are as nice and funny as can be. Yeah, Alvin's got character."

All of a sudden Tom remembered that they still had to get to the salvage yard. "Oops, sorry Mike, but we've got to get out to Savage's to inspect the wreckage."

Mike stood up while replying. "No problem. You two head on out and I'll give them a call and let them know you're on the way. They'll hang on for you."

Tom and Susie got up. Mike walked them to the door and bade them farewell. "Don't forget. Our welcome mat is out all the time."

●

The five by nine-foot sign with green block letters read:

SAVAGE SALVAGE

YOU NEED IT - WE GOT IT

The sign was wired at each of its four corners to a chain link fence fronting almost 1,500 feet along Route 6. From both ends of the frontage the fence receded almost a quarter of a mile to Mustang Bayou. It was unusual for a small town like Alvin to have a salvage yard of significant size. Little towns tended to have little yards; this one belonged in Houston. Relics from the fifties, dotted with a few cannibalized cousins from the thirties and forties, took up the back half of the yard. Tom and Susie drove into the metal graveyard, stopping outside the small wooden building just inside the fence. Fine dust from the dirt entranceway carried over the car on an ever-so-light breeze. Maybe it would be one of the last stifling days of the summer. Maybe not. Tom and Susie waited for the dust to clear, then exited the Buick and walked toward the office. To their left, no more than 50 feet inside the fence, were the three largest pieces of evidence: the remains of the Ford Taurus destroyed 14 hours earlier; a cab, sitting upright, with a partially crushed top and two blown tires on the front; and a flatbed trailer that, except for the one blown tire and some striations along its left side, looked to be in pretty good shape. They walked into the office and were greeted by a hulk of a man sitting behind, and dwarfing, a small metal desk at the back of the room. The air conditioner was working overtime.

"You the ones Chief Mercer called about?" Sleeves rolled up, known by friends and foes as Ham, he looked up but made no attempt to stand.

"Right, we're Tom and Susie Seiler. I don't know if he mentioned it, but we need to see what's left from the wreck on Parker Road." Tom walked over and extended a hand to Ham. Ham's return of handshake almost crushed Tom's fingers.

"Prob'ly saw it when you got outta your car. Go ahead." Ham had no intention of leaving the air conditioning. He returned to reading the latest *Motorworld Magazine*. "If you got any questions, lemme know."

"Thanks - thank you." Both Tom and Susie responded, then walked out into the blistering heat to begin work on what would become the most sensational legal case since Billie Sol Estes roamed Texas.

13

Houston was a steam bath for two million people. The relative humidity topped out at 92 percent with the temperature hovering at a blistering 97 degrees. The streets were silent. Ben Taub is a beautiful hospital; large, yet only a small part of the huge Texas Medical Center complex. Burnt orange brick with beige tiles surround massive areas of windows. Jud entered the main entrance at Taub Loop, the cool air giving him a chill. He shivered visibly as his sweat evaporated in the relentless flow of air. Looking at the crowded foyer and halls, he judged all. *Spics and niggers.* He ignored the cold and focused on playing his role. He stopped at the information counter.

"Got a badly injured brother in the surgery ward. He's real bad."

With Hank's name, the elderly volunteer quickly found his room.

"He's in room 4-E-12. It's in the E corridor, fourth floor. Follow the signs towards the cafeteria and McDonald's until you come to the elevators."

"Yeah, thanks." He walked away, quickly lost in the mass of humanity.

At the SICU reception desk he asked politely if he could see his brother-in-law. The nurse on duty was polite herself but informed him that Hank was not able to receive visitors. Fortunately for Jud, Dr. George stood at the station counter scanning the patient chart for Mr. Henry Monroe D'Arcy.

"How do you know Mr. D'Arcy?"

Jud's mind quickly formed two responses, *What the fuck business is it of yours?* And *He's my brother-in-law. We've been friends ever since I married his sister. He's all that's left . . . he's all I got now.* Jud chose the second response.

"Come on, let's take a look. I'm Doctor Joe George." Joseph George, a first-generation American of good Lebanese stock, extended his hand. "Spent a long time with Hank. He's tough, very tough, but his injuries are massive. Making it

99

this far has been a miracle."

Jud bit down on a hidden smile.

He shook the doctor's hand. "I sure hope he does. He's a good'n." *I hope he's dead before we step in th'room.* "My wife, Sybil - she was killed in the wreck - an' Hank was real close ever since they was kids in Alvin. Don't know what I'll do without her." Jud, hands returning to his pockets, stared at the floor as they walked down the hallway. He was enjoying the role he had to play. *Be smart. This guy's not stupid.* "Can't believe this all is goin' on." *I'm eatin' this shit up.*

Doctor George had gone home earlier to a quick meal of chicken soup and a 45-minute nap. Tuesday afternoons were usually reserved for the golf course; he worked on this Tuesday. Given the nature of Hank's injuries, Joe felt an obligation to return to the man whose life he may, or may not, have saved. It made him no less a man that his return was also dictated by a need to judge the quality of his work. The two men passed through double doors and into room 4-E-12 where Hank lay fighting for his life. Even from the doorway both men were startled at the degree of human devastation before their eyes. His face was no more than rubbery pulp. Very little could be done for his crushed chest and broken jaw. Light casts covered his left arm and both legs. His breathing was labored and tubes and wires appeared from almost every orifice in his body. The pallor of his face was gray chalk. Hank was close to death.

Doctor George pushed gently on Jud's forearm, a signal for him to remain where he was standing. Joseph George walked to the edge of the bed and looked down at Hank, up to the monitor and back to Hank. Jud studied the room. Dr. George motioned for Jud to come forward.

"Jeez." For a split second Jud felt sorry for his brother-in-law; the feeling quickly changed to frustration. Hank's being alive was a major problem.

From a deep sleep, Hank unexpectedly opened his eyes. Under the weight of sedation, they closed. Jud saw rippled movement beneath Hank's eyelids. Slowly, Hank opened them again. An attempt to move his crushed left arm brought on intense pain, far beyond medication's ability to deaden the shattered nerve endings. He tightened, then loosened his eyes, exhaling short, labored, breaths. Hank finally focused on his only living relative. He studied Jud's face. The second hand on the wall clock moved a quarter revolution. Hank's eyelids tightened again, slightly, as though questioning his circumstance. He focused on a blurred picture of his first encounter with a tractor-trailer at Parker Road. No recognition of the driver, just the sensing that the near miss somehow linked with the final tragic collision. Through Jud's eyes, Hank saw the past. *Jud, you . . .* Unable to speak, he relaxed his body and returned to a world of pain and confusion. Doctor George knew that he was being left out of the interaction, but did not know why.

Joe George spoke, "We need to go."

They turned and walked silently back to the nurses' station. Doctor George put his hands in his pockets in an unconscious act of resignation. For different reasons, Jud did likewise.

"He got any chance of makin' it through this?" Maybe a little melodramatic, but also a standard question from someone who may have really cared.

"Not good. Probably the worst I've dealt with. It's not the physical appearance; it's the vital signs. I'm just not sure."

Jud covered his reaction well. They slowed at the nurses' station.

Joe George added, "Jud, I'm sorry. I can't begin to express our sorrow at your losses today. We'll do everything we can to help Hank survive. The next 24 hours are critical. But, even so, people with injuries like Hank's have made it for weeks and then go down with everything from a renal shutdown to heart failure. But I will tell you this. He's already shown incredible strength. His will to survive is probably more than I've ever seen before. If things turn his way he might make it."

Jud looked directly into Joe George's eyes. "Thanks doctor, I b'lieve you already done a miracle. I need t' go, it's a bad day." He extended his hand one more time.

As Jud started down the hall to the elevator Doctor George called to him.

"Jud, before you go. Hank reacted to you. He wanted to speak with you. It's a good sign. I'd like you to come back as often as possible."

A sense of chill, coinciding with a muffled clap of thunder from outside, startled Jud.

"Sure, I'll be back. Soon." Jud's voice was more deliberate than in their previous discussions. "Gotta do my job, but I'll get back t' Hank."

"Thanks." The surgeon gave a sincere smile then turned back towards the SICU.

Walking to the elevator, Jud replayed the last 10 minutes. The look in Hank's eyes. The unmistakable communication. *The son-of-a-bitch knows. We gotta kill 'im.* He picked up his pace, pushed the lighted button several times in an unconscious effort to get away from Hank, and disappeared into the elevator.

●

"Hate to bust your bubble," Jud leaned into the phone, "but our friend might just make it through all this." His voice lowered. "If he does, some folks, not just me, are in for a rough time."

Jud hung up the phone.

Barry placed the phone in its cradle, wiped his mouth and considered the situation.

●

Tom and Susie worked until late Wednesday afternoon on the Flagg Brothers defense. The earlier than normal run proved good for Tom. The line of thunderstorms the day before had been a harbinger of cooler, drier air from the first Canadian high of the year. A fresh shower, peanut butter and toast, and hot coffee provided Tom with a clear mind to work on this new accident investigation. With well over 2,000 already tucked away, Tom always worked simultaneously on multiple cases. But he never worked on such a high visibility case as either this one or the Stetly case. Two major – very major – cases at the same time. Behind the work desks, next to a bookshelf that had been shortened in order to make room for the pictures of the World War II fighters, was a 25-inch television and VCR. The bookshelf was stocked with a 50-50 mix of previous casework and technical reference material. Tom turned on the TV to channel three, inserted the cassette, and then sat down in the overstuffed chair, feet on the ottoman.

"It's showtime." He pushed the play button with his left hand, grabbing the toast with his right. A very predictable person, Tom's most surprising act in his entire life may have been the totally unexpected switch from Peter Pan to Jiffy peanut butter at age 51. Maybe it was his passage through a mid-life crisis. So much for predicting human behavior.

Susie took most of the footage. She filmed the tractor cab first so that the damage to the Taurus could be better related to the configuration of the trailer.

Surprisingly, the cab had sustained relatively light damage in rolling over multiple times. The entire left side made first contact with the roadway, allowing it to absorb the force across a large cross-sectional area. The camera clearly picked up the indented door, scrape marks erasing much of the Flagg Brothers logo and a strange pattern of blood, part elliptical, part splatter. Very little damage was visible on the right side, indicating that it spent the ride airborne, never actually touching the ground. The front was undamaged.

"There's a lot of blood on the left inside door panel. Be careful." Tom's comment coincided with his opening the right door allowing the camera to capture the complete interior of the cab. The caution in his comment also reflected that, educated or not, people still think of AIDs these days.

The cab interior was in good shape, notwithstanding the bloodstains. Only the roof displayed the effects of what had taken place. Even the steering wheel, which by itself caused enough injury to kill Buck, was intact. Tom stood on the hood, then took the camera from Susie to film the strange buckled feature on the cab top.

"The top has a circular, almost bowl-like, feature indicating that it hit a solid object." Unknown to Tom, the indentation was caused by a small boulder on which the upside-down cab landed during the first rollover. Had Buck not been killed a fraction of a second earlier, the boulder would have crushed his skull and broken his neck. A split second later, it was caught between the shoulder of the road and the front left tire on the trailer. Like watermelon seeds pinched between the thumb and index finger, it shot across the road and was never noticed.

The final segment of the cab filming focused on the fifth wheel. Susie filmed again while Tom pointed to specific areas clearly showing the fracture surfaces. Throughout the process Tom jotted down notes on the yellow pad of paper.

* *Left side - scrapes, window down, indented door, blood splatter & ellipse*
* *Right side - clean, no major damage*
* *Tires - both front blown, back, O.K.*
* *Cab top - bowl feature?????*
* *Fifth wheel - fracture, fatigue, mechanical condition - good*
* *Tiedown straps – Kinedyne - 2 foot rupture points*

Before continuing with the trailer Tom asked Susie to stop the filming so they could talk. "Anything stick out?"

"Not much. Only thing is how remarkable it is that one side doesn't even have a scratch. I wonder if the driver was just unlucky in the rollover."

Tom answered instinctively, "Unlucky as hell. A passenger with a tight seatbelt might have walked away. C'est la Vie - or is it C'est la Mort?"

Using the film sequence, specifications of the cab, load factors of the trailer and measurements taken at the scene, Tom later reconstructed a probable scenario of the events related to the cab. His final version would never be proved with certainty, yet it was an almost exact replica of what actually happened.

They filmed segments of the car and the trailer the same way. A single steel tube was still impaled in the Ford Taurus. Without knowledge of the incident, one would guess it had been a victim of a falling building in an earthquake, a terrorist bombing or a bad decision to outrun a tornado. It resembled a crushed beer can skewered by a pencil. Only the front passenger section had escaped complete destruction.

Damage to the trailer was not severe. Tom focused on the tiedown apparatus, including each of the torn webbed straps. Susie filmed Tom holding the frayed ends of the split straps as high above the lifting shackle as possible.

He spoke to the camera. "The vertical length from the shackle to the point of rupture on the front strap is 22 inches. The distance on the second strap is 23 inches. On the third, 22 inches. Twenty-one inches on the fourth." Not shown on the film was Tom's removal of a section from the front piece of webbing. He released the ratchet's grip on the strap, keeping the ruptured end free of his hands, and pulled it free. He rolled the section carefully, placed it in a large Zip-Loc baggie and continued his inspection.

Tom replayed the segment showing him with the tiedown straps. The piece he had taken lay on brown wrapping paper at Susie's feet.

He hit the pause button and spoke quietly to his wife, "I've got big problems with all of the straps."

Susie said nothing.

Tom interlocked and placed his hands on the back of his neck, stretched, then continued. ". . . big problems. I should have taken a second strap section. Damn. This one is, what? About 22 inches? The second strap was about the same . . . and so was the third. Straps just don't break like that. The tensile forces that caused the first strap to break occur throughout the entire length of the strap. It makes sense that, because it's got a tear or cut or it's frayed, it'll break at that weakest section. With the first one gone, the others will have to carry more load and they too will break at the weakest point. That could be anywhere on a strap. For all of them to break at about the same location and on the same side is strange, very strange."

Susie detected urgency in Tom's voice. For the first time since she had known Tom, she sensed fear, both from his non-verbal mannerisms and from her expectation of what Tom would say next.

"Somebody cut the straps." Tom was both exclaiming a hypothesis and asking a question. He bent over and picked up the section of webbing. He studied the specimen for half a minute then turned to the yellow pad on his desk and wrote a couple of notes. He got up and handed the webbing to Susie. "Don't touch the end. Look at the threads across the tear."

Susie stared blankly at the specimen as Tom continued.

"Some of the threads are longer than others. It starts out pretty smooth for about half an inch, then it has stringy fibers for most of the rest of the way across. Then it gets smooth again. There are a couple of places in the middle that are also smooth. It's strange hon. I can see some high school kids vandalizing a flatbed at a truck stop. I've lived through stupid times."

●

The Coke bottle arced through the air, exploding on the pavement five feet in front of the '50 Ford. Shards of glass splintered into near-lethal bullets spraying the front of the car, breaking the windshield and slicing into the driver's left arm. "Oh shit, hit it Seiler, I think I pissed somebody off." Alex Denby's anxious laugh exuded excitement and fear.

Tom looked into the rear view mirror to see a swirl of dust and sand as the Ford spun out of control. "What th' hell did you do?" He screamed at Alex while flooring the gas pedal. The '46 Cadillac slowly responded as it carried the boys over the crest of a knoll. The roller coaster ride in the Texas hill country was a matter of survival to Tom and the others.

Jack yelled over the roar of the car and the whistle of the wind. "The dumbass threw a coke bottle at that car."

The old Cadillac swayed and bounced along the asphalt road at 80 miles an hour. Seeing no car in the distance, Tom relaxed slightly and let off on the gas. Thank God they're gone.

"Oh shit," Alex groaned. "They're flying."

Three hills behind them, the Ford roared over the crest. Alex could see it actually go airborne. Much better on the steep climb than the Cadillac, it was gaining fast. Much too fast.

Tom wished it would stop . . . and it did. The Ford, now two hills behind, swerved just enough to go off on the shoulder. The driver over-corrected and the hapless Ford rolled over like a can kicked down the street.

"Oh God, no." Tom spoke softly.

"Keep on truckin' Seiler. We're outta here." Alex was relieved and upbeat.

Tom repeated himself. "Oh God, no." It was surreal. It just could not be happening.

He slowed the Cadillac and, seeing a small home nestled amongst mesquite trees and rocks, turned into the dusty driveway.

"Jack, make a call to the Boerne police. Then start walking back to the wreck. We're going back . . ."

●

He held out his hand and Susie gave him the strap. Her stomach rolled in reaction to her thoughts. As though it was a newborn child, Tom gently placed the strap, fully extended, on the brown paper and carried it to the lower shelf of the printer stand in the corner of the room. Tom and Susie continued their analysis for another hour; then Susie, nauseous and needing the bathroom, turned over the duties to her husband.

Tom spent the remainder of the afternoon piecing together the incident in

Alvin. He always did his initial analysis on sheets of yellow legal size lined paper. He generally used three pads of paper simultaneously. The first one had a heading that read 'Observations'; the second, 'Scenarios'; and the third, 'Questions'. He drew sketches of the scene on a pad of white grid-lined engineering paper. Analysis data came from a government sponsored computer program, entitled CRASH, used for its ability to recreate speeds, paths, and patterns of damage for vehicles involved in collisions. His references included numerous books on mechanics of materials, statics and dynamics. By 6:00 all three pads were full. Several sketches graphically depicted possible causes of the events in Alvin. Tom made a conscious effort to dismiss the nagging thought that somehow human intent had been involved . . . but the notion of vandalism-turned-deadly inserted itself well into the recesses of his mind.

●

Barry arrived at 7:00. Rules for the SICU are strict at Ben Taub. Immediate relatives are allowed no more than 20 minutes with a patient. Non-relatives are authorized access to these critically injured persons by special permit, and only with the permission of the attending physician. In the case of Barry Douglas Colter, Esq., the matter was simple. He had been retained by Judson Weems, brother-in-law to Hank D'Arcy, regarding an accident in which negligence may have been the primary cause of death and suffering for a close-knit family from Alvin. As attorney for the family of Sylvia Weems, Mr. Colter had a legal purpose in visiting Hank D'Arcy. Doctor George had gone home for the night and did not appreciate the call.

"I'm sorry to bother you at home, Doctor George. A Mr. Colter is an attorney who needs to see Mr. D'Arcy. He does have legal authorization." She had not wanted to make the call, yet Sarah Melton was overwhelmed by the attorney's demanding urgency. She immediately disliked Barry Colter.

Joseph George, doodling small, tight ellipses on the note pad by the kitchen phone, spoke irritably to the young, but very competent, nurse. "Give him 15 minutes, but I will not allow him in unless Mr. D'Arcy is awake on his own. You personally have Mr. Colter wait until you verify that Mr. D'Arcy is awake and alert."

Nurse Melton, already flushed by the sensation that she had somehow violated the doctor, apologized. "Yes doctor. I really didn't mean . . ."

Doctor George cut her off. "Sarah, I'm not mad at you; it's your visitor who gets to me. Sorry."

"I understand, Doctor George. I'll take care of it." She hung up the receiver and returned to the waiting lawyer.

In an unconscious desire to protect her favorite doctor, Sarah Melton explained quite forcefully the terms of his visit. Barry Colter agreed and waited at the nurses' station while Sarah walked to room 4-E-12. She disappeared into the room for no more than 10 seconds. She reappeared shaking her head 'no'.

Barry Colter reacted harshly. "I have other urgent business to conduct and I have no intentions of waiting around all night." Pointing his finger at the nurse, he demanded, "I want you to call the hospital supervisor."

Sarah looked him directly in the eyes. "The only people I will call are the security staff. Take a seat please. I will check every 15 minutes."

He had no retort except to glare at her. He turned to a group of four chairs lined side by side against a mint-green wall. There were no magazines. He sat down, right ankle on top of his left knee, and waited for the next 30 minutes.

On her third trip to Hank's room, the nurse found Hank D'Arcy awake, alert - and in extreme agony. Her instructions required her to administer morphine. It took another two minutes to dull his intense stabbing pains. Hank faded into unconsciousness.

"You need to know that I had to sedate Mr. D'Arcy. At best, it will be another four hours until he wakes up. Even then, he may not be able to speak to anyone." She did not wait for a response before turning towards her station.

Barry glared at her. "Stupid bitch." His comment was barely audible, but she heard it.

He rose from his chair and walked out of the ward.

●

Paige arrived at 7:30 with an almost final product explaining both the damage pattern to the Stetly RV and reasons why Wolfpack Van was the more culpable party among the defendants. Cheeseburgers on the grill, a couple of beers and her announcement that she thought Ross would ask her to marry him were the components of an enjoyable evening that included less than an hour of work on the Stetly case. It was enough. Her analysis of the accident and the supporting documentation, including several computer-generated drawings of forces, stress concentrations and damage patterns, were exactly what Tom wanted to see. She prepared a separate outline providing recommendations for convincing the jury that Belton Trucking was the least negligent of the involved parties, including the unfortunate Mrs. Stetly. Paige's work dovetailed with Tom's reconstruction of the accident - including information from the video received from Bill Newton. The trial would begin in less than six weeks. They would be ready.

14

Barry Colter walked into Ben Taub and joined a sizable crowd bound for various destinations throughout the hospital. A young Mexican, his face almost childlike, shuffled in front of Barry, holding a broken arm close to his stomach. In shackles and orange Harris County Jail garb, the youth was being guided by a police officer larger than Barry. Barry thought quickly of incarceration, then dismissed it. He used his bulk to forge his way to the front of the elevator queue. First in the door, he was wedged to the rear by a dozen other passengers. Sweat, born of his nerves and the Houston humidity, mingled with that of the others. A slight pungent odor wafted throughout the human cage. Barry stepped out of the elevator at the fourth floor, paused in the hallway and looked at his watch. Exactly 2:00. The timing had its advantages. At 2:15 the shifts change; the probability of miscommunication is at its highest during the 20 minutes that bracket the change of shift. The retiring staff would not be as sharp as they were at the beginning of the shift. He was excruciatingly nervous, yet his ability to manipulate others made it easy to make his emotions invisible to the staff. A part of his past, holding bitter memories, bolstered his resolve:

> *October 16, 1968, Cambridge, Massachusetts..*
> *"The Harvard University Medical School Honor*
> *Committee, after thorough and impartial review of all testimony*
> *and related documents . . . do hereby find that you have violated*
> *the core values . . . will be expelled . . . "*

Barry remembered the sting of shame. His parents. His goddamn parents. His father enjoyed a very successful partnership in Clipper Trading Company, an import-export business that specialized in oriental furniture, Persian rugs, and, for the right customer at the right price, any type of contraband that could be routed through the Kellin Shipping facilities in Baltimore Harbor. Barry thought about his father's facade of honesty and integrity. *Sanctimonious bastard.* Ironically, the junior Barry Colter's best display of virtue was that he never blackmailed his father. His mother was an alcoholic. Not that his father would really have cared, but Mrs. Sandra Ames Colter, wife of Barry Douglas Colter, Sr., serviced half the senior management of Clipper Trading and a goodly portion of close associates from Kellin Shipping. On March 28, 1971 both died with another couple in the crash of a corporate jet near Pennington, New Jersey. Barry, Jr., was left $100,000 chump change while his sister received an estate of nearly $12 million. It was the final 'kick him in the ass' from both of his parents. Yet, the younger Barry Colter used his money wisely and finished law school at the Baylor School of Law. Barry found it easier than expected to conceal his past from the Office of Admissions. He didn't mention his Harvard experience and, with thousands of applications, Baylor didn't check. In the final analysis, he won against his father. Neither of his parents had a clue about real wealth - and real power.

Barry's mind returned to events within the SICU. He made note that Hank's nurse had entered the room half a minute earlier. He thought, *She won't take long.* A few things needed to be accomplished before leaving. He pulled a handkerchief from his back pocket and wiped his forehead. Barry waited another half minute before approaching the counter.

There was gentleness in his voice, unlike his earlier visit. "Excuse me Miss, is Mr. D'Arcy still in room 12?" Barry Colter showed the plastic card giving him permission to visit Hank on behalf of Mr. Weems. The nurse, not the one he had jousted with the day before, was finishing her day.

"Yes, he is, go on in," she replied hurriedly, "but please keep it to 15 minutes." She was not concerned with his answer and returned to her work.

"Sure, I was given the rules yesterday. Thanks." Barry's response floated unheard through the air. His normal dress would be a resplendent dark blue pinstriped Armani, powder-blue shirt and a silk burgundy tie accentuated with thin diagonal stripes of aqua blue. The drab blue coat over tan Dockers and white button down shirt with a plain blue tie rendered him very ordinary. Except for his size, he did not stand out.

He gave a condescending wave to no one in particular and then turned towards room 12. His timing was well thought out. The nurse was checking Hank's vital signs and making notations on the medical chart. He walked in, gave the same friendly wave and casually, yet purposefully, moved to the far side of the bed between the nurse and the wall opposite the door.

"How's he doing?"

The nurse continued writing some final bits of information. Then, without looking up, replied, "He's a fighter. I'm putting all my money on Hank . . ." She gently gave a rub to Hank's lower arm while continuing, ". . . to make it through all this." Her tone was almost upbeat and her voice loud enough for Hank to hear.

She finished her duties and turned to leave. At the doorway, she stopped and spoke to Barry, "Hank's awake, but can't speak much because of the endotracheal tube and his jaw. We've been able to have some great talks with hand signals. Raised thumb is 'yes.' Hand down on the bed is 'no'." She walked out.

Barry was not interested in what she had to say, his mind intent on his mission. But not totally intent. He noted a very pretty face outlined with black, loosely wound curls and an exquisite body, tucked tightly in medical garb. He refocused on the man in the bed.

Hank, awake yet heavily sedated, could not recall that he had seen Barry Colter before. Studying the face of the large man looming over him slowly brought forth a sense that Colter would help him out of the hell he endured.

"Hi there, Hank. Don't worry about speaking. I just wanted you to know that I'm here to help you. We'll get you fixed up and take care of any medical bills. Now's not the time, but once you've improved we'll make sure that your future will be far better than it is now. We'll make sure there will be compensation for the hell you've been through."

In Jud Weems' eyes Hank had seen treachery; in the eyes of Barry Colter, Hank saw trust and hope.

Barry, positioned between the surveillance camera and its view of Hank's upper body, placed his left hand on the patient's right arm. He rotated his large frame at an angle to the camera. His position looked natural and gave a completely innocent view of a right arm gently placed on the bed at Hank's side. All looked normal.

"Just relax Hank," came as a gentle order from Barry Colter. He kneaded Hank's arm.

Hank closed his eyes; Barry concurrently checked the venous access line at the antecubital fossa. Barry took no more than four seconds to move his left hand away from Hank's arm to the inside right pocket of his suit jacket. He deftly pulled a syringe, a rubber casing covering a one-inch needle, from the pocket. Without disturbing Hank, he grasped the casing with his thumb and index finger and easily lifted it off of the needle, dropping it into the coat pocket from where it came. He regrasped the syringe in his left hand like a dart.

"That's it Hank. Take it easy." Barry again placed the side of his palm on Hank's arm, the syringe securely held as one would hold a pencil. The sensation of

Barry's palm tracing down his arm was soothing to Hank. He returned to a state in which he felt he was floating on air. It was a release from pain . . . and it left him unaware that the lawyer had moved the syringe to the small rubber cap connecting the venous access line to the rest of the catheter.

His little finger around the rubber cap, Barry Colter easily rotated and pointed the needle. No different than a magician with a repertoire of card trucks, Barry had practiced this form of single-hand dexterity many times. He was quite good at it. His only fear was of someone entering the room in the next 10 seconds. But he was counting on Hank's new nurse spending several minutes with other patients. He drove the needle perfectly through the cap and into the line. In six seconds, Barry Colter injected five cc's of heparin, at 20,000 units per cc, into Hank's arm. A total dose of 100,000 units of heparin, the supreme anticoagulant, began to flow through the body of Hank D'Arcy. In less than 20 seconds Barry Colter was finished. Slick as a whistle.

Barry offered gentle words. "See you later Hank." Blocking the camera's view, he withdrew the syringe, placing it, needle up, into the right inside breast pocket of his coat. Barry Colter quietly exited the room, nonchalantly walked past the nurses' station, and bade a mental adieu to a good man. He quietly closed the SICU door and disappeared down the gentle blue and beige corridor, smiling all the way.

Forty-five minutes later the surveillance camera automatically erased its view of events.

●

The images coming from Tom's color printer were superb - graphic displays of the damage and colored simulations of the movements of the two vehicles before and after their collision. The final sheets were computer drawings Tom created with the physical dimensions of the vehicles and a legend displaying critical data: weight, construction material, and the like. After making the hardcopy products, Tom created color transparencies for display to the jury. Not that they provided any additional information, but, through experience, Tom knew juries like Technicolor. It's more believable. He placed a piece of white paper behind each transparency, arranged them in order of presentation and numbered each, one through 27. The hardcopy prints were numbered on the back in the same order as the transparencies.

Tom walked barefoot down the stairs to the dining room table. From the 27 prints Tom made three rows from end to end on the table. The first row of 10 contained the results of Paige's finite-element analysis. The second row depicted a chronology of the accident. The third included one print of statistics of the Belton Trucking rig, one with the specifications of the Wolfpack recreation vehicle, and a final drawing of the cross-section of the construction of the overhead panel on the RV. Tom saved the portion of the table closest to his body for an arrangement of photos taken at the accident scene and at the salvage yard. He would digitally scan the photos later so that they, too, could be displayed on the screen. Two of the photos were of the traffic light, both taken from a distance of almost 200 feet. He stepped back from the table, massaged the back of his neck, then called towards the bedroom.

"Hon. Got a minute? I need to bounce this off of you."

Susie answered as she walked down the hallway, "On the way babe." She walked into the dining room and behind Tom. She placed her arms around his waist and, on tiptoes, peered over his right shoulder at the collage on the table.

"Looks impressive, whatcha got?"

Tom began to explain his presentation of the facts concerning Jamison vs. Belton Trucking, et. al., as the Regulator clock chimed 3:45 . . .

●

Bernadette Mulligan was unaware of Barry Colter's visit to the SICU. Known as 'Bennie' to her friends, she was far too preoccupied with countless tasks to remember the man she bumped into on the first floor. She entered 4-E-12 shortly after 3:00 for her second visit to the room. Hank's appearance was poor, but that was to be expected of someone in his condition. By instinct, Bennie always looked at the monitor behind, above, and to the viewer's left of the patient. Ninety-nine out of 100 times the digital display reflecting blood pressure and heart rate would be well within the range of data indicating a stable or improving state of health. The visual display of patient heart rate, with its healthy spikes and sinusoidal waves, also served to reassure the medical staff.

No alarm had yet sounded, but Hank's pulse rate accelerated rapidly while his systolic blood pressure concurrently dropped below 100. Bennie leaned against the bed in order to adjust the pillow that had almost worked itself free of Hank's head. Hank awoke from a fitful state of sleep. His response was hidden behind the endotracheal tube, head bandages and bruises that, though dark, had earlier displayed pallid fringes of yellow.

"How're we doin' today, Hank?" Looking down at his arm, she noticed small traces of blood in the catheter. By itself, a little trace of blood was not serious. Coupled with marginal vital signs, Bennie Mulligan was concerned enough to give him a closer look.

The nurse pulled down the sheet and, upon seeing the stains from a bloody bowel movement, gasped in horror. She surveyed his body and found traces of blood at the Achilles heel portion on Hank's left leg cast. The monitor alarm erupted in her ears. His pulse rate surged. Bennie took another look at the catheter - blood had backed up in critical quantity. Just as she started to rush out of the stark room, Nurse Bennie Mulligan looked down to see two eyes, wide open in amazement and fright, pleading with her for help.

Dr. Richard Wilson, the chief resident, was paged in the cafeteria where he was enjoying his first sip of coffee. There was an emergency in SICU - room 12. Less than a minute later Bennie met him at the elevator.

"Room 12. He's bleeding everywhere. Pulse is up. Blood pressure's down. It's bad. Very bad."

Dick Wilson reacted quickly and decisively. His race to the room slowed only briefly at the nurses' station. Bennie Mulligan matched him step for step. He gave a firm, though not abrasive, push to Bennie's shoulder towards the counter. "Call Code Blue. Call Doctor George." He was thinking out loud. He was urgent, yet he was under control. "Five units of blood. Get frozen plasma in here. Now! We need the crash cart." Doctor Dick Wilson had the makings of a fine doctor. This was, however, not his day. "Call Doctor George!"

The young doctor and the senior nurse continued their half-sprint to room 4-E-12. The sight was horrifying. Hank D'Arcy was trembling in his bed, blood oozing from multiple sites. It poured from both nostrils, his stool stained the sheets in a grotesque brownish orange, the IV catheter had turned purple, and areas that were stitched appeared to be artesian wells of crimson. His heart raced out of control.

In spite of his condition, Hank was conscious - and, once again, he knew he was being murdered. *What . . ? Who . . ? Why . . ?*

Doctor George burst into the room. Doctor Wilson looked quickly over his shoulder, then immediately back to the patient. He spoke urgently, but still with an air of control. "He's suffering from overwhelming sepsis with life threatening coagulapathy."

"No shit," Doctor George retorted.

Dick Wilson gave an overview of his early actions. The senior doctor replied with similar commands as his young resident.

"Get the lab up here. I want a CBC, platelets and a PT/PPT. I want the IV wide open." Inside Joseph George's psyche burned a fire that always raged against Death. Beyond the human sorrow, death of a patient was a professional loss. He couldn't believe that he and Will Smith were about to lose a contest they believed they were winning. Their work was too good. Dr. George looked back down at Hank D'Arcy.

All hell was breaking loose. The alarms, the mannerisms and the eyes said it all. Hank was in cardiac arrest. His eyes closed slightly, then fluttered, as he began struggling for consciousness and survival. Hank's chest heaved. Then staccato short breaths. His limbs flinched erratically, he gasped rapidly and his eyes became glassy. Hank D'Arcy began slipping away.

Hank sensed the air being sucked out of his body. He tried vainly to inhale life. The overwhelming sense of oxygen deprivation deadened the ache associated with his physical injuries. He could not feel the pain nor hear the popping sound of his ribs breaking under the external cardiac massage. A cold blackness settled over him for a moment; then came a sense of warmth, soothing warmth. An unfamiliar scene formed in his mind. He was trying to make his way through a field of South Texas cactus. The cactus punctured his body with every step. Strangely, he felt no pain. He eventually came to a clearing in which grass emanated an emerald green, highlighting a car on a dirt road. It was the Taurus. Magnificent mountains towered behind the car. Hank saw Sybil smiling at him from the passenger side. She waved for him to come. He tried to run, but the power of the dream would not let him close in on the shiny Ford. Then, instantaneously, he and Sybil were driving together across the country. It was what they both had wanted to do. It was beautiful. The car came to a stop at the edge of Colorado's Black Canyon National Monument. It was his canyon – and he reveled in sharing it with Sybil. Hand in hand, they walked to the gorge slicing more than 2,000 feet into the earth. The rising sun still floated beneath the horizon, but the rays of sunrise crested the peaks, giving off a hue of pale blue and white painting a brilliant clear sky. It was so beautiful and he and Sybil were so very happy. She smiled at him as they walked toward the sun.

●

"Watcha need?" Ham looked at his watch. It read 4:38.

"I collect antique cars. Actually rehab them almost from scratch." Barry Colter, dressed in dirty jeans, dark green short-sleeved shirt and worn jogging shoes, sweated profusely in defiance of the efforts of the air conditioner. Changing into work clothes in a gas station restroom was not easy. Barry had added 15 years to his age using a gray aerosol spray.

"I'm from San Antonio and was just driving through when I saw the body of that '46 Ford out there. Had a humpback in high school and would love to rebuild one." Again, the affable appearance was disarming. "O.K. if I scout it out and check some of your other cars?"

Ham scratched his forearm where sweat and poison ivy had mixed. "Damn poison. Go on out. Quittin' time is five. Won't be able to move it today, but just lemme know when." Ham surveyed the heat and dust outside. "I need to stay here for the phones."

"Thanks. I'll stop back before I leave."

Colter gave Ham a high sign and walked out the door. He walked towards the rusted body of the abandoned Ford in what was roughly the fifth row of cars at the end next to the fence. Barry owned one in high school and recognized it from the highway. Puffs of Texas dust billowed beneath his footsteps. Instead of continuing to the car, once out of view of the shack he circled around the first row of cars and returned to the empty flatbed trailer. *Need the straps. Only bad evidence.* He slipped his hands into a pair of work gloves. It was simple work unlocking the ratchet cylinder and removing each section of webbing, beginning with the short sections along the left side. Still, he needed to do it quickly. From the opposite side of the trailer he removed the long sections in a similar manner. He rolled all of the webbing together and walked directly to his already opened trunk. As he filled the trunk he contemplated registering a complaint concerning the 'lost' straps. Barry smiled. It had taken less than 20 minutes to complete the removal of the evidence. He walked to the Ford and waited.

Ham waddled out of the shack at 5:15. Seeing Barry's car first, he screened the horizon until he focused on Barry. He didn't want to walk the extra distance, but what the hell, a sale is a sale. It took almost two minutes to make it to Barry and the old Ford. "Thought you was gone already. Whatcha' think? Slick ole lady, huh?" Sweat poured from his face.

Barry patted the back of the Ford where the bowing hump becomes the trunk. "Sure is. More rust than I thought from the road, though. At least it's a good candidate. Have you got a phone number I can call?"

"Sure." Ham pulled a card from his shirt pocket and gave it to Barry. "Open nine 'til five. Course, it's past that now and I gotta lock up."

"Yeah, thanks. Sorry I took so much time." Barry turned simultaneously with Ham and walked him back to the white Acura. Barry endured Ham's crushing handshake, squeezed into his car and drove away.

Barry relaxed. He deserved to relax and dwell on the future. He had the only evidence that could link him to the murders in the trunk of his car. The straps were soon to be destroyed. All except one section.

●

"Tough. Real tough. I thought we had him. He was strong and wanted to survive. Eats at me." Joe George talked into his coffee mug.

Dick Wilson remained quiet. He had seen the quality of Dr. George's work. It was art. The guy should have lived.

Joe took a deep breath and continued. "Cardiac arrest secondary to coagulapathy. No autopsy needed. Same injuries as the other three. Multiple traumas, multiple compound fractures. Hank suffered from D-I-C." Joe George was tired. His physical state admitted defeat. He felt a little nauseous. He lost someone he barely knew, yet admired immensely.

He got up, patted Dick Wilson on the shoulder and spoke quietly to the young doctor.

"Be prepared Dick. You'll have these days. They do hurt."

A reply was unnecessary. Dick watched the veteran orthopedic surgeon shuffle out of the cafeteria.

●

Dr. Joseph George signed the death certificate.

A toxicology study was unnecessary. Two days later Hank D'Arcy, at Jud Weems' request, was cremated. Data from the simple post-mortem laboratory studies were charted and placed in a medical folder. The folder and, with it, any evidence as to the real cause of Hank's death, soon rested in the bowels of the hospital filing system.

15

The benches outside the courtroom were hard, straight-backed and very uncomfortable. Tom sat on the bench nearest the courtroom. He was not privy to the events taking place inside.

"All rise, the 295th Judicial District Court, South District of Texas, Houston Division, is now in session. The Honorable David V. Schultz, presiding." The bailiff was pleased with the authority with which he opened the case of the State of Texas versus John H. Schrauder.

Ms. Elizabeth T. Harker, District Attorney, represented the State. Resplendent in a dress suit of classic navy, a shirt accentuated with blue and white Bengal stripes, and a red coral scarf, Liz Harker scored heavily with the nine male members of the jury before speaking a word. She was a strikingly beautiful woman. Her legal assistant, Malcolm Mitchener, was a diminutive young man wearing a brown business suit, white dress shirt and blue and beige stirrup motif tie. The stark contrast between the two was obvious to the defense and Judge Schultz; it was lost on the jury.

Mr. Travis M. White of Duffy, Guyer, and White represented John Schrauder. The attractive physical appearance of the two legal opponents, one female, one male, added competitive ambiance to the courtroom.

Judge Schultz pulled the sleeves of his black robe to the midpoint of each forearm and leaned forward, chin resting on cupped hands. Surveying the courtroom, he sensed the mood of the audience and immediately reflected on his own state of anticipation. The sensational nature of the case brought in media from all of South Texas, relatives of the accused and the deceased family, including the genuinely bereaved parents of Martha and Joe Stetly and a sizable gathering of curious onlookers. He began the proceedings.

"Are we ready?"

The lead attorneys responded in tandem, "Yes, your Honor. Yes, your Honor."

"Let's have some opening statements."

Elizabeth Harker rose from her chair and walked to a position midway between her table and Judge Schultz. She rotated slightly to the right allowing her to speak directly to the judge and, with a small turn of her head, the jury. She was relaxed, confident and the perfect model of politeness. She was formidable. She was very impressive.

"Your Honor, the State takes no pleasure in prosecuting someone who has previously been a law abiding citizen. Mr. Schrauder has a family whom he loves and has supported for over 15 years." Liz Harker nodded gently to the woman sitting directly behind John Schrauder. Hands folded and resting on her lap, the small, pale woman could not make eye contact with the District Attorney. She could only listen.

The opening statement continued. "However, we, as a society, must draw a line as to what responsibility we have towards others. A line which, when crossed, clearly marks the difference between simple negligence and criminal conduct." Liz Harker's eyes tightened as she walked to the table behind which sat John Schrauder. She looked him squarely in the eyes. "Just as Mr. Schrauder has a loving wife and two beautiful daughters, the Stetly family had loving, affectionate parents and three wonderful children. The real difference between the two families is that the Stetly family . . ." She changed the tempo of her speech to a slow, deliberate, monotone of ominous texture. ". . . Martha, Joe, Andrew and Ben are stone dead. Needlessly and brutally dead. There is a beautiful little girl, Amanda Stetly, asking for her mommy and daddy. She will never know the joy of having a mother and father. Nor will she grow up with her two brothers, who certainly would have been there to protect her."

An inhaled, guttural, sob rose above the voices in the courtroom. Martha Stetly's mother was consumed in grief. Others responded with restrained cries of their own. Despair engulfed the courtroom.

Liz Harker seized the moment to establish a linkage to Belton Trucking and the whole trucking industry. She suggested a policy of gross corporate indifference. "Your Honor, and ladies and gentlemen of the jury, under a different venue we will show criminal conduct on the part of senior management of Belton Trucking. However, the fact remains that the last clear chance to avert this tragedy lay completely with Mr. Schrauder." Travis jotted down a quick note. "Had he chosen to step on the brakes as opposed to the accelerator, we would not be here today. Had he simply stepped on the brakes, costing himself possibly a minute of his time . . ." Elizabeth Harker moved slowly, deliberately, to the center of the jury box railing. She leaned forward, cocking her head first in the direction of the foreman, then continued the dialogue while rotating her head slowly from left to right, connecting directly with each member, ". . . then two young boys would probably be on the playground at school this very moment. A husband and wife, sweethearts since junior high school . . ." The inevitable pause. ". . . might be planning for a family reunion. A young bride might someday walk down the aisle next to her father. But none of it will happen. Four lives wasted, a family ripped from friends. All because," she paused, "John Schrauder wanted an extra minute." Liz Harker pointed at John Schrauder. "He might want to call it 'being in a hurry'," she folded her arms below her breasts, concluding her statement with, "but, as the District Attorney for the city of Houston, Texas, I call it vehicular homicide. Vehicular homicide, exactly as charged."

Travis White watched his opponent with grudging respect. *Smart woman. Hard nosed. Dangerous.* He mentally rummaged through a series of Harker victories. Where the evidence wasn't quite enough, Elizabeth Harker had the power to will juries to a favorable verdict. He quickly returned to the remarks being made.

The District Attorney backed off the railing and turned away from the jury. Out of sight of the twelve jurors, her face clearly showed satisfaction. She returned to stand behind her chair, again facing the judge. "Your Honor, we will present facts, based on physical evidence and eyewitness testimony, that will prove beyond any doubt," she added emphasis, "ANY doubt at all, that Mr. John Howard Schrauder is guilty of criminally negligent homicide. Thank you." Liz Harker sat down.

Elizabeth Harker had no ax to grind against John Schrauder. As much as possible for her nature, she felt somewhat sorry for the truck driver. But John Schrauder was the entry point to indictments against Belton Trucking and, ultimately, Flagg Brothers. Barry Colter was already working those issues. Assuming that a driver, the little person in a trucking firm, would be found guilty, then the prosecution, led by Ms. Elizabeth Harker, would be in a position of psychological strength to pursue bigger fish. New trials, both civil and criminal, against Belton Trucking would present an impression of a poorly trained, underpaid, and overworked stable of drivers.

Of course, in the long run, Flagg Brothers, with its alleged criminally negligent senior leadership, was the real jackpot.

Judge Schultz nodded to Travis. A member of the bench for 24 years, David Schultz had built a reputation of fairness. He also exercised complete control over the conduct of proceedings in his court. Woe to the lawyer who challenged the judge's dominion, either through a breach of ethics or through abrasive behavior in the courtroom. Tall and gangly, he nevertheless had an aura of strength about him. It was once said the he was a good-looking Ichabod Crane. Steel blue eyes, full head of gray hair, and, unlike Ichabod, a Roman nose. He had a commanding presence over the courtroom.

"Mr. White, let's hear what you have to say."

"Yes, your Honor." In his own tactical move, Travis positioned himself to the judge's right and in a direct line with himself at one end, the jury at the other, and the District Attorney exactly at the mid-point. Tit for tat.

He began, "Your Honor," Travis looked through Liz Harker to the jury, "and ladies and gentlemen of the jury. I won't offend you by making light of the prosecutor's opening statement, but I heard one statement that legitimately addressed the case before you. Everything else was directed at your emotions. This case must, absolutely must, be judged on pure evidence applied to the laws of the state of Texas."

It was Liz Harker's turn to watch the opponent. *Son of a bitch.* No, not much love lost between the two.

Travis continued. "This case is not about whether or not Mr. Schrauder may have run a red light. From everything I have been able to ascertain about the unfortunate accident, it appears he well may have. However . . ." Travis paused and directly faced the jury, ". . . it turns out that many factors, very important factors, must be considered. Paramount will be the issue of intent – and intent is the child of attitude. The prosecutor, Ms. Harker, alluded to the principal of 'last clear chance.' The question to be answered is whether or not Mr. Schrauder actually had the last clear chance to avert the accident. And what of the two boys? Where does Wolfpack Van fit into the events of that early evening? Would those boys have died, or even been severely injured, had the cab portion of the recreation vehicle been constructed with the possibility in mind that people, quite likely children, just might be up there during a drive? This, as you will soon see, is not going to be a simple case." Travis, just as Liz Harker had done five minutes earlier, leaned at the center of the jury box railing. "I have no doubt whatsoever that you will do your utmost to try the case as honestly and logically as you possibly can. However . . ." an intense, serious, look seized his face, ". . . the one thing that I do specifically ask you is to put yourself squarely into the events as they are explained to you. Only if you can see the accident through the eyes of John Schrauder will the truth in this matter come to light. I will trust your judgment." Travis White lingered at the rail for five seconds, then spoke, "Thank you." He returned to his place at table.

The State's case against John Schrauder was strong. Very strong. Officer

Bill Newton testified that Schrauder admitted he had run the light. His statement, with quotes, was entered into the investigation report. The prosecution's expert witness, Dr. Muriel Rooney, a University of Houston professor, was compelling. Dr. Rooney, a Ph.D. in mechanical engineering, was confident and credible. She convinced the jury that John Schrauder entered the intersection at almost 65 miles an hour. More notes jotted down. Travis would bounce them off Tom at lunch. An eyewitness, a young woman who had stopped for the light in direct view of the oncoming tractor-trailer, corroborated the expert testimony. Travis questioned her ability to arrive at a specific speed while being totally unaware of the recreation vehicle approaching John Schrauder's tractor-trailer. Only once did Travis object to any of the morning's examination, that being when Officer Newton was asked for an opinion as to how fast he thought the tractor-trailer was traveling as it entered the intersection. Bill Newton was not an expert witness and the objection was sustained. The description of the movements of the vehicles and sources of damage presented by Dr. Rooney fit fairly well with Tom's reconstruction of the accident. The one point of major disagreement was the speed suggested by Rooney. Travis admired the prosecution's presentation of the case, including light inferences painting John Schrauder as not being the model citizen described earlier by the prosecution. It was a good tactic, the prosecution subtly attacking it's own opening statement that John Schrauder had been a 'law abiding citizen'. Two speeding tickets in eight years, one while driving the same rig involved in the accident, helped the prosecution. So did a previous credit card problem. By the time of the lunch recess, Liz Harker's work had damaged the defense. The only positive factor was that Travis was not surprised by the testimony of the witnesses or the direction of attack by the prosecution. He was glad that it took all morning. He would be able to analyze some of the testimony. Travis' cross-examination of Dr. Rooney focused on the degree of conviction she had concerning the speed of the rig. He remembered Tom stating that the rig was not traveling much over 50 miles an hour. Travis made one attack on Dr. Rooney's credibility. In his cross-examination, he planted a seed.

"As a mechanical engineer, do you possess any sort of professional registration, like doctors or lawyers?"

Slightly irritated and aware of Travis' tactic, Dr. Rooney handled herself well. "Mr. White, as I said earlier, I possess a doctor of philosophy degree in mechanical engineering from Texas Tech University. I possess both the credentials and the knowledge to appear before this court."

We'll see about that. Travis thought ahead to putting Tom on the stand.

The morning session passed quickly. Judge Schultz called for recess. "Ladies and gentlemen, it's noon. We'll recess until 2:00. Any problems?" He surveyed the jury. There being no response, he concluded, "O.K., you're in recess until two. Jury out at 11:58."

The noise of the stirring courtroom alerted Tom to the recess. He placed the thin stack of papers back into his briefcase and was ready for lunch by the time Travis and Ed Harvey, the junior attorney on the case, walked into the hallway. With them were John and Sarah Schrauder. Both appeared to be remorseful. During his visit with the Schrauders Tom pieced together an accurate picture of the events through John's eyes. There was no need to go over them again. Tom stood to greet his new friends.

"Hi Sarah, John, you still hanging in there?"

During investigations, Tom occasionally spent several hours with the principal parties. Solving the physical mysteries of accidents often began with understanding the human component of events. In rare cases, a friendship ensued. Tom was different from many accident reconstructionists. Tom thought back to his first meeting with John and Sarah on their porch. This friendship was real.

"Hello Tom," John reached out to Tom, "we're doing our best."

Tom wanted to put his arms around Sarah but was sensitive to John's already failing sense of self-esteem. He shook John's hand, then stepped back, giving them space. Sarah looked at Tom and tried to muster a response. Her attempt to speak was interrupted by uncontrollable sobs as she collapsed into John's arms. Stress, confusion, sadness and anger overcame her. John held her close to his chest without speaking. Sarah Schrauder needed the freedom to cry. She held on to John tightly and cried.

"I'm, I'm sorry. I just don't under. . ." Sarah couldn't get the words out. She sunk her head back into John's chest and closed her eyes. No one moved for half a minute.

"Thanks, thanks everyone." As Sarah straightened up, John released his gentle hold. She turned to her husband and reached for his hands. As they touched, she spoke. "John, I love you so very much. We will make it. Please hold me."

John and Sarah Schrauder embraced again, tears rolling off of his cheeks onto hers.

It was John's turn to speak. "We need some time alone. We'll be back. Thanks."

The three men waited as John and Sarah, his arm around her shoulders, walked out of the courthouse.

"This is all bullshit. Let's go eat." Travis took the lead.

By the time they reached Cosimo's Restaurant, two blocks from the courthouse, the emotional meeting with the Schrauders had receded from their minds. All three ordered a turkey club and iced tea for lunch.

Over their drinks, the legal team discussed events of the day. The first event did not concern the Schrauders.

Travis asked, "Did you get the word about the Flagg case? Husband of one of the D'Arcy's is suing everybody who has a wallet. Colter, Fisher and King have it." He paused, then said, "Have you ever noticed that whenever the D.A. gets a big criminal case, Colter sweeps up the street with a civil case? Yessir," Travis, his jaw tightening, added, "they sure are an unholy alliance."

"Yeah, saw it on the news. Doesn't surprise me much. With Colter involved, I'm surprised he didn't sue before they picked up the bodies. The injuries to the one who almost survived were gruesome, to say the least. He was mangled. Other than not being able to talk to him, it doesn't affect what I'm doing. How's it change things for you?"

"The stakes are going to be big time. No mention of the amount yet, but get set folks. It will be huge and that, coupled with the timing of the Stetly trial, will really bring in the press." Travis finished the first of four glasses of tea. "Brazoria County. We've got problems. Actually, Flagg has the problems." Travis rotated the glass, then lifted it and tapped on the bottom. A single ice cube slid into his mouth. He bit into the cube, chewed and swallowed the tiny pieces of melting ice. With confidence, he spoke again. "Let's just continue to march on that one. For now, we ought to get back to John and Sarah." He spoke of Sarah Schrauder as though she, too, was on trial. She was.

Tom spoke. "How'd the prelims go?"

The sandwiches arrived and were devoured during the conversation. Travis covered the general flow of the morning session. The testimonies of Officer Bill Newton, the eyewitness, and Dr. Muriel Rooney all had been strong.

"So, that's where it is now."

Ed broke in. "We need to counter their testimony somehow."

"Agreed. Other than the McCorkle woman, not much I could do this morning. Newton was very credible. I got in one objection, but it didn't make much difference. He verified that the Stetlys were killed and that John did run the light."

Tom winced, bobbing his head with a tiny cough. "Damn. But we knew it was coming."

Travis leaned back on the back two legs of his chair. He stretched, then continued. "As for Dr. Rooney, she did a hell of a job. Had him at 65 and climbing. So did McCorkle, even though I nailed her on not seeing the Stetly vehicle."

"He wasn't going 65 and I can prove it." Tom took over the conversation. "Here's my view of the events so far . . ."

Tom emphasized that their 'foot in the door' would be Dr. Rooney, but that it shouldn't be done by character assassination. It had to be based on perception as to which witness was the better engineer. He had evidence that he believed contradicted hers. Tom had far more experience, in the field and on the witness stand, than did she.

"Our research verifies Rooney's not a registered professional engineer. That can work to our benefit. As for the eyewitness, from her vantage point, she'd play hell knowing exactly how fast the rig was moving. If she also said 65, then that's pure coincidence with Rooney's testimony. She was coached. We need to hit that hard."

After more than an hour of tactical discussion, the three gave the waitress a generous tip, paid their bill and walked back to the courthouse. The defense plan did not need significant change.

Tom would be on the stand the next morning.

●

"This is Barry Colter."

"It's me. We have a good start. The picture of the family came across strong. Rooney was very credible, as was McCorkle."

Barry made a half-turn in his executive chair. He pulled out the sideboard and crossed his legs on top of it. The project was on target. "Good. It's going as planned. I told you. Keep the focus inside the courtroom on the driver. On the outside put it on the out-of-control trucking industry and the victims. Play up the orphan bit."

"I will. What's the status at your end?"

He looked up at the ceiling, then to a Degas print of the New Orleans Cotton Exchange. His mind surveyed the future. "Timing's on-schedule. I'm pushing to keep it as close to your trial as possible. We're on the move, so let's just keep it going. We can tie strings together in Seadrift." Barry smiled contentedly, lost in his imagination.

16

"Tom, it's your turn." Ed appeared from nowhere, breaking Tom's concentration over the police videotape. Tom looked at his watch. Eleven o'clock. He preferred an earlier start, before a jurist's stomach takes over.

Tom replaced his papers, gave the briefcase to Ed, and then followed him into the courtroom. The walk down the courtroom aisle always evoked a slight twinge of excitement from Tom. He nodded politely to the jury and the District Attorney, stopped at the witness stand and was sworn in. He sat down, looking quite comfortable. Travis walked directly to his witness. They began.

"Good morning, Mr. Seiler."

"Good morning."

So far, so good. Travis continued. "I'd like to ask you to introduce yourself to these folks. Please begin by giving your complete name and tell them where you live."

"Fine. Thomas Mannan Seiler. I live in Houston, actually Clear Lake, Texas." Tom surveyed the jury as he spoke. Eyeball to eyeball. Tall, short, skinny, fat, black, white, smart, ignorant, honest, dishonest – they fully represented the human condition. Yet, if they were like most juries in South Texas, they would begin the trial on the side of the plaintiff.

Time to build Tom's credibility. Tom knew, Travis knew, Liz Harker knew, and even Dr. Rooney knew that Tom was the superior engineer. But the jury did not know. The introduction would be critical.

"Please tell us what you do for a living and a little about your educational background."

"Yes sir. I grew up in San Antonio. Went to Northeast High School, now known as MacArthur. I went to the University of . . ."

Tom had given the story countless times. Born in Texas, son of a military officer, a great deal of traveling, a quick mention of family, even losing his firstborn son in a boating accident and his brother in the Vietnam War – a well painted picture of human events leading to Tom's presence in the courtroom. No need to lead the witness, Travis waited until Tom finished to start making their case. Given the late start, Travis decided to end the session by taking his first poke at the prosecution's case.

"Thank you, Mr. Seiler. Yours is a very interesting life. Let me ask you a question about your professional background. You mentioned that you're a registered professional engineer. In English, what does that mean?"

"Well, the State of Texas licenses engineers who practice in public. In a nutshell, it means that the state recognizes that I've met certain standards to practice as an engineer."

Travis walked closer to the jury. "Does that mean that all engineers in Texas are registered?"

"No, not at all. The registered engineers, called P.E.'s, are only a small part of the whole engineering population."

Travis seized the opportunity. "Would you consider professional registration to be more important than a Ph.D. to practice engineering?"

Liz Harker jumped on Travis' question before Tom could open his mouth. "Objection, your Honor. The question is leading and asks for an opinion about which Mr. Seiler is not expert."

Travis had already made the point. He knew it; Liz Harker knew it.

"Sustained. Mr. White, keep your focus on the witness. Continue."

Travis looked at his opponent, then to the jury. *O.K., they know she's easily pissed.*

"Your Honor, I would like to turn our discussion to the facts surrounding the accident involving Mr. Schrauder and the Stetlys. However, given the time of the day, could I suggest that we recess now and take it up after lunch."

Judge Schultz' stomach made the same plea. "Fine. Any problems?" He knew there wouldn't be. "Please return at 2:00. Have a nice lunch. Jury out at 11:42."

●

"Hi there, good to see you back. Is your sidekick goin' to join you?" It was the same waitress, with a friendly smile on her face. She sat Jud in the same booth, offering him the menu.

"Nope, not today." *Not any fuckin' day.* He smiled and gave the menu back.

"Let me have the special and a Pearl."

"Comin' up sweetie." The friendly smile offered a future invitation to Jud. *I might just let you get into my pants pretty soon.*

Jud read the smile. *I might just have to get into your pants pretty soon.*

The special of the day at Sodbuster's was chicken fried steak. Marinate prime beef in a garlic butter sauce; immerse in flour; fry in fresh oil at extremely high temperatures to capture the flavor and moisture in a golden bronze crust – perfection. This one did not disappoint. It was delicious; yet, the meal, the beer and the promise of a roll in the hay with what's-her-name did not deter Jud from focusing on more important business. Over his meal he pondered what strategy must be applied to Barry Colter. Since the day Barry handed him the $5,000, Jud distrusted and disliked him. He processed his options. Jud finished off the last of his fries, took a final swig of beer and got up to leave. His last thought at the table concerned the esteemed Barry Colter, attorney, esquire and all that other shit. *If I have to, I'll deal with him.*

Again, the tip was large, but, in a way, it was a prepayment for some good times to come. "By the way, what's your name."

"Sandy, what's yours?"

"Joe Jarrick. Sure enjoyed meetin' you. How about us going out one of these days soon?"

That smile again. "I'd love to. Most nights I'm free by 10:15. Give me a call when you can." She pulled out a piece of paper with her phone number and name already on it.

"Count on it, Sandy. I'll be outta town for a couple of weeks, but I'll call you when I get back."

As he walked out into the parking lot, both Jud and Sandy thought simultaneously, *I'm about to get laid.*

●

Two o'clock. Travis opened with a couple of softball questions, then offered the meat.

"What you seem to be telling the court, Mr. Seiler, is that there are several specific causes to the accident. Is that true?"

"Yes, sir."

"Can you simplify matters so that we all can understand?"

"Yes, sir." Tom spoke politely, confidently.

"Please, then, what are the specific components of this case that, based upon your investigation, are critical to this court?"

Tom shifted weight in his seat and looked at the jury. "Basically, there are four major events. They are: first, what took place in the 18-wheeler and why; secondly, what took place in the Stetly van and why; third, what caused the two boys to get thrown through the overhead compartment; and fourth, what physical features at the intersection played a part in the accident."

Liz Harker squirmed in her seat. Tom Seiler was as smart as they come.

Travis looked over at the District Attorney and smiled discretely. No words were needed. He put the notepad back in his shirt pocket and turned to Tom.

"Fine, Mr. Seiler. We'll continue your testimony in that order. But, before we begin, I would like the court to know where it is that we are headed. Do you have specific conclusions related to this accident?"

Tom spoke firmly, showing conviction to what followed.

"Yes sir, I do."

"Please tell the court of your conclusions."

"Based purely on my investigation there are three contributors. First is the City of Houston, Texas. Secondly, shoddy construction of the overhead compartment of the Wolfpack Recreation Vehicle led to the deaths of the boys. Third, Mrs. Stetly drove directly into the tractor-trailer driven by Mr. Schrauder. As for Mister . . ."

Liz Harker responded too slowly and should have objected to Tom's first statement. She allowed herself to be caught up in the testimony, as opposed to parsing each statement to find inconsistencies. She shot from her seat.

"Objection your Honor. The whole city of Houston is not a contributor. It is the jury, not the witness, who determines fault in this case. I request his testimony be stricken from the record and that he confine his remarks to areas of his presumed expertise."

The jury sensed Liz Harker's animosity towards Tom. In other venues a fistfight might have erupted. The entire congregation was alert, oblivious to time and the oppressive humidity seeping into the courtroom.

Judge Schultz agreed. "Sustained." *We've got ourselves a good one.* "I want expert testimony, not a ruling as to innocence or guilt. Proceed."

"Yes, your Honor." Travis rolled the pen back and forth in his hands, allowing a few seconds in which to adjust his tactic ever so slightly. He began again. "Mr. Seiler, I would like you to address the four major events. It's probably best to do it in the order you described. I'd like to show you some photographs. Do you recognize these photographs?"

Travis flipped through a sizable assortment of photographs, then gave the stack to Tom.

"Yes sir." Tom sorted out the first 11 photographs and held them in his left hand. "I received these from you. I took some of the other photographs and my wife took some."

Tom held up a separate collection of photographs, 17 in number. "We believe that these photos are important. I scanned them so that I could show them with the overhead projector."

"Your Honor, we would tender defense exhibits one to 28."

"Ms. Harker?"

"I have no objection, your Honor."

The pair, in fluid give and take, gathered momentum. Entered into evidence was a VCR simulation of the accident. It depicted the paths and relative speeds of each vehicle as it approached the intersection. Their teamwork continued.

"Mr. Seiler, please explain the VCR film that we are about to see. I mean, how does it work and how can it accurately portray what really happened?"

"Glad to." Tom enjoyed telling the story one more time. "Back in the late sixties and early seventies, as the computer began its explosive rise to prominence, a lot of folks were doing research on automobile accidents and set up many trial crashes. Engineers teamed up with computer specialists and began writing programs that would model what happens when two cars hit each other. At first, test crashes that had already been conducted were replicated with pretty detailed accuracy. The early computer programs were somewhat rudimentary. Then companies like Cal-Span, and universities like Cornell and others got into the act, modeling crashes before they actually happened."

Travis interrupted. "Mr. Seiler, let's back up for just a minute. I'm not sure I understand. Why is it significant that they reverse the procedure and model crashes before they happen?"

Tom leaned forward slightly, then continued. "It's based on the fact that you can do just about anything with numbers. It would be possible to replicate a crash using logic and numbers that would work for that single crash but not be applicable to other crashes. Basically, a lot of early stuff was eyewash. Then programs began to sprout up that would predict the movement of the vehicles after impact, to include how they might spin, how far they would go, and in what direction. It was like 'Eureka' to predict a collision scenario and then go and actually run two cars into each other and find out that they behaved very closely to what the computer program predicted."

"So these programs are both accurate and easy to use."

"They are now. Early versions were what I call user-surly in that the time to learn how to use the program was extensive."

Several jurors, victims of computer surliness, nodded in agreement.

"Were you able to model this accident accurately?"

"Yes sir, I was."

"Please explain to the court how you developed the results that you will be showing on the tape."

"Fine. But I need to start with the simple laws of physics. Could I ask to have Mr. White's table moved to the middle of the room? It will help greatly to clarify exactly what I will be speaking about."

Judge Schultz looked over at the prosecution. "Any problems counselor?"

"No, your Honor." Liz Harker really had no choice. She decided to rely on the expert testimony of Dr. Rooney.

The Judge approved. "Fine. O.K. Mr. White, set it up. Mr. Seiler, you may step down."

Using functioning models of a blue Ford Mustang, a red Pontiac Gran Prix and a Hess gasoline tanker, Tom instructed the jury on the basic laws of physics. Force equals mass times acceleration. The consequences of friction. Braking forces. Most of the jury grasped the major concepts. Those who didn't held a blind faith that Tom was speaking the Gospel truth.

Travis knew they were on a roll. Like Rocky Marciano, he would retire for the day while on top.

"Your Honor, I believe this is a good point to end. I would like to begin tomorrow with Mr. Seiler explaining the results of his analysis and his expert conclusions."

●

Tom looked at the strap resting in his hand. Filled manila folders, computer drawings, photos, and his yellow notepad covered the coffee table. The television provided background noise. He examined the severed end as though hunting for ticks on a cat. He did not touch the frayed edges. A slight stain of oil darkened the manila folder where the cut end had lain. No oil was at the other end. His mind searched for benign answers. It found none. The Stetly case represented the largest trial in which he had ever participated; yet he could only focus on the strange bits of information related to the D'Arcy incident in Alvin. He examined what appeared to be areas cut with a razor and areas pulled apart with terrific force. Tom returned to Savage Salvage late that afternoon only to find all of the other straps missing. Ham had no idea as to who might have taken them. Investigators, tow drivers, junk dealers, antique car aficionados, teenagers, and even the curious had visited the yard. He couldn't remember one face. A queasy feeling invaded Tom's body. *Why would anyone even want those straps?* It was a slight touch of fear. He remembered crossing a field at night as a little boy. Somewhere nearby came the low, muffled snarl of a dog. The young boy froze, every hair on his body raised in stark fear of the unknown. Or was it the known? Ever so slightly those feelings invaded Tom's comfortable surroundings.

Susie walked up behind Tom and placed her hands on his shoulders. Startled, he jerked forward and half-spun around before realizing where he was. It scared her.

"Holy shit! Talk about catching me off-guard." Tom tried to play it off, but Susie wouldn't bite.

Her blue eyes focused intently on her husband. "What are you thinking?"

Tom held the strap in his right hand, the ruptured end rising an inch above his thumb and index finger. He rubbed the cut end back and forth across a clean section of manila – a slight stain of oil resulted. He repeated the process using the free end of the strap – no stain.

"Right now everything is a jumbled mess. Here's what I know. First, out at Parker Road you said something like 'the curve can be negotiated'. That stuck with me. Now I find oil on a strap that has been cut. Either vandals did it or we might have an intentional act. Why would vandals oil a strap? And where are the straps that we left with the rig? If not the police, who would have taken the other ones? And why? The driver is dead. Did he plan to kill someone in the car, cut the straps and run the whole show? No way. He did his part but screws up his late-night drive."

He paused long enough for Susie to respond.

Susie asked, "Could someone have wanted to kill the driver?" She sat down.

Tom thought briefly. "No, I can't see it. If you cut the straps, the safest person around would be the driver."

"Then who? Who would be a target?"

"I wonder, could it be a vendetta against Flagg Brothers?" Tom walked in a circle looking up at the ceiling. He spoke to the slowly spinning fan. "If so, wiping out a family would be a great way to do it."

Susie asked, "What about one trucking company framing another one?"

"Interesting. Certainly possible."

"What do you know about the family?"

"Not much. Why?"

"Just strange that an entire family gets wiped out in an accident. It's probably happened before, but it's still a big coincidence. Then there's the *Chronicle* report that the rig was dispatched to Corpus. He was going the wrong way. It seems funny that a family of four gets killed on a desolate road by a rig in the wrong town." She gently bit on her lip, then spoke again. "If I wanted to go after a trucking company,

I don't think I would do it on a road where the driver isn't supposed to be."

Tom stopped walking, then stared at Susie.

Both sensed the dog.

17

Tom spent a fitful night, the events in Alvin hammering away in his mind.

Travis slept like a baby.

The trial began at 9:15, delayed by the late arrival of several jurors. The weather was bad. Heavy downpours accentuated a steady rain fueled by a tropical depression. A fatal accident on the Gulf Freeway created a four-mile backup. Curious onlookers clogged the single open lane.

Judge Schultz did not tolerate tardiness; however, given the weather and the news reports on the accident, he made an exception. In truth, he was pleased to have a few minutes to savor a hot cup of coffee. He walked into the courtroom in better spirits than the poor, damp, souls occupying their assigned seats.

"All rise." Another session, in and for Harris County, Texas, began.

Travis could read people and, on this dismal day, knew that he had to overcome juror apathy. *This is not the time for jokes.*

"Let me bring us back to where we ended yesterday." Travis walked to the rail as he summarized the theory presented the day before. He reminded them of Tom's demonstration in a manner again linking Tom to the jury. The thrust of his remarks emphasized that he, just like the jury, was a neophyte to the world of physics. But, just like the jury, he was able to genuinely grasp the basic concepts. "Your Honor, I would like to call Mr. Seiler back to the stand."

Tom was sworn in for the morning litigation.

●

Barry Colter joined the audience for the start of the morning session. He sat in the rear of the courtroom, analyzing the flow of the proceedings. He would prefer Tom Seiler be Liz's witness. *He's good, damn good.* Mixed emotions ebbed and flowed as he watched the courtroom scene unfold. What was the best outcome for future events? If John Schrauder were found guilty of vehicular homicide, then it would be easy to orchestrate an outcry that Schrauder was a scapegoat for the poor training and hiring practices of senior management. That scenario played well in his mind in that it substantiated a trucking industry with only greed as a guide. But then, suppose sentiment swayed towards Schrauder being railroaded by an overzealous prosecutor. Barry felt more comfortable with the first possibility. He then envisioned a verdict of not guilty. *What then?* Probability, he reasoned, favors a sense that a 'not guilty' verdict would make it more difficult, but far from unwise, to continue with a civil suit. At worst, he would get a settlement out of Belton Trucking. Expressing institutional outrage aimed at the trucking industry over a 'not guilty' finding might be advantageous to the D'Arcy trial. He thought, *I've got to tailor any outcome to supporting the project.* Even subconsciously he labeled it "the project". *But still,* Barry's mind forced itself back to the events to his front, *first things first.*

On file at Colter, Fisher, and King was a written legal agreement to sue Belton Trucking in civil court, signed by Wyman Jamison, the father of Martha Stetly. Barry closed the deal 44 hours after the accident. The lawyer's story that he lost his niece at the same intersection disarmed the family. They could never have back what they lost, Barry reasoned, but they could be part of the process making those having blatant disregard for others pay for their transgressions. Normal fees for taking on a case of this nature were one-third of the settlement. Barry Colter, because of his great affection for and common bond with the Jamisons, had agreed to only 25 percent after expenses. Barry knew that the firm's calculation of 'expenses' would be enormous. He left before Tom testified about Martha Stetly's actions. He had an 11:15 meeting with a Mr. Judson Weems.

●

The interaction between Travis and Tom took almost two and a half hours. The flow was natural. Travis took advantage of his ability to build that imperceptible bond between himself, as the attorney, and the jury, as people in search of the truth. The interplay between Tom and Travis was a delicious recipe of physical science, plausible scenarios and a stage play in which the jurors were unconsciously invited to participate. The rehearsal began two nights earlier over a couple of beers and chicken-fried steak at Bennigan's.

"No bullshit challenges. Schultz doesn't bend to that crap at all. He controls the flow better than any other judge in town. Unless the testimony is blatantly destructive, I won't challenge." Travis spoke matter-of-factly, twisting the Miller counter-clockwise in his hands.

He continued. "We need the jury." Travis leaned back, raising his arm as though asking for permission to go to the bathroom. The waitress gave him the happy nod. Two more Millers on the way. Travis added, "And, my good friend, we've got to carry the whole jury on the dilemma zone."

Tom gulped down the remaining three inches of his beer and interjected, "O.K., I'll play to your lead. We'll screw Harker to the wall on the intersection. That woman is something else. I just don't understand why anyone needs to be such an ass. But, what the hell, it's her decision how to approach life."

The waitress traded full bottles for empty ones, smiled, and moved off to deal with hundreds of other Texans who like beer and wild stories.

Tom added, "You need to study the jury on the finite-elements part. The way I see it, if we can actually teach them the basics, they'll see the truth for themselves. If not, then Wolfpack gets away with some shoddy engineering. If they buy into it, then Paige's work will do it." Tom emptied the top third of the refreshing liquid. "Let me know if I get too technical. Sometimes I get orgasmic with my own brilliance."

"You sure as hell do." Travis laughed.

Another hour of sequencing the testimony and drinking beer. They decided to go over computer-generated simulations at Tom's the next night. They would be ready.

Travis placed the cap back on the magic marker and moved to his strategic location between Tom and the jury. He went through the procedure for admitting the video taken by the two police officers. He made a couple of remarks indicating that the first part was taken the night of the accident and the second part taken two days later. Travis did request that each juror study the video intently since they would return to it later.

Tom waited impassively for the first question.

Travis initiated the testimony, "Mr. Seiler, based on your analysis of the video, the photographs, your investigation of the scene, and your speaking to Mr. Schrauder, how did the accident occur?"

"Well sir, let me retrace the movement of the tractor-trailer. Mr. Schrauder was driving northbound at between 40 and 50 miles an hour when he encountered the dilemma zone to the intersection."

Travis interrupted, "Please explain what is meant by the dilemma zone."

With the judge's permission, Tom walked to the easel. "The dilemma zone defines the distance from a traffic light that, for a given speed, length of a vehicle and the dimensions of the intersection, creates a dilemma for a driver." Tom sketched each component of an intersection on the paper. "In the case of a tractor-trailer, if the driver applies the brakes, will the rig stop before hitting the intersection? If he continues, how much of the rig will make it through the intersection before the light changes to red? For a driver, the unknown variables in the dilemma zone are the length of time the light stays yellow and the dimensions of an intersection."

The lesson was crucial. He spoke clearly, deliberately. "As an example, let's use a tractor-trailer going 40 miles an hour and a yellow light that lasts four and a half seconds." With engineering precision he added a symbol for a light to the drawing.

The jury studied the artwork. *Good.*

He continued. "I simply multiply 40 times the distance of a mile, 5,280 feet, and divide by the number of seconds in an hour, 3,600. The result is 58.1 feet per second. Multiplying that by the time of the yellow light, 4.5 seconds, I get a result of 264.1 feet that the rig has traveled while the yellow light is on."

Tom paused slightly and scanned the jury. They were attentive. *Still have them.* "What this means is, if the front of the rig is at the edge of the intersection at the exact moment the yellow light goes on, it will have traveled 264 feet when the light changes to red." He placed a red magic-marker tick-mark at the approximate scaled distance along the roadway sketch, labeling the distance '264'.

On cue, Travis sat down, leaving the classroom discussion solely to Tom.

"The real question becomes, 'Even though the driver is well down the road, by how much did the back of the trailer clear the ENTIRE intersection?'" He paused again, sensing two or three of the jurors wanting to raise their hands. He still had them. He spoke again. "All we have to do is add the width of the intersection, and in this case the width of Texas 35 is 60 feet, to the length of the tractor-trailer, 62 feet, giving us 122 feet. We subtract that from 264 feet, giving us safe clearance of the back of the trailer of 144 feet."

Tom drew a very neat outline of the rig. He then wrote '144' to indicate the clearance. "What this means is that if the rig is one-hundred and forty-four feet," again adding emphasis, "OR LESS, from the start of the intersection, he would safely pass through it." Using the blue marker, he placed a mark at the equivalent distance before the intersection. He wrote '144'.

Even Liz Harker was engrossed in the lesson. And she didn't like it.

Tom turned pensive, serious. "But what if he is one foot, five feet, 50 feet, further away from the intersection when the light turns yellow?" He could see the confusion in their eyes – and he played upon it. "What most of you are sensing is the result of the dilemma zone."

Liz was alert. "Objection. The witness has no idea what the jury members are sensing."

"Sustained. Keep to facts Mr. Seiler. Continue."

"Yes, your honor."

Tom relaxed his demeanor, aware that he scored a direct hit, and completed the lesson. "The other end of the dilemma zone problem is simply the distance it takes to bring the tractor-trailer safely to a full stop from forty miles an hour. For Mr. Schrauder's rig, given the asphalt composition of the road, that distance is," Tom's voice inflected slightly, "three-hundred and twenty-eight feet." He placed a new tick-mark on the paper.

Tom stepped back from the sketch, moving closer to the jury. "Let me emphasize that these tick marks show the D.Z. very accurately for Mr. Schrauder's tractor-trailer at a speed of 40 miles and hour AND," Tom accentuated the word, "for a yellow light that lasts 4.5 seconds. If his tractor-trailer was between 144 feet and 328 feet from the intersection, he would have been in the dilemma zone."

Tom looked directly at Liz Harker. "Of course, virtually no one really knows how long a given yellow light will last. And, at least for me, that's a dilemma."

In quick fashion, Tom added the envelopes of the dilemma zone for speeds of 50 and 60 miles per hour.

Travis asked, "O.K., Mr. Seiler, what does all this mean in terms of the tractor-trailer?"

"As I mentioned, I visited the scene and reconstructed the accident using all the information received from the police and that which I gathered on my own. I'd like to begin at the point of impact." Tom drew the location on the sketch where the RV collided with the rig. He traced out two long lines that looked like partial fishhooks, cut off just below the barb. The long part of each hook ended at the final resting place of the RV. "Based on the obvious facts that, one, there were no marks from the rig and, two, they came to rest here . . . ," Tom indicated the stopping point for the two entangled vehicles. ". . . then, by simple calculations based on force equals mass times acceleration," Tom wrote '$F = M \times A$' on the butcher paper as he spoke, ". . . and making the assertion that the RV being lodged partly under the trailer constitutes an added braking force, the speed of the tractor-trailer had increased to approximately 52 miles an hour."

The jurors understood the physics.

Tom hesitated a split second, then interjected, "Let me back up for just a second. This model is also based on my observation that, since there were no skid marks from the tractor-trailer after impact, Mr. Schrauder applied the brakes prudently, probably a result of experience and training."

Liz Harker's immediate objection relative to John Schrauder's experience and training was sustained.

Travis bore on. "Mr. Seiler, an expert witness and a witness at the scene stated that Mr. Schrauder was traveling at 65 miles an hour when the accident occurred. What is your opinion as to that speed?"

Tom leaned forward in his chair and asked the question to which he already knew the answer. "Could you show on the sketch where the witness was stopped?"

Travis, this time using green, drew a small box in the left of two eastbound lanes.

Tom's turn. "May I approach the easel?"

"Yes, please do."

Tom walked to the easel and drew two new rectangles, representing the cab and the flatbed trailer, in the right hand westbound lane at a point where someone might become aware of an oncoming truck.

"To begin with, I did run simulations based on 65 miles an hour, but I can talk to that later. Let me just point out that, whether it's a train, plane, or tractor-trailer, it is almost impossible to tell the speed at which an object is directly approaching you. The best examples of this fact are the television advertisements in which a car in the distance approaches the speaker from behind, stopping just as it reaches him or her. At the moment a vehicle passes by, there is a human tendency - I have actual data if it's needed - to overestimate the speed. As for the witness, I don't think she is intentionally wrong, but, given the horrible nature of the collision, everything was probably magnified. I'm a little surprised she didn't say it was a higher speed."

Tom and Travis were surprised that no objection had been raised. The prosecutor knew that the information to which Tom referred did exist. Better not bring more attention to it.

Tom added, "More importantly, my simulations indicate that a non-skidding tractor-trailer colliding at 65 miles an hour could not, under the most favorable conditions to the prosecution's case, have stopped any closer to the intersection than here." He drew a 'P' for 'prosecution' in pink at the spot on the sketch that represented 188 feet further down the highway than where they had actually come to rest.

Travis drove the point home. "How many cases involving tractor-trailers have you worked on, Mr. Seiler?"

"Over 300. About 350 I'd say."

The District Attorney jotted '350 cases with 18-wheelers: slaughter on American highways' on the pad of paper.

Travis asked, "So your opinion as to the 65 mile an hour theory is what?"

"Sir, it is absolutely impossible."

"O.K. then," Travis continued, "give us the bottom line as to the tractor-trailer driven by Mr. Schrauder."

"Mr. Schrauder approached the light at approximately 45 miles an hour. The light changes from green to yellow as he enters the dilemma zone. He decides . . ."

"Objection."

"Sustained."

Travis changed the question slightly. "You need to keep it to the physical evidence. Continue."

Tom cleared his throat slightly. "Sorry. The rig accelerates. As it passes through the intersection the rig has reached a speed of about 48 to 52 miles an hour. Just as the trailer front passes directly under the light, the recreation vehicle driven by Mrs. Stetly, in what is known as a 'T-bone' collision, broadsides Mr. Schrauder. The RV rotates and is wedged under the trailer. Mr. Schrauder applies the brakes immediately, but not so much as to lock the tires, bringing the contact point of both vehicles to rest at a point 240 feet from the impact point, partly in the right lane and partly on the shoulder."

Travis, concluding the current testimony, entered the key points under the event heading 'Event One.' He neatly lettered under 'The Eighteen-Wheeler':

> Mr. Schrauder - 48 to 52 mph
> Struck broadside by Mrs. Stetly
> No braking skid marks - either vehicle
> Travel after impact - 240 feet

The late start time relegated the morning break to 15 minutes. Judge Schultz intervened into the proceedings. He returned to his chambers quickly. A man whose life motto could be summed up in the words 'discipline' and 'integrity' did have one vice. The good judge was addicted to the aroma of Smit & Dorlas, a fine Dutch koffie.

Event two, reconstruction of the movements of the Stetly recreation vehicle, followed a similar format. Tom returned to F equals MA. No skid marks before impact. Excellent visibility. Travis and Tom weaved in discussion of the flight of the two boys through the overhead window and onto the trailer. Travis interjected strong comments alluding to poor construction of the overhead compartment. Why Mrs. Stetly did not brake for the red light was a matter of conjecture. Careful not to evoke an objection by the prosecution, Tom offered his own theory.

"I do know that she was not aware of the impending danger. It's possible that something was in the road or to the side which may have distracted her. Possibly she was responding to her husband or sons and had turned away. No one will ever know. One possibility which I believe has substance is that, given the fact that the sun was setting, she may have seen the glow of the yellow light and judged the light was about to change."

Liz Harker objected to Tom's speculation about what went on in the mind of Mrs. Stetly. Judge Schultz sustained part of the objection. He instructed the jury that a distraction was an allowable statement, but that a specific reason, such as seeing a yellow glow, would be stricken from the record and from their minds.

Travis emphasized Tom's testimony again by writing the key points related to event two, 'The Stetly Van':

> Distraction??
> No skid marks prior to impact.
> Clear visibility.
> Speed - approximately 45 mph.

Travis' natural instinct for controlling the flow of testimony gave him great advantage over courtroom opponents. He kept to a schedule parallel to the biologic time clocks in juries. Travis never told a jury 'we'll get to that later' without actually getting to it later.

"Your Honor, at this time I'd like to ask Mr. Seiler to show his simulations of the accident to underline our position."

Ed Harvey set up the VCR to provide the playback of the computer-generated simulations of the accident.

Tom stood to the far side of a large-screen television facing the jury. Only Travis and Ed had to move in order to see the simulations.

"What you will see are six simulations which track my earlier testimony. The first four are based upon the probable maximum and minimum speeds of the two vehicles. At the end of each scenario I have entered numerical data in text form so that you can gain a perspective as to actual distances. The space between the maximum and minimum stopping distance is what I call the envelope of possible outcomes. My fifth simulation, which I did last night, was based on prosecution statements that the tractor-trailer was traveling at 65 miles an hour. You can draw your own conclusions. The sixth simulation is based upon speeds, weights and pre-impact vehicle locations that result in the final actual location of the two vehicles."

Tom pushed the play button.

●

While Tom captured the jury, a late-morning conversation played out in Barry Colter's office. What the young legal secretary did not know was that the meeting with Jud Weems had been practiced, even written down, three weekends earlier at Barry's beach home in Seadrift. The explanations as to the legal issues, the normal percentage fee for services rendered and the sorrowful comment about the 'accident' seemed normal to Mary Bliss as she furiously took notes. Jud had genuine-sounding anger in his voice as he vowed that Flagg Brothers Trucking killed his wife and must accept the consequences. That he waited a month before announcing his intent to sue had been planned. But, once the process started, Barry Colter moved quickly through the system, aided by the fact that families were involved. You just don't kill families, under any circumstance, in Texas. The D'Arcy trial would quickly follow the Stetly trial.

"Them sons-a-bitches gonna pay for what they did to Syb 'n the others." He clenched his teeth so hard that Mary could see the veins in his neck.

Barry rose, walked to the window and looked out at the breaking clouds over Houston's impressive skyline. He seemed to concentrate deeply for a few seconds. "Jud . . . ," a long pause, ". . . we've never done this before." He turned to Mary and instructed her to take exact notes, then continued. "First, we're going to make a national statement about corporate greed and indifference. We will ask for a joint settlement of $5 million pain and anguish and $253 million punitive." Barry Colter determined the exact amount from a simple analysis: If a professional athlete can get a quarter of a billion dollar contract for hitting and throwing a baseball, then a good woman like Sybil Weems is worth a few million more.

Mary's chest heaved as she sucked in an immediate gasp of air.

"Mary, are you all right?"

"Yes . . . yes, sir. Please excuse me." She took a deep breath and exhaled.

"If that bothered you, hang on for the next one." Barry sat down facing Jud. He leaned forward as though he were about to whisper. "I have discussed this case with my partners at length and they agree with what I am about to tell you."

Jud had practiced his response and was ready. Mary Bliss was shaking all over.

"Jud, you get everything." Barry placed both forearms on the table, hands joined with index fingers pointed at Jud. "As a firm, we will take this case pro bono. You will receive every cent of the settlement. There will be no charges whatsoever."

Barry thought back to the firm's approval of his idea.

●

"For crissake, listen to me. If we do this pro bono and win, and we will win, then we move to the head of the pack. In three years, we will have doubled this sticker price."

Marvin Fisher rose from the table. "I don't like it. We can't just give away $80 million. It's insane." He turned to the third partner. "Murray. You're the tie-breaker."

Murray King was the financial genius of the partnership. He leaned back in his chair, took in a large volume of cigar smoke, and blew two near-perfect smoke rings towards the ceiling. He looked directly at Barry Colter.

Barry, always capable of a dishonest facade, looked directly back at Murray.

Murray cast his vote. "Barry Colter, you're one brilliant son-of-a-bitch. Let's do it."

●

"We may not be able to bring Sybil back, but you stand to gain $258 million. Sybil and the others would be pleased."

Not nearly pleased as me. Jud thought to himself behind the blank facade of his face. "Thanks, Mr. Colter, it'll help some. But it won't bring none of them back."

●

Lunch.

"If they could hang in there on a morning like this, they'll hang the rest of the way. Hell, I think these folks are having a good time." Travis wiped his mouth with the red paper napkin. "You really crushed them on the 65 mile an hour theory." He swigged down some Coke. "That jury is smart and they're paying attention." Travis was on a high and had an appetite to match.

The beanburger, consisting of two slabs of hamburger, melted cheese, crushed corn chips, chopped onions and a layer of bean dip, was one of the few true rivals to chicken-fried steak. Ed Harvey, heavily engaged in learning the Seiler-White methodology, attacked his turkey club.

Travis asked Tom, "How about the finite-element stuff? It's your biggest hurdle. If you can convince them about the construction, then Belton might get out of a civil suit altogether. Hell, I'm fired up on this case. Am I justified?"

Tom finished swallowing the last bite of his beanburger and took a drink of iced tea. "Travis, Ed, my good men, just stand by for a first class show." He grinned at his compatriots.

Ed continued eating his God-awful turkey club. His tongue darted out and captured a small glob of mayonnaise at the right corner of his mouth. He swallowed, then spoke, "Speaking of shows, did everyone notice Barry Colter at the morning session? What's his ugly ass doing here?"

Travis gulped down the remainder of his beanburger. "Probably wants to see where we're headed. Who gives a shit?"

Ed said, "Just thought it strange since I've never seen him at someone else's trial."

Tom thought it strange as well.

18

"... in and for the county of Harris ..."

"Mr. White, you may begin."

Travis looked at the jury members, encouraged that his own spirit was buoyed by the improving weather conditions. He wished the same for them. "Ladies and gentlemen, this is a criminal trial for vehicular homicide. Remember that intent is a key component of the rules of evidence. Inherent in one's guilt is a total disregard for the safety of others. Mr. John Schrauder had a split second in which to react to the light. I wonder what went through his mind. 'Uh, oh, should I hit the brakes? Will it jackknife? Will the light hold? Should I accelerate?' Does anyone in this room really believe he had time to develop a sense of intent? We all know that he obviously reacted in a manner dictated by his physical instincts."

A pause, followed by movement towards the jury. "What would you have done in the exact same circumstances? Ask yourself, 'Have I ever, ever, stepped on the gas when the yellow light appeared?' If so, did you do it with the intent of hurting someone or did you do it in response to a difficult situation? How many of us here abhor a yellow light?" A serious look into the eyes of each juror.

Travis changed the direction of the proceedings. With a voice slightly raised, yet still a clear baritone, Travis spoke. "But what about the designers of the Wolfpack RV?" He quickly turned to the courtroom.

A group of four, two lawyers and two executives, from Wolfpack Van had already taken notepads out. Upon hearing 'Wolfpack RV' all four automatically looked up at Travis, then to the jury, and then rapidly back to their notepads in an uncomfortable choreography of human reaction.

Tom was called to the witness stand and advised that he was still under oath. At Travis' direction, Tom identified the computer graphic pictorials. He reintroduced the jury to blowups of the photographs of the front of the RV, showing the demolished front and the broken out window portion of the overhead compartment. Travis specifically pointed to the four corners.

"Take particular note of the torn aluminum sheeting at each corner. It should strike you as strange that each of the corners failed instead of one, or even two." His manner of speaking suggested that each jury member understood enough about structural mechanics to see poor construction when it was blatantly obvious. "Or, for that matter, that anything tore at all."

The stage was set and the time right to hand-off the lead to the expert witness. "Mr. Seiler, we have, at your request, written 'The Overhead Compartment' on the butcher paper as major event three. Why is this a major event?"

"Well sir," Tom and Travis loved to throw the 'sir' around the courtroom, "I was asked to determine what happened to cause the deaths of four people. Two of the four died because they were not contained in the overhead compartment. Structural failure was the key contributing factor to their deaths."

Travis turned to the jury. "Wolfpack uses the computer program AutoCAD, Automated Computer Aided Design. It's the industry standard design package. What I am going to ask of Mr. Seiler is that he explain the concept of finite-elements to you, then discuss, as a mechanical engineer of 40-plus years, what reasonable engineers should have accomplished in the design of the Wolfpack recreation vehicle overhead compartment."

"Objection your Honor." Ms. Harker rose confidently from her chair. "I am sure that Mr. Seiler is quite good with his computer, but it is totally a moot point. The laws of the state of Texas do not allow people to occupy the overhead compartment in a moving recreation vehicle. The failure of the window is therefore immaterial to this case. All of Mr. White's discourse is irrelevant."

"Mr. White, can you tie this discussion directly to the issue of guilt on the part of Mr. Schrauder?"

Travis hesitated, ignoring the full courtroom. He came out of deep thought, the tight lines of his forehead disappearing into thin air, and addressed Judge Schultz. "I'm sorry your Honor, but I believe that the prosecutor's statement about Texas law just placed some significant blame on Mrs. Stetly. She clearly broke the law."

Liz Harker looked at her legal pad in apparent concentration. She was furious at Travis – almost as much as at herself.

Travis continued. "As for your question about tying the discussion to the issue of guilt on the part of John Schrauder, yes sir, I can . . . absolutely."

He walked slowly towards the pensive Ed Harvey. His mind blistered, searching for a response to the intent of Harker's remark. *Irrelevant? What's irrelevant about two dead children?* Travis hadn't planned for this situation, but he was good on his feet. He quickly turned away from his table and walked to where Tom sat, then turned again to Judge Schultz.

"Your Honor, I need to ask Mr. Seiler a question which I had not thought of before. The answer to it lies at the crux of this issue."

"Ask your question."

"Thank you, sir." Travis asked the question slowly, deliberately – hoping for the right answer. "Mr. Seiler, have you ever been involved with another accident involving a recreation vehicle in which occupants in the overhead compartment were either injured or killed?" Travis offered up a quick prayer of petition. *God, I need you now.*

Tom waited for a fraction of a second, then he answered. "Yes sir, I have." *Thanks, God.*

"Objection overruled."

Travis and Tom transitioned to stress concentrations and Wolfpack. Tom used the example of a sharp corner first, providing the jury, and Judge Schultz, with samples of small metal structures that had failed by tearing at the corners. They had very little trouble understanding that at sharp corners fractures start small but, under additional loading, continue to expand along a path of least structural integrity. It's all caused by high stress concentrations at critical points.

"The problem is solved by rounding off corners, using stronger materials and adding thickness to the structural components." He made it clear that the average person on the street should understand simple structural integrity. "It's really pretty basic stuff." Tom then emphasized the importance of stress concentrations. "I might add that the aircraft industry learned that lesson the hard way . . . and thousands of people lost their lives because of failure due to stress concentrations, many occurring at the windows along the fuselage."

The testimony flowed back into finite-elements. As Paige had urged, Tom began with the power of the computer. From a simple calculation of stress on a block of wood, he went directly to forces acting on the fuselage of an airplane. It was a risky move in that there was potential to lose the entire jury. Tom and Paige had decided to use the airplane example since it was complex. From there he would return to the much simpler example of a window in an overhead compartment. The more he spoke, the more these things called finite-elements became believable to all in the courtroom.

"The smaller the elements," Tom explained, "the better the accuracy." The ability to model the structure and forces on the screen gave authenticity to the computer. Of course, the splendid color output rendered the computer almost infallible in the minds of the jury.

Tom stood between the easels, facing the jury. The easel on the left contained separate blowups from three color-photographs. The right easel contained eight placards tracing the modeling of and solutions to a structural engineering problem defined by two human bodies striking, then passing through, the window of the Wolfpack van. Tom's explanation of converting human bodies into forces acting on the composite aluminum, Styrofoam and plywood assembly was riveting.

"As you can see," Tom said as he brought the blowup photo of the entire overhead compartment, "the actual tears in the aluminum sheeting occur very close to where they were predicted by the stress model from the computer. It's almost exact."

The computer-generated model was intriguing. Colors of the rainbow clearly outlined patterns of differing stress. Light blue for areas in which stress was low. From light blue, the color mosaic changed to dark blue, magenta, green, pink, yellow, orange and finally, bright red. A legend in the lower left corner of the placard related the colors to the degree of stress suffered by the window section of the van. Bright red indicated extreme stress conditions.

Emanating from each corner was a spike of bright red. From the distance of the jury box, the red, a crimson red, appeared as rays of the setting sun slicing through a late afternoon sky. Paige sat spellbound in the last row of the courtroom.

Travis broke the silence. "So, in terms of good engineering design, what conclusion do you have relative to the performance of the overhead window section during the accident?"

"Well sir, it's simple. At best, the design of the overhead compartment and the resulting quality of structural integrity are poor. At worst, they are the manifestation of economics over safety. In either case . . ."

"Objection your Honor, speculation. Mr. Seiler does not have access to the financial records of Wolfpack Van; nor does he know what the basis of their design decisions were for this vehicle." Liz remained standing until Judge Schultz responded.

"Sustained. Strike Mr. Seiler's last statement. Mr. White, rephrase the question and take it in a different direction."

Judge Schultz' response brought back some color to Liz Harker's face

Travis paused momentarily, then asked. "Mr. Seiler, as an expert who spent more than 30 years in hands-on engineering design, what is your opinion of the quality of design of the overhead compartment."

"Sir, I don't know how obvious it is to everyone else, but to me it is unacceptable. The single best word I can find is incompetent. But I also have to say that the world of engineering includes the word 'unethical'."

This time the District Attorney shot from her chair in near rage. "Objection, the witness is intentionally baiting the jury. He just did what you told him not to do. His actions are grounds for a mistrial." She glared at Tom, then Travis and then Judge Schultz.

"I want a sidebar." Judge Schultz seemed clearly irritated with the defense.

Whispered hostility spewed from both sides.

Liz Harker demanded Tom's remarks be stricken with a threat of contempt to be made by Judge Schultz. "He is intentionally baiting the jury. It's a planned move between the two of them and it's grounds for a mistrial."

Judge Schultz admonished her to keep her voice down. ". . . or we'll go into chambers for the remainder of this argument."

Travis, in a low whisper, gave his version of the episode. "Your Honor, all that Mr. Seiler presented are facts. A design is either good or bad. If it is bad, then it could be bad because of either a lack of competence or a case of bad intention. He has over two thousand cases and he certainly is expert in the area of professional design. His comments are more than appropriate, they are an obligation."

Judge Schultz looked at both attorneys, took a deep breath, then announced his decision. "Overruled."

Several jurors could see the loathing in her eyes. Others silently nodded their heads.

Paige beamed.

●

The weather system moved to the east faster than expected. The bright sunshine, the refreshing breeze and the upcoming weekend uplifted the participants to the trial.

Tom downed a couple of beers while rehashing the day's events and leading the strategy session for Monday's testimony. It would bring an end to Tom's contribution to the immediate defense of John and Sarah Schrauder. . . and be a determining factor as to potential trials down the road. Ed Harvey outlined the cross-examination to be expected of the prosecutor. No one was particularly concerned about her ability to impeach Tom. The payback for Tom's work could be worth millions. It might also save a man's life and dignity.

19

The weekend allowed the jurors to relax at home with their families, content in knowing the trial was coming to a conclusion. John and Sarah Schrauder spent time with their daughters. Save the respite of attending Methodist services at their small church in Bellaire, neither could escape the unrelenting weight of the decision soon to change their lives. Tom and Susie took the Stinson out both days. His plan called for freedom from the Stetly trial until Sunday evening. He and Susie drove out to the fatal intersection one last time. Travis would call around 8:00 at which time the final strategy would be established. They would be ready for what each hoped would be a final "coup d' grace." Others handled stress differently.

●

"Mmm . . ." her moans, quiet and peaceful at first, became urgent as he slowly inched his index finger towards the small, moistened bud that awaited him. Gentle circles decreased in size until she could stand it no more. "Now, oh please, now." Adding slight pressure to each circle, his own throbbing fell into rhythm with the sweet waves sweeping over her. Her hand, responding to the spasms of pleasure, squeezed his smooth, warm shaft tighter with each convulsion until the delicious sensations slowly ebbed from her body. Two deep breaths, a moment of silence, then, barely above a whisper, she spoke. "Mmm . . . like fine wine. I can't get enough of either."

She rolled over and, with long hair falling from both sides of her neck, quickly straddled his expecting body. She guided him into her, leaned forward and kissed him seductively on his forehead, and began the slow vertical and circular gyrations that, once again, brought forth explosive spasms of masculine pleasure.

"It's here . . . oh, God, it's good, yes, it's good . . ." The intense crescendo of delight peaked and, to every man's dismay, subsided much too quickly. He lay motionless as she raised herself and rolled back to her side. She added a few additional strokes to his subsiding penis. Slowly her fingers moved up to his chest and traced lazy circles through the salt and pepper hair. She rolled over on her back. She started thinking of other things. It was quiet.

He broke the silence. "Where are you? What's going on in that remarkable brain of yours?"

She turned to her partner, staring at the gray outline of his face. "Sorry, I drifted back to the trial. It should be open and shut, but it's not. White and his asshole expert, Seiler, have the jury eating out of their hands. If I lose this one, your civil trial is in trouble. It'll cost us a lot and that just pisses me off." She turned back, looking up at the black ceiling above her. Her hand no longer gave pleasure to him.

"I know. They're formidable. I've gone after Seiler before. A great engineer and good on the stand." Barry shifted the compliment. "But you're a better lawyer, much better in the courtroom." He moved his hand to the back of her neck, giving her a gentle massage. He smiled unconsciously, adding, ". . . and unbeatable in bed." Then he regressed. "The jury's smart and I can't judge how they'll vote. But losing this one doesn't mean much of anything. The important thing is that the two cases are in quick succession. If the verdict goes bad, you'll be outraged in front of television screens and public opinion can still take over. No different than the O.J. Simpson case. And who knows, this jury could still end up with an emotional verdict. That's the key." Barry rolled towards her. He reached through the darkness and found a small but perfectly shaped breast. His fingers traced to her nipple, bringing it to an erection of its own. His mind was changing gears but still focused somewhat on the discussion. "If you lose the criminal trial, we still have the papers and TV. We can still set up a civil trial with a jury full of Stetly sympathizers. There's a big difference between a poor truck driver and a rich CEO." His fingers continued tracing along their path of delight.

"Look Barry, I don't lose and this is not the time to start." Almost unconsciously, she arched her pelvis upwards. "If I win the criminal case here, then the D'Arcy case will be worth the quarter-billion price tag."

Barry was only slightly concerned. He was upbeat, physically and mentally. His physical state was dominating. "Just don't lose sight of the big picture. This case, and everyone in it, is just an appetizer."

"You're right. Screw 'em all."

He slowly moved his hand down to her stomach and beyond. "Good idea." He instinctively closed his eyes. "Why not start with me?" The gentle push was exactly where it needed to be.

"M'mmm."

She opened her legs and reached into the dark.

●

Tom watched Travis refresh the jury on the key factors addressed in his testimony. Judge and jury were alert, the judge glad to be back in the courtroom and the jury refreshed from the weekend at home. All anticipated that closing arguments would be heard by early afternoon, allowing them the opportunity to enjoy the late fall afternoon. On Tuesday they would receive the judge's instructions and would be sequestered until a verdict could be reached.

"Mr. Seiler, you placed the intersection at the crux of one of the events and you listed it last in your discussions. Why?" Travis placed both hands in his pockets as he handed off the final and most critical element to winning the case. Unnoticed by all except Elizabeth Harker, Travis walked slowly to the edge of the juror's box. He was one of them.

"Some of my work involves the physical laws of nature." Tom needed the jury to understand that what took place dead center in the intersection was the key to the accident. He panned across the faces looking at him. "I use my natural grasp of physics to explain why my view of circumstances makes sense." He glanced over to Harker and sensed her getting ready to interrupt. "In this case, deducing the major cause of the fatalities only required a stopwatch. All I needed to do was time the yellow light. It was much too short."

Travis reentered the videotape taken by the two police officers. He asked Tom to tell the jury about the tape and its consequences.

It took all the mental strength Liz Harker had to keep her composure. *The tape? Newton gave them the tape. Sonofabitch.* That the tape could not be withheld from the defense was irrelevant to Liz Harker. *Sonofabitch.*

"When I learned that the officers had taken a video of the accident scene that night and also two days later I requested to view the tape. The District Attorney, Ms. Harker, and one of the officers, Officer Newton, saw the tape with me." Tom, at Travis' suggestion, needed to make sure that the jury knew Liz Harker had personally seen the tape. "Before leaving, I requested and received a copy of the tape from Officer Newton. If I could, sir . . . ," Tom asked Judge Schultz, ". . . I'd like to discuss the tape in front of the TV monitor." Given permission, Tom moved to the monitor and addressed the jury.

Before describing the video, Tom reinforced the concept of the 'dilemma zone' to the jurors. Next, he addressed the timing of the light.

"Secondly, Texas state law mandates the length of time that a yellow light is to remain on before turning red." He cleared his throat. "The prescribed time is a function of the type of road, dimensions of the intersection and the expected volume and speed of the traffic."

The jury followed along.

"Finally, at intersections considered potentially dangerous, a timing feature showing red on all four faces of the light for a short period of time is required. This feature is known as red-on-red."

Travis interjected, "And did this light have a red-on-red feature?"

"Not before the accident." Tom stopped talking, leaving the jury at the end of an unfinished statement.

Travis entered the technical guidelines governing timing of traffic lights into evidence.

The District Attorney squirmed in her seat.

Travis gave the floor back to Tom. Standing beside the screen, Tom explained key points to the playing video in a business-like manner. Following the showing of the second drive-through, Tom paused the VCR and stepped in front of the screen.

"The final segment shows the third run through the light." He stepped back and pushed the play button. The film rolled on. "It shows exactly what happened to John Schrauder. Here the officers are coming to the intersection. Now watch for the movement of the camera and then the top light." Tom pointed not to the yellow light, but to the unlit red light. The light changed from yellow to red. "There? The light has changed to red and is on the film. The two officers ran the red light. They accelerated the car and ran the red light themselves. Just like John Schrauder. They ran the red light."

"Objection." Liz Harker didn't have a reasoned response. Clearly exasperated, she blurted out, "My men didn't kill anybody. He killed four." She pointed angrily at John Schrauder. "And they're still dead." She sat down. Her number two pencil rolled off the table and onto the floor, breaking the point.

The entire courtroom went silent. Everyone seemed confused as to the significance of her statement. Judge Schultz returned the proceedings to order.

"Overruled."

Travis stepped in quickly. He turned off the TV, returned to his table, picked up two thick manuals, and turned to the jury. "Ladies and gentlemen of the jury," he lifted his left hand, "this is the Manual on Uniform Traffic Control Devices for Streets and Highways, published by the United States Department of Transportation Federal Highway Administration." Repeating the process with his right hand, he continued, "and this is the Texas manual of the same title. It implements the

federal statutes for the State of Texas. I would like to tender these as exhibits..."
Travis entered the manuals into evidence. He continued with Tom's testimony.
"Given what we have just seen, and your experience with the manuals, Mr. Seiler,
what is your conclusion as to the traffic light at the intersection of Stryker Avenue
and Texas State Highway 35?"

"Sir, the yellow light was set to two-point-five seconds in violation of the state
mandated minimum time for this type of intersection of four-point-five seconds.
With no red-on-red feature, it's a certain recipe for accidents. Six people have died
at that intersection since 1985. When I saw the light change in the video I decided
to time the light myself. In the video taken by my wife and me . . ." Tom referred
to his video already entered into evidence. ". . . I timed the changes from green to
yellow to red. That's where I got the actual timing for the yellow."

Before continuing, Travis entered evidence giving statistics for accidents,
including fatalities, having occurred at the intersection.

Travis pulled the noose tighter. "Have you had the occasion to visit the
intersection since your initial investigation?"

"Yessir. I returned to the intersection yesterday and timed the yellow light
again."

Travis had to turn away from the jury. It was wrong to be enjoying a trial
so much, but, after all, Liz Harker was a first-class bitch. He recovered, turned
to Tom, and continued. "Did you notice anything of substance relative to this
trial?"

Tom had to look away from Travis. He spoke. "Yes, sir. The timing on the
yellow light had been changed to 4.5 seconds." He regained his composure. "And
the red-on-red feature is now in operation."

Travis lifted a letter-sized piece of paper from the table. "Your Honor, I have
here a maintenance request to the Texas Department of Transportation, requesting
a change in the timing and red-on-red features of the traffic light at Stryker Avenue
and Texas State Highway 35." He studied the piece of paper, allowing his remarks
to sink in. "The call came from a Mr. Detmer of the office of the Houston District
Attorney." Visible shifting could be seen among the jury as the impact of Travis'
statement sank in. The revelation that the prosecution was aware of the mistake in
timing the light and, based on a quick phone call to the state highway maintenance
division, actually initiated the request to change the timing, the jurors smelled the
same rat as did Tom and Travis.

Before continuing, Travis entered the short video of Tom's previous night's
trip to the intersection into evidence. He returned to the butcher paper and entered

under 'The Intersection':

> Short yellow
> No red-on-red
> In violation of Texas highway guidelines
> Changed since accident

Almost humbly, giving added stature to Tom, Travis spoke to his witness. "In conclusion then, Mr. Seiler, what were the true significant causes to the deaths of Joseph, Martha, Andrew and Ben Stetly?"

Cattle to the slaughter.

●

It took the jury 38 minutes to return a not-guilty verdict. That the District Attorney's cross-examination lasted less than ten minutes was not lost on the entire courtroom. They didn't even find John Schrauder guilty of a misdemeanor for running the red light. He was a free man. The scene in the courtroom was euphoric, save the prosecution table, the group from Wolfpack Van and a lawyer from Colter, Fisher and King. The underdog won. Several members of the jury could not refrain from smiling at the scene of John, Sarah, Travis and Ed hugging each other at the defense table. Most poignant of all, and captured for the evening news, was the scene of Amanda Stetly's grandfather shaking hands with John Schrauder. Had Tom Seiler been present, he would have been in the middle of them all. He was always good, but this trial was his masterpiece. As it was, however, that special moment in time was spent with Tom and Susie going over key points to the structure of his analysis of the incident in Alvin. Like it or not, the Alvin case was on the docket for the end of October. Time was not an ally. The Alvin case went beyond physics. He knew it included free will and intent. Susie heard the news of the verdict first when she clicked on the television in the kitchen. She yelled up to Tom and they took a small break to listen to the breaking news. A quick hug, a couple of "Hot damns!" and it was back to work. They would catch up with the details at the New Bay Brewery that evening.

●

Four couples in jeans and sweatshirts enjoyed the fruits of victory at the New Bay Brewery. The mid-October evening turned cool, forcing the party inside. They placed two rectangular tables together in the center of the floor. Voices raised in competition with other gatherings reveled in the retelling of different episodes of the trial. Hardly 30 seconds could pass without laughter erupting from the table. Most of it came at the expense of the prosecution.

Time after time Travis, his fist slamming on the blue tablecloth, proclaimed, "We won the whole thing. Not guilty. Can you believe it? Not guilty!" He would no sooner get the words out than another story would unfold.

Travis raised his bottle, followed by all. "Here's to the arrogant Elizabeth T. Harker, may she lose 'em all." Clicking glasses and a quick moment of silence while each savored his or her beverage of choice.

Michelle White, as petite as Travis was large, called out over the din, "I wonder what the 'T' stands for?"

Tom jumped on the question. "Tightass!"

The crowd erupted.

●

Ross squinted into the oncoming streaks of light. After-midnight traffic can be heavy. He considered this family he was being drawn to.

He glanced quickly at Paige, then back to the road. "Paige, I don't know when I've enjoyed people more than tonight. You've got quite the family. The dynamics are, uh, just different than any family I've met. Can't put my finger on it, but you, your dad, Susie, Steve . . . the whole gang, are just in sync. They're real." He quickly added, "I've watched your dad and Susie flow in and out of each other's space in sort of a natural rhythm." He eased off slightly on the gas, not wanting to get Paige home too soon.

She took a deep breath, breathing in good will. "I wish I could explain it. I've always sensed that we are different as a family. Don't know how . . . or why. I've wondered if others feel the same way."

Ross pressed to know more. "Tell me about your dad."

She pictured Tom in her mind. "He's the most remarkable person I've ever known. Grew up in a military family. Two brothers and a sister. My Uncle Jack was killed in Vietnam. Bothers Dad to this day. Somehow he feels guilty about Uncle Jack failing out of college. When Tom, Jr., died my dad could at least grasp that it was a cruel chance happening. He felt responsible for Uncle Jack. My grandfather was a fighter pilot in World War Two. A general. The family traveled all over the country. Dad learned how to work and play. That's what he did – and still does – works hard and plays hard."

Ross formed perceptions of his own. He also considered a long-term relationship. "I hope I get to know him better. He's forceful, but he's gentle.

Seems like he takes everything in stride."

She smiled. "As a rule. But he has a boiling point. He'll do anything for anyone alive, but he can't handle intentional dumping on other people. Uncle Donald's told stories of Tom getting into fights with guys who were pushing other kids around. In the good sense of the word, he's sort of a vigilante. And he's honest. Tells you things straight up." Another smile. "A friend of mine in high school, Erin, stopped over one day sporting a new hairdo and asked my dad, 'Mr. Seiler, how do you like my hair?' He looked at her for a few seconds, then said something like 'looks good Erin.' About five minutes later he comes back in the kitchen and says, 'Erin, I just can't lie, your hair looks like hammered shit.' That's Tom Seiler."

They both laughed. Ross savored their conversation.

"What happened to Tom and your mom? I've never heard him say a bad word about her. When she calls to ask for help, Tom's there in a minute." Ross unconsciously moved to the slower lane and then continued, "And if he weren't at home, then Susie would be second in line to help her out. They both blow my mind."

Paige searched quickly through the years. "The strains between my parents went mostly unnoticed to three teenage kids living in their own worlds. I wish I knew. I think they tried to love each other, but, bit by bit, it seems that things just unraveled." To share more meant she had to trust Ross. "I remember, as they contemplated divorce, him saying 'I'd come home, see her car in the driveway and I'd sometimes just keep driving.' "

Ross remained silent, allowing her to continue.

"It had to hurt both of them. Now they're friends, good friends. In some ways I wish it had been different."

He asked, "What do you mean 'in some ways'?" A quick glance.

She thought for a moment, then answered by example. "I've got two cousins who ended up divorced. Their parents saw the train coming but couldn't get either of them off the tracks. By the time they realized what was going on, both were pregnant. Both had beautiful little girls. Had my cousins not gotten married, Alyssa and Lynn would never have existed. And, by my understanding of God, those young ladies need to be part of this world. Both cousins remarried decent, hard-working guys. One had another little girl. Talk about a real pistol. She'll either be president or doing hard time. My other cousin picked right the first time and she has three beautiful daughters without having gone through the mill." More smiles. Paige looked at Ross, putting her hand on the back of his neck. "I think Tom, Jr., Steve and I fall into the same category. And," she added emphasis to her statement, "I believe my mother is happier today having lived with Dad."

"How about Susie? Where does she fit into the whole scheme of things?"

Paige responded. "That's the whole point. I believe that my dad was meant to end up with Susie as well, and that the three of us . . ." She hesitated a split second, contemplating why God had taken Tom, Jr., from them. ". . . I believe the three of us were meant to be who we are."

Paige began a story of Susie's entrance into the Seiler household. "Susie's added so much to his life. She has the same attitude about people that he does. She's very affectionate, but gives him the space he needs." She focused on the woman who was more a friend than stepmother. "Susie's smart, real smart." Paige mused at life's turns. "She sort of fills in the holes in his life and he does the same for her. I remember the first time we met . . ."

When Paige finished speaking, Ross patted her knee. He loved the whole family. Paige felt warm, secure. Contentedly, she turned and smiled to the oncoming traffic. Life was very good indeed.

●

Elizabeth Terese Harker stared at the Houston skyline. The balcony of her 22nd floor apartment offered a spectacular view of the teeming life below. On the streets and in the shadowy boxes of gray concrete, steel and glass cascading in front of her, thousands of human dramas were playing out their daily subplots. The full moon, changing from pale orange to a brilliant off-white, looked down on her from its luminous perch above the Hamilton Towers. Clad in purple sweats and brown furry slippers, she fought off the effects of the cooling October evening. The drink in her hand helped. Small potted ficus trees accentuated gray and white striped patio furniture. It had all the trappings of serenity. Except in her mind.

Elizabeth Harker could not believe the case had been lost. An image of her cross-examination would not go away. Tom Seiler beat her to a pulp with his responses to question after question. *I may as well have been his fucking witness.* *'No Ma'am, I'm not confused at all, and since only two of us are talking . . .'* It cost her dearly. She had never done this poorly. She saw Barry's Alvin case going down the toilet. Her left index finger unconsciously stirred her fourth glass of wine. It was impossible to change what had happened. It was impossible to change her thoughts. *You bastards won't get away with this. White, I swear you'll regret this day. You'll pay. Along with Seiler. Bastards.* Intermingled with her noiseless epithets were thoughts of doubt. *How could this happen? I'm going to be a fucking D.A. all my life. Maybe I'm not very good. Governor? Not any more.*

It never occurred to her to concede that John Schrauder never was guilty of a crime. She could not have cared less.

20

"It's going to be this way for a while. These people are corporate thugs and our reputation is at stake." Barry Colter explained the need to work late on the Alvin case.

Betty Colter sympathized with Barry. "I understand." It didn't matter if he were screwing a whore on the living room rug, Betty would find it in her to understand. Once again she would leave his dinner plastic-wrapped in the refrigerator. "Wish you could join me for a nightcap." She smiled at the floor and slightly slurred "I'luv you." She hung up and returned to the lanai with her Manhattan.

He placed the receiver in its cradle, then turned and smiled warmly at the young woman.

Mary Bliss was an easy target. Still, work before pleasure.

"Bring those witness folders over here." Barry pointed to a small stack of manila folders on his desk.

Mary retrieved the folders and brought them to the conference table. She stood silently looking down at the mahogany surface. Neither Mary nor the others knew that she was the ninth secretary Barry Colter had slept with since joining the firm. For her part, Mary never wanted it to happen, but now she was trapped. Once seduced, always seduced . . . and she had accepted a sizable pay raise. She saw herself as a whore.

"As I call out each name, place the folders in witness order, starting on the left." Barry moved around Mary, placing his hand around her waist for only a second. He still had work to do.

Mary's body tightened. Recovering slightly, she placed each folder in sequence along the table. Barry instructed her to tape a blue 3 x 5 card, labeled by name, to the inside of each folder. On each card were a series of bullets.

Barry covered the card with his hand, then spoke quietly, in monotone. "Frank Berringer. Knew Tallant. Drinking buddies. Will speak to weak training." He took his hand away, smiled confidently and started sorting through background papers concerning the witness. When he encountered a card for which he couldn't recite each bullet correctly, Barry would turn the folder over, returning to it later.

One by one, the process continued. "Clay Wilton. Vice President for driver operations. Not very bright. Lazy. Unfamiliar with driver logs . . ." It took 45 minutes for him to visualize the courtroom scene, analyze the testimony and personality of the witnesses tucked neatly in each folder, and then reposition them in an ever-strengthening sequence. He was a brilliant trial lawyer.

He was a sexual predator.

As if returning to a folder, Barry walked to the end of the table next to Mary. He moved behind the young secretary, this time wrapping both arms around her, one hand on her breast, the other moving downward from her stomach. She felt the pressure rising from his groin.

●

Barry arrived late for his 10:00 meeting with Judson Weems. He entered through his private entrance and buzzed for his personal secretary. There was no immediate response. His work on the upcoming case consumed him until midnight. Compounding the disarray of the morning, Mary Bliss called in sick. The senior executive secretary, Barbara Kelty, was not pleased. Her gruff, almost masculine, voice fit her stocky frame.

"That's her third absence in the last month alone. Barry, I need to fire her. We can't do business like this. No one can afford a secretary who makes her own hours. She always sounds so depressed and gives such poor excuses. Will you at least formally counsel her?" Her tone exuded contempt and, at least to Barry, alluded to his relationship with Mary as being something other than strictly professional. She slammed home her sentiments curtly. "Her pay raise was a joke."

"O.K., get me a counseling statement. I'll talk to her." Barry was more irritated than defensive. "On the other hand, Mary worked with me until ten last night on the D'Arcy trial. I didn't see anyone else working late except the cleaning team." He took off his overcoat that signaled the first cold weather of the year, then walked to the conference table. His glance at the couch brought forth a delicious remembrance of the night before. A tingling sensation filled his groin. He cleared his mind and leaned over the rows of papers and folders that lay before him in military formation. "Barbara, ask one of the girls for some coffee and send

Mr. Weems in."

Barbara grumbled to herself as she stomped out of the office, "Worked on the case. Yeah, right."

Jud followed a member of the secretarial pool into the office. He looked out of place in blue jeans and lightweight red jacket. In addition to coffee for Barry, the secretary carried a stenographer's notebook.

Barry walked over to Jud, smiled and reached out to shake hands. Mirroring his co-conspirator, Jud smiled back and shook Barry's hand.

"Good to see you Mr. Weems. I see Sharon has taken care of your coffee." He turned to Sharon with the same comfortable smile. "Thanks Sharon. I need a few moments alone with Mr. Weems. After a quick cup of coffee I'll need you to take some notes. Thanks."

She smiled to both men and left.

"Have a seat." Barry started to offer the couch to Jud but quickly diverted his arm movement in the direction of two chairs in front of his desk.

Jud sat down as Barry stepped around the other chair to his desk. He held up his hand to keep Jud from speaking and checked to insure that the intercom and other taping devices were turned off. The smiles on both faces disappeared.

Quietly, Barry spoke first. "Just follow my lead when the secretary arrives. I need to have an official record of this meeting. We'll discuss the final details in Indianola. Have you got any problems?"

Jud slouched in the chair with his legs outstretched and touching the desk. He unconsciously pulled his upper teeth vertically across the unshaven stubble beneath his lower lip. Staring blankly at Barry, Jud responded, "Nope. I'll do my part. You do yours. Jus' r'member not to screw with me when this is over." The blank stare grew intense. Barry understood.

"Don't worry, once it's over we go separate ways." Barry lightened up slightly. "As for the case, it looks good. Very good. No one's out asking strange questions. The investigation concluded it was an accident. You're the only relative. Even my television interviews have gone well. You need to stay out of the picture."

"I don't give a shit about bein' on TV. I'll leave that horseshit to you." Jud drew his legs underneath the chair. He stared impassively at Barry.

"Fine. Everything's a go. We need to meet one last time at the airstrip. The trial will have started. I'll give you an overview of the case and any actions you might need to take. While you're there, get rid of everything." Barry pushed a button on the intercom. "Sharon, I'll need you to take some notes now. Thanks. Oh, also, please bring in some more coffee."

●

Tom placed the three stapled stacks of yellow paper on the dining room table. The fact that he turned off the television was significant. While Susie heated their coffee in the microwave, Tom removed the staples and arranged three columns corresponding to 'Observations', 'Scenarios', and 'Questions.'

The straps had nagged at him incessantly. Try as he might, Tom could not release himself from the conviction that they were involved in a murder. His naiveté wanted to carry him back to the vandals scenario. The evidence dictated otherwise. Tom brought up the straps and his concerns about the deaths of the D'Arcys the day following the Stetly trial but Travis did not accept his view of the incident in Alvin. Travis' reluctance to open his eyes to the possibility of murder bothered Tom. Had Travis lost his zest to 'fight the good fight?' Had he learned not to rock some boats that might capsize? Where was the Quixotic Travis White? With two weeks to go until the D'Arcy trial Travis finally agreed to an evening meeting at Tom and Susie's. He knocked on the door simultaneously with entering. It was 8:10.

"Hey mis amigos, who's got a beer?"

Tom sat at the table, his coffee cup already empty. Susie automatically opened the refrigerator and grabbed two Miller Lites.

She called from the kitchen, "Hi Travis. Come on in."

"Mi amigo. Que tal?" Tom welcomed Travis in his broken Tex-Mex.

They exchanged casual greetings and moved to the great room. Tom and Susie took the three-cushion couch and Travis sat in the Ekornes recliner, almost dwarfing it. Tom had an urge to turn on the TV but thought it better to get right down to his analysis of the events in Alvin. Susie would be an equal partner. The section of webbing lay on the coffee table. By the end of the second round of beer their discourse became intense, eased only by the interruption of Tom returning for more beer. Susie accepted one of her own for this round.

"That's my bent on the whole thing. I've done 2,000 of these and this is the only one in which murder jumps out and grabs me. Look at these." Tom remained standing and motioned Travis and Susie to join him along the side of the dining room table, detouring only enough to grab the strap and turn the rheostat for the overhead light. Travis heard Tom's concerns earlier, but it wasn't until he could visualize Tom's argument that he gave it any real credence. Interesting and plausible, but not convincing enough.

Tom addressed the papers under the 'Observations' heading. First, he removed those papers on which were written the physical phenomena of the incident. On a single sheet he listed the items of his analysis which bothered him.

1. Web section - deliberate cuts. Unusual pattern.
2. Cuts – motor oil? Vandals???
3. Lawsuit against Flagg – huge. Why not Kinedyne?
4. Tractor-trailer - head east towards Houston. Why?
5. Weather - clear.
6. Visibility - unlimited.
7. Other web sections taken from salvage yard. Why? Who?
8. Video - other web breaks at approximate same location. Not normal.

Thrusting his index finger at the written numbers, Tom spoke. "Shit, Travis, one, two, three, four, seven and eight tell me something is wrong, very wrong. Why don't you buy it?"

Travis leaned over the yellow sheet of paper, momentarily frozen in thought. He stood erect and took a large swallow of Miller. "Tom, I'm not saying it's totally out of the realm of possibility. I will say it won't hold up in court. It's that simple. There are answers, some good ones, which explain away your concerns. The cuts may be deliberate but I've worked cases in which vandals have cut straps before. So have you."

Tom interrupted. "Vandals my ass. Vandals might cut straps, but vandals don't zigzag their cuts and cover them with motor oil." Almost squinting with tension, Tom looked Travis in the eye. "Since you're the lawyer, answer this. Why in the hell are they going after Flagg for a quarter-billion and not Kinedyne?"

Travis looked up in hesitation. He hadn't even thought about it. Tom had.

"I'll tell you why." Tom lifted the bottle to his lips, took a voracious swallow, then continued. "Because someone on the plaintiff's side of the line knows that the big screw-up was putting oil on the straps after cutting them." Tom's words were accusatory. "A suit against Kinedyne, who, by the way, makes the best cargo handling equipment in the world, would bring a whole shitpot of focus on the straps." Tom exhaled, then drew a deep breath. "It's fucking murder and, to be blunt, the rig driver isn't the only one involved."

Travis returned the volley in kind. "Why don't you just shut up for a few seconds and let me continue. I'll grant you that the pattern and the oil on the strap . . ," Travis rotated the strap, bringing the cut end closer to the three of them, ". . . is unusual, even disconcerting. But, as I already told you, in a court of law it doesn't necessarily mean someone is a murderer."

"And it never will if no one has the balls to present it." Frustration and anger streamed from his lips.

Travis deliberately ignored Tom. "As for the amount of the suit and who they've gone after, hell, you know the dollar value is based more on deep pockets than on the degree of fault. They picked Flagg because they don't want to be seen as using the shotgun approach. One defendant, one very wealthy defendant."

Tom's face reddened with anger and beer.

Travis continued. "Even your observation about the direction of travel has an explanation. The guy had no next of kin so the police checked his place out. They found airline tickets to Aruba with an early September departure date out of Corpus. It's reasonable that he was rushing home to retrieve the tickets. We'll never know that one, but I, for one, don't think he had the brains to create such a strong alibi."

Tom cut in, "That's part of my point. This guy was not that smart. It would take someone else to think that up. Can't you see a possible set up in which Flagg Brothers comes out a big loser."

"Sure, it's possible. But as it stands now, what you're telling me would be shot down in flames. The cut straps all at the same location are different, to a point. A screw up like that supports the idea that vandals, not professional killers, were to blame. The oil is significant, but, unless linked to other major evidence, it doesn't mean much to anybody except Tom Seiler. I haven't got a clue as to why all the webbing was taken from the trailer. Might be souvenir hunters. Might even be private investigators like you." Travis' tone of voice relayed the message that he was not pleased with Tom's taking of the one section of webbing. "How I'll explain your taking the one section is a bigger mystery than all the others."

Tom responded angrily. "If I hadn't shot the video and taken this goddamn thing, there wouldn't be any evidence at all." He yanked the strap from Travis' grasp.

Travis, with great restraint, was ready. "You're absolutely right. And who really gives a shit? Flagg Brothers hired us, not Kinedyne. Losing the webbing may help our case. I didn't steal them, but I don't care if they're never found. The piece you took is more of a problem than a solution."

Susie recoiled at the sight of Tom and his best friend in a face-to-face confrontation.

"And all this shit about 'someone beyond the driver' sounds like you've been watching 'Law and Order' too much.

Tom answered, "You tell me then. You sure as hell ought to be looking at who stands to gain on this. Have you even thought about the plaintiff, other trucking firms or anyone else?"

"No, I haven't. But I can tell you right up front, you've got shitty suspects. The surviving husband, from what I hear, is a simple sodbuster. I don't buy for a minute another trucking firm doing this. There would be a million better ways to screw Flagg Brothers."

"What about lawyers?"

Travis gave Tom a half-assed chuckle. "Like me, I guess. No, Colter and his firm need blood money as much as we need syphilis. Hell, they're taking the case pro bono."

Tom shot back, "Sodbusters can kill just as easy as anyone else. And because you're an honest lawyer, you think none of those other assholes aren't corrupt? When you get a chance, read up on the name Chillingworth. A judge in Palm Beach. Murdered by another judge named Joe Peel back in '55. Peel had the world by the tail but wanted more. He had two goons kill Judge Chillingworth and his wife by throwing them overboard from their own boat. Even tried to kill the killers and another judge. There are a million Joe Peels out there and their stories aren't funny. Don't give me this judicial purity crap."

Susie couldn't take any more. "Both of you shut up," she snapped. Her total change of character dumbfounded both men. "We're supposed to be on the same team and you sound like kids." Susie, face reddened with frustration, moved around Travis and took a new position in the middle. "At least give each other some respect." Though the fuse smoldered, her interruption abated the hostility. "Let's focus on winning the trial. At least listen to each other." She walked back to the living room, sheepishly followed by the two combatants.

Travis fell into the Ekornes. Without noticing, he partially crushed his beer can in his clenched fist. He looked at Susie. "O.K., you're the sounding board. We'll listen. What do you think?"

Susie just wanted it all to go away. But it wouldn't. Still standing, she looked down directly into his eyes. Her voice, steady and serious, gave weight to her statement. "Travis, I don't think anything. I know."

Travis was surprised at her forcefulness. He leaned forward to hear what she was about to say.

Her stare pierced Travis. "It's murder." She repeated, "Murder." She sat down next to Tom.

An uncomfortable silence ensued. Sinister visions played in their minds.

Travis, still reacting to Susie's comment, slumped against his chair. He gently placed the can on the rug, drew a large breath, and, shaking his head, exhaled heavily. "Damn." He focused more on Susie than Tom, then concluded the conversation.

"Tell you what. I'm honestly not convinced it was deliberate murder, but I will promise that if future evidence, solid evidence, is found to indicate murder, I will pursue it. I may be a cynical bastard, but you know I keep my word. And I'll sure as hell keep my integrity."

With Travis' compromise, the discussion transitioned into the physical sequence of events, structural aspects of the damage to the two vehicles, the explosive breaking of the webbing and the flight of the steel tubing from the bed of the trailer into the Ford Taurus. Tom and Travis had a fourth beer and watched ESPN Classics replay of the 1985 'Hail Mary' Boston College upset over Miami. Doug Flutie's pass was monumental. Susie went to bed. It was after midnight when Travis and Tom called it an evening. While Travis relieved his bladder, Tom placed the beer cans in a plastic recycle bag. Travis returned and headed for the front door as a thought penetrated Tom's mind.

As Travis opened the front door, Tom said, "Sorry about losing control, but I can't shake this thing. Shit, it's consuming me."

Travis sensed the substance of Tom's conviction. "You might just be right. Hell, I don't know."

"Just think about it. Might keep you awake on the way home. Adios, amigo."

"It will. Adios." Travis walked to his white Buick, squeezed in and turned the ignition.

Travis gave Tom a thumbs-up as he accelerated down Bar Harbour. Tom walked into the house and to the refrigerator for one last beer. The meeting with Travis had ended on a positive note. Travis said he would go after solid evidence and that was all Tom really wanted to hear. Yet, Tom was restless. Nagging thoughts continued to feed his conviction that someone among the four victims had been targeted. *But why? Who would take out a whole family for revenge? Who was the driver and had he tried to kill them somehow only to screw up? Was he related to one of the women? Who orchestrated murder? Could the sodbuster be a killer?* He looked down at the aluminum can, aimlessly read the label, then put it back in the refrigerator. He turned off the lights and picked his way through the darkness to the bedroom. He undressed as quietly as possible, slid under the light covers and turned to kiss Susie.

She was awake. "I'm scared. I just can't believe this is happening. I'm so scared."

Tom rolled over on his back, reaching beneath Susie's neck and around her shoulder. They looked into the darkness.

Tom thought of the human condition. "I just don't understand it all."

"All of what?"

"Power, arrogance, greed and all those other human frailties that tend to turn the world into a cesspool. I think of beautiful babies born with pug noses, rosy cheeks and bubbly smiles. They all start out the same, then pass through turbulence of some sort. To some, it leads to growth; for others it is far too difficult. My take is that there's a fork in the road of life for everyone. Maybe a lot of forks. I guess some people pass through the turbulence to lead productive lives. Others get swallowed by it."

Susie closed her eyes as tears stained her cheeks. Tom felt her shake and held her tight. He continued. "You know who I envy?" He didn't wait for a reply. "I envy those souls who are content to live simple lives, enjoying the punch of a clock and the freedom to keep the job outside of the home."

Susie opened her eyes and rolled her head towards Tom. "But what about respect? Who do you respect?"

"Oh, I don't know. Probably those who have an internal value system that calls to service. The clergy, the military and the social work communities seem to have a majority of those people. They don't make much money but their lives have value because of some sense of a higher calling."

"Like Mother Theresa?"

"She's probably the best example out there. I'm no religious fanatic, but she fits the mold of what a religious person ought to be. I watch some of those folks on TV, with all the jewels, makeup and ornate crap all over the place, and I get sick to my stomach. But Mother Theresa, now there was a beautiful woman. She walked the talk." Tom's reflective journey moved to the other end of the spectrum. "But what really hurts is that for every Mother Theresa there must be a hundred out there who are classic users. Sons of bitches. I guess we all have a price." Tom went silent, reflecting on his own possible price.

Susie turned on her side towards Tom. Her knees touched his leg and she placed her hand on his chest. Their touching was intimate – no arousal, all affection.

She almost whispered as she asked, "Who is it Tom? And why?"

"It's got to be someone higher in the food chain than the driver." He studied her question deeply. "I see the amoral."

Tom focused on a single word. *Amoral. The saddest, most despicable form of life. No right. No wrong. Just a piece of shit sitting at the middle of the Universe.*

He reached down and gently stroked her hip. Then, lost in thought, spoke to the ceiling. "Amoral. There is a human trail based on greed. Just follow the trail."

She traced her fingers across his chest. "Can you see the trail?"

"No, at least not clearly. An attack on someone in the D'Arcy family is most likely, or maybe the trucking firm. In either case, the husband is a possible suspect. Who else stands to gain the most in all of this? The husband, probably with the dead driver is our starting point." He considered an attack on Flagg Brothers. *Who would attack Flagg Brothers?*

Barry Colter slithered into his mind.

"I'll get another shot at Travis soon. Very soon. He's processing it all right now on his way home."

Susie patted his chest.

Tom sighed, then asked the ultimate question of human nature. "Is there a God? If so, He – or She – must really be pissed."

Susie responded, not with words, just the gentle tracing of her fingers.

Tom, still staring into the darkness, silently asked again. *Why is there so much evil?*

The other side of his question lay next to him, giving him a rebuttal. *There are also beautiful people on this Earth.* He rolled over and kissed her.

Susie responded in beauty.

21

Wednesday morning. Judge Sandra Piazze entered the courtroom promptly at nine o'clock. All rose, the jury to Judge Piazze's left, the packed courthouse and the legal combatants directly to her front, and the single television crew selected to film the trial to her right front. She began the proceedings with an announcement.

"Before we start, let me inform all participants to this trial that I have an important engagement this Friday. We will proceed today and tomorrow and then recess for a three-day weekend." Her words resonated well with the entire courtroom. "Now, Mr. Colter and Mr. White, are you ready to proceed?"

Just as the Stetly trial generated great interest throughout South Texas, the D'Arcy case had the press feeding at the Brazoria County Courthouse like shark on chum. The three major networks along with CNN and Fox joined in the frenzy when word got out that the pro bono lawsuit would be fought over more than a quarter of a billion dollars. While punitive damages belong to the jury, Colter, Fisher and King had already planted the huge sum in the minds of those concerned with the case. Media speculation ranged from drunk driving on the part of either or both of the drivers to an animal in the road. The original police investigation lasted less than a week and then faded behind a workload that only grew with time.

Jury selection concluded with the selection of eight men, two black, three Hispanic and three Caucasian, and four women, all Caucasian. The normal jockeying for position had taken place with but a few challenges for cause. Neither side was particularly pleased or distressed with the jury.

The well-tailored dark blue business suit, accentuated with light gray pin striping, formed perfectly over Barry Colter's large frame. The conservative alternating blue and dark red-striped tie complemented his light pastel blue shirt.

173

His thick, almost black hair benefited from just a dusting of gray. It gave the perception of wisdom, not age.

Travis White was dressed almost as a twin to his adversary. But Travis wore a genuine smile.

Barry went first.

●

Barry opened strong, covering highway death statistics involving the trucking industry, the uncaring attitude and greed of the corporate leaders and specific reference to the woes of Flagg Brothers Trucking. He told a clear tale of what the D'Arcy siblings went through in the final seconds of their lives. His concluding remarks were piercing. Standing in the middle of the open area before the judge, Barry Colter spoke to the entire courtroom.

"When the witnesses from Flagg Brothers Trucking take the stand, I ask you to look each one in the eye, listen carefully to their responses, then make your own judgment whether you sense evil." Walking to the front of the railing, he bore into each juror. "If you sense evil, evil manifested in guilt, then you must eliminate it. Over 200 years ago, Sir Edmund Burke might have been speaking to each of you tasked to provide justice for our people." Barry slowed his speech, then spoke powerful words. "The only thing necessary for the triumph of evil is for good men to do nothing." He repeated, "for good men to do nothing." He waited, allowing the words to sink in. "This trial is about evil. Evil people committing evil acts." Eyeball to eyeball. Some maintained the eye contact; others lowered their eyes. "You are good men and women. You must not just do nothing." He turned his back on the jury, paused, then return to his chair.

Travis' opening remarks were not as emotional as were his opponent's. He used Barry's comments for the jurors to see the proverbial 'other side of the coin'. After urging the jurors to judge the case on merit rather than emotion, on the rule of law rather than the rule of the mob, he closed gently.

"And I too believe that evil will triumph if good men and women do nothing. But I also believe in the words of Gandhi, 'You have to do the right thing'. I believe you will do the right thing." He returned to his seat.

●

A cruiserweight brawl ensued with Barry Colter easily winning the first three rounds. Each witness for the plaintiff came across crisp, knowledgeable, very believable. Highway patrolmen, EMS workers and local Alvin residents who heard the collision then saw the carnage all told stories painting a picture of an out-of-control tractor-trailer. Grotesque photographs were placed on an easel in clear view of the jurors and the gathering of fight fans. If the early part seemed good, Barry Colter could only lick his chops about getting the Flagg Brothers corporate executives on the witness stand. He savored thoughts of a crushing knockout blow.

Travis, against the ropes, jabbed and parried at every opportunity. He judicially objected when feasible, wrote notes in response to Barry's attacks and carved out small changes to the defense plan. He needed to go over the defense with Tom.

"Ed, get Tom Seiler on the phone and tell him to meet me at my office at 5:30. Order some burritos and a couple of six-packs of Miller."

"Got it."

More salvos came his way. By the end of the day, Barry Colter was way ahead on points. But the fight was not over.

●

Judge Piazze's giving everyone Friday off was a godsend to Barry. During lunch he called Liz Harker.

"The weather's going to clear and Piazze gave us Friday off. Let's make it a three-day weekend. A little bit of business with Jud Shithead and then a plate full of pleasure. You on?"

Liz perked up at the other end. "I need three days away from the office. I'll cancel my schedule with some sort of emergency."

"How about meeting on Thursday night. We can start the weekend off with a bang."

They both laughed, then Liz said, "Sounds like your friend is already there."

They laughed again. Life was good.

At home that evening Barry invited Betty to go to Seadrift with him for a weekend of fishing.

"The fishing will be great and, even if you don't go, the sun will do you good."

"I could enjoy a good murder mystery and the fire at full blast, but fishing is out." She remembered the unabated vomiting and had no intention of ever setting foot on a seagoing vessel again. "I'm also hostess for the DAR luncheon on Saturday."

Betty felt both guilty and relieved that she had to stay in Houston. Barry knew Betty had the luncheon; he only felt horny.

The business side of the weekend was not going to be nearly as enjoyable as sleeping with the beautiful Elizabeth Harker. He scheduled a Friday noon meeting with Jud Weems at Indianola. Assuming all went well, it would be their last meeting outside of Houston. Barry was well known in Houston. Not yet to the stature of a Joe Jamail but certainly a Houston lawyer of great prominence. Meetings in the office were risky and fishing trips along Mustang and Matagorda Islands had been part and parcel of his free time for over 20 years. Once Barry recruited the two men, he held three meetings at the airstrip.

●

At the first meeting, Barry introduced Jud and Buck, then went over his concept of the operation.

"Do you both fully understand the risk this involves?" Barry looked at the two men sitting across from him.

Both recruits smoked furiously, filling the dingy room with bluish haze.

Jud responded first, "Yeah, I got it. We fuck up and we get fucked up." He inhaled deeply, then dropped his cigarette to the concrete floor. He stepped on it, twisting his foot back and forth.

"Yeah, I'm not stupid." Buck spoke righteously.

"You need to know that if you execute the way you're supposed to, then keep your mouths shut, you will lead a life unknown to every working schmuck out there." Barry took a sip from his water bottle. "You say one word about it, and each of you buys Huntsville." The consequences seemed pretty straightforward.

Jud took another cigarette from its pack. He lit it, sucked in the delicious drug, then asked about the plan. "Before I go the last step, I need to know exactly how we're going to do it."

The inside of the office was stifling. Humid, smoke-filled, dark, it represented what their lives would endure were they to screw things up. All three sensed the environment.

"Fine." Barry took a single sheet of paper from his briefcase. He turned it upside down and pushed it away from himself, affording Jud and Buck the freedom to read the words. "We're going to use this airstrip to prepare. It's been abandoned for years. No one comes out here."

All eyes remained fixed on the sheet. Barry continued.

"There are four simple parts to the project. First, we set everything up here." Beside a '1' on the paper were the words 'Setup – airstrip'. "Then comes the practice phase. Both of you need to work together on this part." Next to '2' was 'Practice'.

Number '3' involved the execution of Barry's plan.

Jud and Buck read number '4' in unison with Barry's repeating it. "Shut up – shut up – shut up."

He outlined each man's actions in detail. The meeting lasted another two hours. He finished with an explanation of how the received funds would be handled. "After Jud gets the settlement, he pays every cent of tax required and puts the rest in a bank account. Jud gets his part right off the top." Barry took a handkerchief and wiped his brow. "I'll provide the instructions for the remainder to be transferred to a bank in the Cayman Islands. After a short period, Buck and I will split the off-shore money."

This time Buck lit up another cigarette. "So we split in thirds, right?"

"No, that's not right. I'm doing this equitably, not equally."

Buck didn't understand, he only knew his cut was going to be less than the others would get.

Barry added, "But, Buck, don't worry. You will pocket no less than $10 million. Do you think that is enough to last a lifetime?"

Buck was a little slow on the uptake, but he easily compared his share against a $38,000 a year job. "Yeah, it'll do." He smiled ever so slightly.

"O.K., this is it. We all agree and don't look back," he paused, "or we walk out of here without ever meeting again. What's your decision? Buck?"

Barry asked Buck first, knowing the answer.

"I'm ready to go all the way."

"Jud."

Another deep drag on the cigarette. Jud took the cigarette from his mouth and held the cigarette over the table. He tapped it, a large segment of ash falling to the table. "I'm in."

"Good."

Barry took Buck's lighter from the table and ignited the paper.

"Any questions?"

"Yeah." Buck looked seriously at Barry. "What's a schmuck?"

●

The second meeting was logistical in nature. Jud used his Ford pickup truck to bring in paint supplies and surveying equipment. Seven five-gallon buckets of black paint and a two-gallon can of red exterior paint sufficed for recreating the centerline of Farm Road 1462. Barry verified the location, both on the ground and from 1,500 feet in his Cessna 182. Over the years of prosecuting highway carnage lawsuits, Barry developed a civil engineer's ability to visualize the landscape.

Preparing an outline of the highway onto a grid was relatively easy. To expand his engineering drawings to actual painted lines and arcs on an airstrip was difficult only in the effort it took to explain the process to Jud and Buck. Four hours were needed to measure out the appropriate distances and produce an exact replica of the horizontal curve at the intersection of Farm Road 1462 and Parker Road.

●

At the third meeting in August Barry and Jud watched Buck make the first of several trial runs along the black snaking stripe. The steel tubing was delivered to the site in increments, unnoticed by the unrelated suppliers from whom it came. Over 60 lengths of nylon tiedown straps were gathered from sources throughout South Texas, mostly from suppliers in the Corpus Christi area. Only Kinedyne straps were procured.

Barry understood the basics of the tensile strength of the straps. Explaining it to Jud and Buck was difficult.

"Pay attention to the exact patterns of the cuts I'm making into the straps." Barry used manila templates to indicate the exact location and length of the cuts. With box cutters he followed the lined markings. "Any questions?"

"Yeah," Buck was already distracted, "how we gonna do this in the middle of night?"

Barry retorted, "You're not. You drive. Jud cuts." Both men would be physically tied to the deaths in the D'Arcy family. First-degree murder if they get caught.

Jud followed the instructions closely. Even the depth of cuts across the back width of the webbing was explained in exact detail. With practice, the straps would break as intended.

For the first run the steel tubing remained nestled securely on the flatbed, held down with four lengths of untampered webbing. Satisfied that the entire system would work, Barry left the airstrip before runs were made with the altered straps. Barry knew that the key to success lay not in the events at the intersection but in everyone's actions after the deaths of the D'Arcy's. Colter's greatest fear was that either or both of these accomplices would end up bragging at some bar. He brought eight newspaper clippings from the *Houston Chronicle*, each describing a murder or armed robbery that had been solved through the perpetrator's loud mouth. Most of Barry's efforts focused on Buck and the role he needed to play in dealing with the police and news media. A simple need to return for vacation tickets coupled with an animal in the roadway would provide the alibi. Before leaving, Barry tabbed Jud as the point of contact and provided him with a schedule of phone calls to be received at the public telephone on Calhoun Street. As he drove away from the scalding airstrip Barry entertained thoughts ranging from *What in the hell have I started?* to *I'm about to be one rich and powerful son-of-a-bitch.*

●

As for Jud Weems, he intended to be inconspicuous during and after the trial. The only change in his behavior since Sybil and her siblings died had been the decline in his work schedule. Understandably, he was so upset that he had been given a reduced schedule as a tractor-trailer driver. He explained to his supervisor that, even though he knew he would be able to work through it, each time he climbed into the cab of his rig visions of the terrible accident filled his mind. He was convincing and, save an occasional short trip when other drivers were scarce, spent most of his time watching television at his - at least it would soon be his - home on South Park in Alvin. Jud Weems had become reclusive. From time to time he ventured out to Sodbuster's for a meal and conversation with Sandy. Jud was smart. Sandy was certainly willing, but Jud never invited her back to the house for physical pleasure. He wanted nothing to do with television reporters or questions from his fellow drivers at Bettis Trucking.

Eight o'clock. Jud had enjoyed the fajitas, beer and conversation with Sandy. His mind consumed the drive home with details of his interactions with Barry Colter and his subsequent concerns about whether Colter constituted a real threat in the long term. Possibly his mental arguments for killing his co-conspirator had been premature

Slowing on his way down South Park, Jud saw the crowd on his lawn. "Shit." He pulled into the driveway only to be mired in lights, people and microphones.

"Mr. Weems, Bill Gagne from Channel 8."

Jud was angry.

"We'd like to ask some questions about the D'Arcy trial. Did the pro bono . . ."

"Get the f . . ., uh, I got nothin' to say 'bout the trial."

Jud quickly drew his teeth over his lower lip. Relaxing slightly, at least in appearance, he spoke to the aggressive reporter. "Please jus' let me be. I lost my whole family and I've got nuthin' to say. They was outright killed and I trust that justice will be done." Again, the habit with his lower lip. "I gotta go. Thanks."

Jud walked directly between the two and made his way to the kitchen door. The cameramen followed, filming until Jud disappeared.

"It's a wrap. Call the station. We're good for the 10 o'clock."

22

Travis walked in the door, haggard from a three-hour strategy session following the 5:00 adjournment.

"Hi, Hon. Talk about a full day. I'm just plain beat."

Travis' request for a four-week delay was denied. The D'Arcy case followed the Stetly victory much too quickly, forcing Travis and his team of four lawyers to put on a two-week full-court press. The work was exhausting. Tom's interjecting the murder scenario ate at Travis. Still, he understood that Tom's arguments would not stand up in a court of law. The silver bullet tying everything together could not be found. Travis' opening statement had gone well enough, but he felt discouraged by his inability to discredit any of Barry's witnesses. He pictured the jury, then thought of Barry Colter. *He shovels them shit and they eat it up.* The basis of the defense argument would be that the actions of Buck Tallant in trying to return to the Houston area were in direct contradiction to Flagg Brothers' policy. The tractor-trailer, including the tires and mechanical components had been well maintained. As for the straps, the defense position was that they had been checked and declared serviceable on the 15th of August. That they were Kinedyne straps spoke well to Flagg Brothers' use of top-of-the-line equipment. If they had been cut, and Tom was prepared to testify that they were, then it was probably a case of vandalism turned deadly. Given that the required number of straps had been used for the load, no culpability of any nature should rest on the shoulders of Flagg Brothers Trucking. Except that the company had insurance.

"Care to unwind with a nightcap and a lap?" Michelle greeted Travis with a kiss, then traded a glass of Undurraga Cabernet Sauvignon 1995 for his jacket and tie. The bouquet was just right, earthy but not overpowering. Her glass was half full, his a bit more than a touch. It allowed him to sip wine with his head resting

181

on Michelle's lap.

"All in all, the day was a real bitch - long as hell." Travis sat down on the couch and bent over to untie his shoes. In 20 seconds he confirmed that Michelle's lap was, indeed, the best place in town.

The wine was soothing. "We're still on track to present next week. I'll put Tom on for a day and a half. There's a recess scheduled for Friday."

"Good. Try to take some of the day for yourself. No, let's take it for both of us." Her hands massaged his head gently.

The conversation gave way to the 10:00 news. Travis started to nod off as the second topic began. It concerned the trial. Both Travis and Michelle had only a mild sense of interest in the story line . . . until the tape played showing the plaintiff, Jud Weems. Travis' reaction was at first inquisitive.

". . . justice will be done. I gotta go. Thanks."

Almost magically, the subject drew his upper teeth over his lower lip.

The image triggered an awakening in Travis. An old tape playing in his mind, Travis shook as ice ran through his veins. He bolted up, startling Michelle. Somehow, Travis knew he was looking at the bullet. The strange mannerisms, particularly the movement of teeth over the lower lip, the look of the eyes and the slow, deliberate Texas drawl. Travis was looking into the eyes of the tiger.

"Michelle, I know him. I've seen him before." Travis finished the wine in a single swallow. He was wide-awake.

Michelle was puzzled. So what if Travis knew the stranger on television? Is it important enough to affect the trial? Her thoughts were confused, yet she sensed something ominous.

"And I don't think I like him." He pushed the wineglass away from him on the table, then stood up. He thought out loud. "It's a trial from before. He's been part of a trial that I worked before. Gotta check this guy out."

When in a hurry, Travis' gait was that of a giraffe. He covered the distance to the hallway in four steps.

"Travis, you don't need to solve it now. It's late. Tomorrow's a rough day. Travis!" Michelle realized she was talking to the wall.

Travis' private office was a two-room suite at the end of the hall. Two guestrooms and a full bathroom separated the office from the master bedroom. Huge mahogany pocket doors receded into the walls, separating the two rooms. His desk was antique, made of oak. Its surface was uniquely large considering the postal hutch that rested on top. Each of the four square openings held letters and reference materials for his use. The sides of the hutch extended almost to the front of the desk, both made of glass framed by beautiful curved strips of oak. To the rear of the desk, a half rotation in the plush swivel chair, French doors opened to a magnificent lawn and garden. Wealthy as they were, Michelle cared for the unique menagerie of bluebonnets, pansies and cactus, letting professional lawn-care specialists cut the grass and prune the other shrubbery. A fireplace filled the majority of the wall to the right of the desk. The wall-length bookshelves were stocked with legal statutes, references for landmark cases and a collection of mystery novels . . . Grisham, Patterson, Parker and Burke leading the way.

Travis walked hurriedly to the second room. Along the wall, opposite windows overlooking the garden, were more bookshelves. At the far end were two pairs of louvered doors behind which stood eight sets of shoulder-high filing cabinets. Travis began with the lower drawer of the far-left file cabinet. The typed heading on the drawer label read, 'January - November 1981.'

●

"Son-of-a-bitch!" Jud punched the "off" button on the remote and walked to his bedroom. In bed, he looked up at the churning blades of the fan. He felt violated. Never mind those who he had violated. The predator had become the prey. It was one-thirty in the morning before he fell asleep.

●

One-thirty in the morning. Travis was into the top drawer of the fourth cabinet. He removed some 50 Blue Sheets – weekly synopses of trial cases - and placed them in two piles on the desk. He was dead-tired and had committed to himself that the two stacks would be the last ones he would look at before going to bed. He was discouraged.

Four Blue Sheets remained when Travis opened the one for September 20, 1993. In the third case on page 11 the plaintiff was Judson Weems, claiming soft tissue neck and back injuries when rear-ended at a traffic light the previous June.

Travis' face lit up like a kid on Christmas morning. "Got it." Travis whispered to himself as he gave a short jab to an invisible opponent. He traced his right index finger across each line. The attorneys for Jud Weems were James L. Neal and Barry D. Colter. For the defense, Travis White.

"Can't win 'em all." Travis' response to reading the verdict was nonchalant.

The expert witness for the defense was Martin Hulsey. His analysis was that the defendant did rear-end Jud Weems' small truck, but at a speed no more than six miles an hour. Travis recollected that, even though they lost the case to the tune of $44,000, Jud Weems was lying through his ugly teeth about injuries he sustained. Travis read over the case three times, then placed the Blue Sheet in the center of his desktop and went to bed. Sleep was elusive. *So what if Colter represented Weems before? If a lawyer wins a case, the same person'll hire him the next time.* He rebutted his own thought. *But Weems was a liar then. Is it more than coincidence? Tom and Susie might be right. What about the truck driver?* It wasn't until three that he was able to drift into sleep.

●

Travis called his office 10 minutes before the start of the Thursday morning session.

"I need the file badly. The trial was held on 6 and 7 September, 1993. Plaintiff was Judson Weems. Attorney firm was Neal, Fisher and King. Not much to it but it might just impact this trial. Can you do it?"

"I'll have it there by the mid-morning recess." The confident Dana Schmidt was reliable. Travis knew she would deliver it on time. His biggest problem for the morning was to concentrate on the trial proceedings.

●

"You're the director of human resources and you have no records stating that Mr. Tallant had been court-martialed and dishonorably discharged from the Marine Corps?"

"Uh, no sir." The witness, sweating in terror, stammered out a response.

"Do you, or does anybody at Flagg Brothers Trucking, know anything about Mr. Tallant other than he died in your truck?" Barry Colter spoke in mock disbelief and frustration.

"Objection. Badgering the witness."

"Sustained. Straight forward questions Mr. Colter."

Barry Colter walked, almost marching, to the edge of the witness stand. He leaned forward, hands on the rail, and invaded the witness' personal space.

"What about driving while under the influence? Did you know about two convictions for DUI?" Barry Colter reduced the witness to an image of a bumbling, incompetent, bureaucrat.

"Uh, no sir, but he had been a good driver since . . ."

Barry caught the sweating, fidgeting witness in midstream.

"Your Honor, all I need is a yes or no response to the question."

"Sustained. Mr. Becker, just answer the questions without additions unless asked to clarify your response."

"Uh, yes ma'am."

The dishonorable discharge. Two DUI's. One misdemeanor assault charge. The morning had not gone well for the defense. Travis made only the one objection. Barry, satisfied that he had hung Fred Becker out to dry, sat down.

In cross-examination, Travis did what he could to salvage Becker's credibility and the reputation of the deceased driver. Facts about Buck's length of service, miles driven and, fortunately, an incident in which Buck pulled an elderly man from an overturned car that caught fire shortly thereafter, provided minimal damage control. There was some positive information, but certainly not enough to counter the attack of his opponent.

●

While Travis engaged Fred Becker, Barry allowed his mind to move on to other concerns. *Remove items from the airstrip. Brief Weems. Proceed with strategy.* He jotted down 'Friday – Airstrip - Weems – LH' on top of a legal pad. Lost in thought, he surrounded the words with a doodling of concertina-wire circles. His last thought was explicit, driving him to add 'G.L.!!' below the other words. He smiled.

"Mr. Colter! Do you agree or not?" Judge Piazze admonished the inattentive lawyer.

Jolted back to reality, Barry responded. "Sorry your Honor. I have no objection." It was a lucky guess on his part.

"Thank you for joining us. Jury out at 10:20."

●

Dana met Travis in the hallway. She breathed heavily, the price paid to keep the promise. She had run two blocks from the closest parking lot. She reached out towards Travis, releasing her firm grip on the manila folder.

"As promised. I agree it's not much of a case. I glanced over it. Poor Mr. Weems seems sensitive to slow moving cars." Dana shook her head, giving Travis an ironic smile.

Travis took the folder and held it up in the air. "I don't care much for Mr. Weems. I hope this stuff confirms my feelings." There was confidence in his voice.

"I think it will, Mr. White. Good luck." Dana turned towards the bright Texas sun at the end of the hall.

Travis looked down at the folder. He opened it and glanced at the synopsis of the 1993 trial. Engrossed in the written information before him, Travis walked back to his courtroom table without making a restroom stop. As he turned towards the left he noticed some words on a yellow pad at Barry Colter's table.

"Friday – Airstrip – Weems – LH" barely escaped his mouth. Travis registered the information, including the initials 'G.L.!!' in the short-term recesses of his mind. He sat down in his chair and copied the information exactly as he remembered it. His self-imposed questions from the night before were answered with a hunch.

●

Dana took the second call from Travis during the lunch recess. She understood that the trial papers concerning Jud Weems would somehow affect liability for Flagg Brothers. When Travis interjected a new name, Dana reacted with a touch of nervousness. She didn't know any specifics, but she knew the trial was expanding.

"His name is William Buford Tallant. How far back do our Blue Sheets go and do we have them all?"

"I know we have a huge file of them. It must go back several years."

"Great." He was excited and Dana sensed the bloodhound in Travis White being unleashed. "If we do have them, let's bracket the years 1989-1994 to see what pops out. While you're at it, please check out the entire D'Arcy family as well. I need to know the relatives."

"We'll start as soon as I hang up. I'll give Houston Trial Reports a call to see if they have a database program that can key on his name. Might save us some time." Dana's enthusiasm, subdued only slightly with apprehension, followed Travis' lead. The many days of operating by rote are sometimes interrupted by a few that are spine tingling. She couldn't put it all together, but Dana knew this was one of those spine-tinglers.

"Thanks Dana. Just leave everything on my conference table. I'll stop by the office on the way home. Take care."

"Good luck again, Mr. White."

●

"We'll recess tomorrow for a three-day weekend. Do the attorneys have any matters that we need to address before Monday?"

"No, your Honor. That will be fine." Travis immediately began packing his briefcase and trial bag.

"No, your Honor. Nothing that three days of fishing can't solve." Barry Colter's mood was upbeat.

"Jury out at 4:45."

●

Knowing it might be another long night, Travis met Michelle at Morrie's for a quick, yet pleasant, dinner. One glass of Chardonnay for Michelle and the first of two Lone Star beers for Travis.

"You're looking pretty chipper tonight. Must have been a good day at the trial." Michelle smiled, looking up at her partner of 27 years.

"Yeah, it really was. I managed to do some damage control. More importantly, Dana gave me some information on Weems." Travis glanced at the passersby on the street. In the flash of an eye he gathered in two teenage boys exhaling cigarette smoke and laughing, an old, terribly tired, woman shuffling along as best she could, three executives, two female, one male, probably discussing mergers or whatever young executives discuss, and a happy little girl holding her father's hand while asking a multitude of questions beginning with 'Why?' He could not escape asking which ones were honorable and which ones weren't.

He looked back at Michelle as he half finished his first beer. "The guy's a dirtbag."

"Does he scare you?" She was vaguely uncomfortable but gave a valiant attempt to disguise her concern.

"No. Not really. It was several years ago but I remembered that he lied on the stand." Travis was not totally truthful with Michelle, but why frighten her at this point? "I haven't had a chance to work on it, but I'm going to see if I can find a way to show that he's a liar."

The waitress arrived with two servings of stuffed flounder. Travis requested, "One more Lone Star when you get a chance. Thanks ma'am," and waited for her to leave.

He continued. "Even if I do, it won't help with proving that Flagg Brothers has no liability. But, I might be able to sway the jury into not wanting Weems to get as large a settlement as is on the table. We'll see. Enough on that. Did we get the tickets to 'Rent' yet?"

The conversation moved away from trials and towards those things a strong couple would discuss. Both sons had called the day before. Their new daughter-in-law, a very welcome addition to the family, was two months pregnant. The younger boy had just been transferred to Rochester, New York with an optics research group of Durning Electronics. Travis lost focus from time to time, drifting back to a visual picture of Jud Weems. The tightening in the pit of his stomach bothered him. Each time Travis felt it, he would force himself back into the conversation.

"OK my love, it's your call. Antigua or a cruise to the Western Caribbean. The whole gang. Let's just make sure that Monique has conquered morning sickness." They laughed first and then frowned at the downside of motherhood.

Despite Travis' mental meanderings, the evening had been very pleasant. According to her invitation, if he got home quickly, it would get better.

They kissed goodbye at Michelle's car. Travis declined her offer for a ride, enjoying the half-block walk to his car. It only took him ten minutes to return to his office and peruse the second packet of information from Dana.

●

A single Blue Sheet lay in the middle of the conference table, a paper clip marking page 10. The yellow tablet had notes from Dana. She found nothing concerning the D'Arcy family. Travis gently placed his jacket on the back of the leather chair, loosened his tie and sat down. The wall thermostat read 88 degrees. It was warm, too warm. Looking quickly at the pad he noticed a single word written by Dana, underlined and in caps. 'BINGO!!!' His heart quickened in concert with the adrenaline surge. His finger grazed over the paper clip, pulling open page 10. Underlined in yellow highlighter, the third case read:

<u>CASE NUMBER</u>
Harris County, County Court
#2 - Judge Trent
611,642

William B. Tallant
vs.
Margaret Sullivan

Scanning to his right, he read the second column:

<u>ATTORNEYS</u>

P – B. D. Colter, E. T. Harker

D – A. A. Brant

The basic description under <u>TYPE OF ACCIDENT</u> provided a quick synopsis of the events:

> Auto - Def. pulled from service station and prepared to make left hand turn into two-way street. Plt. struck Def. on left front fender. Plt. contended Def. was in roadway. Def. claimed Plt. saw her vehicle and could have avoided collision.

The claimed injuries by Buck Tallant were soft tissue neck and back. Medical costs were estimated at $8,000, lost wages ran $9,000 and property damage was $2,000.

As for expert witnesses, the representative for Buck Tallant was superior to the witness for the defense, resulting in the final column:

<u>VERDICT OR DISPOSITION</u>
Week of 5-14-91

Found Def. was neg., awarded
$19,000

Pre-trial demand: $25,000
Pre-trial offer: None

He spoke to himself, "Damn, it's true." Then came reflection. *A bereaved husband who had hired Colter before is reasonable. Except that this one is a crook. A dead truck driver who also hired Colter in the past. No way.* Something else triggered his brain. He looked back at the second column and winced. He whispered, "Well I'll be damned. Harker too." As a young lawyer, she worked with Barry Colter on the case involving Buck Tallant. Travis was unaware of the perspiration trickling down his forehead. He opened his briefcase and pulled the 1993 Blue Sheet out, placing it next to the 1991 Blue Sheet. He stared at the two cases. The linkages among the three men wound together as steel wire. *And what about Harker? She might be in on this shit, too.* First Tom and Susie; now Travis joined with them – the D'Arcy's were murdered. A single bead of sweat splashed between the two Blue Sheets.

Travis picked up the phone and made a call to Tom. Three rings and the message came on. Tom and Susie were not home. Not wanting to alarm Susie, Travis decided against leaving a message.

"Damn." Travis placed the phone in its cradle and stared down at the Blue Sheets. He wrote 'Coincidence vs Murder' on a new sheet of yellow paper. Drawing multiple circles of graphite around the words, Travis realized that he could no longer deny irrefutable evidence. The new information swung the pendulum fully to Tom and Susie's version of the events in Alvin. Travis remembered Barry Colter's statement that he would be out of town fishing. The words seen on the scratch pad - 'Friday – Airstrip – Weems – LH' and 'G.L.' leaped out to herald a meeting between Colter, Weems and, if he read the initials correctly, possibly Liz Harker. If it were on the 'up and up' a meeting would be held in the law offices of Colter, Fisher and King. *Didn't Colter say he would be fishing over the recess? Is the 'LH' for Liz Harker? Why an airstrip? What airstrip? Who or what is G.L.?* If illegal matters were to be discussed, the meeting would likely be held elsewhere. He continued his one-person conversation. *There's no coincidence. It was planned. What do I do now? How do I get the evidence?* He answered his questions instantly with recall of the infamous Faria case. Another claim of whiplash in an accident in which neither car traveled faster than four miles an hour.

●

When Jesus Faria, the plaintiff, limped into the courtroom sporting a neck brace Travis felt a mixture of nausea and angered tightness. His emotions had much more to do with the dishonesty of the lawyer representing Jesus than with the poor manipulated plaintiff. The whole setup was straight out of a grade-B Hollywood movie. In this case, however, Travis took some movies of his own. On the afternoon before the trial was to go to the jury Travis followed the young Mexican laborer back to a family gathering not far from the intersection of Carlin Street and Irvington Boulevard. It was simple to document the full extent of Jesus' injuries with a camcorder. The next morning Travis, then the junior attorney for the defense, entered the last item of evidence - a videotape of Jesus Faria. It would have been hilarious had it not also been pathetic. Jesus was the picture of health. Beginning with the removal of the neck brace, the camera had caught Jesus jumping from his pickup truck to a group of waiting, celebrating friends. Though somewhat garbled, the audio system was clear enough to capture the repetitive word "dinero, dinero" as he grabbed a happy little girl and swung her around and up into the air. His festiveness was one day early.

●

"I nailed one son-of-a-bitch. I'll get two this time."

Travis searched the computer database for the address of Judson Weems. He copied it down and placed it in his shirt. He rose to leave, then remembered something else.

He sat back down at the computer and accessed the Google search engine. Letting Google do the work, Travis typed in the keywords CHILLINGWORTH, MURDER and PALM BEACH.

The rest of the night would belong to Michelle.

23

The wind blew cool and crisp across his face. Travis walked briskly to the white '99 Park Avenue, shrugging off the sensation that his jeans were tighter than necessary. He did not tuck in his red flannel shirt. Inside his gym bag were a video camera, coffee thermos, a sweater depicting the Texas University 1945 Southwest Conference football champions, binoculars, a Texas map and a white baseball cap with PETRILLO written in black. Hiking boots completed the ensemble. He buckled his seat belt, pushed the reset button on the trip odometer and turned the ignition. Travis glanced at the side of the house gliding past him and reflected on his note to Michelle:

> *Michelle,*
> *Sorry I left so early. Couple of things I need to get done and they'll take most of the day. Yep, it's trial stuff. Nope, it's not dangerous. Be back by seven tonight. How about dinner at Pappasito's. Speaking of tonight, I'll take a thousand more like last night!*
> *I love you,*
> *Travis*

He stopped at Mellon's Texaco on Freeman Drive, topped off the gas tank and purchased gum, a day-old ham and cheese sandwich and a large coffee that he poured into his thermos. As an afterthought, he added a bottle of mineral water. Twenty-five minutes later, with dawn invading the night sky, Travis arrived at South Park in Alvin.

Travis whispered to himself, "OK, Weems, where are you?" He pulled the

193

piece of paper holding Jud's address from his shirt pocket, verified the house number, then put the paper back. Passing by small, neat, cloned homes, Travis picked out the home where Jud and Sybil Weems had lived. The dark green Ford F-150 truck was parked backwards in the driveway. South Park is basically a 'U' with both ends terminating on Gordon Avenue. He continued driving and found a small alley with a view of both ends of South Park, backed in, and waited. It was a short wait.

In the gray murkiness of the new morning, Travis did not recognize the truck until it rolled through the stop sign and headed south on Gordon. He allowed two early morning travelers to pass by, then began his journey to seek out the contents of Tom's version of Pandora's box. Jud headed southeast on Texas 35 and cleared the city limits of Alvin. The chase was on - where it would lead him was an intriguing mystery. The rising sun at his back and the generally straight section of highway gave Travis unobstructed visibility, allowing him to keep a good distance from his target. Time to call Tom. He first tried Tom at home, then his cell phone, and finally back to Tom's home.

". . . and we'll get back to you just as quick as we can."

Unknown to Travis, Tom and Susie had flown to San Antonio for a mixture of business and pleasure. As an unfortunate coincidence, the cell phone Tom always took with him was sitting neatly on the floorboard center of their truck, abandoned in the forgetfulness of two friends engaged in affectionate bantering.

"Hey folks, where are you? Give me a call on my cell phone when you wake up. I'm hot on the trail of our friendly plaintiff. He's headed down the coast on Texas 35. I'll check in every now and then until I hear from you. By the way, Joe Peel was a dirty SOB. Did you know he died of cancer as soon as he got out of the slammer? Deserved it big-time. Adios." Travis pulled a voice recorder from beneath his seat and made the first of several reference messages.

In West Columbia Jud pulled in at a McDonald's, parked and walked in for a short stop in the bathroom, two egg McMuffins and a cup of coffee to go. Travis continued on and made a quick pit stop of his own at a Texaco. He waited inside looking at maps that over the last 20 years increased in price from free to $5.95. As Jud drove by he seemed to take a quick, deliberate, look at the vehicles parked at the fuel island. Travis walked out, his senses heightened, and watched the truck vanish into the horizon. Whether Jud knew he was being followed or not, it was obvious that he was both careful and nervous. Travis continued the pursuit.

●

Liz Harker slowly shifted in bed, pulling the covers tightly around her shoulders. She could ignore the sun's intrusion into the bedroom, but not the captivating aroma or the pressure on her bladder. She surrendered and quickly took care of her personal needs, wrapped herself in Betty Colter's terry cloth bathrobe and walked to the kitchen for her first cup of Colombian coffee. Looking through the window, she smiled unconsciously at Barry, similarly robed, looking out over the water. She poured two steaming cups of coffee and walked into the crystal blue morning. She joined Barry on the double-tiered deck overlooking San Antonio Bay. From behind, Liz gently placed the cup on the drink stand to his left side, bent over his shoulder and gave him a quick upside-down kiss on the lips.

"Chilly but beautiful isn't it?" She didn't wait for a response. She walked around him to the edge of the deck, loosed the ties on Betty's bathrobe, and twirled in a mischievous pirouette, arms outstretched and head back. No inhibitions. Her lithe body, her small raisened nipples peeking out from perfect soft breasts and the warmth of an inviting black triangle called to Barry from beneath the wings of the robe. "This is how we ought to spend the rest of our lives. Making love, drinking coffee and living on the beach. Who needs Houston?"

"Come over here." Barry pulled the arm of her chair and helped maneuver her next to him. His long arm reached her right breast. Her hand moved between the folds of his robe. His fingers traced gentle circles. She ever so lightly stroked his rising penis.

Barry, almost hypnotized with tingling pleasure, tried to extract his thoughts from his groin. "Yeah, it is nice. I'm going to have us a home in each of the 10 most beautiful places in the world." He sipped his coffee, lifting slightly towards her fingertips, then pointed to a gull gliding overhead in search of its own version of breakfast. "See that gull? He knows he could fly anywhere he wants, yet he picked our beach."

The gull circled back around and slowed just above their heads. Barry talked to the bird. "Yeah, you're one smart son-of-a-bitch. Travel the world but always return here. I swear, Seadrift is the grandest spot on God's green earth." It was rare that Barry Colter used 'God' as a one-syllable word.

Liz reflected on the serenity of the moment. The water, the breeze, the man sitting next to her. *And we can do this every day of our lives once the trial is over. Well, every day after I'm the Governor of Texas.* She smiled into the breaking day. *Once the trial is over.* Her mind focused on the trial, giving birth to an image of Jud Weems juxtaposed in front of the tranquil water, entered her imagination. *Barry has a meeting with Jud Weems.* Unconsciously, her hand ceased its pleasant stroking. Her thoughts changed in mood, the serenity countered by darker thoughts. Jud Weems was a problem.

"Barry," her tone anxious, "how long will you be with Weems? He's nothing but bad news."

Snap. Barry stared blankly over the glassy surface of the bay. His mood switched from amorous to hostile. He removed his hand from her breast. "Shit, can't we spend five minutes together without talking about that asshole? The trial. Yesterday on the phone. Last night. Now. Are you trying to drive me stark raving nuts?" Barry stood, closing and tying his bathrobe. He walked to the deck railing, looking out over the bay while seeing nothing.

His reaction stunned Liz.

Thoughts swirled in the epicenter of Barry's mind. Meeting with Jud never sat easy with him. Try as he would to judge otherwise, Barry saw the core of Jud's persona – who he really was, the total lack of personal integrity, the greed – as a manifestation of himself. Only the ability to exercise power differentiated the two men.

He turned and glared at Liz. "Two fucking hours. I'll be back by 2:00. Damn." He walked back into the house, slamming the door.

The sun reached over her back and enveloped the vast expanse of San Antonio Bay, warming everything except the cold chill surging through her body. She was shaken. Tears streamed down her face. She could only ask herself. *What have I done? What in the hell have I done?*

●

Another phone call. "Just passed Bay City. Our man is up to something today. I may have hit the big-time. Ten-to-one he has a meeting with Colter today. Give me that call when you get back." Travis made a similar statement into the recorder, then returned attention to his coffee and, finally, to the small truck almost a mile to his front.

When Jud turned on Farm Road 1862 at Blessing, Travis was faced with a key tactical decision. Farm Road 1862 was a minor, desolate road cutting through the flat, open Texas landscape. The visibility would make it relatively easy for a suspicious Jud to figure out he was being followed. Conversely, a quick reconnaissance of the Texas highway map showed Farm Road 1862 to be a natural shortcut, bypassing the town of Palacios, before linking back up with Texas 35. Travis continued past the turnoff for half a mile, then returned to Farm Road 1862. Reaching speeds of 85 miles an hour, he was able to catch a glimpse of a small vehicle turning back on to Texas 35 towards Port Lavaca.

●

"I'll be back later, I've just got to get out of here. Might be two, might be three." She was depressed and lonely. It seemed that the whole world was falling inward on her.

Once in the car, Liz gathered some composure and began thinking of items to buy in Port Lavaca. Twenty miles east of Seadrift on Route 238, Port Lavaca lay as one of two parcels of land in this part of Texas that resembled a city. Fifteen miles further away was the slightly larger city of Victoria, but Liz reasoned that neither offered what she really needed – she simply had to get away. At least she could enjoy a milkshake from the Dairy Queen. Reeds, cactus, empty cotton fields and the warming Texas sun accompanied her along the way. By the time she reached the Port Lavaca Dairy Queen her thoughts had returned to contemplating power and wealth. Her fix for the day would be to find something exquisite in a non-exquisite town.

●

Jud turned south on Route 238 at the outskirts of Port Lavaca. The road, four lanes of smooth asphalt, seemed out of place. Vestiges of days gone by, Shooter's Sports Bar and Priddy's Oyster Bar, sat abandoned and bedraggled at roadside. Travis kept a safe distance, but was concerned about losing Jud in unfamiliar country. Jud made one more stop for fast food in Port Lavaca. One thing Port Lavaca has is a great Dairy Queen.

Travis pulled to the right side of the road just beyond a small group of mobile homes and wooden cottages. He waited.

"Greasy food, greasy scumbag," Travis whispered to himself while looking at Jud ordering at a small counter. Even if looking right at Travis, Jud would not know who he was. Still, Travis decided not to chance an encounter. He unwrapped the ham and cheese sandwich.

Liz stopped and waited for an oncoming car to pass before turning into the Dairy Queen. Just as she started her turn into the parking area, she was stunned at the sight of Jud walking out of the Dairy Queen, bag in hand. Concentrating on his keys, Jud was oblivious to her. Fear and disgust bore into her gut. Her chest seized around a pounding heart. Liz Harker turned the wheel and centered the car back into the northbound lane. Her fear had barely begun to subside when her eyes caught sight of the occupant seated in a white Buick.

"Oh, my God!" She gasped at seeing the large frame of Travis White looking down at his lap and then towards Jud's truck. Placing her left arm up as though shielding her eyes from the sun, Liz stepped hard on the accelerator. She had to get out of there.

●

Liz pulled over into a 7-11 convenience store parking lot. She poked at the numbers erratically as the cell phone shook in her hand. It took three tries. Barry answered before the second ring.

"Are you sure? Are you absolutely sure?" His voice was firm, yet worried. Barry had traveled only a quarter of a mile when she called.

"I know Travis White. It was him. He's following Weems. Why is he following him? What in the hell is going on?" She was pleading for a reasonable, even safe, answer.

"Did he see you?"

"No. No. I'm sure he didn't."

"How in the hell did he know?" Barry was talking out loud to himself. He began responding to the new situation. "Was he headed to Indianola?"

She thought it a stupid question. "He's following Weems."

"Get back to the beach house. Grab your stuff, everything, and get back to Houston. I'll take care of White."

Under most circumstances she was equal to Barry Colter and did not allow him to dictate to her. Sex, power, intelligence, greed. Many of the forces that drove Barry Colter also guided Elizabeth Harker. This whole day was different, though, and she realized that she must escape the certain web of suspicion that Travis White had cast over the deaths in Alvin. Her motivation was changing from a need for power to a need to distance herself as far, and as quickly, as possible from Barry Colter.

"What are you going to do?" Her question seemed stupid.

Barry shot back, "I won't do anything dumb. Just do what I say." Then he added. "And once you get back, make damn sure you get seen by a bunch of people. Get back and get seen before tonight." Urgently, he asked a new question. "Does anyone know you came down here?"

"No. Nobody at all."

"Good. Make sure no one does."

"O.K., just be careful. Call me as soon as possible." Her tone wavered.

"I will." He hung up the phone, braked the powerful Lincoln, and made a U-turn to return to the beach house.

Barry eased into the three-car garage, then closed the automatic doors. Between the garage and kitchen was a 10-by-14 foot workshop. A smooth counter lined one entire wall and a commercial circular saw was situated optimally in the center of the room. Hammers, pliers, screwdrivers, measuring tape, levels and other assorted tools hung from pegboard. A large, well-stocked tool chest lay open on the floor. Barry loaded the chest, a sledgehammer, a 'D-handle' shovel and a black crowbar into the bed of his truck. He walked to his bedroom and took a loaded Smith and Wesson .357 and box of 40 cartridges from the bottom drawer of his nightstand. He changed into his duck-hunting clothes and placed the pistol into a shoulder harness beneath his loose denim shirt. Seadrift lies at the southern end of the great American flyway and, save the Aransas National Wildlife Refuge 10 miles to the west, offers some of the finest hunting in the United States. For a fleeting moment, he craved going duck hunting.

Barry loaded his gear into the bed of the black GMC Sierra, activated the garage door simultaneously with starting the engine and backed out of the driveway. His major concern was how to rendezvous with Jud Weems without Travis seeing him. He considered simply not driving to the airstrip at all, but reasoned that if Jud eventually drove to Seadrift, he would have Travis in pursuit. Thoughts rambled in his mind. *Can't have the truck at the runway. Park it to the south of the inlet.* His call to Jud's cell phone went unanswered. Barry considered possible scenarios to explain his meeting with Jud Weems at the airstrip. An offer of fishing to a grieving husband; a day of duck hunting; or an opportunity to allow Jud Weems to have a respite from the stress of the accident - all would hold up in court. Yet, they could not stand beneath the weight of reality that Travis White would not be following Jud Weems if he didn't suspect that Jud was involved in the deaths of the D'Arcy family. Did Travis suspect Barry as well? How did Travis know of the meeting?

●

Five miles south of Port Lavaca the road splits. Route 238 turns west towards Seadrift and Route 316 continues south. The terminus of Route 316 runs into Indianola just beyond the Historical Marker for Angelina Bell Peyton Eberly. A Texan by way of Tennessee, she was noted for rescuing the original records of the Republic of Texas. She died in Indianola in 1860 but her actual burial site was lost in the storm of 1875. From the marker a small asphalt road winds for less than a mile to the southeast and the monument to Sieur de la Salle. Tall reeds and small cactus dotted the otherwise desolate landscape. Rabbits, lizards, scorpions and mosquitoes were the most plentiful inhabitants. From the monument one would have to back track around a small lagoon to the Indianola fishing village. The few homes, including Diana's Stained Glass shop, lie along South Ocean Street. With Matagorda Bay to the east, the road passes an area of concrete debris, John's Fishing Tackle, the small shrimp boat marina and a series of one-room derelict cottages. A private road with a "Keep Out, No Trespassing" sign seemed to signal the end of the road. The road splits at the sign; the road with the sign belongs to a private owner, the other, mostly covered with sawgrass, continues almost a mile and a half to the airstrip. Without prior knowledge, no one passing by would suspect the airstrip existed. The road curved left, tracing the eastern end of the runway and ending at the beginning of a once majestic docking terminal area. Years of storm debris sealed off the terminal from the rest of the world. The one remaining hangar separated the loading ramps from the runway.

Still concerned that he would be noticed, Travis carefully closed the distance from Jud Weems. Jud seemed to be in no hurry. At the split in the road Jud continued south towards Indianola. Travis followed, hoping that, if Jud noticed him at all, he would judge him to be a fisherman. Jud continued past John's Fishing Tackle and the "No Trespassing" sign. Travis needed to assess his options. He pulled into the parking area for John's Fishing Tackle. Travis stopped in the shop and rented the smallest fishing tackle available, bought a half-pound of dead shrimp and a new bottle of water. He exchanged a few pleasantries with the locals before moving on. While in the shop, Travis casually asked what was down the left fork.

"An old abandoned airstrip 'bout a mile down the road. Fishin's better up here, but there's a few good spots."

Travis replied, "Since I'm new, think I'll scout it out a bit." He gave the group a genuine smile and walked out into the warming sun.

He relaxed enough to pleasantly take in the quaint charm of this remote piece of the earth. Two little girls, perched on the edge of a small wooden pier, shrieked at the sight of the small croaker fighting for its life at the end of their hand-held line. Shrimp boats, weatherworn with time and hard work, lined the dock. Travis imagined noble histories for the Pat F., the Shirley C., and the Miss Melody. He returned to the car and placed the fishing equipment in the back seat. It was getting hotter. He eased himself into the front seat, turned the ignition and waited for the refreshing wave of air conditioning. Aware that he would not be able to drive much further down the road into which Jud had disappeared, Travis analyzed potential courses of action. He decided to take the rod, shrimp, water, his baseball cap, the camcorder and the binoculars. He faced a dilemma: should he leave the car at John's? Doing so would make it harder for him to be seen. But it also made an escape less likely. Driving the car partway down the road did provide for escape and might give the appearance of a fisherman simply hunting for an isolated fishing spot. He decided to drive. He placed his small hand recorder back under the driver's seat and secured it with Velcro straps sewn by Michelle. Travis slipped into drive and proceeded quietly past the Charlotte Ann and the "No Trespassing" sign.

●

Tom and Susie requested a late checkout from the Hyatt Hotel in San Antonio. His deposition concerning a multi-vehicle accident on I-10 near Luling rambled on from Thursday afternoon until noon on Friday. The lengthy deposition delayed their linking up with Nancy for a three-day weekend at her small cottage on the Guadalupe near New Braunfels.

Tom punched *99 to receive the playback of messages. Paige called Thursday afternoon to see if Susie and Tom would meet them at Fish Tales in Galveston on Sunday night. Two other late Thursday calls came from legal secretaries in hopes of setting up depositions concerning upcoming trials. The only messages on Friday morning were from Travis. Tom replayed the messages a second time, writing down the key bits of information.

"What the hell are you doing?" Tom spoke into the receiver.

"What'd he say Tom?" Susie asked in response to the serious look on Tom's face.

He hung up the phone. "Travis is following Weems down the coast. Said that Weems and Colter are meeting at some airstrip. Got two messages. The last one . . ." Tom said as he squinted his eyes to read his watch, ". . . couldn't have been more than half an hour ago. He added the possibility of the District Attorney, Harker, being there too."

Next to Tom's briefcase was the planner he carried sporadically. Although he had taken the time-management course associated with the commercial planner, Tom's transition from sticky-notes and extraneous pieces of paper was not complete. But he was trying. He picked up the planner and thumbed through the address list to 'W'. Tom knew Travis' home phone but not his car phone. His index finger went to the fifth listing and he began dialing 9 - 1 - 281 . . .

The computer-chip ring on Travis' car phone announced itself crisply, but not loudly. Travis was less than 25 feet away, but the light breeze carried what little sound had escaped from the sedan away from him. With each ring, Travis was one more giant step removed from Tom Seiler.

From thousands of miles beyond the Earth's surface it would be possible for a sophisticated EOS satellite to focus on the hangar and surrounding terrain. If directed at Indianola, it would identify the signature of three humans. Jud Weems exited the Ford truck. Travis White moved from a white Buick Park Avenue on a dirt road just south of Indianola. Barry Colter moved along an inlet one mile south of the runway. A later pass of the satellite would verify that the three tiny signatures were converging on the hangar at Indianola.

24

"Damn. He's not answering." Tom turned to Susie. "I just don't like this at all."

•

"Shit." Barry whispered breathlessly as he moved towards the hangar. His was the toughest route.

•

What the hell am I doing? Travis questioned himself with each step taken.

•

"That fucker better be here." Jud looked around but saw no trace of Barry Colter. He parked at the east end of the hangar and opened the padlocked door to the personnel entrance. He went inside, flipped the light switch – the lights didn't work - then surveyed the inside. The hangar smelled of rust, salt and mildew. Hot, humid air blanketed its interior. The once sliding aircraft entrance doors along the near side had been roughed up in the tornadic storm of 1980 and no longer worked. A wooden framework of storage bins rose to a height of 12 feet along the far side and both end walls of the hangar. Dirty windows, some with broken panes, all covered by corroded steel mesh, had been cut into the walls to allow some natural light to filter into the cavernous building. A lone room with four metallic chairs, two small windows, and a weathered wooden desk greeted Jud with indifference.

He tried the light switch with the same negative result. Irritating. A quick scan revealed no signs of human life. Mice scurried to shelter. Jud took out a cigarette, lit and inhaled it deeply, then turned and exited the hangar. Twelve o'clock, high noon.

●

Saltwater pulsed from every pore in Barry's body. He discarded his duck vest 10 minutes into his trek. The unrelenting sun and the soft muck giving way under his feet made the mile-long trek along the inlet excruciating. Barry didn't know where Travis might be, but he clearly knew that Travis was closing in on him. *Got to stay hidden. Got to get there first.* His thoughts returned to the heat and the parched recesses of his throat. It seemed an eternity from the time he first saw the tiny image until the hangar manifested itself as an oasis in the desert. He seethed at the circumstances of fate, sun and desolation that were working together to destroy him. Barry staggered to the hangar only to realize that he had left the padlock key at the beach house. He slumped against the corrugated metal siding, sensing only misery. He cursed God, his parents and his own stupidity for his present residence in the fires of hell. A waft of air from the east brought a touch of relief . . . and the gentle sound of an idling truck.

●

The Guadalupe is a small, winding river traversing a path from the Hill Country near Kerrville, in and out of Canyon Lake and gently to the Gulf through New Braunfels, Seguin, Gonzales, Cuero and Victoria. Along its banks are thick stands of mesquite and oak trees, providing idyllic opportunities to relish the natural beauty of Texas. During the spring, summer and fall, inner-tube rafters caravan down the river to the overture of mockingbirds calling from the trees. Hickory-smoked aromas invite all to feast on world-famous Texas barbecue. Chains of rafters are commonplace, floating effortlessly downriver to the French culvert at Gruene. Locals know to pronounce it "Green." The rafters hook themselves together by locking their feet around the torso and into the inside of the tube belonging to each preceding human link in the chain. Except for occasionally having to share the river with a water moccasin or two, life on the Guadalupe is gentle, lazy and very sweet.

The barbecue ribs at the Guadalupe Smoked Meat Company in Gruene should have overtaken Tom's thoughts. Often Susie and Tom wouldn't even get out of the car when they reached Nancy's river cottage. A quick "beeeeep, beep, beep, beep,

beep, . . . beeep, beeep" on the horn and the three were off. On Saturday nights they would sometimes return to Gruene Hall for a night of good Texas country dancing. Not much for the complicated line dancing, Tom always enjoyed his Miller Lite and the Texas two-step. Today was different.

A second call from the Austin Highway. No response. A third call at the turnoff to Nancy's. No response.

"Damn, where is he? I thought he'd have his cell phone on." Tom was clearly concerned.

So was Susie. "I don't like it either. I don't like it for you." Her voice reflected her fear for Travis and, knowing Tom, for her husband. "Tom, shouldn't we take this to the Houston police? We're losing control very fast."

One hundred yards from Nancy's, Tom veered left on the rutted dirt road bordering the river and stopped the car. He had to bring closure to their conversation.

"Not yet. And let's don't bring Nancy into this. She doesn't need the grief and it's still possible that other explanations exist." He was right on the first point and both knew he was wrong on the second.

"Tom, I need to know what you're really thinking about all of this. I found you by the grace of God. Before, I lived in crap, and now I have my own brass ring. I don't want to lose you. You do know I love you, don't you?" Susie's smile was betrayed by a slight quiver of her lower lip.

They looked at each other. They leaned to each other and kissed gently.

Tom spoke. "And you're my brass ring. It's a promise. No hidden thoughts or agendas. I'd go to the police in a heartbeat if I thought they'd respond on our behalf. But they won't. Right now I don't trust them." He visually recalled the night Donald was shot by a Houston cop. *One Bill Newton for every 10 shitheads.* "I'll keep calling until I get him. If we don't make contact by tonight then I'll call Michelle. I'm sure Travis knows what he's doing. Let's grab Nancy and head out to Gruene."

●

Once in the truck, Barry blurted out, "What've you got to drink? I'm dying." He relished the coolness of the air conditioning.

"Got some melted ice in th' cup. Here." Jud removed the paper and wax cup from its window holder and gave it to Barry.

Barry gulped down the water, then tapped the upside-down cup forcing it to relinquish the few remaining drops of precious liquid. Barry's thoughts turned to the unfolding events. "Get the truck over to the entrance, out of sight from the road. You've been followed by White the whole way." He was disgusted.

Surprise, then violation, grabbed Jud. "Who the hell is White?"

At that very moment Travis rounded a tight bend in the road and into view of the hangar in the distance.

Barry's lips tightened. "He's the goddamn defense lawyer on the trial and he sure as hell wouldn't be out here if he didn't think you were involved in the shit in Alvin." Barry Colter emphasized second person, singular, to absolve himself of murder. "He's out here somewhere, so move the truck."

Jud put the small truck in gear and tossed a small barb at Barry. "Sound's though you got a big fuckin' problem." A smirk.

"Just move the truck and let me think." Barry began to think of his options.

As Jud backed into a tight semi-circle, a reflective bundle of sunlight bounced off the windshield, traveled one-half a mile and passed through Travis' eyes into his brain. He quickly focused on a truck backing around the dilapidated hangar in the middle of nowhere. Two thoughts flowed in quick succession. *So there you are Mr. Weems* and *Why are you backing around the building?* Travis knelt on the sandy soil. A small king snake slithered deep into the reeds.

Cat and mouse.

●

"Brother Tom, where are you? The barbecue that bad?" Nancy considered Tom's withdrawn behavior as very unusual for her brother. He was finishing only his second beer, a real oddity considering the afternoon heat and thirst-birthing meal.

"Naw. Just thinking about the trial. I need to get in touch with Travis and he's not home. Not real important, but it's time sensitive." Tom rose from the table. "I'm gonna give him another call. Order me a beer, if you would."

Nancy waited until Tom was out of earshot distance, then turned to her sister-in-law. "O.K. Susie, what's up? You guys fighting today?"

"No, not at all. Tom's concerned about Travis. You know him and loyalty. Travis called early today and asked Tom to get back to him. As usual, it's Tom's fault if someone else doesn't answer the phone. Your brother may be outrageous in many ways, but he's also the nicest guy in the world."

Nancy smiled as she pushed her plate to the center of the table. "If you'll add hard headed as hell, then I'll agree with you." The reserved chuckles lessened the tension.

They ordered one more round of beer.

●

"Tom. What else did he say? What did he specifically say to you? Tom, you're my friend." Michelle trapped him and he knew it.

Tom regretted making the call. He should have known Michelle would answer. A sense of remorse fell over him. *Now, why in the hell did I do that? I've scared the hell out of her.* Michelle was already concerned and Tom's call had only heightened her sense of dread. He tried being nonchalant but they had been friends much too long and had shared too many times of both joy and despair. Michelle read Travis' note to Tom. Tom was not as forthcoming, other than Travis had called him twice. Michelle challenged him. He could not betray her.

"Travis is tracking the plaintiff guy down the coastline. Sort of pulling off another Faria video job." Travis' video had made it all the way to the 'Sixty Minutes' coverage of fraudulent lawsuits.

Tom continued. "Tell him to call me at Nancy's when he gets back. I'm sure he's fine. It's not the first time your wacko husband has gone goofy on us." His attempt at levity was a dismal failure.

As he hung up, his expression mirrored his mind. *Shit.*

●

Jud had not forgotten his keys. He padlocked the hangar door, returned to the truck and drove out the same way he came in. Travis hid behind a small mound of dirt and peered through the scrub brush as Weems drove by. For the first time since leaving Alvin he considered that following Jud might have been in vain. There was no sign of Barry Colter. Even if there had been a meeting, it had probably been quick and was over. He was thirsty and contemplated the time it would take to get back to his car. A quick look at what the hangar contained wouldn't take long and then he could return quickly along the dirt road. Still, he knew that caution was in order. Travis waited until only billowing dust could be seen from Jud's truck as it headed apparently back to Houston. He stood up and surveyed the area. No sign of life. He placed the PETRILLO baseball cap on his head and moved forward. The cool November morning turned scorching in the midday sun. Rather than take a straight-line advance to the hangar, Travis continued to walk along the road in the hopes that the tall reeds would keep him hidden. If Jud did return, Travis did not want to be caught in the muck and mire of the swampland. He half-strolled, half-crept towards the hangar. Eventually the road inclined up a small man-made slope to the concrete loading platform. The eastern side of the platform straddled the remains of a once-marvelous natural inlet. The depth of water lapping against the vertical concrete wall never exceeded 10 feet. Decades had passed since the inlet was last dredged. Weathered lumber, frayed pieces of rope, driftwood and sand blanketed the loading dock area, deposited haphazardly by the infrequent, but intense, storms of the Gulf of Mexico. In the next storm, all would be carried miles away, replaced by a new offering of sand and debris.

Travis scanned the landscape. Relieved by the quiet, he began walking normally, his muscles relaxing with each step. He walked to the east end of the hangar. Unaware that he had been under observation for 20 minutes, Travis swallowed the last of his water and tossed the bottle among litter waiting for the next blow. He rotated the baseball cap backwards on his head, cupped his hands around the side of his face, and peered into the cavernous building. Dirt, embedded into the panes of glass, obscured his view. An entire broken pane above his head offered better observation. Travis stepped back and turned around to survey the area. A pile of concrete block, most of it broken and partially covered by sand and weeds, lay but a hundred feet away. He found six usable blocks and fashioned stairs of three blocks, two blocks, and one block. This time he could see most of the interior of the building, illuminated by rays of light that struggled through the translucent glass. What he could not see, but might have heard, or even smelled, was a human being, prone on the shelf, nine feet above the floor. Their heads were less than 18 inches apart.

Barry lay motionless, flat on his stomach with his head turned towards the window. He opened his mouth, inhaling and exhaling in short rapid succession, in hopes that his breathing would not betray the silence. The loaded pistol rested in his right hand.

"What the hell's he got in here?" Travis spoke to himself quietly, yet easily understood by Barry Colter.

Travis stepped down from his precarious perch and proceeded around the hangar. The personnel entrance door was locked, the sliding aircraft doors wouldn't slide, and the steel mesh on the windows were still too strong to be taken down without significant effort. He completed a three-quarter lap around the hangar, stopping at the edge of the runway. He resigned himself to the fact that nothing he had seen could be construed as evidentiary matter. Yet, he maintained his steel-hot conviction that Barry Colter and Jud Weems had met in that hangar - and that the meeting was related to the events in Alvin. Travis had not anticipated coming up empty, but he was hot, tired, and thirsty. He began walking along the edge of the runway towards the dirt road and his car. He was thinking about water.

Except for a few seconds needed to climb down from the shelving and move to the window in the northeast corner of the hangar, Barry Colter watched every move Travis made. As Travis neared the far edge of the runway Barry felt the tension ebbing ever so slightly. The crisis seemed to be over.

"Keep going, asshole." Barry whispered the command.

As if in response to Barry's plea, Travis stopped and turned to the west. He hesitated for a few seconds, then drew binoculars to his eyes. The sight pierced right through Barry Colter. Travis White began walking along the length of the runway, in the opposite direction from the dirt access road.

25

Travis surveyed the horizon. The runway was in remarkably good shape. An occasional pilot still used it for practice touch-and-go landings. The only thing that seemed out of place was a scrap pile of steel tubing. Most of it was off to the side of the runway; a few pieces were lying haphazardly on the fringe. From the distance of several hundred feet they looked like pickup sticks. *Only those . . . his mind continued to process the image . . . aren't pickup sticks. Those are pieces of steel tubing.* He put the binoculars to his eyes and focused on the random scattering of steel.

Jud Weems arrived at Barry's truck. Barry had given Jud the keys while taking Jud's cell phone. His instructions were clear. Get to Barry's truck, grab his cell phone and wait for further guidance. Things were happening too fast. He didn't have to wait long before the phone rang.

"Yep."

"Listen carefully. The son-of-a-bitch has started walking to the steel. If you'd gotten rid of the goddamn stuff we wouldn't be here sucking wind." Barry didn't wait for a reply. "Stay there and wait for my next call. Once I see what he's up to, I'll call back. Don't leave that phone. Any questions?"

"Nope, 'cept I drove by his big fuckin' car half a mile from the runway." Jud didn't wait for a reply. He pushed the 'end' button. He kept the engine running in order to enjoy the cool relief from the air conditioner. In a slow two-syllable twang Jud articulated his perspective of the phone call. "Fuck you."

Travis walked along the rectangular sections of concrete. He noticed a black paint stripe converging from the far side towards the path that he was taking to the main pile of abandoned steel. He stopped at a point where a red stripe crossed orthogonal to the black. Looking generally to the southeast, he could see the black

211

paint finishing out its curve. To the west, it curved back until it was parallel to the runway axis for another 100 yards. Travis continued towards the steel by walking along the black stripe. From eye level the curving black line would have no meaning at all. To Travis White, its meaning was crystal clear. In his mind's eye, he was looking down Farm Road 1462.

"Damn, it's the same stuff." Travis spoke quietly to himself. Pieces of the puzzle were rapidly falling into place. Over 100 sections of four-inch steel tubing marked the center of a testing laboratory for vehicular homicide. He pulled the camcorder from his shirt and began to film.

Data unfolded as quickly as Travis could process it. Next to the pile Travis noticed several lengths of webbed tiedown straps. He knelt down over a small clump of assorted ruptured straps. He picked up a single piece and studied it closely. He read the partial name of the manufacturer. *K-I-N-E-D-Y-*. Strands of hair stood up from his arms to his back and danced to the music of fear and self-preservation. The strap in his hand appeared identical to the one Tom took from the salvage yard. He rolled the length of nylon into a tight coil and placed it inside his shirt. With one slow sweep of the horizon, Travis concluded his investigation. The camcorder took it all in. His only stop before reaching the dirt road was to once again stand at the point of intersection of red and black paint. He knew he was in danger.

Jud answered the phone.

"He's headed to the access road back towards Indianola. Get over here and pick me up. Bring everything that's in the back of my pickup. Everything." Barry did not want his truck involved in the unfolding events. "Use the trail off of Powderhorn but watch out for the soft sand." He had settled upon his plan. "On the way, find a spot where we can surprise him. We don't have time to screw around." Barry had a hard time swallowing. "And bring the bottled water in the front seat."

"It'll take 'bout five minutes." Jud knew they now had to deal with Travis. On the way out he scouted the desolate landscape. The absence of homes or other structures would afford them the advantage they needed over Travis. He selected two positions in which he and Barry could be hidden from view but also within a few feet of the car.

Jud looked over to the bottle purloined half an hour earlier. "Screw you, asshole." He savored the taste and didn't care that less than a quarter of the bottle remained.

Liz Harker's phone call forced Barry into cold fear. But fear alone could not diminish his thinking process. Travis White had not physically seen Barry Colter. He had seen Jud Weems. Still, it was obvious to Travis that Jud must have come to Indianola to meet someone. It was an odds-on bet that Travis knew the someone was Barry Colter. The urge to deny the obvious screamed inside Barry's head. Travis followed Jud. He walked the runway directly to the steel tubing. *Goddammit, why didn't they get it the hell out of there?*

Travis stopped at the painted facsimile of the intersection at which murder had been carried out. He inspected the frayed tiedown straps. The confluence of Barry's multiple thoughts gave birth to Barry's two final decisions. He had to kill Travis, or have Jud kill him. Eventually he would kill Jud.

Twelve minutes, not five. The truck eased comfortably through the brush and onto the concrete. Barry pushed the aircraft entrance door strongly outward, making enough space to squeeze through. Barry jumped into the truck and grabbed the bottle of water. Empty save a small swallow. He looked at Jud with contempt.

"Did you have to drink the whole damn bottle?" He emptied the remaining drops of water. Still, swallowing did not come easy. "Let's go. Can we beat him back to his car?"

Jud smiled faintly as he accelerated back to the southeast. Their circuitous route back to the vicinity of Travis' car still delivered them in time to hide the truck and walk to their concealed positions well in advance of Travis.

The cool morning was history. The afternoon sun penetrated Travis' shirt and seared his back. Once-vivid thoughts blurred in the relentless heat. He fumbled slightly as he tried to insert the key into the door lock. In his focused concentration to unlock the door, Travis only became aware of movement as the shadow of the shovel crossed his eyes, followed instantaneously by a crushing blow to the left side of his face. His head jerked back and to the right under the force of the blow, then bobbed to the left as he dropped to the ground. Blood flowed from a wide laceration tracing the outline of a fractured skull.

"No! Put the shovel down. Put it down." Barry screamed at Jud, his intercession saving Travis from certain death.

Jud hesitated, wildness reflecting in his eyes and face. He turned defiantly towards Barry. For a split second both understood Jud's urge to turn the shovel on Barry. He thrust the spade into the ground, where it stood, almost vertical, six inches from Travis' head.

The shock absorbers were no match for the incessant sand moguls. Travis' first conscious thoughts focused on the ache radiating in seismic waves from an epicenter somewhere deep in his brain. He was too weak, and in too much pain, to move from his fetal position in the blackness of his own trunk. As the scrambled cells of his brain began to reorganize themselves into a functioning neural network, the sense of his danger overtook Travis. He needed to think clearly, yet his body only wanted to sleep. His first clear thought was that since he hadn't been killed outright, there was an opportunity for freedom. Travis reasoned his escape had to be an outcome of his mental strength. Physically, he was badly injured. At least he could move his arms. Each small depression in the road amplified the cluster migraines in Travis' head.

●

With Travis shoehorned in the trunk, Barry and Jud drove to the hangar. Barry unlocked the padlock with Jud's key and entered the building.

"Get the fuck out of the car or I'll crush your goddamn skull." Jud, pistol in one hand and crowbar in the other, didn't bite on Travis' feinting unconsciousness.

Travis, dazed and weak, struggled over the lip of the trunk, fell once, then rested on one knee to gather strength.

"Get up asshole. Through the door." Barry Colter stood unseen behind an interior wall next to the office. Travis had not seen Barry Colter that day. Barry still had hope that there was some way out of this despicable caldron of trouble. Killing an insignificant family of four was not any more difficult than shooting jackrabbits. There were other consequences in killing a respected Houston attorney. While Travis lay unconscious on the road, Barry told Jud what questions to ask.

"Nobody follows me. I got ev'ry right to blow your ass away. What the fuck you doin' trailin' me?"

Three of the tiedown straps were used to tie Travis to the chair, one around his chest and seatback, one making multiple wraps tying his wrists behind his back, and the third tying his ankles to the bottom legs of the chair. While in the trunk, Travis, among other things, had anticipated the question.

"I . . . I've done this several times before. I've videotaped people to see if . . .", Travis struggled to clear his head of the throbbing pain, ". . . to see if I can gather evidence to help my case. I never found shit following you." Travis tried to take the offensive. "So, why are you so pissed at me?"

Jud shot back. "For two reasons, asshole. I don't like nobody following me and also because you're a lying sack of shit." He left the room.

Jud returned in less than a minute, carrying the camcorder. "I saw your fuckin' movie. You talk too much. Well, guess what asshole, ain't nobody gonna see your ugly face again."

Think fast, think clear. "Jud, before you go and do something stupid, let me tell you what else I know." Travis, ever so slightly, began working his wrists back and forth. "You might think differently about who you think are your enemies and who you think are your friends."

Jud wanted to know how much of his participation in the Alvin killings was known by other people. And he wanted to know who the other people were. So did Barry Colter.

"Start talkin'."

Travis' thoughts flickered back and forth from responding to Jud to figuring how to free his wrists. "At first I concentrated my defense case solely on the pure physical evidence such as speed, time of night and things of that sort. As you know, the trial hasn't been looking good for my side." Travis sensed a slight lessening of Jud's hostility. He continued. "Then, strictly by coincidence, I saw you on television. I remembered you from an earlier trial. I didn't like you because you were lying." *And I sure as hell don't like you now.* "So I spent almost the whole night a couple of days back checking over cases until I found one in September of '93 in which you won a few thousand bucks. For no other reason than that, I . . . " Travis paused just long enough to make a decision.

Travis preferred to use ignorance as the method to freedom. But Jud brought the camcorder with him. Travis knew Jud was not stupid. His fingers picked up their effort at the nylon webbing. Time was his only ally - time to gain strength and time to loosen the straps. Surprise would be his only weapon.

"I . . . well let me back up a minute to give you the full story. Then I'm sure you'll make your own decisions." Without moving his body, Travis worked deliberately at the straps. By slowly rotating his wrists back and forth, he began to effect his goal - the straps started to loosen.

"On Thursday I returned from the morning recess before your attorney did and noticed some writing on his legal pad."

Barry listened intently from next to the door and, as he did, the words on the pad imprinted themselves in his mind. *Goddammit.*

"Two of the words were 'Weems' and 'Friday' so I knew you were going to meet Colter today. That's why I followed you."

Almost miraculously, Travis hooked his right little finger on the leading end of the strap where it could be pulled from the knot of which it was part. He still needed more time. Travis shifted in the chair in an apparent motion to ease the agony of the straps cutting into his wrists and ankles. The knot was loose but Travis still had to unwrap the binding without exposing it to Jud. He wouldn't be able to untie his ankles or chest but, if he could get close enough to Jud, his size and survival instinct would more than compensate for the minor disadvantage of still being bound to a chair.

Jud was getting agitated again. Just a few seconds more.

"Jud, have you considered your long range situation?" Holding the loose wadding of nylon in his left hand, he was able to pull his right wrist free. He only needed to remove his left wrist.

"Like what asshole?" The decision to kill Travis had been made, but Jud still wanted all the information he could get before carrying through with one more murder.

"Like what your chances are of living more than a couple of weeks past the trial." It was time to play the trump card. "You know it and I know it. Just like Colter had you and the driver kill your whole family, he'll have someone kill you. Another unfortunate accident, but your ass will end up dead as a doornail. As for me, I say good riddance to a no-good son-of-a-bitch. The only bad news is that Colter goes free. And you know what, he'll do it in a way that will leave him with all of your money."

Jud turned to make a statement to the door. As soon as his focus left Travis, the prisoner became the aggressor. Travis, still tied to the chair at the chest and feet, thrust his arms and body forward, simultaneously springing his feet at hinged ankles. He caught Jud from the side. An All-Southwest Conference defensive tackle at Baylor in the late-'60s, Travis enveloped Jud's body like a python. He slammed Jud's hand onto the concrete floor. A single shot rang out as a bullet ricocheted off the floor and through the exterior wall of the building.

Jud screamed as Travis pried his finger backward against the trigger guard, snapping it like a Popsicle stick. Travis was fueled with rage. His full concentration was centered on destroying the despicable animal under him.

'Thwump!' The sound was that of breaking open a cantaloupe with a baseball bat. The full force of the crowbar split the back of Travis' head, crushing the skull and driving splintered bone into the webbed-shaped cuneus of his brain. The first blow was fatal. A second blow fell swiftly from Barry Colter's raging arms. Then a third . . . and a fourth.

26

The call came at 5:00 in the morning.

Its stinging ring, a harbinger of events to come, woke Tom from unsettled sleep. Shaking away his confusion, he sat up, fully sensing the coming conversation. Susie breathed heavily beside him. The only phone in Nancy's cottage was in the small living room. Tom threw off his half of the sheet, leaving Susie warm and unaware. His urgency did not allow him time to put on his clothes. Bent over at the waist so he could find his way along the bed, Tom edged his way to the bedroom door and down the hallway to the living room. He clipped his small toe on the rattan couch, evoking a muffled "shit" before finally reaching the phone.

"Hello. This is Tom Seiler."

"Tom. Oh, Tom, he's dead. Travis is dead."

For reasons he would never fully understand, Tom was prepared for the news. He would find out later that he was the first phone call on Michelle White's list. Over the years Tom and Travis had become as brothers. In many ways, Travis was likened to Tom's brother Jack. Like Jack, Travis could make friends with a lamppost. Crowds swarmed around this congenial, gregarious, man like drones around a queen bee.

●

Tom and Susie dropped Nancy off at her home in Windcrest on the northeast side of San Antonio. Once nothing more than brush country, Windcrest was now a modest city with its own government. Many such municipalities had been deposited by the city as it expanded in all directions. With Hemisfair and less-stringent liquor laws, San Antonio flourished in the '70s and '80s. Major hotel

217

chains joined the St. Anthony and Gunter to change the San Antonio skyline, almost swallowing the Alamo in the process. The restaurants, bars and shops along the Riverwalk transformed the tiny San Antonio River into a setting of charm and romance. Those who were overwhelmed at the Alamo in 1836 would not believe all that transpired over time to that sacred ground.

They turned in the car at Enterprise and were dropped off at the airport by a good natured, but unappreciated, driver. Susie attempted to respond civilly to the insipid questions about whether it was their first trip to San Antonio and the prospects for the Spurs basketball team. Tom was lost in thought concerning the past 24 hours and what actions he needed to take in the next few weeks. Tom didn't give a shit about an early report that Travis fell asleep at the wheel. No one was going to screw over Travis White without facing judgment. He rotated his head vertically back until it rested on top of the rear seat, closed his eyes, and thought of the immediate future. Tom's boiling point had come to pass.

As the Stinson lifted off into the early morning sun, Tom decided on his next move.

"Hon, take over the controls, I need to do some planning."

●

The tinny ring bounced off the cubicle walls like BBs on a metal roof. *Even on a Saturday.* Bill Newton lamented the life of a cop. He put his coffee cup down and picked up the receiver.

"Bill Newton."

"Hey Bill, it's Tom Seiler. You got a couple of minutes?"

"Sure, Tom. What's up?"

"Travis White was killed yesterday or early this morning."

A short pause. "Oh, no." Bill sincerely hurt for his friend. "I'm sorry Tom, he's a great guy and I know you're friends. I'm really sorry."

"Thanks Bill, I appreciate it." A quick visualization of his best friend appeared. "To get straight to the point, I need to meet with you on some concerns I have about the Alvin accident, and about Travis."

Bill sensed the tone. "Fire away, Tom. I'll help where I can."

"It's complicated and I'd rather talk about it in person. Someplace else."

Bill switched hands on the phone, then grabbed a pencil and notepad. "Name the place."

Tom answered, "I'm on my way over to see Travis' wife, then on to Alvin. How about meeting in the bar at the Clear Lake Hilton?"

"OK. I have to wrap a few things up. I can make it around 5:30."

"Great. See you there."

●

Well-wishers had already arrived, trying to do the right thing, whatever the right thing may have been. None were upset when Michelle told them she needed a few minutes with Tom and Susie in the kitchen.

"I can handle it Tom. Just tell me what to do." Though tears clung to her cheeks, Michelle stopped crying and looked straight into Tom's eyes. She sensed Travis telling her to listen to Tom. *Listen to every word.*

"Demand a complete autopsy. Have them concentrate on the exact nature of the wounds to his head." Tom surveyed the notes he made in the Stinson.

He continued. "But don't let anyone, not the press, the police, or friends, know that you think anything different than it was a horrible accident. I'm heading down to Markham to go over the car. I've got a friend in the Houston Police Department who might help us out. I have no doubt about there being some form of evidence."

Sitting across the kitchen table from Tom, Michelle lifted the glass to her lips. The iced tea was tasteless. Nothing had taste to Michelle. She wondered about the secretive nature of Tom's instructions. "Why don't you want the police to know what your theories are? Can't they conduct the investigation?" She sensed Travis' presence again. *Listen to every word.* "But, I'm with you Tom, no matter what." Her lower lip quivered ever so slightly. "Please . . . please be careful. I can't handle anything happening to you. I'll . . . ." Michelle began to cry out loud. She cupped her face in her hands and slumped forward, elbows on the table.

Tom moved to her and placed his hands on her shoulders. He never felt more awkward in his life. He owed her more information.

Michelle sat up straight and wiped her face clean. Tom squeezed her shoulders and returned to his seat before speaking.

Tom made a decision. "Michelle, from this point on you will know everything I know. I am sure that more people are involved in this than just Jud Weems. I don't know who, but this whole thing has exploded." Adding fear to the gathering, he said, "and I can't eliminate people in law enforcement. I'm afraid that if someone with influence is involved, then I don't want him . . . or her . . . or them to know that it's not the perfect crime. If whoever it is gets wind of our knowledge, then whatever evidence is out there will be destroyed." He swallowed his tea. "And, yes, we do have to be careful. You play dumb, I'll play dumb." He lifted her hands slightly into the air. "But I promise you this and I promise Travis . . . someone will pay in full." He squeezed and then gently let go of her hands.

Michelle looked in his eyes. "Tom, you're Travis' best friend. He would not want you hurt."

Tom ignored the statement. He took a single step back. "I've got some things I have to do this afternoon. I'm going to get some help on all this. I'll be back late tonight."

Susie spoke to Michelle, "If, and only if, you'd like company, I'll be glad to stay and help with visitors and anything else you need."

Michelle, wiping her eyes with her forearm, answered, "I'd like that. I want you both to stay the night."

●

The afternoon sun began its drop towards the horizon. Tom sat on the trunk watching children laughing and yelling as they played innocently at the Alvin elementary school playground. He reflected on the irony of having to move from idyllic children's games to solving the death of Travis White. The intersection, where it all started for Travis and Tom, had pulled him back with unrelenting force. There was no more evidence to be gathered there, it was just the center of a maelstrom of human events and human failings. He thought, *What really happened to Travis? And what is my place in this? What kind of person is even capable of murder?* He raged with vengeance. The children played happily. He mentally tasted the pure pleasure of a struggle in which he brutally beat Jud Weems to death. There was a contradiction – the satisfaction of killing a murderer with his bare hands bounced off his realization that the vengeance he sought was not about Travis, it was about Tom.

Tom sat quietly for 15 minutes, drifting in and out of his own struggle. The intersection did not want to let him go. He mentally tried to force time backward. Finally, more confused than when he arrived, Tom called Susie.

Susie answered the phone. "White residence. This is Susie Seiler."

Tom was glad that Susie answered and Susie was glad that it was Tom calling.

"It's me, hon. I'm at Parker Road and 1462. Checked out the curve one more time." Tom leaned against the car. "I'll take a few more pictures then head to the Hilton to talk with Bill. I can stop by and pick you up."

"Did you find anything new?"

"Not really. I walked out into the fields to see what might turn up. Nothing. The curve isn't that bad." He paused.

The sun, hanging lower in the late afternoon sky, provided a spectacular backdrop to an oncoming beautiful evening. Farm Road 1462 stretched to the horizon. It was the kind of day couples should be together. Tears came from nowhere.

Tom collected himself and continued. "Anyway, I'm about done. I can pick you up in 45 minutes. You may have some insights for both of us."

"I'd love to," Susie smiled into the phone, then turned serious, "but you need to talk to Bill alone and Michelle does want me to stay with her. Maybe you can pick something up at Fudrucker's on your way back."

"Sounds good. I'll call when I leave the Hilton. Love you."

"Love you."

Tom placed his cell phone in his shirt pocket, turned and opened the car door. He surveyed the few houses surrounding the Alvin Elementary School, thinking of small-town America. He thought of the children. He thought of their parents. *These are good people. Small towns have good people.*

⬣

Bill walked into the Hilton shortly after 6:00. The large, modern, Hilton bar was smothered behind a surging mass of humanity. The dominantly young crowd lounged in large, soft chairs around small cocktail tables. Very few barstools remained empty. Smoke rose in ribbons from every table. Tom sat talking to the bartender at the far end of the bar. The seat next to Tom was occupied. Bill lumbered over.

"Hey Tom, sorry I'm late. Traffic beat me up."

Tom, Miller Lite in his left hand, turned around and extended his right. "My screw up. Forgot about the time and traffic around here." A sheepish smile crossed his face. "I drank your beer. Next one's on me." He turned to the bartender, "Two more Gabe, when you get a chance. And a bowl of peanuts."

The lanky young man behind the bar answered over the din of the crowd. "Beer and nuts. Got it, you're next."

Tom surveyed the situation. *Too crowded.*

"I sure picked a helluva place and a helluva night. Let's take a walk."

Bill replied, "You lead the way." He wasn't big on the smoke either.

Tom called out, "Gabe, we'll be back. Keep the tab going."

"No sweat, Tom. See ya." Gabe stepped back and was enveloped by the thirsty, demanding throng.

Tom offered Bill the peanut bowl. A huge hand grabbed almost half a bowl of peanuts. Tom took what he could of the rest. They walked out of the lounge and through the main lobby. A natural inclination for nature directed them towards the east and the small, beautiful sight of Clear Lake.

"Isn't this where some woman ran over her husband about a hundred times with the family Mercedes?" Bill looked back over his shoulder at the façade of the Hilton.

"That's what they say." Tom chewed a couple of peanuts, took a swallow, and began. "Bill, I'm convinced that the deaths in Alvin were murder . . . and I'm just as certain that Travis was murdered as well. I need you to help me on the quiet."

Bill stopped and turned towards Tom. "Wow. I knew something was up, but this . . ." He frowned, shook his head, then spoke again. "Before you go any further, I have to tell you that, as a police officer, I have an oath keeping me from hiding evidence. You need to be careful what you say to me." They started walking again.

Bill's comment did not surprise Tom. He expected it.

From east to west, Clear Lake is shaped somewhat like a boomerang, with the bend pointing to the north. A few small sailboats were taking in the last vestiges of wind and warmth.

"Bill, let me tell you some things that come from my gut. No convicting evidence yet. Just the reasons why I have come to you." Finishing the beer, Tom wished he had ordered two for himself. "Hang with me." They passed a trash container into which Tom placed his empty bottle.

"OK, I'm willing to listen." Bill wiped the top of his half-full bottle of beer and offered it to Tom. "I'll just throw it out."

Tom took the bottle, then spoke to the string of physical evidence of which Bill was already aware. They walked a good distance along the edge of the lake.

Tom delicately maneuvered his case to enlist Bill Newton. "Bill, I can go into the courtroom and spout all of this out. If I tell the jury what I have told you, they'll eat my lunch, Flagg Brothers goes down the tubes and no one pays for murder. That, in itself, would be stupid on my part. I have a good idea who might be involved. I have some circumstantial evidence and I think I know where I can get conclusive evidence. The only problem is that I need your help."

"Why me. Why not see someone in HPD and do it properly?"

This time Tom stopped. Another swallow. "Because you have ethics. You want the best for others. You give a shit about the world we live in. I believe that a specific person in your organization has a direct role in all of this. If that person, and others outside of HPD, learn what's going on at this point, everything will fall apart." He took a deep breath and a final, deep swallow. "To me, there is vengeance and reprisal, but there's another part to it. It's about humanity, about people using others. It's about not only getting away with murder, but profiting from it as well. It has to be stopped. I am willing to put my life on the line, and I have to ask you to trust me and, basically, risk yourself."

"Let me think."

Bill started walking back towards the Hilton. Tom joined him, neither man speaking. Seagulls, facing into the failing breeze, sat atop small, concrete pilings, carefully watching the two men. Tom tossed the last bottle into the trash bin.

Just outside the Hilton, Bill stopped again.

"Tom, who is it?"

Expecting the question, Tom answered, "Barry Colter and, to some degree, your district attorney, Harker."

Bill showed no emotion. He lifted his cell phone from his belt and punched a few numbers.

"It's me. Something urgent has just come up. I'll be home by nine."

Tom said, "My place is one minute from here. I can tell you everything I know."

Gabe had to wait a week to close the tab.

●

Michelle spoke to the coroner earlier that afternoon and secured his promise that she could speak directly to the pathologist before and after the autopsy. Her participation in moving towards retribution for Travis' death assuaged the biting remorse ever so slightly. A sliver of defiance, born hours after her husband died, wedged its way between despair and anger.

It was early morning before sleep took control. Michelle paced robotically through the house, being quiet not to awaken Tom and Susie. Disbelief overwhelmed her. Dark, massive waves of grief crushed against her. Finally, her body had suffered enough. She sat down on the edge of the bed, then took a picture from her nightstand. A friend had taken it moments after he won a Teddy Bear for her at a carnival.

●

"O.K. Michelle, here we go." Travis rubbed his hands together, proudly accepting the challenge. The carnival lights, the music from the carousel and the laughter booming from smiling faces provided a festive backdrop for the young couple. This big, gentle bear had captured her. With stick and string, Travis looped the wooden ring around the end of the reclining Coke bottle and gently began lifting. She was breathless. She held her hand over her mouth to keep from interrupting his quest for the prize. A simple carnival game was so important to her. Her mind conjured up a monumental thought. He loves me. He loves me. He loves me. He . . .

"Up." The taught string responded to Travis' command. The bottle inched towards the vertical. "Whew." A slight quiver almost created disaster. A touch more. Almost there. "Come on pal." Travis whispered. He coaxed the string and bottle one last time. The bottled rotated, loosening the grip of the string. It rocked straight up and then past the vertical. Both hearts stopped as they gazed at the rocking dance of a simple, yet so important, Coke bottle. The bottle, ever so slowly, ended its tormenting dance.

He may as well have slain a dragon. That was the moment she knew she had fallen in love with Travis White. They were perfect for each other. Travis, the soon-to-be lawyer, won a teddy bear. Michelle, the nursing student, won a husband.

●

The salvage yard in Markham was open on Sunday. Gaining access to the car was a simple matter.

"Just need to close the books on this one. It's pretty standard." Bill Newton flashed his badge to identify his purpose. "By the way, did they tell you not to dispose of the car until we give you a release? The city of Houston will pay the storage fee." Bill Newton's natural friendliness did not fit the stereotype of a police investigator.

The Park Avenue rested next to the front chain link fence. Given the degree of damage, the car did not appear an instrument of a fatality. The autopsy report was not finished, but Tom's suspicions were rock solid. Travis' head wounds had nothing to do with the damage to the front end of the car.

Tom took the lead. "Bill, I know you're expert at this, but I'd like to ask you to do a bumper-to-bumper while I check out the inside. Then we can switch. I don't want to compare notes until we've each looked at it separately." Tom handed Bill a pair of rubber gloves. "Just in case we run across some interesting finger prints. I don't think we want to mix them with ours."

"No problem Tom. It's your show. Just let me know what you need." Bill walked to the front of the Buick, took out a pad of paper and pencil, and began his inspection.

The two men scoured every possible inch of the car separately. Tom began with the driver's compartment. Tom's first move was instinctive. He reached beneath the driver's seat, then let out a deep breath. The small recorder, a potential treasure of information, was securely fastened with the Velcro straps. Whispering, "Thank God," he placed it in his pants pocket and continued the search.

The full investigation took an hour and a half. Despite a gentle breeze, both men were covered with sweat. Crawling under the car, leaning into the engine compartment, searching under the seats and combing every inch of the trunk made it a very physical exercise. Photos were taken inside and out. Once finished, they began comparing notes. Bill Newton noted that the damage to the front end, though significant, was not consistent with a high-speed collision. He also noted that the trip odometer read 2 – 0 – 7. Two hundred and seven miles. The mileage information may or may not have been significant. Though he was not aware of the autopsy report, Bill also noted that the front windshield was still intact – a more violent impact would usually be required to cause fatal head injuries. He finished with an analysis of the matting in the trunk.

"The matting has certainly been roughed up and this," he pointed to a dark irregular stain near the wheel well, "could be blood." Bill wiped his forehead. "That's about it Tom. How do I track with you?"

"Dead on . . . if you'll excuse the unintended pun. I'd just add two things. First, none of the tires blew out. I haven't seen many high speed car-to-concrete impacts where all the tires went undamaged." Tom then started towards the trunk. "And your comment on the matting is critical. Look at this."

Lifting the trunk, Tom pointed to the wiring going to the taillights. They had been pulled loose.

"I remember a woman locked in a trunk who yanked out the wiring. Sure enough, the cops stopped the car and one rape and murder case was averted. I think Travis did the same thing."

"Tom, we've got some problems. Tying everything else you have related to this tells me that we do have a murder. At this point, Weems is the logical suspect. It's a far stretch to tie Colter to this. Much further for the District Attorney." Bill wiped his brow and continued. "Assuming they are involved, I'll guarantee you that this car will be gone in less than 48 hours. We need to get good fingerprints and a DNA sample of the stain. That might mean bringing someone else into this. What do you say?"

Tom reacted cautiously. "I'm not so sure they will take the car. If it disappears, suspicions about murder will erupt. Colter understands risk, and right now he's faced with a big decision. I hope he chokes on it. Still, he might take it and lie his way out." Tom thought for a minute, then spoke. "Bill, I asked you in because you're honest and you're good. I trust your judgment. If you bring someone in, make sure he's locked-lipped. Who do you have in mind?"

"Unfortunately, no one for now. Let me work on it. I'll also start checking out the relationship between Colter and Harker."

"It's a deal."

Bill looked aimlessly around the metal landscape, seeing nothing. "I guess we're done for now."

"Except for one thing." Tom reached into his pocket.

●

"For I am convinced that neither death nor life, neither angels nor demons, neither the present nor the future, nor any powers, neither height nor depth, nor anything else in all creation, will be able to separate us from the love of God that is in Christ Jesus our Lord." The words of Romans resonated from the Reverend John Kelly's deep baritone voice.

Tom squirmed in his seat, the message failing to take root. Try as he might, Tom could not free himself from bitterness. Tom, Jr., and Jack walked into his mind. *And now, Travis. Love of God? Then why this? It's all random chemistry. That's all we are. Nothing more, nothing less. But, for whatever it means, some son-of-a-bitch will pay full price.*

The good reverend spoke eloquently about a young boy who, in his acceptance of Jesus Christ, grasped the concept of unconditional love in a manner that should have been the model for all non-perfect Christians. He told stories of a high school athlete whom, win or lose, was sincere in his congratulations to every player he had lined up against. Then Reverend Kelly recaptured the moment of Travis' decision to become a lawyer.

His voice booming, Reverend John Kelly narrated the fork in Travis' life. "Travis looked me straight in the eye and told me the path he was to travel, 'Reverend Kelly. I thought and prayed about it a lot. I know that the Lord thinks I'll save more lives by being a Christian lawyer than by being a minister. It's just the way I have to go.' And he carried out what his heart told him to do. He wasn't just a good lawyer. Travis understood the need to never lose sight of the human component of the Justice System. Travis White was a great lawyer."

Travis was a great lawyer. The words sunk deeply into Tom's core. Travis was a great lawyer. *Better than that, he was a great friend.* Tom faded out again, shifting uncomfortably in his wooden seat. He pictured the two of them drinking beer after coaching the kid's baseball games. He remembered the political debates and discussions on morality and God. Save some salty language and a total lack of guilt about drinking beer, Travis struck Tom as, if you're going to be one, what a real Christian should be. And the laugh, the irrepressible laugh. Several trials passed through his mind; they sure won more than they lost. Good days. Gone. *Why?*

The reverend then spoke directly to Michelle White. His words could not heal her, but his tenderness and reassurance of Travis' station in the eyes of God did serve as another step in the healing process.

"In this moment, Travis is reaching out to you. He's not asking you not to cry. It is your right, just as it is your right to be angry. But Travis would not want his life measured in the despair of those who have loved him. Rather, he wants your tears to change as the seasons . . ."

Michelle tried to focus on the words. Images of Travis overpowered what was said. She wanted to run away, but forced her way to the end.

". . . comes the promise of a day to come when your memories will be filled with the stories, some large and some small, that have bound you together forever."

●

Ed Harvey took over the defense following Travis' death. He asked for and received a two-week delay in the trial despite the objections of the plaintiff's attorney. Tom and Ed met on Tuesday, Wednesday and Friday of the second week in November. At the first meeting Ed went over the details of Tom's upcoming expert witness testimony. Save a five-minute discussion at the start of their meeting, there was no time to dwell on Travis' death. It was a straightforward rehash of the physical sequence of events - speed, location, time, visibility, and on and on. Ed would be able to cover the same ground that Travis presented earlier, though not with the same eloquence. Throughout the second meeting they developed a strategy of sequencing and wording the interaction between them. Each played the devil's advocate for the cross-examination that they knew would be hard-hitting. They concluded the meetings with a full-blown rehearsal.

"My bent on it is that they'll say you're simply using the shotgun approach, throwing out a slew of numbers hoping something will snag on the jurors. He'll want to make you a junk scientist." Ed rolled down his sleeves, then continued, "What's your response going to be when he calls you an incompetent, money-grubbing ambulance chaser?"

Tom looked down at the yellow pages before his eyes. He thought for a moment, then answered, "How about if I call him an asshole and punch his fucking lights out?"

Ed laughed heartily at Tom's sarcasm. Tom didn't laugh at all. Tom's emotions cried out to him to do exactly as he had said. He was convinced that Mr. Barry Colter, Esquire, Attorney at Law, and all that other shit, murdered his best friend.

"That's a great note to end on." Ed felt much better about his chances to compete against Barry Colter.

"Yeah," Tom paused, then added, "Colter is such a joke."

●

Tom met with Susie, Steve, Paige and Ross the night following the funeral. Light from the fake Tiffany lamp surrounded the conclave.

Susie was terrified. In the years they had known each other, she had grown to love a man who placed loyalty at the top of his list of human values. His oft-quoted prose of Robert Service, 'A promise made is a debt unpaid', echoed in her head. If Tom said he was going to demand payback for Travis' life, then he would either recoup full payment or die in the process.

"I've tried to keep everyone out of it, but at every step I just get deeper and deeper into murder. It's unbelievable. I really don't think I'm in any danger at all, but I do have to be careful. Travis White died because of information I gave him. I can't go to the police right now because it's possible that some involvement may concern the District Attorney's office. I do have someone inside HPD working with me. He gets found out and he's gone."

Steve listened intently, his mind sharpening. "Dad, what specifics can you share with us?"

Tom stared down at several legal sized envelopes. He addressed the group. "I've made copies of everything I have to this point. Take one and safeguard it." He gave an envelope to each, then continued. "I'll explain the contents, so don't open them now."

Paige felt weak. She had a slight tingling sensation just above her knees. She was nauseous, fighting against fear.

"Daddy, I'm scared. You've got to turn this over to someone – the police, the media. You're in . . ."

Tom cut her off quickly. "Paige, listen to me. The police department is the last place I need to go right now. Don't worry. I'm working on a way to bring this to an end. In the meantime, you have got to keep this to yourself. Do you understand?"

Paige struggled to keep her composure. Tears beaded in her eyes. "I, . . . I do. This is so terrible."

"I agree. For now, put the packets away so I can give you everything I have firsthand."

Tom, once again using meticulous notes and Travis' testimony on the voice recorder, told a story of circumstantial evidence pointing loosely, but with gathering strength, at the plaintiff, his attorney, a deceased truck driver and, just possibly, the District Attorney for the city of Houston. He finished with the playing of Travis' voice recorder.

No one wanted to leave the house that night, wanting to protect Tom and Susie. Shortly before midnight Tom finally urged them home. They needed the sleep and he had to finish an overdue task. While Susie, also sleepless, took refuge in the shower, Tom went to the executive suite. He rested his head in his left hand, pen in his right. Graph paper lay before him on top of a Texas highway map. He solved a simple math problem.

The entry read:

> Odometer: 207 miles.
> Crash site: Concrete abutment, overpass, routes 1468 and 35,
> vicinity Markham, Texas – 2 November

Had Travis not been killed he would have continued driving the 82 miles from the crash site back to Clear Lake. Adding the untraveled miles to the odometer indicated a round trip of 289 miles. Division by two leaves a one-way trip of about 145 miles. Tom then calculated the 126-mile distance between Clear Lake and Port Lavaca, Travis' last known location, and subtracted it from the one-way distance. A result of 19 miles. Travis White was killed somewhere within a circle having a radius no further from the center of Port Lavaca than 19 miles. The math corroborated the voice recorder. Using a 1:250,000 JOG sheet Tom drew a circle with a 19-mile radius. He then drew a second circle extending a new radius outward another three miles to account for possible accuracy problems. He looked intensely at the southeastern quadrant of the circle. The hodge-podge of Texas towns stared up from the map.

That's where it all played out. Travis, if it takes me forever I'm going to find out what happened - and where. It's time to pay. You can bet on it amigo.

Tom had his first good night's sleep since Travis' death.

●

What Elizabeth Harker failed to realize was that her attempt to hide from Jud and Travis at the Dairy Queen in Port Lavaca failed. Her rapid turning and over-accelerating caused Travis to look up at the last moment. His glimpse was fleeting, but it was unmistakable. The event was captured on his voice recorder.

27

The morning broke clear and cool. Susie followed the scent of bacon into the kitchen. A smile broke across her face at the sight of her husband. Tom was more upbeat than he had been in several days. He hadn't had bacon and eggs in two weeks.

"O.K. Sherlock, what's up?" She placed a second coffee on the placemat.

Tom smiled. Holding his right hand as though it were a pistol, he took an imaginary shot at the far wall and said, "I've got almost everything I need. I still have to confirm a few things and then figure out when and to whom do I give my evidence."

The stress still lingered. Susie nevertheless sensed that maybe it would end soon. She hoped it would.

"And then I hope we get our lives back." She gave a quick, soft, glance at her husband.

"We will honey. As a matter of fact, I'm going to take some time off today to take the Cub out. Want to make it a twosome? No barrel rolls, I promise. We'll be back by four."

The lightheartedness had been a long time in coming.

"What's the weather like?"

"Damn, I married a sissy girl. Small craft warnings along the coast. Southwest winds. Warm and windy, but it's supposed to be clear as a bell."

Susie's mental picture included vomiting in the small plastic bag they always kept for such purposes. "No thanks," She reached down, put her right arm around his chest and whispered in his ear, "but I'll have something ready to rev your engines when you get back."

Tom was pleased. Pleased for her invitation which he would accept and

231

pleased that his invitation had been rejected.

●

The defense case was underway. Tom wasn't scheduled to testify until Wednesday. Before taking the Cub up, Tom called Ed Harvey.

"The dumb asses. They all knew that Colter would intimidate the hell out of them." Tom spoke of the previous witnesses with frustration. They couldn't stand up to Barry Colter's relentless assaults.

Tom was the final witness for the defense. They needed to get the less-important witnesses on and off the stand as quickly as possible. Caught between a rock and a hard place, the defense needed to establish that the company operated under specific policies pertaining to hours driven and improper private use of any tractor-trailer. Their witness was lousy. Barry Colter hammered away at the intent of the company leadership.

●

"Mr. Wilton. I don't believe you for an instant. Do you expect this jury to believe something as ridiculous as . . ."

"Objection, your Honor. Mr. Colter's words are inflammatory and he's calling the witness a liar."

"Sustained."

It was to be Ed Harvey's only victory of the day.

"Let me rephrase my question. Mr. Wilton, as the vice-president for driver operations at Flagg Brothers Trucking, have you ever studied a driver's personal log?"

"Uh, yes I have." Clay Wilton was obviously uncomfortable.

"Then you do consider the driver's log to be very important. Is that correct?"

"Yes, it is."

Barry Colter walked over to his table and took a small manila card into his hands. He held it in the air in front of the jury. He had it entered into evidence. Then he turned again to the jury.

"This, ladies and gentlemen, is known as the driver's log. Mr. Wilton has established its importance."

He lowered the card, studied it for a few seconds, and then walked into the personal space of a very nervous witness.

Deliberately looking into Clay Wilton's eyes, Barry Colter spoke coldly at the witness. "Mr. Wilton, other than name and address, can you tell us the headings of any of the rows or columns on this card?"

Clay Wilton shifted in his seat. He was dead in the water. "Well, it's got, uh . . . please excuse me, I'm somewhat nervous. It's . . ."

"That's all right Mr. Wilton, you've already answered." Barry stuffed Clay Wilton deeper into the meat grinder. "Just one more question. We've established two things, your job responsibility and the importance of the log. And you did say that you have had the opportunity to review, shall I say, at least one log. Is that correct, sir?"

"Er . . . yes."

"Remembering that you are under oath, I want you to tell this jury exactly how many driver logs you examined in the year preceding this accident."

Clay Wilton looked at the jury quickly. Each member stared back intently. He looked up, looking for divine intervention, and then back to Barry Colter. In a voice no more than a whisper, he responded.

"None."

Barry Colter demanded more. "Please speak up sir!"

"None."

"I have no further questions."

●

Bill met Jenna Smith at the Subway on Dowling. With sandwiches and Cokes, they walked two blocks to Emancipation Park. Sitting on a park bench among a throng of waiting pigeons, they chatted small talk for a few minutes, then turned to the subject of the District Attorney.

"I'm much happier now. I don't feel any stress. People treat me fine. They're good people."

Jenna left the Houston District Attorney's office a few weeks before.

"Why did you leave?" Bill asked.

The slender, young woman stared at her soft drink. "I had been there three years when the new D.A. arrived. Until then, everything went well. Under Philip Borders we felt we were working for someone who cared about the office, getting the job done. I'm sure you remember."

Bill thought back to the period that Philip Borders served as the Houston District Attorney. Eleven years. They were good times, though not easy. A heart attack. A new district attorney. Yes, times had changed. Where Borders made a habit of coming around to all the offices to 'shoot the bull' over coffee with the detectives, Elizabeth Harker had not been in Bill Newton's office unofficially since the second week of her tenure.

Jenna served in the same suite of offices as the District Attorney and knew far more about Elizabeth Harker than did Bill Newton. She continued her story. "When Harker arrived, it all changed. We still went after the bad guys, and we did it with a vengeance. But the character of our office changed drastically. I don't know exactly why you are asking about her, but I can answer your central question. She is a bad actor."

"But the others have stayed. Why not you?"

"It was personal. Straight up, I think it was because I'm competent and I'm not bad looking." Jenna's comment concerning her looks was a huge understatement. And, also true to her comment, she was very competent indeed. Jenna continued. "She didn't like that and she made me suffer for it. The snide comments, the unnecessary workload, the keeping me hidden. I'm not a weakling, but it got to a point that I detested her and I detested coming to work. There were times when she purposely chided me in front of others. Given her position, there was little I could do. When I realized how unhappy I was, I started looking. Chambers and Herzinger offered me a position and I took it. As I said, they're good people. I'm much better off and I'm sure the D.A. is happy beating up on some other slob."

"Was she ethical in dealing with people?" Bill was digging deep.

Jenna proceeded with caution. "I'm not sure where you're going with this. The word 'ethical' is a strange word. Did she out and out break the law, and I think that's what you want to know? I wasn't privy to that. You probably know more about that personally than I do. What I do know, from talking to some of the detectives out of homicide, is that she put severe pressure on them to prosecute cases. To answer your question, she probably couldn't be convicted of criminal wrongdoing, but, yes, she's unethical."

Bill thought of Jenna's statement, *she probably couldn't be convicted.* He tucked *probably* away.

Time passed quickly. Both had finished their Subway sandwiches, save a small chunk of French bread resting on the paper on Jenna's lap.

Bill decided not to wait for another lunch to make some connections. "Do you know a Mr. Barry Colter, principal with Colter, Fisher and King?"

Cocked eyebrows and a wry smile answered before words came from her mouth. "Sure do. And, yes, they've got something going." Breaking the bread into little pieces, Jenna smiled into space. "You can ask anyone still there. Colter and Harker make such a cute couple. Makes you want to barf. If they think their love interests are lost on the office, they shouldn't be in this business."

"Anything specific?" Bill asked.

"For one, their private meetings, on average, lasted longer than meetings between she and anyone else." Jenna shifted herself uncomfortably as she continued. "Personally, I once saw him grab her rear end. Enough said."

Both shook their heads. Jenna added a couple of personal stories concerning Elizabeth Harker's character and interpersonal skills. She also provided Bill with the names of coworkers, some of them friends of Bill's, who could add to the stories.

"Unfortunately, I need to get back to the office. I appreciate the lunch." She smiled gently, sincerely. "It's good to see you again, Bill."

"Before we go," Bill added unnecessarily, "I need to ask you to keep this to yourself. At some point I will tell you more, but I can't right now."

Jenna took the broken pieces of bread and tossed them on the sidewalk. Against the backdrop of gathering pigeons, she answered, "Don't worry, I knew the minute you called what kind of conversations we would be having. Great lunch."

They walked away, leaving the pigeons to fight over the bread.

28

The weather report called for clear, breezy conditions up and down the coast. It took Tom an additional half-hour flying to Port Lavaca using the Cub rather than the Stinson. The advantage of the Cub was that it had a stalling speed of about 35 miles an hour. Flying into the westerly breeze, Tom would be able to hover the Cub above any area that might provide information. His flight path paralleled Texas 35 past Angleton, Bay City and north of Palacios. He flew seven miles northwest of the center of Port Lavaca and began an east-west-east search pattern, each pass offset one-quarter mile south of the previous pass. Tom made one refueling stop at Palacios, then resumed the search. He passed over Indianola shortly after 1:00. As predicted, the brisk wind blowing from the west-northwest allowed him to fly over the runway with a ground speed less than 40 miles an hour. On his first approach Tom flew along the northern length of the runway. His attention focused immediately on the black stripe - and then to the stack of steel tubing. As Travis did just days before, he identified the steel very quickly. What Tom did not see was Jud Weems. Jud had just finished dumping four sections of tubing over the docking platform into the brackish water. Jud saw the Piper Cub from half a mile in the distance. He turned off the ignition, climbed out of the forklift, and, as Tom flew behind the hangar, ran to the eastern end of the building.

Jud had no idea who was in the plane. He only knew he didn't like it. "Son-of-a-bitch."

Tom decided to reconnoiter the runway again before landing. His second flyby revealed no signs of life, only an empty forklift near the dock. No vehicles were anywhere in the vicinity. What Tom didn't know was that Jud had carefully parked his truck close to the hangar entrance. The facility looked uninhabited.

His third pass, again from east to west, took him directly over the black stripe.

The steel tubes, the curve and the red paint . . . Tom was riveted. He could visualize the practice runs made at the airstrip and then, suddenly, the savage death of his best friend. He grabbed the Nikon and took numerous pictures as he circled the evidence. Still, he knew he had to physically touch the debris and paint. As the runway and hangar passed beneath the right wing of the Cub, Tom pushed the joystick sharply to the right and slightly down. He pulled the throttle, slowing the propeller speed to allow for a gentle nosedive towards the pavement. A smooth landing. He taxied back to the black stripe and followed it to the red paint. Several pieces of steel tubing remained strewn at the edge of the runway.

Once Jud saw Tom roll to a stop in front of the steel, he ran from the hangar back to the forklift. He grabbed the pistol from the pocket of his denim jacket hanging in the small driver's cab. He ran back to the hangar, leaving a box full of cartridges in the forklift, and returned to his vantage point at the northeast corner. Jud lowered himself into a prone position and waited to see what Tom would do next. His mind whispered. *I don't know who you are, but if you get over here, you're dead.*

Tom mimicked Travis' action taken two and a half weeks before. The ruptured tiedown straps, steel tubing and a long curving line of black paint registered a murder in Tom's brain. Jud Weems watched him from a football field away.

The hangar appeared empty to Tom. *Did Travis die in there?* Tom walked slowly towards the hangar, believing that some of the mystery would be revealed there. His direction of advance veered slightly to his right towards the northwest corner. Once he was certain where Tom was headed, Jud slowly inched his way back, got up, and moved quickly, quietly, into a new position at the far end of the hangar.

Standing fully upright, Jud waited for his prey to arrive. His plan was simple enough; wait until Tom was no more than three feet from the corner and then shoot him - first in the chest and then in the head. He was not concerned with disposing of the body at the moment; that would have to come later. Jud could hear Tom's slow shuffle as he neared the corner. Jud moved his right hand, with his middle finger on the trigger, towards the middle of his body and cupped it in the grasp of his left hand. Jud's broken index finger pointed along the barrel of the pistol. Tom walked closer.

⬢

Susie looked at the clock. Two p.m. It was too early to start to worry, yet her stomach churned and her worry increased with each tick. *He should be heading home by now. Please Tom, please come home. I need you. Please. Please.*

●

Tom was wired to the physical world. But, at that single moment in his life, the intuitive reigned. No more than 10 feet from the corner of the hangar, his defenses stiffened. He saw nothing, smelled nothing, heard nothing. He slowed his walk, gaining a valuable second. They were six feet apart when Jud sidestepped to a position directly in front of Tom. The alignment of the pistol barrel moved toward Tom's heart. Instinct dominated - Tom rushed Jud, lowering and rotating his body slightly as he moved towards the killer. Jud fired.

The first bullet tore through Tom's left arm. It made pulp of the tricep muscle, nicked bone and grazed the upper side of his back. The second round took a small chunk out of his right ear. A third shot was propelled into the air as Tom hit Jud in the chest with his right hand, knocking him backwards. Jud's body clipped the corner of the hangar rotating him as he fell to the ground. Jud managed to hold onto the pistol and immediately began a roll that brought him rapidly to his feet. There was too much distance to hit Jud again before he could fire a second volley. A split-second decision put Tom in full flight to the next corner of the building. His camera swung madly in the air, flailing erratically from his wrist. Not nearly in the shape he had been years before, Tom nevertheless was in far better condition than Jud. Jud got off the fourth round just as Tom rounded the next corner of the hangar. It missed. With each step Tom distanced himself from his pursuer.

"You ass . . ." The short run was already overtaking Jud. His lungs were on fire. "You fu . . ." He stopped at the edge of the building, gasping for air.

Tom rounded the northeast corner and ran halfway along the east wall before changing direction due east into the brush. He had to get back to the Cub. From where he entered the brush, Tom's escape route would take him east to the dirt access road, north to the back side of a small rise, west along the northern edge of the runway following what he hoped would be a series of depressions and then straight south to the Cub. Even as he ran from the hangar, Tom conducted a risk analysis. He realized that Jud was not in good shape and would not be able to follow him for any great distance. Tom's next reasoning brought him to the conclusion that Jud would expect Tom to go straight to the fishing village to seek help. His stride was powerful, his body momentarily ignoring the wound throbbing from elbow to shoulder. Tom turned north at the access road, glancing to his left to determine the danger from Jud. Jud had stopped a few yards from the hangar and was just looking at his escaping quarry, arms down at his side with the pistol pointing at the ground.

"I'll still kill you, you son-of-a-bitch." Jud whispered into the wind.

Tom Seiler understood fear, but he could put it into perspective. He could deal with it. His driving emotion changed from self-preservation to anger. His anger, controlled yet seething, gave him sense of purpose. You don't piss off Tom Seiler.

Tom spoke into the same wind. "You're going to rue the day you were born. And right now, you're one scared bastard." He stopped and knelt down on his right knee. It was then that the camera, swinging gently from his wrist, gained his attention. The distance was problematic; they were several hundred yards apart but Tom squeezed off one picture just before Jud rounded the corner of the hangar. Then the pain set in. He took his handkerchief and, clamping one corner with his teeth, tied it just below the shoulder joint. He used the top of his head as support for raising his left elbow as high as possible, reducing both the blood loss and the throbbing that stabbed at his shredded arm. He squeezed his ear to stop the bleeding. The blood made the wound appear worse than it was. He moved towards the Cub. He repeated himself. "Yeah, that's right, you're one scared bastard. One sorry, scared, bastard." The camera swung in rhythm with his stride.

Jud sensed that he was hunted more than hunter. What he had just said out loud did not track with what was going on in his mind. Jud silently pleaded with Tom. *Just get outta here!* Never before had he experienced unmanageable trembling. He leaned over, head down with hands extended to his knees. He took three deep breaths, stood up, and started walking to the hangar. He had to think the whole situation through.

One thing could be said about Jud. Regardless of what went on around him, he never lost his capacity to consider consequences and courses of action. As he watched Tom disappear towards the Indianola fishing village, Jud contemplated what Tom might do in this situation and what his response needed to be. Instinctively, he changed his focus to the Cub.

That's it. You want to get back to the plane. Jud estimated the distance and time Tom would be in the open if he made a run for the Cub, then judged his own running time. He could make it. *Go ahead. You're dead meat.* He put the pistol in the waistband of his dirty jeans, brushed the remnants of sand, dust and straw from his shirt and walked to the hangar door. Once inside, he climbed up on the dunnage and then to the shelving where he could look out from the top of the window towards the runway and the Cub. Jud decided that he could wait for possibly 40 minutes, then he would have to return to Houston. He reloaded his pistol, peered through the glass and thought of his adversary and the incredible bad luck that brought them together.

The crackling of brittle weeds died in the wind. Tom's low silhouette provided him cover from all but the top window of the hangar. Jud peered through the window and scanned the view to his front. Twenty minutes passed before Tom reached a position directly north of the hangar. Jud didn't respond the way Tom expected. Tom dropped to his hands and knees and crawled to a small knoll covered with sawgrass. His eyes swept the horizon and the building directly to his front. Tom was sure that he hadn't heard a car or truck engine and reasoned that Jud either was still in the area or had left on foot. Tom continued to scan the area while approximating his distance to the Cub and that from the hangar to the Cub. If all went well, he would be in the open for no more than 15 to 20 seconds before reaching the relative safety of the Cub. Another 10 seconds to prop the engine and a final 20 seconds to be airborne. Just under one minute. Could Jud make the almost 300-yard run in less than a minute? The wind was problematic. *Should I take off into the wind or with the wind?* was the question passing through his mind. If Jud were still in the area, he most probably was still at the hangar. Taking off into the wind would be quicker, but it would also mean that the plane would have to travel from east to west, bringing it temporarily closer to the hangar. Taking off to the east would take the plane away from the hangar, but, even with a Cub, it also provided very little runway for a plane moving in the same direction as the wind. He chose to fly into the wind. Tom low-crawled over the knoll towards the edge of the runway. Jud, from atop the shelving inside the hangar, saw him.

Tom bolted from the brush.

Jud jumped from the upper shelf as Tom rushed towards the Cub. Jud ran through the personnel door, already applying pressure to the pistol trigger. Running as fast as he could, Tom noticed the few pieces of steel tubing still on the runway. "Shit!" constituted an involuntary reflex at realizing he would have to turn the Cub in a small, yet dangerous, arc towards the hangar before beginning his move towards the west and safety. Tom was no more than 20 feet from the Cub when he saw Jud running across the apron directly at him.

Tom gauged the distance between himself and the man who was possessed with killing him. A little more than 200 yards. *Open the door with my left hand . . . pain or no pain. Mag on. Pull the chock. Pull the prop. Do it right.*

Jud, too, was fighting for survival. He fought through the burning sensation tearing at his lungs and continued his relentless run at the man and machine standing between him and freedom. He was closing on the Cub faster than Tom predicted. Less than 200 yards. At full running speed, Tom rounded the propeller and pivoted towards the left side door of the Cub. The sand on the runway responded to the sideways thrust of Tom's foot - giving away beneath him. He fell full force on the concrete. Unaware of his chipped right elbow, Tom focused on getting into the plane. Knowing the lost half-second was critical Tom rose to his feet and almost leaped to the door. The camera hit the side window hard. Pulling on the door simultaneously with rotating the door handle caused another mechanical dilemma. The door didn't open immediately. *Slow down - get it together.* He pushed the door slightly, rotated the handle a second time and opened the door. Ninety yards. His left elbow erupted in excruciating pain as he reached for the mag switch a few inches above where a pilot would be sitting. He fought through the pain and hit the switch. Two factors were in Tom's favor. Only 32 minutes had passed since he landed. He had a warm engine. Warm enough to effect a first-try start. Tom also had placed the throttle on a small mark he scratched out years before to start up at 750 rpm. It would start to move once his homemade chock was removed, but it would start slowly. He reached in, this time the searing in his arm taking his breath, and engaged the primer. Tom turned quickly to his left and kicked the chock from where it rested beneath the front left wheel. He raced to the front and began the ritual of starting the engine. Ignoring his injuries as best he could, Tom pulled the propeller downward. On the first pull, the propeller hiccupped briefly, then eased quickly into its loyal counter-clockwise rotation. *Thank God.* Tom – only 60 yards separated from Jud Weems – moved quickly around the propeller to the cockpit of the now moving airplane. He bolted into the seat and pulled back on the throttle. The blades swallowed healthy bites of the Texas air, forcing it towards the rear of the Cub. The thrust of air pushed the small yellow plane forward. Tom made it. He knew exactly how the plane would behave under these circumstances. Now he was in his environment. Now he had some options.

Fifty yards. Jud was staggering, but he continued to close on Tom.

Several random sections of steel blocked Tom from exiting in a straight line. Pushing on the right brake, he forced a clockwise turn of the plane. He gunned the engine.

Forty yards.

Gasping as he ran, Jud nevertheless was able to take advantage of the angle at which he closed on Tom.

Thirty yards.

Jud raised the pistol on the run, his extended arm jerking with each step. He could not stop for a well-aimed shot. He wailed internally at Travis - *goddamn broken finger!* He knew he needed to get within point blank range or hit Tom with a lucky shot. He pulled the trigger.

Thwap! The first round tore through the left windshield and traveled at an angle out the right rear window. The bullet would have hit a backseat passenger in the chest. A second round cut through the air just above the wing.

Fifteen yards.

Tom and Jud looked into each other's eyes. Tom felt Jud's cold, murderous, stare.

Six yards. Point-blank range. Survival instinct. Then rage.

In one swift maneuver, Tom engaged the left wheel brake and turned left, simultaneously applying full throttle. Another round crashed through the front windshield, cracking at his ear as it passed two inches from his head. It was the last shot.

Jud wasn't ready. Stark fear locked him in place. He stopped running, dropped his arms simultaneously with dropping the pistol onto the hot concrete.

"Goddamn son . . ." Tom screamed at Jud as he closed the distance.

Jud didn't move. "No." His whisper was cut short.

The whirling propeller caught Jud from the knees up. It sliced into flesh and bone, lifting what remained of Jud's body quickly off the ground. Blood and entrails exploded onto the windshield and wings. Small hunks of meat flew into the air. It was over immediately.

Gaining speed, the Cub jolted as the left wheel rolled over Jud's lower leg. Blood covered the windshield. Tom pushed down on the throttle and braked the plane to a stop. He shut down the engine and climbed out. The pain was almost crippling. Tom's body also shut down. He slumped to his knees on the hot concrete runway, not 20 feet from the remains of Jud Weems. Struggling for balance on an injured arm, Tom Seiler shook the battle-worn camera from his wrist, leaned forward slightly, then threw up.

The process to clean blood and human matter from the plane lasted until the lowering sun lost its power to warm the November air. Tom walked the quarter-mile to the edge of the loading area. Several plastic two-gallon containers lay in the sand, remnants of crab trap markers. He filled two and, using his newly, but less seriously, injured right arm, carried both back to the plane. He used spare rags, always in the back waiting to be used, to clean the blood from the engine cowling, windshield and front section of the plane. It was all right-handed work. The stabbing pain returned with each movement of his left arm. What remained of Jud grotesquely lay on the concrete. Only once did Tom stop and linger at the partial corpse. *It could have been me.* Exhaustion, wounds and the cooling afternoon breeze sucked away at his strength, slowing him down. Had he finished earlier, he still would have waited until near evening to depart. He did not want blood to be apparent in the bright sunlight when he refueled in Palacios. The small Piper J-3 lifted off into the sinking sun.

Twelve minutes later, Tom approached Palacios from the northwest, landing on runway 13. All that remained from a military airport of half a century earlier were the runway, a single hangar and a small office building. Fortune fell his way.

A dim light shone through dusty windows. Shortly, a young Mexican woman opened the office door and hurried to the refueling truck. She seemed preoccupied. In the near-dark she noticed neither his condition nor that of the Cub. *Good.* The non-negotiable price was fair. He gave her his credit card, then made his way to the restroom to clean up as best he could. The lack of warm water disturbed him, but the cleansing soap did its job. Pain numbed his elbow and arm; yet the cool water revived Tom. He dabbed his left arm gingerly with the wet paper towel, then spent five full minutes washing his face and hair. He did not touch his ear. Another minute to put on his University of Houston sweatshirt. The woman had just started in the direction of the restroom to see if anything was wrong. Tom met her at the corner of the wooden building, miraculously signed the bill and mustered all the energy possible to say thanks and wish her a pleasant evening. He felt like shit.

Tom walked slowly to the plane as the pretty Mexican maiden parked the truck. She stopped at the door, surveyed her last customer of the day and entered the office. The lights went out.

Unheard to Tom, a sensual male voice called into the darkness, "Ven papa aca, preciosa."

●

Tom sighed and groaned simultaneously as the Cub lifted quickly from the Palacios runway. The small machine, its yellow cloth covering light steel tubing, befriended Tom Seiler one more time. Lights from the many towns along the coast of Texas clicked on one after another. They provided a beautiful demarcation between land and sea. The constant hum of the engine prodded Tom to close his eyes and go to sleep. He fought the urge by trying to put structure on what the next few days would hold. Barry Colter accompanied him for much of the trip, if only in the recesses of his mind. He followed the coastline to Freeport before turning north towards the glowing embers of the Houston skyline.

The La Porte airport tower was closed. Still, the two rows of lights provided an easy target for runway 12. A smooth landing and thoughts of home countered the unrelenting pain now emanating from both arms. The absence of other pilots and their families meant that Tom would be able to put the Cub in the hangar undetected. He could worry about further cleaning in the morning. *Oh my God. I've got to testify.* With the weight of the world on his mind, Tom taxied off the runway, down the dirt and grass path, and around the corner of the hangar. In the darkness he thought he saw a silhouette.

It was Susie.

29

Tom's wounds, ugly and painful, were not serious. He and Susie drove to Michelle White's, stopping at home only long enough to drop off the truck, grab some notes concerning his analysis of the murders and listen to phone messages. One message from Bill Newton was important. The others were saved. He called Bill Newton and asked him to come to Michelle's. His customary post-flight beer remained in the refrigerator. Michelle responded to their phone call by putting on a hot pot of coffee and gathering a significant cache of general medical supplies. Until their second son was born, Michelle had been a registered nurse.

"Ayhh! Whew. That sucker smarts." Tom grimaced as Michelle scrubbed the wound in his upper arm with a Betadyne shower packet.

With lidocaine one could go about cleaning a wound of this nature as though scrubbing dirt off a potato. Without it, exposed nerves screamed in response to each stroke. Michelle backed off on the severity of scrubbing, but not by much. Thorough cleansing took precedence over comfort. She gripped a large handful of Tom's arm, exposing the exploded flesh, and compressed the nerves as much as possible. She vigorously washed the damaged muscle. The kitchen counter was their makeshift operating room. The patient sat on a small chair from the breakfast nook. Susie could barely look at Tom's face. The torn flesh made her nauseous.

Tom sucked in air through tightened teeth. "Ayeee, shit!"

"You're lucky I'm not mad at you." Michelle gave him a strong smile, an indication that she had started the return journey from her personal hell. "Almost finished. The cleaning has to be good and thorough before closing it." She switched the conversation to their agreement of 10 minutes earlier. "One day Tom. You've got one day and then you're going to the hospital."

Tom exhaled. "One day." He knew he was fortunate that both Susie and

247

Michelle would give him 24 hours before he had to go public with his wounds, his encounter with Jud Weems and his accusations.

Michelle repeated the procedure with the entrance wound. It was an easier task. As for the bone injury, Michelle was able to ascertain, albeit not without further pain to her patient, that the bullet had only chipped off a tiny piece of bone fragment. His left arm would probably not need any casting. His chipped elbow certainly needed to be immobilized.

"Susie, take Tom's arm and pull the wound together here." Michelle began closing the exit wound.

Susie fought off a gag reflex. Garnering every ounce of intestinal fortitude, she used the index finger and thumb of each hand to partially close the wound. She looked at it only long enough to place her hands at opposite ends of the open flesh. She quickly looked away. Michelle placed a piece of gauze gently over the wound and applied strips of tape. The first strip was placed firmly on the edge of the wound midway between Susie's clenched hands. Michelle secured one end of the strip tightly against his skin, then pulled it over the top of the gauze toward the opposite side of the wound. Using the thumb of her left hand to move the previously free side towards the taped end of the strip, she pressed down. The tension on the tape closed the wound significantly but not completely. Michelle did not want a complete closure. An ugly scar would be the result, but she was concerned more about infection than perfection. The wound needed to heal from inside out. From the center strip, Michelle applied four more strips, alternating each side from the middle of the wound towards Susie's hands.

"O.K. Susie, let go."

Michelle admired her work. Susie, sweating profusely, sat down, putting her head between her hands while resting her elbows on two trembling knees. Tom looked stoically at Michelle's work.

The chipped elbow received only Betadyne, a temporary sling and ice. Casting would have to wait one more day.

Bill's timing was perfect. He missed the local version of E.R..

Michelle heated some chicken tenders and red potatoes in the microwave. Tom was hungry and still charged with adrenaline. Bill had already eaten but was good for a few links of fowl. Michelle picked at her food. Susie did not touch the meal. It wasn't until Tom finished eating that he focused on Jud Weems. It was time to recall what had happened. Over coffee, Tom told the grisly story of his trip to Indianola. Susie copied down everything as Tom spoke. Michelle and Bill listened intently. Tom repeated himself often so that Susie could keep up.

Following the dictation of the Indianola story, they moved to the patio and made plans. The natural inclination of the two women was to turn all of Tom's evidence over to Ed Harvey and the police. Tom disagreed adamantly, emphasizing that it would end up in the hands of the District Attorney's office. There it would be used against him.

"Nope. I just can't do it. Not yet anyway. Add all that happened today to the evidence that I already have and we have the start of a case showing Colter is a killer. I'm certain Colter has his radar out to the max. He certainly knows that poorly planned murders leave evidence. He's probably running scared and I know he's alert." He looked at each face staring at him.

Bill ended the silence. "Tom's right. This is too big to be heard by too many people."

Tom used Bill's comment to continue. "Here's what I've got. Travis researched Blue Sheets from the past. Two were found on his desk at the office. Colter represented Weems several years ago. No big deal. Happens all the time. But," he pointed his finger aimlessly into the air, "Colter also represented Tallant before. He represented the man who killed the D'Arcys. That is one hell of a coincidence. And damned if Harker wasn't part of the Tallant case. It may be circumstantial, but it is evidence. Then we have Travis' voicemail stating that Colter and Weems were having a meeting more than 100 miles from Houston. He also mentioned Harker might be involved. Again, in and of itself, it won't convict, but it does tighten the thread. The fact that a mega-million dollar trial is being handled pro bono reeks of a set-up. He conned his partners. A perfect opportunity to share the money with Weems, our dead friend Tallant and, quite possibly, Elizabeth Harker. The son-of-bitch killed Travis." He looked away from Michelle, then continued. "Problem is, what's pretty clear to us may not be clear to a jury and the rules of law favor the defendant. Also, he's powerful and has people in his hip pocket. He's the worst there is. A very smart sociopath."

Bill held the last chicken tender in his huge hands. "Tom, you'll be glad to know that I did some footwork on Colter and Harker. They're about as discreet as nuclear war. Plenty of people can verify a physical relationship. I also have some background on her conduct as district attorney. Sleazy but not criminal. I'll drop my report off tomorrow."

Before Tom could respond, Susie broke in. "But, what about you once he finds out you killed the Weems guy? He's going to have you killed, too." Tight lines accentuated Susie's pallid forehead.

"Susie's right, Tom. You can't let this go on and on. He's got to be worried and on alert. He'll come after you."

"Nope, again. Not if I do it right. Remember, he doesn't know me from Adam. Thinking about my survival kept me awake during the flight back." Tom started to lean forward and extend his arms in a clarifying gesture. Shooting pains forced him back into the wicker chair. "Ooh. Aah!"

"You don't look very safe to me right now." Michelle spoke as she rose to get the coffeepot. "To be honest, if I were Colter and learned that Weems was dead, I'd be very alert. Seeing you stagger into the courtroom looking like pulp wouldn't make it too difficult to figure out who killed him. One quick check to see if Tom Seiler is a pilot, then a check to see if he possibly filed a flight plan today. You know what, we then have you as the next candidate for murder." Michelle was Susie's surrogate.

"One day to think it out. Can everyone make it to our place tomorrow night? Steve, Paige and Ross also need to know. Pizza at seven if you can make it. I'll call the kids."

It was already midnight. Tom needed to make two phone calls.

●

The unsure, half-slurred voice at the other end indicated Steve's interruption from a deep sleep. As Tom eased into a quick synopsis of the day, Steve struggled to clear his mind. He sat up in bed, turned on the table lamp and instinctively reached for the nightstand drawer. Kelly didn't budge.

"I need you to add all this to the evidence I gave you in the envelope, then tell me the best way to get it into the system. If it gets suppressed, I'm in big trouble. Can you do it?"

"O.K. Dad, I can check it all out. What's the time frame on this?"

"Has to be resolved in the next day or two. And, by the way, you also need to let me know just what can they do to me, especially given my encounter with Weems."

Steve jotted one-word notes on his pad of paper. He was wide-awake.

"Count on it Dad. What else do you need?"

"How about pizza over here tomorrow night? Make it around seven. Paige, Ross and Michelle White will be here. We've got to get real smart on this."

"I'll be there. Dad, you O.K.?" Steve's mental picture of his father was identical to Tom's actual physical condition.

"I feel like hell but everything's working. I just don't believe all of this is happening. Sorry to wake you - just consider it payback for the 500 times you woke me in the middle of the night."

Both Tom and Steve smiled. "You got it, Dad. Full payback."

A similar phone call was made to Paige.

●

Tom and Susie switched positions in bed. As sore as his right elbow was, it was a poor second to his left arm in terms of pain. Susie propped him up with two pillows supporting his back. His left arm rested gingerly on three additional pillows taken from the guestrooms. His right arm, bent 90 degrees at the elbow, lay across his mid-section. Susie lay on her left side and gently stroked the right side of his head. Neither said a word. Tears rolled quietly over the bridge of her nose and across her cheek onto her pillow. For Tom, the percocet worked. He fell asleep. Susie cried silently.

She asked God over and over. *Why?*

The room was stone silent, except for the deep breathing of the man she loved so much.

30

The incessant beeps announced morning's arrival. Six o'clock. Tom groaned slightly as he tried to shift his position in bed. He hurt.

"I'll get the coffee. How're you doing?" Susie spent most of the night awake; her senses programmed to respond to Tom's each move. It had been a rough night for both of them. Still, Susie noticed that the percocet did its job. Tom would wake up each time he moved; once his new position was established, the percocet succeeded in pulling him again into an unconscious state of unintelligible dreaming.

"Feel like hell, but I did get some sleep. How'd you sleep?"

"Took me some time to fall asleep. But once I did, it was all over." A small lie wouldn't hurt at this point in time.

"Great. Now, how about that coffee?"

Susie eased out of the bed and returned in three minutes with two hot cups of coffee. The early morning discourse went from Tom's injuries to an overview of the testimony he needed to give. Susie joined him in the shower to give him a shave. She kissed him several times, then nuzzled her head into his chest. Tom held her as best he could. A gunshot wound to the arm, a chipped elbow, bruises all over, and, of all things, an erection. Unfortunately, proof of his full recovery would have to wait.

●

The usual crowd assembled at the courthouse. The defense case had not been very strong. Barry Colter was good; he chewed up the defense witnesses one by one and pretty much spit them out. Tom would be on the stand before the noon recess. Ed Harvey assured Tom that it would be at least 10:00 before calling him to the stand. The pain of bending either arm dictated holding his notepad as far out on his knees as possible. Still, his lettering was perfect. He was fully prepared to testify to the physical evidence. Turning circumstantial evidence and assumptions into a conviction was a different story. Before the trial started, Ed showed Tom an animation given by the prosecution's expert witness. Tom assured Ed that the exaggerations in vehicle movement could be refuted.

●

"Mr. Seiler, they're ready for you."

Tom started to check his watch but, given the radiating pain, decided it wasn't worth the effort.

Walking into the courtroom was different this time. Gone was the insatiable excitement he had remembered as pre-game jitters. His only feelings were gnawing sensations of uncertainty and pain. Even his first trip to the witness stand, when he perfectly described the concept of rotational inertia for a dozer rolling off a flatbed, carried more assurance than this one. He had studied the physical evidence over and over, yet everything seemed scrambled in his brain. He couldn't even muster the friendly gesture for the jury. One by one, they briefly appeared through the fog only to quickly disappear. Tom was aware that he needed to overcome his injuries and speak with forceful authority, but his body seemed to betray him at every step. He plodded his way to the witness stand.

"Place your left hand . . ."

The bailiff's instructions faded into the air. Tom's efforts focused on placing his left hand on the Bible. He couldn't do it without raising his entire shoulder. *Lower the Bible, dammit!* His eyes pleaded but there was no response.

". . . you God."

"I do." Tom sat down, small blisters of sweat forming on his forehead.

Ed walked to a position directly in front of Tom. He offered a quick, polite "Thank you, your Honor" to Judge Piazze. He unbuttoned his suit jacket, pulled a pen and small notepad from his shirt and initiated his first testimony with Tom Seiler.

Ed asked Tom to introduce himself in the standard manner. Following Tom's replies about hometown and college, Ed went straight to the subject of engineering. "Mr. Seiler, please give us some background into the work you do as a mechanical engineer."

As best he could, Tom took on an almost philosophical look, first looking up and studying the ceiling, then fixing his gaze on the jury. "Well, mechanical engineering is just kind of the day-to-day practical application of the laws of Nature. It's one thing to be in the physics laboratory doing, you know, wild sorts of things; and it's something else to take those laws and put them in the marketplace, put them in the mainstream. And that's what I do, just take the basic laws of Nature and turn them into everyday useful items."

Tom felt sick, dizzy, sweat almost gushing from his pores. He bore on. "I started working for the National Aeronautics and Space Administration, NASA, at the Johnson Space Center. I spent 32 years with NASA as an on-the-board practicing mechanical engineer, doing mechanical design. Even designed some lunar hand tools. Because of weight restrictions, several of my tools were left on the moon. I may be the first lunar polluter."

A chuckle broke out across the courtroom. Slowly, but definitely, the men and women of the jury were becoming allied with the witness. Tom Seiler was just a normal, down-to-earth, guy. He was just like the men and women of the jury.

A strange phenomenon occurred. As bad as he felt, as angry as he was, and in spite of working for the first time with Ed Harvey, some of the old Tom Seiler began to flow.

"I was one of the early designers on the Shuttle Program. It was exciting work."

"For clarity Mr. Seiler, give us an example of your work."

Tom intentionally paused. "Sure. I worked on the commode. As . . ."

The courtroom erupted in laughter and muffled chatter. The tension relaxed. Judge Piazze took command.

"Silence. Continue Mr. Seiler."

Tom seized the moment. "As inglorious as it may sound, everyone goes to the bathroom. Being able to do so in a sanitary manner while in a zero-gravity environment is no small task. Add to that the fact that men and women are built differently . . ." Again, the noise level in the courtroom raised ever so slightly. It quickly abated. " . . . and you have yourself one great engineering problem. I spent six months developing a commode system that was gender neutral. I not only worked with other design engineers, I also worked closely with Dr. Judy Resnik and Lieutenant Colonel Ellison Onizuka. As a matter of fact, it was Judy Resnik," Tom leaving off the formal title to imprint in the minds of the jury that he was close friends with a true American heroine, "who made the rest of us feel more comfortable with male and female anatomy. It involved vacuum apparatus, airtight seals, containment vessels for fluids and solids, and anatomically friendly attachments. I won't get graphic, but I will tell you that it worked quite well on the flights that followed Challenger."

The commode dialogue had little to do with traffic accidents. It had everything to do with establishing Tom's credibility. The remainder of the morning provided the link between Tom's expertise as a forensic engineer and the deaths in the D'Arcy family.

Ed felt more comfortable. *Keep it going Ed. Come on Tom, help me out.* "Mr. Seiler, before you give an explanation as to the cause of the accident, would you please state how many cases you have worked on?"

"Over 2,000."

Time to plant a picture of Tom's honesty in the minds of each juror. Travis had been expert at it. Ed began. "Have you ever had a situation where your analysis differs from the position you were hired to support?"

"Many times. I'd guess close to 400."

"Please give us an example of those times, Mr. Seiler."

Tom leaned forward in his chair. He fought against nausea. "Well, there are actually two scenarios. The first is the situation where a legal firm will ask me to take a look at information on a case before they hire me. In those cases, I look, I see, and I form some sort of a quick-look opinion. And, if my quick-look opinion is different than what they are looking for, I don't always get hired."

Mimicking Travis, Ed slowly walked towards the jury box and calmly placed his hands in his pocket.

Tom noticed. He hoped the jury did not notice. *Don't overdo the Travis bit.*

Ed hesitated, then turned back towards Tom as he spoke. "What about the other scenario you mentioned?"

"Well, sir, sometimes at first glance my quick-look opinion agrees with the folks who hired me. But after investigating the incident in detail, I realize that it didn't happen that way. So I tell them."

"What happens then?"

"Generally, there are two new scenarios." Tom wanted to wipe the sweat from his forehead; the pain in his arms stopped him. He forged on. "Sometimes the firm asks me to either adjust my figures a little or to maybe disregard something."

Ed responded with a direct question. "Have you, Mr. Seiler, changed your figures or disregarded anything, in any case, that would alter your conclusions about the cause of the incident you were investigating?"

"No sir." Tom made his statement very matter-of-factly.

Ed asked quizzically, "Well then, what does the firm do since they can't put you on the stand to give evidence that hurts their case?"

"It's pretty simple, sir. And that's the second scenario. Since they hired me, they just keep me on a retainer but don't allow me to testify. Then they either try to settle out of court, or they go get another accident reconstructionist."

Barry Colter thought about objecting to some of Tom's statements since they were opinions. He chose against it. *Get him on the cross-examination.* He wrote bullets of information on the yellow legal pad before him.

Ed was buoyed by his initial interplay with Tom. *Here comes the meat.*

"Ladies and gentlemen, we will be showing you . . ." Joe DeMarco, the new assistant to Ed, began preparing the television and VCR for a showing. ". . . a simulation of the movements of the Flagg Brothers tractor-trailer and the D'Arcy car." Ed paused, allowing Joe to finish his task, then continued. "Before I ask Mr. Seiler a few questions, please recall that the plaintiff's expert witness presented an animation of the two vehicles. As you recall, it was a pretty fascinating video." Ed turned towards Tom. The substance of a new relationship between attorney and witness began.

"Mr. Seiler, although you weren't present for previous expert testimony, we were presented with what the plaintiff's attorney described as an animation of the accident. You speak of a simulation. Are these just two words to describe the same thing?"

"No sir, they are quite different." Tom neither increased nor decreased his volume. It was just a matter of fact tone that he displayed.

"Please explain the difference."

"Well, a simulation actually replicates the laws of physics." The words he used weren't much different than he had spoken so many times with Travis. The delivery would be critical. "I guess the best description is to use the old cartoon character Wylie Coyote. In an animation, Wylie goes running off the edge of the cliff in pursuit of our friend the Roadrunner. He continues in a straight line until he is way out over a three-mile deep canyon. He stops in mid-air; after a second or two of motionless befuddlement, a light bulb goes off in his head; all of a sudden, boom, he goes straight down. And the roadrunner gets away again. That's an animation."

"O.K., how is that so different from your program?"

"The fact is, in a simulation, if Wylie Coyote runs off the edge of a cliff, under the influence of gravity, his movement will immediately describe an arc through space. He's going to be falling faster and faster until the air - it will feel like a hurricane to Wylie - pushes back on him with the same force as gravity. That will happen when he is going down at about one hundred and thirty miles an hour. That top speed is known as terminal velocity. He will continue at that speed until he unfortunately hits the ground. The key to the simulation is that I can predict Wylie's movements, and, if he ran off the cliff at the same speed as I plugged into the program, and he remains the same size and weight, and the air around him hasn't changed, then his path to the ground would be almost exactly the same as was simulated. If he did it a thousand times, the results would be virtually the same."

"In this case have you reviewed the animation done by the prosecution's expert witness?"

"Yes sir, I did early this morning." Tom replied, deliberately moving eye contact to Barry Colter and then to the jury.

"What is your conclusion about the animation." Ed moved away from the jury.

Barry, clearly irritated that Judge Piazze seemed allied with the defense, objected. "Objection, your Honor, the witness is being asked for an opinion about a program of which he is not expert."

Ed had done his homework. "Your Honor, in my work with Mr. Seiler, I am aware that not only is he familiar with animation programs, he has worked with the Dyna3D program used by the plaintiff's witness."

Judge Piazze took over the questioning. "Is that true, Mr. Seiler, and, if it is, how much experience do you have?"

"Yes, your Honor, I have used it on occasions when I need to enhance the motion of vehicles, or, in some cases, aircraft. In all cases, though, I only use it to animate the motions that resulted from my simulation program. I will admit that the animation presents a more spectacular view of things; however, it does not follow physical laws, it only replicates what is plugged into it. My simulation provides the most accurate picture of the vehicle movements approaching the Parker Road intersection in Alvin."

"Overruled."

Ed sighed with relief. Barry was slightly miffed. Tom felt like shit.

Thus ended the high point of Tom's afternoon testimony. Slowly, but surely, Tom's energy faded. As they entered the specific elements of the Alvin incident, the teamwork began to break down. No fluid give-and-take; too many hesitations on Ed's part. Not all of the problems were Ed's fault. Tom's injuries were a great distraction. Where Ed was failing at presenting a strong buildup to their defense, Tom was doing very little to help them maintain their initial momentum. His answers, though correct, soon lacked the story-telling component so characteristic of the White-Seiler team. They were losing the jury.

Barry Colter, sensing the kill, leaned over to his junior lawyer. "Fred, pretty soon you're going to witness the best dissection in the great state of Texas."

Both men chuckled.

The time of night. Visibility. Speed. The straps. The pattern of deadly steel. Tom responded to each question in a manner which, though accurate, was delivered without one shred of conviction. Tom was getting weak, a wave of nausea sweeping over him. In South Texas, facts without conviction don't sell juries. With Travis, the testimony would have lasted until late afternoon. Travis realized early on what a great witness he had in Tom Seiler and always tried to time Tom's appearance so that they would spend lunch in a strategy session to map out a powerful conclusion to the testimony. And, no matter what, the timing always left the jury fresh with that little thirst to actually hear more. Travis often paraphrased the renowned Houston lawyer, Joe Jamail, "Tom, you're the best fucking expert witness in the State of Texas." Not today.

"Eh, I have no further questions your Honor." Ed Harvey knew they had lost their momentum. Not only had he ended poorly, he knew Tom was left open to Barry Colter's vicious counter-attack. Ed turned around, tapped his pencil twice on the table, and sat down. The expression on his face conceded defeat.

Concealed in Tom's mind was a spellbinding tale of murder.

Barry Colter turned and smiled to the jury.

Judge Piazze closed the proceedings. "All right. Given the time, we'll break for an early lunch. Court will reconvene at 1:15. Jury out at 11:23."

●

"Without White, they're dead meat. Mr. Weems is about to be one rich son-of-a-bitch and we're about to be the most well-known law firm in the country. By the way, did he call?"

"I don't believe so Mr. Colter. He's a loner."

"Sure is, but not for long. By this time tomorrow, he should have more pussy running after him than he could shake a stick at. He's one lucky shit." Barry inhaled deeply. Alive, strong and in command of all that he touched, Barry loved walking the thin, dangerously exciting line.

"That he is, sir." Fred responded as an image of the unattractive Jud Weems flitted across his mental screen.

"Tell you what Fred, stick close to me at the post-trial press conference and you'll be seen on half the TV screens in the country." Barry was too excited to sit down.

"Mr. Colter, I'll be hanging on your coat sleeve. I appreciate the exposure but I've got to tell you, just watching you in the courtroom has taught me more than law school and the last two years combined." Fred Stadler was caught up in

Barry's relentless attack. "I'm already licking my chops about this afternoon."

"Hang on to your hat, Fred. It's going to be an unforgettable lesson in trial law. Let's grab a bite to eat."

●

Tom didn't have the energy to go for lunch. Joe DeMarco brought back sandwiches and Cokes from the deli. The three men pondered damage control.

"Don't crucify yourself, Ed. I stunk the place up. By the way, I'm not worried about Colter. He's an arrogant bastard and I hold my own against those guys. Facts are facts and I won't back myself into corners by twisting them." Tom gently picked up his sandwich, stared at it, then put it down. "Help me out of my coat."

Both lawyers helped Tom out of his suit coat. Neither realized that Tom was injured until he was sworn in. How they had missed it, especially his split ear, spoke volumes about their preoccupation with the case.

"What the hell happened to you?" Ed looked at the repairs to Tom's arm protruding from his light blue and white striped short-sleeved shirt. "Holy shit, your elbow too."

"Too stupid to talk about. Have you ever fallen off a stepladder onto a concrete floor with a protruding lag bolt. Don't try it. Damn near killed me." Tom took two Motrin from his briefcase, swallowed them with the Coke, then took his only bite from the sandwich.

Tom changed the subject. "We need to brainstorm what Colter plans to do this afternoon."

●

"Thank you, your Honor." Barry Colter was impeccable. Following a quick lunch, he had gone home, showered, shaved, and put on a new, identical, suit.

Susie, Steve, Ross, Paige and Michelle White sat stoically in the last row. To their good fortune, Michelle went unnoticed by the media. In contrast to outward appearances, each of them was caught up with visions of life, death, hate, love, treachery and loyalty.

Pleasantries faded fast. A verbal fistfight followed the very polite "Good afternoon, Mr. Seiler, you seem uncomfortable. Are you all right?"

"I'm fine sir. And you?" *You sorry son-of-a-bitch.*

The questions were hostile, insinuating incompetence.

"So you actually consider yourself a competent engineer?"

Tom responded in kind. "I imagine I'm as good an engineer as you are a lawyer."

The interaction was white hot.

"In disclosure, we were made aware that you had taken a section of the webbing. Did you have permission to take it from the salvage yard?"

"No sir, I didn't. No one told me not to take it. If I didn't take it, nothing would . . ."

"Hold it, Mr. Seiler." Barry Colter emphatically raised his hands in the air.

Tom continued to bore through with his answer ". . . have existed."

Judge Piazze leaned forward and took control. "Mr. Seiler, simply answer the questions without interjecting commentary. The jury will disregard all after the answer 'No, Sir'."

Tom looked placidly at Barry Colter. *That's the last sir you'll ever get from me.*

"Did you, Mr. Seiler, ever see the other straps? Yes or no."

"Yes."

Barry implied the taking of the other straps belonged to Tom.

"Well, let's go one step further. Did you take the other straps?"

"I did not take the other straps. Did you?"

Judge Piazze snapped. "Mr. Seiler, did you hear me? Unless instructed otherwise, you will answer the questions without additional commentary. Do you understand?"

Tom looked at the judge and tightened his lips. "Yes, your Honor. Sorry."

Fifteen minutes into the cross-examination Tom's nerves were frayed.

"Your reasoning, Mr. Seiler, would suggest it wise to investigate other tiedown straps belonging to Flagg Brothers. Did you make the effort to check the condition of other straps on other Flagg trucks?"

"Actually, that would go beyond the scope of what I was asked to analyze. But I did notice that the Kinedyne Corporation made the straps. They are recognized as the best in the industry."

"Your Honor, you have asked Mr. Seiler to give direct answers. His insistence to ignore you is wasting everyone's time, particularly the jury's."

Before she could respond, Tom erupted, "Your Honor, he's asking me if I still beat my wife. I'll give the same dignity to my answers that he gives to the questions."

The jury was waking up.

"Both lead attorneys, come up here."

Tom looked dispassionately at the judge and the two antagonists. Shifting his weight in the witness stand, he was unable to ease the throbbing in both arms. He felt miserable. He was mad, very mad. Tom glanced at the jury. No rapport whatsoever. Next he scanned the rows of onlookers. He thought *If they only knew.* He looked out at the reporters, freelance writers and a single courtroom artist. For no particular reason he shifted his line of sight to the back of the room. There they were. First, he saw Susie. *Susie? Why are you here?* Pretty red hair; friendliest smile in Texas; his best ally. At that specific moment he felt the full affection of loving someone and knowing love has been returned. Susie turned away but found it impossible to resist returning to the look in his eyes. Tears welled up and rolled down her cheeks.

Garbled discussion at the judge's bench became heated. Tom did not notice.

Tom might have continued to gaze at Susie had she not been nudged by the person on her left. *Paige.* A memory tugged at him. He could see her climbing over the side of her little plastic pool and running to hug him as he stepped from the car. She exceeded every expectation a father could have for a daughter. *God, she's beautiful.* Then to Ross, just the right man to take his place in her life. Steve, still looking 15. He was going to be a great, honorable lawyer someday. *I hope we work together in the future.*

He almost overlooked the other two. It was an eerie sensation. No sooner did Tom look back towards Susie than he saw Michelle White on Susie's right side. On occasion, Paige or Steve had watched him give testimony. But never the whole family. Standing directly behind Michelle against the back wall of the courtroom was Travis White. *Travis. What the . . ?* Large as life, the imposing figure seemed content to wait for his cue to take over the defense testimony. And just in time. But, he didn't move. And the suit. It was a dark blue, somewhat rumpled, sport coat and Land's End cotton twill trousers. Not Travis White's. Something more suited to Bill Newton. *Bill Newton.* It was Bill, not Travis. Tom focused to make sure. His spark of hope cooled to an ember. *No. Travis is dead. Dead at the hands of a man no more than twenty feet away.* But still, Bill Newton was there to support Tom. *Bill Newton. Damn. That's great. The best cop in Texas.* Tom's mind began to clear. He shook his head briskly. The clearing of his senses was precursor to a fluid, smooth functioning thought process. Tom sat up and, to the amazement of the few jurors and spectators watching him, raised his bent right arm into the air and took a shot at an imaginary figure in the vicinity of the prosecuting attorney. It wasn't imaginary to Tom. Susie nearly gasped out loud.

The lawyers returned to their benches as Judge Piazze addressed Tom.

"Mr. Seiler, the three of us have agreed to the manner in which questions will be asked. I expect you to join in the spirit of that agreement. If you don't, I will hold you in contempt."

"Yes, your Honor. I hurt myself on some concrete yesterday and I'm not quite up to par. Could I ask the bailiff for a glass of water?" The tone in Tom's voice changed from confrontational to conversational.

The bailiff, irritated to be given such a menial task, handed the cup to Tom. It was delicious. He felt better.

For the first minute of the resumed cross-examination Barry Colter held true to his word, then let it slide back into character assassination.

"Objection your Honor. Irrelevant. Previous cases have nothing to do with this case." Ed Harvey was livid.

"Your Honor, the answer to the question has everything to do with this case. A pattern of faulty analysis has everything to do with the credibility of the witness. Please recall Mr. Harvey's question to Dr. Simonis."

"Overruled, but be careful Mr. Colter."

"Yes, your Honor." Barry turned to Tom and waited for the response.

"Yes, I testified in the Hilger and Neff cases.

Barry homed in on the witness. "How did you fair in those cases?"

"We lost both." To himself, he added, *because your expert witnesses lied through their teeth.*

Other inflammatory questions were interjected in a subtle pattern.

"Have you ever adjusted, even slightly, the results of an analysis to favor the position of the side you represented?" Barry Colter was close, very close to Tom. He was in Tom's space. Before allowing Tom to answer, Barry interjected, "And feel free to answer the question fully."

Tom remained in control. "In a very rare case where it was a 50-50 call, I, by human nature, may have assumed a favorable scenario. But as for lying, which is what you're implying . . ."

"Never mind, Mr. Seiler, you've already answered the question."

Tom looked directly at Judge Piazze. For one of the few times during her tenure on the bench, she averted eye-to-eye contact.

The clock showed 3:45 when Judge Piazze told Barry Colter to wrap things up for the day. Barry had the perfect closing to imprint in the mind of each juror. Ed Harvey failed to object to the questioning.

"How much beer do you drink Mr. Seiler?"

Where the hell is the objection? This is out of line. "To be absolutely honest, when I'm not flying or working, I probably drink a six-pack at night, sometimes more." Tom looked over at Ed, lost in thought.

Tom's stare finally caught Ed just in time to object to Barry's fraudulent question about Tom's being convicted of a DWI. It was stricken from the records, but not from minds. Then came his final question of the day.

"So, to this point there has been a line of reasoning on your part that what we have is an unfortunate accident through no one's fault."

Tom responded with mock politeness. "Are you asking me a question or just talking to all of us?"

A slight stirring permeated the courtroom.

In an irritated gesture, Barry Colter pointed to Tom and, in raised voice, stated, "Mr. Seiler, everyone here is tired of your arrogance. We all are exhausted because of you."

Exhausted? Tom thought to himself, *You don't know the half of it.*

Barry continued, "Let me finish with a scenario. It involves a tired, poorly trained, driver falling asleep at the wheel. You've rambled on with a litany of little insignificant blips about physics. Why haven't you considered the possible scenario of the driver, as happened unfortunately to Mr. White, just falling asleep at the wheel?"

Falling asleep? Michelle White almost shot from her seat, only to be grabbed firmly by Susie.

Tom gave Barry a calm, almost placid, stare. Somewhere in the recesses of his mind, Tom expected the question. He controlled the anger. His thoughts brought back a smirk. He was not reacting in a manner preferred and expected by Barry Colter. He initially wanted to wait until after the family meeting scheduled for that evening. But no, he couldn't wait. The time was now. He owed it to Travis. Before responding, Tom searched the room for Michelle White. It took a few seconds before she looked back at him. Tom looked intently into her eyes, then smiled. She understood. *O.K., Tom.*

"Did you hear my question, Mr. Seiler, or are you tired too?"

First, Tom spoke silently to Travis. *O.K., amigo.* Then he spoke silently to Barry Colter. *O.K., asshole, get set for a ram.*

Tom turned to Judge Piazze. "Ma'am, I realize I am under oath. I am certain that I can answer Mr. Colter's question to everyone's satisfaction except his. I only ask that I be given the freedom to answer the question fully, without constant interruption from Mr. Colter. He seems to have an affinity for rudeness."

The crowd noise verified that Tom was confronting Barry Colter. Barry did not respond, caught by a quick stab of discomfort.

Tom finished, "I know the driver did not fall asleep."

The Judge quieted the courtroom. She ignored Tom's remarks on rudeness. "As long as you are directly answering the question. Any problem, Mr. Colter?" She squinted her eyes ever so slightly at the lawyer for whom she held such contempt.

"Not at all, your Honor." After all, the verdict was signed, sealed and almost delivered. He could easily handle Tom's crudeness. Still, Barry knew he was relinquishing control to one hell of an engineer.

"Mr. Seiler, the floor is yours."

"Thank you. I do need to use the courtroom easel." He slowly moved from the witness stand and nodded to Ed Harvey.

Fred Stadler looked at Barry Colter. Barry's eyes were locked on Tom.

Ed and Joe took the hint and moved the easel from the far side of the courtroom to a place directly in front of the defense bench, facing the jury. The angle was fine for Judge Piazze. Fortunately, it was a large easel and Tom used a wide, black magic marker. Tom asked Ed and Joe to help him remove his coat. Bloodstains had seeped through the gauze covering his left arm. His right elbow was swollen and bruised. The jury sat up in their seats. Noise rose, rolled through the courtroom, then abated slowly to absolute silence. Barry Colter's senses tightened.

"Thanks." Tom then turned back to the easel and, very slowly, neatly wrote DRIVER/WHITE – FALLING ASLEEP. Beneath the statement he wrote PHYSICAL on the left side and DECEASED on the right side. His finished product read:

DRIVER/WHITE – FALLING ASLEEP

PHYSICAL	*DECEASED*
SPEED	WILLIAM TALLANT
VISIBILITY	SYBIL WEEMS
STRAPS	HANK D'ARCY
WEATHER	MARLA D'ARCY
TIME	ZEBULON D'ARCY
ROAD SPECIFICATIONS	TRAVIS WHITE
ANIMALS	JUDSON WEEMS

Judge Piazze overruled Barry's objection to the title concerning Travis White and the initiation of the column under DECEASED. He could state his objection after the easel had been set up.

Barry Colter almost pleaded. "Your Honor, my question related to the physical causes in this case, not the unfortunate people caught up in it."

Judge Piazze relented. "Mr. Seiler, is there a direct link between the names on the easel and a direct response to Mr. Colter's question?"

"Yes, your Honor, there is."

"Objection, your Honor." Barry Colter's voice was loud, but this time it was more urgent than arrogant. "Mr. Seiler doesn't even have his facts right. Mr. White's death has nothing to do with this trial and Mr. Weems is the plaintiff, not a decedent."

"He's right Mr. Seiler." Judge Piazze ceased speaking when she saw Tom turn his back to her.

Tom walked to the jury box railing. He gently placed both hands on the rail, something he had always wanted to do. Then, in a very strong, articulate, voice he made his position to the jurors.

"No, your Honor. He is not right. Mr. White's death has everything to do with this trial. And, as for Mr. Weems, he is dead. I killed him."

A single gasp lifted from the courtroom.

Tom waited for the noise to subside. Judge Piazze was speechless.

Tom backed away from the jury railing and walked directly in front of Barry Colter, sitting stunned behind his table.

Ignoring pain, Tom swept his bent arm across the table towards Barry Colter while speaking directly to the jury, "As an expert witness, as a practicing engineer, and as someone who has studied the events in Alvin in more depth than anyone else in the state of Texas, it is my expert opinion that, other than Mr. Judson Weems, everyone else on the chart died at the hands of Mr. Barry Colter, a despicable son-of-a-bitch."

Tom looked into Barry's eyes, turned his back, and walked to the witness stand.

He turned around again and addressed Judge Piazze. "And, your Honor, I personally ask you to impound Mr. White's Buick Park Avenue in Markham."

31

I DID IT - YOU DID IT!!
WITNESS KILLS ONE, ACCUSES LAWYER OF MURDER

In a stunning move, Mr. Thomas Seiler, defense expert witness in the D'Arcy wrongful death suit, accused Mr. Barry Colter, lead attorney for the plaintiff, of premeditated multiple murders. Before an incredulous courtroom, Mr. Seiler also admitted that he had killed the plaintiff, Mr. Judson Weems . . .

Street sales of the morning edition of *The Houston Chronicle* exploded to a record level. Similar reactions moved across the country. Late evening television news bulletins flashed across millions of screens. Investigative reporters spent the night putting together background stories. Descriptions of the courtroom scene by eyewitnesses played over and over on CNN, Fox, MSNBC and other cable news programs. Details of the alleged murders and Tom's killing of Jud Weems were sketchy because Judge Sandra Piazze terminated the court proceedings almost immediately. It didn't take long, however, to identify Buck Tallant and Jud Weems as former clients of Colter, Fisher and King. That both won their cases under the representation of Barry Colter added intrigue to the exploding story. Buck Tallant's Marine Corps record was a tantalizing hors d'oeuvre for the insatiable appetite of the press.

Fortunately for Tom and Susie, they spent a good deal of time at the Clear Lake Regional Medical Center where the orthopedic staff improved ever so slightly on Michelle's work. After recleaning the wound, they casted Tom's right arm from mid-forearm to mid-upper arm. Fortunately, Tom looked far worse than he felt.

267

Susie drove the car, Tom satisfied to keep every body part still.

"I've got to tell you, I was impressed at what they said about Michelle's work. She really knew what she was doing." Susie felt a sense of well being.

Tom chuckled, looking over at his wife. "To be honest, they hurt me more than Michelle or Weems put together."

They rounded the corner and saw the crowd. Susie beat Tom to the punch. "Shit."

Tom and Susie drove through a cordon of reporters to the garage. The gaggle followed the car down the driveway.

"Mr. Seiler. Do you have proof about Mr. Colter?"

"Why did you kill Mr. Weems?"

"Do you know why you haven't been arrested?"

Tom thought about the last question long before it was asked. *Harker has to know that I see her involved in this. She's being cautious.*

Tom raised his left arm as best he could and partially waved to the gathering. "Sorry, I have nothing to say. My lawyer has already commented on the situation." He pushed the remote to the garage. Wounds and all, he stepped quickly around the car to open Susie's door. Without stopping to grab a beer, they disappeared into the house. Ross and Paige had taken the day off from work. Michelle arrived earlier in the afternoon, before the reporters. Steve and Kelly negotiated the maze 10 minutes later. Tom was slightly concerned when told that Bill Newton called, saying he couldn't make it. He was given an investigation that was immediate and time sensitive. Tom thought about Elizabeth Harker, then dismissed it from his mind.

Paige and Ross brought the salsa, tortillas, tomatoes, peppers, onions and Monterey Jack. Ross grilled the chicken while Paige and Michelle prepared the filling. Corn chips and beer topped off the chicken fajitas. There was plenty to eat and plenty to discuss. The discussion around the dining room table fell far from family discussions of the past.

Tom finished his third fajita and took a large swallow of beer. He looked pensively at the others, and spoke. ". . . but what was most interesting, was that I saw Harker at least three times during the day. What a bitch. Each time she'd have some private conversation with an investigator - I think I talked to three different ones - the tone of the interrogation would change. Each time things would go downhill. I know they believe me, but she grabbed them by the balls. She's orchestrating a deliberate move away from what the hell happened at the airstrip and my evidence about Colter to possible inaccuracies in my version of things. Basically, she wants to make a liar out of me." He chuckled slightly and continued. "You know what else, she made sure they pumped me for any possible involvement about other conspirators. I played dumb as hell. At this point I see two things with Harker. First, she's scared as hell that I know something about her relationship with our friend Barry. On that one I'm happy to let her sweat. But, secondly, because she is involved in the plotting of the Alvin murders, I think she's more dangerous to me than he is. Right now, if anything happens to me, Colter, not Harker, is in very big trouble. Anyway, I'm a little surprised she didn't hold me overnight in the slammer. Ed made a great case that I am not a flight risk." Tom shook his head and smiled. "I drove him crazy today with the investigators. Long way to go to fill Travis' shoes, but Ed's getting there."

Everyone recognized that Elizabeth Harker was a danger – would she try to kill Tom?

Ross spoke bluntly. "What concerns me is that her actions are going to be strictly governed by her self-interest. If that's true, maybe the best question is 'Why would she not try to kill you?'"

Susie didn't speak at all. Her mind raced with horrible thoughts.

"I've thought about that also." Tom rose and walked to the refrigerator. "Who wants a beer?" Only Steve accepted the offer. Tom returned and sat down.

He popped the tab on the can, then drank. He looked around the table. "The one big thing in my favor is that, if Harker would kill me, then all eyes would turn to Colter. She knows it; he knows it. He would be enraged knowing that she has just sold him out. He'd go after her. If he can kill everyone else, he would certainly not hesitate to kill her. She understands how Colter ticks."

Steve offered his input. "But we're looking at numbers. There are at least two people who want you dead. Both are capable and willing. Maybe you ought to confront Harker in public in order to put her on the potential killer list as well." Wise advice.

One by one, the Seiler family, with Ross as a full member, offered possibilities about what Barry Colter and Elizabeth Harker may or may not do. Tom, following one of his trips to the refrigerator, grabbed a paper pad and pencil. Opinions and thoughts about the unfolding play were written on the pad. Only Susie had failed to contribute.

After many scenarios were presented, Tom asked everyone to give him a couple of minutes to think things through. He tore the used sheets from the pad, separated them in front of him and thought silently for five minutes. He wrote two lines on the fresh page. Tom, looked up at his family and offered them his wisdom. "Here's what I intend to do. You tell me what's a better idea."

They were up until midnight. Tom called Ed Harvey before everyone left. Time to let Ed know exactly what was going on. Tom's next interrogation was to continue at nine in the morning.

Tom, still high on the events of the previous 36 hours, and Susie, in fear beyond an ability to sleep, volunteered for kitchen duty. Susie was putting the dishwashing detergent in its receptacle when the phone rang. She looked at the clock then grabbed the receiver and spoke.

"This is Susie Seiler."

After a short listening pause, she stretched the line towards Tom. She frowned slightly.

Tom took the receiver, aware of the time of night. "Hello, this is Tom."

"My name is David Salk. I was a client of Mr. Colter and the District Attorney a few years back. I need to talk to you privately."

●

By early morning the weather had turned bad. A cold, steady rain fell from gray, nimbostratus clouds. Raw weather is not unheard of in Houston, Texas. The mood in the small unattractive office matched the weather.

"You know what? Yesterday you offered me a hot cup of coffee, you asked some sensible questions and at first you treated me like I had some dignity. Excuse the language, and I duly note the recorder is on, but let me ask you . . ." Tom paused briefly, taking just enough time to make eye contact with each of the interrogating officers. ". . . why are you treating me like a fucking criminal?" Before they could respond, he added, "Has someone in the district attorney's office ordered you to treat me this way?" With the recorder taking in his every word, Tom had defined the change in the interrogation.

Ed Harvey winced, but said nothing.

Without speaking, one of the officers got up and left the room. He returned in five minutes. The hot coffee was delicious. Tom took a small sip, put the cup down, and waited for the next question.

"But, in a plane that takes off in, did you say 200 feet, why didn't you just take off?" The shorter, stocky investigator kept turning the focus of the questions to Tom's need to kill Jud Weems. "If you suspected the accident in Alvin was a murder, why didn't you turn the evidence over to us long before we got to this point? Doesn't it seem strange that you had to kill someone first?"

They questioned Tom for a full 30 minutes without mentioning Barry Colter. The lawyer's proclamation of outrage on national television had imprinted itself in Tom's mind. *Play it close to the vest* he told himself.

His answer was sardonic. "Well, first of all, and I've already told you this, I was trying to find out what happened to my best friend. Then, guess what, after tracing the possible route of travel when Mr. White died, who do I run into but the guy I think was involved in murder over in Alvin. Now that's coincidence. And, of course, I think someone else was the mastermind behind it. Of course, you guys don't have the brains, or the balls, to pursue that angle. Well, once again, let me explain. The bastard has shot me, I escape and get to my plane and try to get the hell out of there. In a mad race, he closes within 10 feet of me, puts a round through the cockpit and is doing his very best to kill me. I had two choices – get killed or kill. I chose the second option. My only chance was to attack him with the Cub. I did and I'm here to tell you about it."

The interrogation clearly showed that the emphasis had, indeed, changed from Barry Colter to Tom Seiler. The evidence Tom turned over was, as he knew it would be, circumstantial. The savage fight with Jud Weems was credible. Tom told the investigators, with Ed Harvey's concurrence, that his flight to Indianola was the result of a voicemail from Travis. When asked about the voicemail, Tom replied, "Damn, I may have erased it." He hadn't erased any of the messages. Still, the linkage to Barry Colter was not as strong as Tom asserted on the stand. On the other hand, Tom hadn't turned over all the evidence in his possession.

His third session with the police investigators was held on Friday. Rather than piece together the actual chain of events that cost seven lives, the investigator's focus was to find inconsistencies in Tom's repeated answers and possible flaws in his character.

"You're free for lunch. Give the office a call at 1:30 and we'll let you know when to come back."

Ed and Tom walked out of the bland office.

Ed offered to build a strategy. "We need to nail down a lot of things. I appreciated the brief this morning, but I'm still getting too many surprises in all this."

"Ed, you're doing great. And getting better with time. You've done a helluva job in first, letting me speak, and then challenging them on some of the bullshit." He patted him on the shoulder. "I'll give you everything when I get back, but I have a date with Susie and she sure as hell comes first."

●

Tom and Susie split the distance between downtown Houston and Clear Lake, meeting at Friday's just off the Gulf Freeway.

"As far away from smoking as we can get. Thanks." Tom was relieved that his face, almost immortalized on television and in the newspapers, was unknown to the waitress. She led them to a table in the back. Barring one table of six, which recognized him immediately, the couple enjoyed relative privacy. They needed it.

Sitting directly across from Susie, both hands resting lightly on the table, Tom said, "They absolutely know I'm telling the truth. What I can't fathom is that they seem like pretty forceful guys who know what's right and what's not. How can they prostitute themselves so much? Honey, it's almost comical looking at their disgust with themselves. I don't know how she does it, but Harker is really putting on the pressure. I'd quit before taking that bullshit."

"But, what about Harker?" Slight furrows appeared in horizontal rows across her forehead. "We both have seen it so many times. There's justice and then there's justice. The truth be damned. Tom this . . ."

The waitress placed a Miller Lite and an iced tea at the table. Susie waited until she smiled and left, then continued.

". . . this is a nightmare and I don't see us waking up soon. Or ever."

Tom reflected on Susie's statement. *How will this end? Will it end?* He represented a serious threat to Elizabeth Harker as well as Barry Colter. He knew Colter was capable of murder, but wasn't as sure about her. The link between the two of them was there. Still, her position 'in and for the County of Harris, Texas', gave her immense power. She could crush him like a bug. *I need to attack. But how can . . .*

"Honey, are you with me?" Susie broke his train of thought.

"Oh, sorry. You're right. This might never go away. Unless we make it go away. It's probably time to put last night's discussion into action."

The waitress arrived with two blackened chicken sandwiches. Both plates were heaped with french fries. His first bite brought on a voracious appetite. Between bites and swallows, they tried to speak of other subjects, but it kept coming back to Tom's involvement in the Alvin incident. They finished their meals and Tom rose to make his obligatory call to the detectives. Next to the bar was a pay phone. It was occupied. He could have used his cell phone, but waiting for the young woman to finish her call afforded both of them the opportunity to watch the events unfolding on CNN. Barry Colter was speaking, surrounded by a throng of news reporters and cameramen.

"I have no idea where this strategy is coming from. I do know that Mr. Seiler's testimony brought the trial to a halt and there are people who would benefit from a mistrial. At this point we're more interested in the parties, and their motives, which forced such an outrageous statement from a witness who clearly had not been credible."

The woman hung up the phone and turned to nod a smile at Tom. Before he could respond in kind, the smile drained from her face.

Will it ever end? He picked up the receiver and dialed.

"We want you back at two." Detective Chartran placed the phone onto the cradle.

Tom whispered into the air. "Shit."

●

Most of Jud Weems' remains had been collected from the airstrip during the night. It was a gruesome task compounded by the effects of almost 24 hours exposed first to sun and heat, then to cold, steady rain. Large body parts were placed in separate bags and labeled. Assorted bits of remains were collected in groups and placed in small baggies. Jud's undamaged pistol was found next to his left leg.

"At least they can identify this guy's hand." The paramedic held up a clear bag with Jud's hand, broken finger attached, in it.

The Cub was impounded for evidence. Because of the rain, it would remain in Tom's hangar for two days. Although they could not get near the Cub, a full complement of pilots, families and friends converged on the La Porte Airport. They watched from a distance as forensic experts took samples of Jud Weems' remains from the propeller and front of the fuselage. Samples of Tom's blood were taken from inside the cockpit. It was a mess. Two accident experts, casual friends of Tom, combed over the damaged propeller and the entrance and exit bullet holes. Their investigative reports would later state that it was fortunate the laminated wooden propeller did not shred during the return flight. Tom flew as low and slow as possible for that reason.

●

The afternoon questioning was more of the same. Tom grew frustrated with the repetition. The show belonged mostly to Tom. Other than a few interpretations of questions asked and points of applicable law, Ed was comfortable with Tom's handling of the interrogation. On two occasions he did persuade Tom to settle down.

"Tom, it's what they have to do."

"Well, how about us switching places and you guys let me ask the stupid fucking questions?" He glared at the men he decided were Liz Harker's eunuchs.

The questioning ended at 5:00. No charges, only the admonition that he was to remain in the area.

Tom walked to the door, paused while directing Ed to lead their exit, and addressed the two detectives. "How do you look at yourselves in the mirror? We all know what I'm saying is true and you're about to let a killer off the hook. For the rest of my life I'll remember you both. I'll always ask 'why?' and every possible answer will include the word 'pathetic.' Just plain pathetic."

Both investigators wanted to respond but were silent. Tom walked out of the door and joined Ed in the hallway. They made a quick stop in the restroom before departing. Ed draped Tom's blue rain slicker over his shoulders in preparation for the rain. Once outside they turned right on Calhoun. The impossible events, the bitter interrogation and the rain weighed on Tom. It was all too heavy. Tom suddenly stopped. *It's time.*

"Shit. I left two folders on the sink in the men's room. Hang on, I'll be right back." At the doorway Tom turned around and called back to Ed. "Hey, it's raining. Let's call it a day. I'll give you a call tonight. Thanks Ed, I almost lost it."

"Yeah, O.K. Tom. Hang in there pal." Ed placed his hands in his pockets, hunching his shoulders together for protection from the nickel-sized raindrops. He picked up his pace.

Tom walked briskly into the building.

32

Tom half jogged up the front stairs to the elevator for the short ride to the second floor. He slowed his pace and walked down the hall. The receptionist walked out at three minutes after five. She didn't lock the door. The District Attorney was still in her office. Tom pulled his slicker from his shoulders and let it drop to the floor.

He opened the main door, walked past the empty receptionist's desk and proceeded to Elizabeth Harker's office. An eternity had passed since his last visit. It crossed his mind that the greatest victory to that point was the Stetly verdict. The loser was Ms. Elizabeth Harker. *The rare winner was the American Justice System* Tom thought. But that was history. He paused briefly at the door, contemplating knocking first. *No, that would be a sign of respect.* He walked in.

Elizabeth Harker sat at her oak desk, head down, writing notes on a legal pad. The same beautiful dark hair, only this time tied in a French braid. She wore a white silk blouse with blue scarf. She was a stunningly beautiful woman. She was startled by the noise of the turning doorknob. Tom's appearance through the opening door brought forth two quick bullets of emotion – loathing followed by fear.

She sat up straight in her chair, eyes turning evil. "You just get the hell out of my office right now."

Liz Harker buzzed her secretary, then realized it was past 5:00. Pushing down brusquely with both hands on the oak desktop, she stood up. She pushed the play button on a small recorder behind a small potted plant, and then walked towards the door. "You're about to be arrested."

Tom sat down in one of the burgundy leather chairs. "Go ahead, bitch. I have a lot of evidence on Travis White's death and you're a main character."

275

Liz slowed her pace but continued towards the door.   She grabbed the doorknob as Tom continued.

"For instance, you were near Indianola on the day Travis White died.   Go ahead, I've got enough on you to make your head spin."

How does he know this?   She released the doorknob and, in doing so, relinquished control of the situation.

He added matter-of-factly, "By the way, you can tape all of this you want to. Your recorder is ideal. Or, if the intercom is open, the more the merrier."

She returned to her desk and sat down. Pushing the stop button on the recorder signified guilt. Tom was not sure of the degree of guilt, but guilt nonetheless.

"All right Mr. Seiler, tell me about all of your hidden evidence linking me to the so-called murder of Mr. White." She continued to put on an air of innocence which both knew was a façade. The house of cards was coming down. The only question was who would be taken down in the collapse.

Why didn't Weems just kill the bastard?   The thought seared her brain.

Tom seemed to sense her mindset. "For starters, what I will share with you is safeguarded in multiple locations."

Her options to have Tom killed were eliminated by his statement.

At least in the short term, she thought.

Tom continued. "And let's be accurate. We're not talking about Mr. White. Actually, I see you as only an accessory after the fact to his murder. But I know for fact that you are intimately linked to the murders of the entire D'Arcy family. Not only are you an arrogant bitch, you are evil, a leech sucking off society. When I think of Travis White and then look at you I have an almost uncontrollable urge to reach across this desk and choke that sleazy fucking neck of yours until your brain explodes." He realized that he was leaning forward in the chair, almost out of control. He wanted revenge. Tom sat back, took in a large volume of air, then exhaled slowly

Liz Harker was clearly frightened. She tried to assert herself. "You still have not mentioned anything of substance Mr. Seiler and I'm getting tired of this discussion."

Tom leaned forward again, lips tight, eyes piercing through to the back of her skull.

He spoke. "And I'm tired of your bullshit. Once you've listened to what I'm going to play, you have exactly two choices. You can continue to act like a righteous bitch, in which case I, or persons I have designated, turn state's evidence. Or, you can sit down, listen to what else I have to say, then be prepared to accept some terms I have for you."

To this point the playing out of events was going exactly as Tom had envisioned it.

"Play it."

Tom, ever so gingerly, took a palm-sized recorder from his left breast pocket. He held it out, almost pointing it at Liz Harker. "I knew Travis White always carried this in his car. Sure enough, when I inspected the car at the salvage yard, there it was tucked away with a Velcro strap underneath his seat. I'm only going to play one of several messages." He pressed the small red circular button.

A short crackling sound preceded Travis' voice. Liz recognized immediately that it was authentic.

". . . oh, hey amigo. This is unbelievable. Scumbag Harker just drove by me headed back towards Houston on Texas 35. Damn, Tom, I didn't get it on the camcorder, but that was her, Mercedes and all. She saw me and tried to hide. Damn, this is great. I'm at the turnoff to 316 in Port Lavaca. She came from the direction of Magnolia Beach or Indianola. It's high noon, the second of November. Looks like what we have on her, Colter and Weems is solid stuff. Only one I haven't seen yet is Colter. Got to make a choice here, so I'll keep following Weems."

. . . what you have on her . . . haven't seen . . . Colter. Color drained from her face with the knowledge that Tom did have circumstantial evidence. She just didn't know the strength of the evidence.

Tom pressed the small black square button, stared at the recorder for a couple of seconds, then turned his gaze back to Elizabeth Harker.

"Just to make things real, I can add your participation with Colter on the Tallant case in May of '91. Your fingerprints are all over Colter's beach house in Seadrift. Beyond the record I also have Travis on the phone answering system at my home. He mentioned you, Colter and Weems. Even checked with his credit card companies. Travis White purchased some items at a place called 'John's Fishing Tackle' or something like that. And guess what - it's in Indianola." Tom paused to allow the information to sink to her brain. "Of course, it will be very easy to check to see if you made any purchases in the area around Indianola."

Liz had difficulty swallowing.

"Take a look at your accomplice." Tom took a photograph and dropped it on the desk in front of her.

Liz stared in disbelief. The figure was small but the picture quality was quite good. Jud Weems could be seen walking to the hangar in Indianola – clinching a pistol.

The assault continued. "Now, asshole, pay attention. In your mind you are weighing the possibility that what I have told you is all I've got. In and of itself, it might not be enough for a conviction. Even Travis White thought I didn't have enough – for a while. But his last messages were nothing short of euphoric about sacking both you and Colter." He relaxed in the chair. "What I'm saying is that I just might have enough evidence on you and Colter to send you both to a lethal injection in Huntsville. In California, you might get away with it; in Texas you get to be the next Carla Faye Tucker. Take your chances. You've got 10 seconds before I walk out the door."

Liz Harker mustered her last ounce of bravado. "What you've got wouldn't convict anyone." She pleaded with whomever her God was that there would be no more.

Tom smiled. "Well, dumbass, Travis' message on the voice recorder is backed up by a note we found in his office. It refers to a note written by Barry Colter linking you, Weems and Colter at an airstrip. Two other initials, 'G' and 'L' obviously stood for 'Get laid.' You might want to check out your wardrobe. You left a pair of your panties at the beach house in Seadrift. And I don't want to be crude but there are stains on them that have all the DNA needed to put you and Colter in bed together. And speaking of DNA, a section of stained carpet from Travis' trunk is being analyzed for DNA right now. So, don't think for one minute that murder can't be proved. You've talked to Colter and you know what went on in that car. Finally, after listening to the recorder, I did enlist the help of a friend who was more than willing to dig into your relationship with Barry Colter. Remember when he forgot to zip his pants coming out of your office? Other folks do. Must have been a great blowjob."

Tom stood up, then leaned over the desk and spoke one last time. "I could go on. Of course, maybe I don't have any more. Maybe the information that a third person was recruited by Colter is false." Liz had been told of the recruiting process and knew the existence of a third person, although she couldn't remember the name. "In that case, you'd be free. Maybe just a little taint of adultery. But then again, maybe I have a lot more. I am prepared to go to the press to assert that you are involved."

A door closed a couple of offices away, startling Liz Harker. Tom saw her reaction.

He added, "The press, local and national, would jump all over this and you know it."

She stared blankly at Tom.

"And think of Barry Colter. You know exactly what he is. If he gets wrapped up in this . . ." Tom waited to allow her to think, ". . . and he will . . ." Another pause. "He will not go down alone. He would drop you in a second."

It was all over. She realized that only one option existed that offered her possible freedom. The urge to cry like a little lost girl welled up inside her. The image of Barry Colter made her shudder. To accept Tom's mandate was to betray

Barry. Then she realized that the voice message left only one person unseen – and possibly free from the whole mess. Barry. *Who betrayed whom? He's supposed to be in love with me. He got me into this mess.* She was fixated on freedom.

"That's it Ms. Harker. Take your chances." Tom turned around, placing the recorder in his shirt pocket, and walked towards the door.

She looked up at him while still lost in thought. He reached the door by the time she snapped out of her trance.

"I accept." Liz Harker spoke quietly but firmly. Cold droplets of rain raced each other down the large panes of glass. It was a miserable day.

Tom didn't have more evidence. What he did have was personal conviction.

●

"Yeah, the guys were talking about it big time. Colter was one unhappy camper."

Bill Newton spoke to Tom across the table at Marty's Café. Until now, their association had been clandestine.

"As soon as they loosened the grip on you, they brought him in and started getting personal. I've only seen him a couple of times, but I can tell you straight up, he was furious." Bill sipped the steaming coffee and continued. "I missed it but others said they could hear him screaming at Harker through two sets of doors yesterday afternoon."

Tom followed suit and sipped at his coffee. "Yeah, those two deserve each other. Wonder how all this will play out?"

Bill changed the discussion. "That reminds me. Tony Chartran didn't know you and I were friends. We just happened to be shooting the bull this morning before Colter arrived. He believed everything you said. He felt bad that . . ."

Tom interrupted brusquely, "The guy's a pissant. If he knew I was telling the truth, ask him why he caved in to the point of selling his soul."

Bill was caught off guard by Tom's outburst. "Hey friend. Give him hell, not me."

"Sorry Bill, I just have a hard time with the low price so many people put on their value system." Tom took another sip of coffee. "Good old Tony and his benevolent friend gave me the weekend off. I'm going to turn the day over to Susie. I've really slammed her with all this stuff. And it's sure as hell not over with." Tom looked up and focused on Bill. "Anyway, let's discuss your situation. If you hadn't checked things out at Colter's place and her office, things would be very different. I appreciate what you've done."

"Tom, we're pretty much the same. Had I not come to the same conclusions about Travis' death, I would have turned you down. Had I asked you to do something unethical, you would have turned me down," Bill answered. He added, "I've got to tell you something else. I'm Catholic. Pretty hard-nosed one at that. Since meeting you, I've come to realize that religions have no monopoly on ethics."

Tom, caught off-guard by the depth of the compliment, lifted his cup in Bill's direction. "Thanks, Bill." Holding off wetness in his eyes, he quickly changed the conversation. "Any problems with letting people know you've helped me on all of this? It's going to come out one way or another."

"Nope. None. Either they'll fire me on the spot, in which case I'll come to you for handouts, or they'll promote me." Bill exuded a huge grin matching his physical presence. "Here's to tomorrow."

A delicious breakfast arrived.

●

Saturday afternoon eventually belonged to both of them. Tom knew that Sunday required a return to working on an orderly assemblage of facts pointing to Colter but not immediately to Harker. The transition of focus from murder to his wife was steady, though not easy. They left the house for Galveston. The rain and clouds dissipated and their spirits lifted. The surge to normalcy was halted only temporarily at the point where Route 528 crossed the Gulf Freeway. Susie watched the distraction on Tom's face as he glanced at the highway sign directing travelers towards Alvin. It lay quietly eight miles to the southwest. It's a nice town, well kept for the most part with mostly modest homes in which friendly families carry out their day-to-day lives. The D'Arcy kids grew up in Alvin – nice kids, all of them. Downtown Alvin is replicated across the State of Texas – a small municipal center, several stores holding assorted commodities, and the proverbial tasty restaurants in which politics and religion are overshadowed only by baseball and football. The townspeople know that Alvin holds a national treasure in Nolan Ryan, the Hall of Fame baseball pitcher. Sybil's father had played high school ball with Nolan. On a more notorious note, Alvin also holds the national record for most rainfall in a 24-hour period – 43 inches. But, for all its pleasantries, Alvin was one of two places to which Tom did not want to ever return. The other was Indianola.

Susie wanted to speak but left Tom with his thoughts.

Galveston was beautiful. The last vestiges of clouds continued their move to the east, leaving azure skies and beige sand beckoning to lovers. Tom and Susie parked at the Convention Center and walked to the beach. Their sweatshirts were perfect windbreakers. Another couple, hands held, strolled the beach to the southwest. The breeze was cool and fresh, each wisp carrying them further away from Alvin and Indianola. A few seagulls flew nearby in hopes of a friendly handout. Tom and Susie stopped and sat down just far enough from the water's edge not to get damp. Off came their shoes and socks and up rolled their trousers. Susie did the honors for her beaten-up husband.

Susie, head and hands resting on her knees, stared out to sea. Tom gingerly scooped up a handful of sand and poured it onto a small pyramid. The sand danced. A small tinge of pain came and went, but it was a small price to pay for the catharsis of the sand. He poured another small scoop on top of the first. Then another.

"It's the story of life."

"What?" Susie turned to her husband.

"The sand. It's just like life. The grains pass through my hands, just like the passing of time." He lowered his left leg so Susie could see the tiny mountain forming beneath his curled hand.

Susie responded. "I wonder how many more grains the good Lord will allow us?" She placed her hand under his, catching the stream of sand.

Tom took another scoop, again allowing the sand to cascade on top of the growing pile. "Each grain looks like the others, yet each one is unique. Just like us. When they join together . . ." Tom moved his hand just above his growing sand castle, then let a new stream join the other grains, ". . . creation occurs. Even the grains in the center, though unseen, contribute to the others."

Susie took her own handful and gently poured it on Tom's masterpiece – a pile of sand.

"I wonder why all humans can't be like these?"

Tom studied the pile. "Oh, all the sand isn't contributing. Watch." He poured again. "Watch that some simply bounce off the pile. They don't contribute at all. Yeah, sand is life. Sometimes beautiful, sometimes not."

Head down, Tom sat motionless, silently caught in another world.

Susie put her hand on his back.

He spoke quietly. "You know, at the moment I killed Weems, I wasn't thinking about self defense. I was thinking about killing. I think I enjoyed it." Head down, speaking to the sand.

"You had no choice."

"I know. But I enjoyed it."

She squeezed his neck gently. *Please God, give him back to me.*

A cold gust caught their attention. Tom looked up, then at Susie.

"Time to move on."

They got up, Tom helped by Susie, brushed themselves off and walked to the damp sand. Both made sure they did not disturb the mound of sand they had created – time, wind and water would take it away soon enough.

Tom and Susie walked along the beach, making footprints in the sand. With each small wave, the water, still possessing warmth from the long, hot summer, washed over their bare feet.

Susie turned to Tom as they walked. "Let's take Aunt Tillie on a cruise. Or skiing in Austria. God knows she deserves it."

Aunt Tillie was a figment of their joint imaginations. When their schedule became overbooked, an entry to visit 'Aunt Tillie' would be logged into the calendar. Aunt Tillie was their saving grace.

Tom stopped and awkwardly turned Susie towards him. "You're on and you're in charge. Don't even tell me where, just give me one day to pack and we're out of here." He raised his arms, saying, "Forget the skiing." They laughed, then kissed, her arms wrapped tightly around his back. As best he could, Tom held the woman he loved. Their toes touched.

The evening, spent at the Galvez overlooking the seawall and beach, took Tom and Susie infinitely away from all that had surrounded them.

●

Tom walked out of the bathroom, hair combed, teeth brushed, and stark naked. Susie looked up from watching the morning news. "Not a bad body for someone so old. M'mm," Susie purred, "maybe I could be enticed."

Tom's reaction quickly took fruit. The pseudo-teenager proudly looked down and exclaimed. "Check this out." An adolescent smile proclaimed victory against age. As far as Tom was concerned, the old man in the mirror in Clear Lake was a stranger.

As he walked around the bed, Susie took the remote to turn off the television. She clicked it off . . . then clicked it on. "Tom!"

Tom turned to the set in time to see two seconds of a still photo showing Barry Colter. Bill Balleza was finishing a rare appearance on the KPRC morning news, "Police are withholding comment pending the coroner's report. We'll bring you updates as this story unfolds. In Sugarland, a hit and run . . .". Susie clicked it off.

Tom grabbed the phone and began dialing. Eight-fifteen.

Ed was waiting for the call.

"Hello."

"Ed, it's Tom. What's up on Colter? I just caught the end of a news report."

His voice was controlled, yet urgent.

"Tom, where the hell have you been? Colter's dead. Gunshot wound to the head. I don't have anything more on it than the news. It happened late last night. Found him in his car slumped over the steering wheel. It was suicide." The same controlled urgency. "By the way, where were you last night?"

"Galveston, with Susie. Where'd it happen?"

"Out at the Bear Creek Golf Course. Couple hundred yards off of Patterson Road on a golf cart trail. A pistol was with him. Don't know make or caliber. How soon can you get over here? We need to talk."

●

As expected, the police did want to talk to Tom. But the line of questioning was above board. To Tom, maybe it was a little too much above board. A few questions establishing his whereabouts were followed by those related to Tom's evidence against Barry Colter. The previous legal representations of Buck Tallant and Jud Weems bonded to other circumstantial evidence. The phone messages from Travis speaking of Barry Colter. The pro bono nature of the civil suit. The time gap between Travis' last message and his discovery near Markham. Not one piece standing alone meant anything. Juxtaposed one with another, the evidence painted a picture of suspicion around Barry Colter. If he were guilty, the blatant accusation and the gathering volume of evidence against him might have sent Barry Colter over the edge. Even if he were innocent, the damage to his reputation would be a major blow. His ego was very large - and possibly very fragile.

Tom returned home at 6:00 Sunday evening. He parked the old Buick Le Sabre beneath the basketball rim, walked the 20 feet to the garage refrigerator and took three Miller Lites. One was for Susie. A quick kiss but no real discourse. Tom wanted to see what new information had been gathered on Barry Colter's death. The thrust of the news report confirmed that he died of a .22 caliber gunshot wound through his right temple. The gun was found in his hand. No note was found in the car or at his home. His wife was still in shock and could not be reached for comment. The most significant aspect of his death, at least to Tom, was that Ms. Elizabeth Harker, the District Attorney, had taken the lead in investigating Barry Colter's death and the accusations of Mr. Tom Seiler.

She certainly has stature. Tom mused as Liz Harker spoke to him through the television screen. She needed no prepared notes and her delivery was perfect. "In consultation with Mayor Gillette and Police Chief Dudevoir, I am leading the investigation into the death of Mr. Barry Colter. We will also be investigating the recent allegations from Mr. Thomas Seiler, the defense expert witness in the

D'Arcy family wrongful death suit." She paused briefly to clear her throat, then continued. "I believe I speak for the entire community in stating that the incident is most unfortunate and our condolences go out to Mrs. Colter."

Tom shook his head and sighed. "What a bullshitter. Like she really cares one whit about poor Mrs. Colter. Sounds like she's up for re-election."

The television audio continued. "Though not often, I have worked with Mr. Colter in the past. He was a brilliant lawyer who served the citizens of Houston with great dignity. As such, I would ask the community not to make judgments about his manner of death or any guilt or innocence in the D'Arcy case. And let me emphasize that even if the preliminary indication of suicide is confirmed, that, in and of itself, does not presuppose any guilt in the deaths of the D'Arcys in Alvin."

Tom listened intently, thinking out loud as she spoke. "That's it. Home free. Harker's going to find it as suicide, probably cut off any murder investigation, and get as far away as possible from Houston. All of South Texas will be distraught over her departure. All except us."

Susie, sitting next to him on the couch, spoke quietly. "I really can't even begin to comprehend all of this. It's totally surreal."

Tom lifted his wounded arms and examined them. "Except for these, I'd agree with you." He slumped back into the couch, crossing his legs on the coffee table. "But for us it's coming to an end. And you know what, I'm not sure I'm happy with the ending. Colter shoots himself, so he's off the hook. He deserved to think about death for a few years first. As for Harker, who knows? I've got a lot, but I don't think I really have enough to hang her. Hopefully, she's not sure of what I have. But I suspect she'll skate on all of this. She'll leave Houston. I already feel pity on the poor souls she meets during the rest of her miserable life."

Susie gently cupped her hand on his, then asked, "Is it really over for us, or will we carry it on our shoulders for the rest of our lives?"

Tom turned to her and spoke quietly, pensively. "It's not over completely, but we'll pass through this, just as we've passed through hell before. We really haven't changed essentially. Except for Travis, whom we'll always miss, our friends are the same. We still have the same way of living our lives. Most of all, we have our family and each other."

Tom released his hand from hers. He walked to the CD player, switching off the television with the remote. He switched it on and selected the third CD in the queue.

"Come here, friend."

Susie joined him in the middle of the room. To the music of Enya, they swayed back and forth. He kissed the nape of her neck. It felt right.

Epilogue

Early December.   The absence of snow has little effect on Christmas celebrations in Houston. In some neighborhoods there are gentle reminders of the season – the subdued sprinkling of tiny white lights and a few green wreaths. In others, the competition for finest decorations is boisterous, bright and sometimes outrageous. Even Buddhist, Hindu and Muslim families have been known to join in on the secular festivities. For Tom and Susie Seiler, there was reason to celebrate. Colter's death had been ruled suicide. A crowbar was recovered from the water in Indianola and forensic experts were analyzing it as the possible weapon used in Travis' murder. The police notified Tom that his participation in the D'Arcy investigation was no longer needed. No charges would be filed in the death of Jud Weems. The lawsuit against Flagg Brothers had been terminated. There never would be a final conclusion as to Barry's guilt or innocence. Ms. Elizabeth Harker, with great fanfare, announced regretfully her leaving the practice of law. She would return shortly to her roots in New York where she would pursue a new career in writing. Tom and Susie made quick calls to gather the clan. "Wear warm clothes. We'll be outside."

A party of 13 whooped it up on the porch of the New Bay Brewery. They confiscated three round tables, each with a set of four rocking chairs, adding one more chair from an empty table. With the exception of one holdout, everyone chose the Dinghy Blond pilsner. Tom stuck with his Miller Lite.

Tom chastised the others. "It tastes better and who the hell wants to pay $3.50 for a beer – any beer?"

In ragged unison the others disagreed with Tom on both the taste and the fair market value of Dinghy Blond.

Everyone bantered back and forth. No one was free from friendly roasting, not even the bereaved Michelle White. She laughed full-hearted at the tales Tom yelled out to the group. The story of Travis being told by a judge that his fly was unzipped broke everyone up, even causing the inside patrons to wonder what was happening on the porch.

". . . and you know what Travis said?" Tom cracked up, started again, cracked up again. He barely finished the story, ". . . he said, 'Oops, oh well your Honor, it's NO BIG THING!" Hysterical laughter erupted.

Woe be to their daughter, Kerri, and her new boyfriend, Randy Travis. Only thing was, this Randy Travis couldn't sing a lick. The group made him prove it.

As for Ross, he had waited long enough. It had been a long time since the family experienced pure joy. Fortified by his third pilsner, he rocked forward and stood up to center-stage attention. "I have an announcement and a request of Paige's parents." He took another swallow as the noise died down. All eyes traced back and forth between Ross and Paige.

Before Ross could continue, Susie corrected him with a genuine smile. "Ross, if this is about what I think it's about, you better address yourself to Tom." She turned to see the squinting eyes and the almost hidden smirk on Tom's lips. She was so happy.

Tom was as uncomfortable as Ross was. Call it what you want – respect, tradition, archaic rite of passage – Tom felt it important that Ross sought his permission to marry Paige. Ross clearly understood.

"Tom, uh, er, Mister Seiler . . ." Ross trembled, but forged through his memorized dialogue, bolstered by the hand cupping his. "Sir, I think you know how much I love your daughter. I'll make Paige very happy and I'll treat her with respect. Sir, . . ." Ross looked down at Paige, gave her a weak but sincere smile, then finished, ". . . I'm asking your permission to marry Paige."

Twelve gazes shifted slowly, deliberately, from Ross to Tom.

Ever so slightly, but easily noticed by Susie and Paige, a quiver actuated along Tom's lower lip. A touch of redness accented his moist eyes. Tom looked across the table at Paige. "You love Ross, don't you?"

"She sparkled. "Yes Daddy, so very much." Paige glanced at Ross, then back to Tom. "So very, very much."

"Ross," Tom spoke to everyone, ". . . take care of my daughter." He raised his Miller, stood up and announced, "To the future Mr. and Mrs. Ross Turlow."

Everyone scrambled to attention. In unison, they responded, "To Ross and Paige."

The Dinghy Blond disappeared from the mugs, followed by boisterous cheering, bear hugs and demands for the next round of beer. What a great time.

Tom slowly retreated, reflecting on the unfolding party in front of him. It was overwhelming to a man who had always kept sentimental emotions in check. These laughing, happy people were his friends – his family. John and Sarah Schrauder smiled at each other in the warmth of a new life. Nancy, unfazed by a 200-mile drive from San Antonio, was engaged in telling Steve and Kelly a side story of her brother. Michelle, sitting comfortably between Kerri and Randy, looked as happy as he had ever seen her. It was as though Travis was going to join her any minute. Ed Harvey seemed relaxed among people he barely knew three hours earlier. He had proved his mettle in the courtroom. *He's not Travis, but he will work out fine.* Paige sparkled, as did Ross. Susie sat next to him. Without turning toward him, she unconsciously put her hand on top of his.

The urge to cry begged for release. His mind quickly balanced the previous three months against this evening. *What a mystery. How life changes. It doesn't get better than this.* But, unexpectedly, fleeting visions of Elizabeth Harker and Jud Weems appeared. The smallest tinge of anxiety entered, uninvited, into his mind. Tom asked himself one deep question. *Have I been after justice or revenge?* It washed away as other memories flooded Tom's mind. Good memories. Jack and Tom, Jr., joined Travis at the party, if only in his mind. He looked across the table at Bill Newton. Something about Bill looked familiar, familiar from the past. Bill Newton and Donald Seiler. *Could it be? The one good cop when Don was shot.* Tom quickly shook it off as the restaurant door opened.

He called to the smiling waitress. "One more Miller for the father of the bride and another round of that trash for my friends."

●

Elizabeth Harker stared coldly at the teeming life below her. The Christmas lights had no power to lift her spirits. She added a down jacket over her dark green sweats to protect her from the cold night and her inner depression. With the depression came anger. There was always anger. Unconsciously stirring the glass of Simi with her finger, Liz Harker could not shake vision after vision flooding her mind.

●

"Now, asshole, pay attention. In your mind you are weighing the possibility that what I have told you is all I've got. In and of itself, it's not enough for a conviction. What I'm saying is that I have enough evidence – overwhelming evidence – to send you both to a lethal injection in Huntsville . . . the next Carla

Faye Tucker . . . 10 seconds before I walk out the door."

●

Liz remembered the rain on the window, the piercing gaze of Tom Seiler, and the sinking feeling in the pit of her stomach. She remembered losing control.

●

"Fine. A wise choice." Tom continued. "First, just in case you have doubts or some sordid thoughts, let me tell you about the linkage between the evidence and my health. Several people, not just family, have copies of it. I also have it in two separate safe deposit boxes. On the day I die it will become common knowledge. If that's tomorrow, so be it. I'm 63 and in very good health. I could go on for another 30 years. It's certainly in your best interest that I live a long, very happy, life."

"Do you think I would actually have you killed?" She smiled, the right corner of her mouth curving up in a sneer. "You think too much of yourself and I think you're a joke." She looked down at her desk.

"Look at me Harker." The veins in Tom's neck bulged. He hated this woman. Partly because she was evil, partly because he feared her. "Every time I look at your goddamn face I see Travis White. You just shut up and listen."

Liz Harker slumped back into her chair.

"To begin with, you're going to take over the investigation and conduct it properly. In effect you're going to fuck Barry Colter in a manner different than you have in the past. If you do it properly – and you will – Barry Colter will be convicted of first-degree murder. How you disengage yourself from him is your problem. Knowing how you deal with people, I'm sure you can pull it off."

Before Tom finished his sentence, Elizabeth Harker began a mental search to solve this dilemma and win her full freedom.

Tom added one more demand. "Once it's all over, you're going to announce, with great regret, that you are leaving the legal profession to pursue other avenues of life." He looked directly at her. "If I learn that you use your legal background in any manner, the evidence gets released. Go ahead and write a book, but if it has one line with a legal term, kiss yourself goodbye."

●

Staring at the glass, Liz Harker watched, in her mind, Tom walking to the door. She hated him. His final word rang out to her.

"*Despicable.*"

Tom's apparition faded as that of Barry Colter appeared.

●

Liz expected Barry's call. "Hello."

"All right, goddammit, what in the hell are you doing to me? Don't you screw with me." Barry screamed into the phone.

"You just wait a minute." Liz was fighting fire with fire. "You're the one who let the whole thing get out of control. I'm your only hope."

Before she could continue, Barry broke in. "What do you mean, my only hope? You're up to your ass in this, too."

"Look Barry, why do you think I asked to take over the investigation? All information is coming to me. The process needs to be straight forward." She was assertive, not aggressive. "I'm the one who makes the decisions. As long as you don't overreact to the questioning there won't be a problem."

●

Liz took a swallow, pausing a moment to savor the dry wine, then allowed her mind to continue.

●

She enjoyed being in control and Barry's acquiescing to her leadership triggered a sense of strength. He did his part.

"Liz, I don't like the phone. We need to meet tonight." His voice calmed down to a conversational tone.

His comment made it easier for her. "Fine, but not here. Too many people. Make it our spot at Bear Creek. But not before ten. We don't want anyone following us and I need to go over what the investigators wrote about your questioning. I'll be able to determine what the direction is and you can handle it from there."

●

A cold gust of wind buffeted her. She drew her arms in tightly around her, just below her breasts, sealing off passageways of chill. Still, a surge of unforgiving coldness passed through her body. Another look at the wine – another vision.

●

Her changing tone of voice disarmed Barry. "I'll tell you what else I can do about all of this." By the time she finished speaking, her voice was little more than a seductive purr. "I'm bringing a bottle of wine. We can talk business and decide what to do. Then we need to change to my finest bottle of Tomzante Pinot Grigio. I need to be held and touched. You need to be touched. I can almost feel it now."

Barry's morale improved. His spirits weren't the only thing beginning to rise.

"Ten o'clock. My car." Barry's mind miraculously switched from dread to anticipation.

"Perfect."

●

Barry arrived first that night, at 9:45. An earlier announcement that he needed some time alone was good enough for Betty. She was going to snuggle up in front of the television with a freshly made Manhattan. That he left without a word or kiss on the forehead left her a little disappointed. But she understood. She always understood.

●

Barry turned off the ignition but left the radio on. Local host Marvin Bates was baiting another antagonist on the evening talk show. Barry's early arrival afforded him time to listen to political discourse being carried on at an eighth-grade level. Responding to the computer chip timing device, the radio went off after 15 minutes. Barry quickly turned the ignition on and off to catch the next few minutes of an angry debate. Engrossed in the program, he was barely aware of Liz' arrival.

The talk show continued. "Well, if you're saying that oral sex with an intern is not really sex, then I guess that the Enron executives were just being creative."

Liz parked directly behind Barry, turned off the lights and gathered all her paraphernalia from the front seat. Then she arranged everything in the order of its use. Once outside, she walked to the passenger side of Barry's car. His head, outlined in the far-off glow of Houston, was cocked slightly to his right. She could tell that he was engrossed in a radio program. One more glance across the landscape. They could be alone together. She lifted the door handle with her left hand. As she opened the door the radio went dead.

"Oh, shit." Barry grunted in irritation.

It couldn't have been at a more inopportune time. Without even looking at her, Barry reached for the ignition key in order to turn the engine back on. Liz slid into her seat and, in one fluid motion, reached into the bag and out again. The car started and the radio program resumed.

Barry didn't feel anything. The bullet entered his head between his right eye and ear, exiting out of his left-side hairline and through the window. He was dead before his head slumped against the steering wheel. Barry started to roll towards Liz, blood spewing onto her denim trousers. She immediately propped him up against the seat. She pulled a pair of leather gloves from her purse, put them on, exited the car and opened the driver's door. Taking a dishtowel, she cleaned off the pistol and placed his right hand on it, manipulating his fingers so that prints engulfed the barrel and trigger housing. She accepted the risk of discovery and pointed the lifeless arm out of the open door. The second shot, muffled by the car interior, could be heard in the immediate area but not at a distance to the nearest house. In the investigation that she would lead, Liz Harker would insure that Barry's right hand be examined for powder burns. She manipulated his left hand to place additional prints. She cleaned off the inside and outside passenger door handles. Before closing his door, Liz Harker pushed Barry forward to the steering wheel. She increased the volume on the radio program, picked up the shell casing from the second shot, then backed out of the car and closed the passenger door. The car idled in neutral; the radio program continued. Walking away, Liz took one last look in the window. "You caused this."

A dark mosaic of quiet shadows graced the landscape. On the edge of the golf course fairway, weeds moved gently in the cool Texas breeze. Liz was very calm, methodical. She thought the entire process through. A suicide ruling would be the only possible cause of death. Liz drove forward a few feet, then executed the required moves to turn her car around. She drove quietly by the white Lincoln and its dead passenger. Unfortunate would be her response to the press.

Unheard by Liz Harker, Marvin concluded his intense conversation. ". . . and that's what morality is all about."

●

Midnight. Two people looked into the Texas sky.

Tom Seiler thought pleasant thoughts. *Tomorrow Susie and I ought to fly down to Matagorda Island. Maybe we can spot some pirates.* The wind blew crisply across his face. It felt good. He surveyed the beauty of the heavens, feeling a profound sense of well being. Then he walked into the house. "Hey Susie."

Twenty-three miles away, Elizabeth Harker stared into the icy wind, contemplating the future with bad intentions. *Someday you're going to pay. This is not over.* She walked quickly into her almost vacant apartment, ignoring the beauty of the night.

Below her, the winds buffeted the street. Sand danced in the vortex.

$$P_0 + \iota P_0 = (1 + \iota) P_0$$

$$(1 + \iota) P_0 + \iota (1 + \iota) P_0 = (1 + \iota)^2 P_0$$

$$\vdots$$

$$(1 + \iota)^{20} P_0$$

$$\frac{P_{20}}{P_0} = (1 + \iota)^{20} = 1.5$$

$$20 \ln (1 + \iota) = \ln 1.5$$

$$e^{\ln(1+\iota)} = e^{\frac{\ln 1.5}{20}}$$

$$1 + \iota = e^{\frac{\ln 1.5}{20}}$$

$$\iota = e^{\frac{\ln 1.5}{20}} - 1$$

Example $\ln 2 = 0.68 \approx .7$

$$1 = e^{.035} - 1$$

Printed in the United States
92067LV00003B/148-192/A